24690

BOOK 1

A. A. DARK

CONTENTS

To Twisted Sisters. I love each and every one of you crazy bitches. Bring on the dark.

PROLOGUE

BRAM

Only in the darkest recesses of one's mind would they ever find true freedom. To push the limits of what they were capable of, to have their character revealed when there were no restraints to restrict the desires within—that was what defined who they were. But where there was a perpetrator, there was a victim. The actions and trials of both were not without consequence. To know fear in its purest form was to live, and life was the greatest gift we were bestowed.

It took falling in love with a slave for me to open my eyes to what I'd been blinded to for so long. Power, money, and status—I'd been born with the world served to me on a silver platter. I had also been born to carry the vilest secret that existed amongst the wealthy and sadistic: Whitlock.

The subterranean fortress was like stepping into heaven and hell. For those looking for pleasure evoked from pain and death, the place was what dreams were made of. But dreams weren't one-sided. For the slaves trapped inside, it was a nightmare so horrendous, most found ways to kill themselves to escape the torment within.

Slave Vicolette had attempted to take her own life once, and the unsuccessful endeavor casted her into my arms. I was a young man then, barely twenty-three, and she was only fourteen, but her beauty had woven a web around me. I watched her grow, and with her age came a deep-rooted obsession. No matter how hard I tried to convince myself, I couldn't deny my feelings. I loved her.

Emotions came in many forms, and love appeared in mass shades. Mine was as dark as it came, and the fixation just happened to develop where hadn't belonged. Slave Vicolette could never be mine, even if she were free of her Master. My position allowed it, but I refused, and it wasn't for her. *It was for me.*

Whitlock was mine now, passed on to me after my father's death. To be attached any more than I already was would have been condemning myself to a truth I also couldn't deny. I was my father's son. I harbored evil, just like every man who walked through our doors.

Love may have taken residence in my heart, but love killed. And here, she was safer with the monsters than the devil who tracked her every move. At least, for now. I wasn't sure how much longer I could hold off.

I was always watching, *waiting*—murdering for the one I'd never escape: slave twenty-four-six-ninety.

CHAPTER 1

24690

"It wasn't me. I didn't do this. P-Please!"

Fingers crushed into my bloody bicep and slipped down to my elbow as the guard jerked against my fighting frame. My sobs made the words pouring from my mouth barely recognizable, but I continued to plead my innocence as more uniformed men stepped through the door of my small, luxury apartment inside Whitlock.

"Please, listen to me. I didn't do this! I swear, if you only—"

"You expect us to believe anything you say? You're covered in your Master's blood and your eye is nearly swollen shut. I'd say you took matters into your own hands this time."

Another guard stepped forward, reaching out toward me, and I flung my free arm away, trying to use my weight to break the other's hold. The angle landed me face to face with my Master's dead body, and I cried harder, lunging toward him with everything I had. The slip of the guard's grip left me surging right for the older man who had owned me since I was ten. It should have given me comfort knowing he'd never be back to beat me again, but it didn't. With his death might as well have come my own.

My knees hit the wood, hard, and I slid sideways through the massive amount of blood pooled and sprayed along the floor. Jagged wounds were shredded along his chest from the knife still sticking out of his left eye. *The same eye he hit me in.* I cringed, but didn't hesitate to crawl back up to him. This felt like a dream. Was I still sleeping? I had to be. Although my Master was mean to me on occasion, everyone loved him. Even I had grown to have feelings for him over the years. He didn't always lash out. Where he had rage, he had tenderness. He loved me. *He was all I had.*

"Grab her! What the hell are you waiting for?" Torrance, the lead guard known as the high leader, stopped by the entrance, whispering something to three men beside him. I watched as all but two left: a dark-skinned older guard and a younger one with blond hair. The moment the door shut, my pulse exploded. Torrance had short, dark hair, and his sharp features were handsome, but the look he held in his dark eyes was one I knew all too well—one I'd spent years hiding from within the halls of Whitlock. No one was to be trusted. Not the Masters who lurked in the shadows, and sure as hell not the guards meant to enforce the laws within this fortress.

"No..."

I crawled over my Master's body, trying to move away as they came closer. With how small the quarters were, there was nowhere left to go. If they got their hands on me, it was all over with. I wasn't owned anymore. I was fair game. Their toy to do whatever they pleased. They'd beat me worse than I already was, then rape me—something I hadn't had to undergo for quite some time. I couldn't bear experiencing that pain again. I couldn't.

"We'll shower her first."

One order—a million evil thoughts reflected in their eyes.

I reached for the large black handle of the knife, feeling the contents of my Master's brain gripping the blade as I ripped it free. Pleasure had Torrance's mouth pulled back into a slight smile. He didn't say a word as his built frame broke from the other two and began circling around me.

"Stay away. Don't come any closer."

"Don't be stupid, slave. You know better than this. Put down the knife and follow us into the restroom and you won't get hurt."

"You lie." My voice cracked as I moved to counter the actions of the leader. The other two were inching closer by the second and panic had me slicing the blade down toward them. "I said stay away!"

Still, they came, ignoring my threats as if I wouldn't try to fillet them alive. They were so wrong. I had nothing else to lose. With my Master murdered, it was to the White Room for me—the place where slaves went to pay for their crimes. *To die*. I couldn't go there. I couldn't be tortured until death for a criminal act I didn't commit.

Torrance's eyes flickered to the blond. I quickly glanced over, slashing toward him as he stayed just out of reach. Adrenaline surged to an all-time high while I searched for a route that would allow me to escape. But there wasn't any. Even if I managed to get through the door, more guards were outside.

"I didn't do this," I yelled again. "I was asleep. I heard something. It woke me."

"You're telling us you slept through a gruesome murder? You're going to have to do better than that."

I threw something between a glare and a pleading look toward the leader as he seemed to slow in his approach.

"I swear. There are pills in my Master's lockbox under the bed. He usually gives them to me after he…" On instinct, my free hand went to raise to my eye, but I stopped it before swinging the knife in the direction of the two guards as they shifted closer.

"I heard *nothing*," I stressed. "The pills put me into a deep sleep. You have to believe me. If you'd look, you'd find them there. My Master…he felt bad for what he did. He just wanted me to rest. To feel better. *I swear…*" The words got trapped in my throat from the sob that wanted to come. I could still see him leaning over me, kissing my split lip while he begged my forgiveness. He was so unlike the other Masters here. He was different. *He loved me.* He told me he did.

"So, if you didn't kill your Master, who did? Who else would have the motive more than you?"

My mouth opened, only to close. "I don't know. He didn't mention anything to me. He has friends over sometimes, but… he's liked by everyone I know."

Dark brown eyes swept over my face and lowered to my body before he shrugged. "Are you so sure about that?" At my confused silence, he continued. "Say I believe you, or at least give you the benefit of the doubt. You're still going to have to face the Whitlock Board. Do you really think they're going to believe a worthless slut like you? You're nothing, slave. You're a used-up waste of space. Even if they did find you innocent, no one is going to want to buy you again. Why would they when they could have a virgin?" Crossing his arms over his chest, he glanced at the other guards before turning back to me. "I'll tell you what. I'm feeling pretty generous today. You've been here for a long time. Why don't you do us all a favor?" He paused. "Go ahead," he said, flicking his wrist. "Turn the knife around. Let's see what you've got."

"What?"

"Don't pretend you don't want to leave this place. It's okay. It'll only hurt for a minute."

My head shook as tears raced down my cheeks. "I wish to request a meeting with the Whitlock Board. I don't want to kill my—"

Weight crashed into me from the side so hard, air exploded from my lungs as I connected with the floor. Even without oxygen, I scrambled to get the knife that was suddenly gone from my hand.

Whack!

Lights blinded me as the blond guard reared back and struck my cheek. The next blow was harder. The roar in my ears was constant as someone grabbed my wrist and pulled my limp frame toward the restroom in the back.

Warmth ran from my nose, tickling my top lip, triggering my survival instinct. My legs shot out and I tried twisting to add resistance. Screams poured from my mouth, ending almost immediately as the dark-skinned guard kicked my stomach. Bile surged to the back of my throat, and I gagged at the impact. The room was spinning—or I was. I wasn't sure as I fought for breath.

"Turn on the water. Let's get this bitch clean. We don't have much time."

The saturated white silk camisole top I wore was torn off, and the matching shorts followed. Water echoed around me, drowned out for only moments as I screamed at the hand squeezing into my breast.

"No! N—"

Whack!

"If you don't shut the fuck up, I'm going to drown you. Do you fucking hear me?"

Torrance's fingers pushed through my knotted hair, jerking back and forth before he pulled me to my feet and placed me in front of the ice-cold water. Although my head remained immobile, I tried turning out of his hold.

"Billy," he growled. "Keep the bitch still while I wash off this blood."

"Get off me! Get off!"

Louder, I yelled. Seeing the blond reach toward me, my nails tore into his bare forearms. A hiss left his mouth, and I knew what was coming before his fist reared back to hit me. Pain exploded over my mouth and blood sprayed along the white shower wall only moments before the other side of my face was smashed against it. Vertigo gave me the effects of falling, but I remained erect while a muffled voice broke through the haze of my mind.

"Move. Fuck this. Good enough."

Pressure pushed into the middle of my back and the water was suddenly off. How I was managing to stay upright was beyond me. Something told me one of them was closer now, holding me up. I couldn't tell. I could barely see.

"Arch those hips. Come on."

An arm suddenly wrapped around my waist. It pulled up against my lower stomach, making it almost impossible to get footing. The tip of my toe brushed against one of the combat boots and I blinked through the clarity, screaming as I tried twisting against the arms that felt like they were all over me—everywhere at once. One was barred over my shoulders while someone pinched my nipple. The arm around my waist tightened, and I thrashed, screaming as pain locked up my entire body.

"Fuck, she's tight. God dammit."

The thrusts were brutal and fast. Air kept getting trapped in my throat. The screams that started out strong, grew raspier, then silent through the force in which I yelled against his palm.

Torrance withdrew his cock, then slammed back into me, laughing as I sobbed through the pain. "I think I might buy you. I could get you real cheap. Would you like to be mine, slave? You like this cock, don't you?"

Again, he pounded into me. Sounds went in and out as I tried to get my voice to project, but nothing matched the disgust I wanted Torrance to hear.

"I'm going to convince them you might not be guilty after all. Then I'm going to come back for you in that cell where you'll be held. I'm going to—"

The hand over my mouth jerked away as warmth gushed over my back. I collapsed to the bottom of the tub like dead weight, sliding on the crimson flooding down on top of me. Torrance was hunched over above, his eyes bulging as a blade was pulled from the middle of his throat. The massive form of the guard dropped, hunching over the tub practically on top of me. But I didn't see *him.* I saw nothing but a thin, straight nose, full lips, square jaw, and a pair of cobalt eyes that burned into mine. Whether it was forever or only a fraction of a minute that I held that stare, I'd never know.

"Mr. Whitlock…Main Master. I was just following orders. I was—"

"Get out."

The words were directed at me, and the harsh tone made me hesitate for only a few seconds before I tried pushing to stand. The blond rushed from the room, and I barely managed to get to all fours before a strong hand grabbed my bicep, pulled me from the shower, and dumped me on the floor. Mr. Whitlock stepped over me, and…*more blood.* It sprayed out in all directions, strike after strike as he stabbed the dark-skinned guard.

I didn't think. I clawed along the floor, sliding and scrambling to get away. Agonizing screams mingled with gargling until they faded into nothingness behind me. Until they died, just like I was going to.

CHAPTER 2

BRAM

Red. All I saw was red as I let the guard's body fall to the bottom of the shower. He'd been standing at the far side, holding slave Vicolette when I'd burst into the restroom. I hadn't even remembered he was there after I saw Torrance raping my slave. Nothing mattered in that split second but killing my cousin. Blood related or not, Torrance disobeyed my orders —orders I was very specific on. *Situation in room two-fourteen, detain the slave. Don't hurt her.*

I turned, heading back into the bedroom. The covers were pulled back on the bed, no doubt from when the girl woke up. She'd been sleeping when I left this apartment. Then again, her Master had also been alive then.

"Slave." The name came out more as a growl, and I took a deep breath, trying to calm the fury inside. "Don't make me call you again. If I have to look for you, you're going to be in a lot of trouble."

A few seconds passed before dark, wet hair swayed into view from the entrance of the closet. Blue eyes peeked out, giving view to her thin nose and full lips as she took a step. She was beautiful, even with the tears sliding down her cheeks. She eased closer, pulling the robe around her tight. "I didn't do it. I swear, Mr. Whitlock. I didn't kill my Master. Please don't send me to the White Room. I swear—"

"Enough."

A sniffle left her, and her head lowered as she sobbed. I walked around the bed, narrowing my eyes, and she glanced up through wet lashes.

"You're to be sent to Slave Row. Your Master is dead. You will be resold. First, you'll follow me and do exactly as I say. If you do not, the guards will escort you to the board where you'll face trail."

Wide eyes flared through her internal panic. I knew that expression. She was terrified, as she should have been. Trial almost always meant certain death. Slave Vicolette wasn't ready to die. Not yet.

"Come."

I headed toward the door, catching a glimpse of my blood-drenched self in the mirror as I breached the living room. The splatter speckled my face and my white shirt exposed behind the dark suit jacket was drenched. The sight was enough to have me slowing. This person, this monster, was me. *The real me.* Compared to the famous lawyer everyone knew as Bram Whitlock, this man was a stranger. Hardly even recognizable to me anymore. There was no warm smile. No honor or nobility. I liked this version more. Here, I didn't have to pretend to be normal or sane. This underground fortress was *mine.* I ruled here. My word was law, and I had authority even the most powerful men in the world didn't hold. They were under my roof, *obeying me.*

Slave Vicolette's reflection stopped next to mine, and I met her red-rimmed eyes for only a moment before her head lowered again. But her vision didn't go to the ground. It went to her Master's dead body.

"Are you happy to be rid of him?"

"What?" At my silence, her stare rose back to me. "No. God,

no…" she trailed off, unable to hold in the sob that left her shoulders shaking.

"He beat you, yet you seem to have cared for him. Am I correct by my assumptions?"

"He may have beaten me, but he was kind. Gentle. He used to hold and sing to me. He was a g-good man."

Brainwashed fool. "He was a pedophile piece of shit. You wouldn't know a good man if he was standing before you. Do you so easily block out what he did to you the first day he bought you? How about when I found you at fourteen years old? You didn't try to kill yourself for nothing. He raped you for years before he broke you. And that's what you are—a broken toy for sick, twisted fucks who have a lot of money. Although, this time, I don't believe you'll do as well as you did with your previous Master. You've been shielded from the horrors of this place for too long."

Without waiting for her reaction, I turned, heading for the door to the apartment and swinging it open. Five guards stood outside, but it was hard to pay them any attention when I felt my slave's presence so strong behind me.

"Have this mess cleaned up. Master Vicolette and Torrance's bodies are to be brought to the holding room. Slave Vicolette—" I glanced back at her. "Slave Vicolette is to be showered and then escorted to Slave Row. She's no longer claimed. She's dead like her Master, therefore loses her title. Twenty-four-six-ninety. That's who you are again," I said, glaring into her light blue depths.

"P-Please, Mr. Whitlock." She shook her head back and forth in small movements. The long length of her hair was curling from the dampness, and I hated how I'd gripped the beautiful tresses in so many of my dreams, loving how I could almost feel the softness between my fingers. *Feel something I never would.* Perhaps I was bitter and cruel but being around her made me soft. I couldn't afford that, and neither could she.

"You're to be stripped of your title and your finery." I reached out, ripping the delicate gold chain off her neck. The heart pendant made me sick. I knew when she'd gotten it—Christmas, four years ago.

"When they get you cleaned up, you're to go to Medical. Afterward, your hair is to be cut short. Slaves don't have the luxury of long hair. If I hear of you giving anyone problems, I will deal with you personally. I'm still on the fence about having you taken to the White Room. Don't give me the excuse I need." I let my stare come back to the guards. "No one touches her. Do you hear me?"

"Yes, Master."

The words echoed through the hall around me and I met Billy's gaze. The blond guard wasn't getting off so easily. Once I viewed the tapes and saw exactly what he'd done, his time would come.

"I want word when she's locked up. Lyle, you're promoted to high leader. I expect a full report."

"Yes, Master. Thank you, Sir."

My hand rose, pointing to twenty-four-six-ninety. "Anyone lays a hand on her in any way that's inappropriate, kill them. If you don't, your life is mine. Don't for one second think I don't see everything that happens here. The shadows hide nothing, and she's going to make me money. It may not be a lot, but no one messes with my investments."

"She will remain untouched."

Again, my attention went to Billy. He had his head lowered, but his eyes were cut up to mine. The anger he held couldn't be hidden no matter how hard he tried. A smile tugged at my lips as I stared him down. When he dropped his gaze to the ground, satisfaction soared. I turned, heading down the long hall. I needed to get back to my quarters and find out what the fuck happened.

"Don't leave me with them, Mr. Whitlock. I b-beg you. Please!"

I slowed, clenching my jaw and closing my eyes. My love for her burned in my chest like a hot poker, stirring things inside me that were dangerous to acknowledge. Yet, I turned, withholding all emotion as I stared at the woman I'd known since she was a girl.

Everleigh Davenport. That had been her name. She'd been born to a wealthy man—a man Mr. Vicolette hated. But he hadn't hated *her*. The sick fuck loved her. Even at the tender age of ten, when he'd had her taken and brought here—an act that almost had my father killing him. That wasn't how we worked. We acquired our own slaves. We were responsible for their disappearances. No one else. Yet, my father pardoned him and allowed the girl to stay. He even had her parents killed at a hefty price to Mr. Vicolette. But it had to be done. There were no loose ends when you ran the world's largest funhouse. Celebrities, politicians…they all took up residence here when they weren't pretending to be someone else. We couldn't afford the risk, not that I worried too much about the outside law. Our pockets were deep, and my five Main Masters had influence and connections in all the right places.

"Don't leave me alone with them. I'll do anything! Please!"

The drawn-out plea had me walking back toward them. Not once did I break eye contact with my slave. *Mine*. Because no matter who bought her, she'd never belong to them. Her future buyer may hold the title of Master, but I owned her very breath.

"Who is it you think you're talking to, your savior?" I stopped inches before her, grabbing her face so tight, she cried out. "You are nothing. No one. You are not entitled to requests. I gave them an order, and they will follow it." I paused, easing my hold and sliding my hand over her bruised and swollen cheek. The evil in me retreated as my stare swept over her. Even beat to hell, she was the most beautiful woman I'd ever seen. Maybe even more so like this. “Your fear is unwarranted,” I said softly. “Let me show you.”

Dropping my hand, I brought my attention to Lyle and looked between him and Billy, unable to hold in the sadistic grin. My finger rose and I pointed to the guard who I knew took part in my slave’s rape and beating. “I have no tolerance for anyone who disobeys orders. High Leader, cut off his left hand.”

“What? Wait!” Billy stumbled back, shaking his head. “I *was* following orders. We were to secure the scene of a hostile situation. I did that. The bitch had a knife!”

My gaze lowered to slave twenty-four-six-ninety and my hand dropped. “Did you hold a weapon?”

“I…did. They were going to rape me. I tried to tell them I didn’t kill my Master. They didn’t care. They were going to hurt me anyway.”

“So, you didn’t have a weapon until *after* they arrived?”

“No,” she rushed out. “I took it from my Master’s body when they sent everyone outside the apartment. I requested to go in front of the board, but they wouldn’t listen.” She peeked over at Billy. “He tackled me down and started beating me. That’s when they pulled me into the bathroom and…”

I let one of my eyebrows draw up as I gave Billy a look. “Is this true? Was she denied her request to face the board? Did you hit her?”

“Torrance was my leader. He denied her. I was following *his* orders.”

“I am the Main Master here! You follow *my* orders. Did he specifically tell you to beat her? Her—a woman not even half your size?”

The disgust in my words had him shuffling back, but the other guards were already circling him, even as they glared at my slave.

“Well…no. But she was fighting.”

“As would anyone faced with *rape*. The difference here is

once her Master was killed, she became mine. You know that. So, what it comes down to is you beat *my* slave with the intention of following in this rape. There's nothing left to say. You're lucky all you're losing is your hand. Touch her again, your dick will be next."

I snatched up my slave's arm and jerked her forward as I led her down the hall. The howls in the distance turned to screams, and I soaked them in, letting the hate inside take over.

Doors opened ahead and the Masters quickly returned to their safe haven after seeing me. This may have been their sanctuary, but they had good reason to hide. I held the key to their filthiest kinks, their sickest sins—and I had the power to take it all away.

CHAPTER 3

WEST

"Slave Vicolette."

My head dipped in respect for her Master but stopped short at the new bruising covering her face. She hadn't been that bad off when Bram and I had seen her sleeping earlier.

"She's not a Vicolette anymore. She's slave twenty-four-six-ninety now."

I went to speak but stayed silent as I stared between her and Bram. He held her roughly, tugging at her arm as he led them toward his bedroom door.

"Pull up the footage of their apartment. Have it ready for me. I want to see what the fuck happened after we left."

"Footage? You have cameras in—" The soft voice was drowned out by Bram's growl.

"No questions, slave. I wasn't talking to you. *You hear nothing.* You are no one."

They disappeared into his room, and I walked over to his desk. The shower started, and I couldn't help but let my eyes drift up to where they'd gone. The moment I had the apartment pulled up, I turned to the bar, pouring myself a drink. And again, I looked ahead.

"You got it?"

Bram swept through, and I glanced over, nodding. "All ready to go." The pressure of the water changed, and I tried to ignore the fact that she was in the shower. *His shower.* Here, within the same walls as me. We were so close.

Bram took a seat behind his desk and clicked the play button. We were walking away from Mr. Vicolette, his expression still furious from our argument. The Master intended to acquire a new slave at the coming auction—another girl who was barely ten he'd witnessed on his stroll through The Cradle. Bram wasn't having it. The outrageous sum was meant to deter the old man, but he was persistent in his bargaining.

Since Bram had taken over, things had changed. The Cradle housed all those under legal age. Not long ago, they were given to anyone who could pay the price. Now, they were off-limits to the perversion that once reigned supreme. The Masters were allowed visitation with their slaves, but only supervised, and never for anything sexual until they were a certain age. Master Vicolette didn't like the new rules and argued over the old ways but lost in the end. He couldn't afford the price—not that anyone could. Even I was shocked by the sum. But Bram's dislike of the man was evident. And I knew why.

Back and forth, the old man paced. When his head snapped up toward the door, the screen went black.

"What the fuck?" Bram clicked buttons, then spun to pin me with a stare so full of blame, my hands rose.

"Don't look at me. I haven't touched anything. I did as you said and pulled it up."

"Only a select few could have erased the video. If it wasn't you, then who? We separated after we left that apartment. Where did you go before coming here?"

He asked the question, but turned back to the screen, typing something in I couldn't see. When the bedroom came into view and slave Vicolette lay there sleeping, I stepped forward. Not even seconds later, the living room reappeared on the monitor. And with it, a masked man stabbing away.

"I went to get some coffee. Then I came here."

"You inquired about the girl, West. You asked Mr. Vicolette what he meant to do with her if he got himself a new slave. How do I know that's not you?"

The blade thrust into the old man's eye and the darkly dressed figure stood from his body, heading straight for the door.

"Pull up the other cameras. You'll see I went straight to the dining hall and returned here. That's not me."

Bram switched the view to the hallway and followed the stranger through the labyrinth of tunnels until he was slipping through a secret door. It was so far down in the fortress, it could have led anywhere underground.

"Where did he go?" I whispered. "Do we not have cameras down there?"

"No. There's another underground road that leads here. It hasn't been used in quite some time, but I'm guessing that's what he took to get in. How he knew about it and was able to slip past the guards is what I want to know."

Bram rewound the footage, going back to slave Vicolette's bedroom while the murder was being committed. It wasn't until seconds after the door closed that she stirred. The expression she held was one of sleepy confusion. She knew something wasn't right, even in her slightly drugged state. And I knew she was drugged. Mr. Vicolette told us as much when Bram asked about her well-being.

"She was telling the truth." Bram's low voice turned angry toward the end as he shut off the recording of her rape and stood. I couldn't help but follow him as he headed farther into the living room.

"Will she go to Slave Row?" I paused, unable to stop the next question from coming. "Will she be put on auction?"

Blue eyes pierced mine as his lids narrowed. "You know

that's how it works, but that's the last thing on my mind right now. I want to know who that motherfucker was who got inside my walls." He took a step toward me. "You have been my best friend since grade school. You're my business partner. We grew up in this place. Never once in all these years have you shown interest in buying a slave. Yet here you are, asking about her again, when we obviously have bigger problems. Are you implying you want to bid on her? You want to anchor yourself deeper in this world?"

My stare went to the bedroom door. The water was off. Was she dressing? Eavesdropping on our conversation?

"I was wrong to put her before the intruder. But yes, I think maybe I do."

He shook his head as he let out a loud exhale. "I never thought I'd see the fucking day. *You know what's here.* This isn't you, West. You don't belong in this world."

"You know what I've done over the years. Same as you. Are you so sure about that? I'm telling you I want her. I want to *buy* her, Bram. What does that tell you about me? Obviously, I'm no better than any of them."

"But you are."

Bram continued to shake his head as he paced, deep in thought. When he glanced toward the bedroom door, he stopped. Moments passed when suddenly he jerked his head to the side.

"You can't afford her."

"Excuse me?"

"You heard me. You can't afford slave twenty-four-six-ninety. I know how much you're worth. You don't have the money."

I cocked my head to the side as anger filled me. "I'll find it."

"I said no."

"No, you said I didn't have the money. I'm telling you I do. *Are you* saying no? Is that it?"

"You're better than a used-up slave. Find a real woman, West. A wife."

I laughed under my breath, but it was anything but happy. "I don't want a wife. I want her. Besides, you owe me. I've covered for your ass over these years and haven't asked for anything in return. I'm not saying don't charge me for her. Just give me the option to buy if that's my choice."

Bram's jaw clenched repeatedly as he stared at me. "Fine. You want your chance to bid, you've got it. But don't think you'll win. There are men out there willing to pay hundreds of thousands for their chance to use her as they see fit. If you think you can find the money to win her, have at it. I won't stop you. Just know you'll be bidding for nothing."

Cautiously, slave twenty-four-six-ninety emerged from the entrance of the bedroom wearing the same white robe she'd come in. Her stare lifted right to me, but I didn't turn away like I usually did. I met her gaze with everything I had. There was no point in hiding my want anymore. She was free. To me, she was already mine.

"Let me have her now. Name your price. It's yours. There's no reason for her to endure Slave Row. I can take care of her."

Bram's eyes flared with fury as his eyes shot to me. "That is asking too much. You know that's not how it works here. She *will* go to Slave Row, and if you want her, you *will* bid. End of discussion."

My lips pressed together in a thin line. I wanted to argue, but it was pointless. I had known Bram most of my life. When he was set against something, swaying him was impossible. He didn't want me to have her. That was clear. But I had a chance to win. And I *would*.

"Slave." I tore my gaze from Bram's and headed toward the dark-haired woman who'd captured my attention from the first moment I saw her on the monitor. "I make no promises, but rest assured, when the day comes for you to be bought again, I will do my best to make you mine." I paused as I took in her beaten face. "Would you like for me to own you?"

"You?" She looked to Bram, only to come back to me. "I…I would be honored, Mr. Harper. Master," she rushed out.

"I'm not your Master yet," I said, smiling. "But perhaps soon. Until then, Mr. Harper will do."

She gave a nod, then walked to Bram's side as he impatiently signaled for her.

"We'll talk when I return. This isn't over, West."

Bram may have thought it wasn't, but the conversation was at an end. He was going to try to get me to change my mind. Little did he know, I'd come too far to go back now. Slave twenty-four-six-ninety was going to be mine. I'd made sure of it.

CHAPTER 4

24690

"You would be honored? The correct response would have been, 'I'm not worthy of you, Mr. Harper.'"

"You're right, Mr. Whitlock. I am unworthy of Mr. Harper. I apologize. I don't know what I was thinking."

I continued to take in the white tiles lining the floor as we walked to Medical. My response was ingrained. The words came from deep within, barely even registering as I said them. *Honored.* Yes, I would have been honored to belong to Mr. Harper. I was guessing he was in his early thirties, and he was extremely attractive with light brown hair, brown eyes, a thin, straight nose, and nice lips…but I would have been even more honored to leave this place. My mind said it was wrong to think that, but the other part of me—the rebellious part I tried to lock away—couldn't be muted. *Honored.* I hated being owned. I hated not having choices or a life of my own.

A guard opened the door as we approached. We walked through, taking a left into a slightly curved hall leading deeper into the round fortress.

"Do you know who killed my Master?"

Bram slowed, coming to pin me with those intense eyes. The

attraction I harbored for him was something I had a hard time controlling. I'd felt it from the first moment I met him, when he held me as I bled out from cutting my wrists. I thought he was an angel then, destined to take me far away from this place. That wasn't the case. Far from it.

"Maybe I should be asking you. Do you know who killed your Master?"

"Me?"

"That's right. This person wore dark clothes and a mask. He slipped through a place that has been closed off for a very long time. He knew things he shouldn't have. Perhaps you've been conspiring with him the entire time."

I blinked through the news, unable to contain my shock. "I haven't conspired anything. I don't know anyone who would want my Master dead. I swear it."

"You've seen nothing suspicious? No one has been giving you attention that maybe you haven't mentioned?"

Flashes of the last few times my Master had guests over blinded me. They were all other Masters within the fortress. Rob, a famous actor. Yahn, a billionaire banker. And a handful more. A rock star I didn't get the name of because I was excused almost immediately. My Master rarely let me in the room when his acquaintances were over. He was very jealous, and the others looked at me. *A lot.*

"Nothing out of the ordinary. I wasn't allowed around other men."

"I know." Bram closed the distance between us, and inch by inch, I retreated, until my back was against the wall. And he didn't stop adding his weight when he made contact. Not until I looked up. The moment I did, his finger slid under my chin, making me keep my eyes on his. "What was it this time? Why did he beat you? Did you look at someone? Take interest in a younger man instead of an old, sick fuck like Master Vicolette?"

I jerked my head to the side, unable to stop the action. "You know it was you."

The chuckle left my body shaking from his laughter. "I saw you looking at me this morning when I came by. Do you like what you see, slave?" He moved into me more, and I tried with everything in me to fight my automatic arousal toward him. It mingled with the pain I still felt from my rape, twisting my mind with sick possibilities.

"I returned later, after I left. I saw what he did. I almost killed him myself but withheld when I saw you were sleeping." He paused. "Did you know your Master was looking into buying another slave?"

Pain lanced my heart, but I had no idea why. Betrayal? Perhaps. I loved my Master just as much as I hated him.

"Another slave?"

Mr. Whitlock's thigh pressed between my legs. I winced at the stinging, and it only made his grin pull back more. He paused, gazing at my lips before bringing his eyes back to mine.

"A little girl. Ten years old. The same age you were when he bought you. You do know he's the reason you're here? That your first auction wasn't real? He had to have told you the truth after all these years."

My mouth opened, but nothing came. Nothing but the tears that blinded me.

"I guess you didn't know. He's the reason your parents are dead. He hated your father. He had you taken as part of his revenge. Everything that has happened to you is all his doing."

"That can't be true."

"Oh, but it is. I know this to be fact. I know everything about you, Everleigh."

I couldn't stop the gasp that exploded from my mouth. The name was like a fist to my gut. How long had it been since I'd been called that? *My name*.

Fingers grasped around my wrist, pulling my arm up to be

pinned against the wall. In a slow decent, Bram traced his thumb over the scar running from my wrist to the middle of my forearm. "Do you remember taking that blade to your skin? Do you remember me sitting on the floor holding and rocking you while your very life flooded all over me? Do you remember what you said to me?"

The tears escaped down my cheeks, and I closed my lids as his touch stopped midway.

"I begged you to let me die or take me away from here."

"And what did I say to you?"

The blue of his eyes seemed brighter as I met them. "You said if I lived, you would watch out for me. You promised I would be okay."

"I was barely a man then, but I held true to my word. The rape from your Master stopped, didn't it? He didn't force himself on you again after that day, did he?"

"N-No."

I sobbed, remembering how the beatings increased right after. But the rape…it *had* stopped. It was two years before my Master touched me and I consented. He'd always pulled back at my no, but I hadn't said no, then or afterward. He'd grown gentler during that time. More wooing. I thought it was because of my suicide attempt, but it wasn't me at all. It was Mr. Whitlock.

"Thank…you?"

Bram's fingers began to trail down, sweeping over my bicep before easing along my shoulder. His grip was firm as he locked onto one of my breasts. I tensed even more, unsure of how to react. "Like I said before, I'm not your savior. I do nothing for free."

And just like that, he was off me and walking away. My pulse was pounding so hard, I nearly fell from the adrenaline numbing out my limbs. I tried to catch up, but in truth, I was scared to. I knew what he was implying, and knowing the position he held, it frightened me even more. Especially after what I had just gone through with Torrance and the guards. There was no one who would stop this man if he wanted to have his way with me. I ached already. Would Bram be just as savage when he finally did come?

I caught up to his towering frame, glancing at his hard features. *Yes.* He might very well tear me apart. Then again, did I know him at all? I saw moments of gentleness. A caress here, a brush of his fingers there. We'd been going about this now for years.

"Hurry up."

We took another turn, and a door appeared in the distance. I swallowed hard, braving the question that scared me the most.

"Will the guard…Billy have access to me in Slave Row?"

Mr. Whitlock spun on me so fast, I stumbled back, half expecting him to throw a punch.

"You still doubt me? Even after I had them remove his hand?"

"I'm sorry, Master. I don't mean to doubt you. I just—"

"Just *nothing*. You're a scared little mouse. Maybe I made a mistake. Perhaps I should have him go to your room every night and have his way with you. Maybe then you'll stop fearing what you *need not fear*!"

The last was yelled only inches from my face. Where the slave in me wanted to curl into a ball and beg forgiveness, the spark within me burned with fire. Had I any sense, I would have doused the flame on recognition, but I didn't. I leaned forward, pressing my lips into his.

"Thank you." And just like that, I began to walk, leaving him there. My eyes widened through my stupidity, but something was happening—an invigorating feeling I hadn't experienced before. It surged through me, feeding the woman I had chained away inside of me.

After a few seconds of only my footsteps, I turned to see Mr.

Whitlock staring at me. Just…staring, as if he was lost. His shock appeared as great as mine.

"Don't ever do that again."

The words came out harsh, but his expression was anything but. It was still lax and slightly confused. There was no slash of his lips or narrowed angry eyes. Quite the opposite. He was beautiful unmasked.

"Do you hear me?" He stalked toward me, and it took everything I had not to cower.

"As you wish."

"That's it? Where's the apology?"

One would apologize to a Master if they were in the wrong. And I should have, but I couldn't drown out this new feeling.

"I'm not sorry," I said, peeking up at him.

"You're not sorry? I give you one speech on toughening up and this is how you behave? I should have you whipped."

I did cower then. My shoulders drew in, and on instinct, I took a step back. I'd seen enough lashings in the old days to know it sometimes killed slaves.

"I forget myself, Master. Please forgive me. It won't happen again."

Bram stepped in and used the wall to his advantage once again, showing me there was nowhere to go. My back pressed against the stone in an attempt to avoid contact, and I turned my face away as a sign of respect. It was routine. It was who I was. I couldn't forget that.

"Look at me."

It took seconds before I obeyed. I was shaking through the possibilities of what he could do. When I turned, his face was so close, all I could see were his eyes. They held mine as his palms flattened next to my head.

"There's still an Everleigh inside there. I thought she died long ago." He pulled back, but only a few inches. "I'm sorry for that, slave. For your sake, I wished she *was* dead. I fear she may not like what her future holds. Way back in your mind, I know you're holding onto West Harper's declaration, but I'm here to tell you right now, he will not win your bid."

"But why? He thinks he can." My voice died out. I couldn't deny that he was right. I held hope for West. I wanted to believe it was possible. That there may be happiness for me in this hell I was cast into.

"Do you want him to be your Master? Like, want him, as a woman would a man? Or are you wanting his kindness?"

Tread lightly. The statement rushed through my mind as darkness edged into his depths.

"He has always been kind."

"But do you find him attractive? Do you hope he might fall in love with you if he buys you?"

"Love?" I asked, breaking our connection. "I'm a slave. I do not deserve love. I only live to please my Master, whomever that may be."

Mr. Whitlock stepped away. "Such a robotic response, but a correct one. West won't find the money, and your new Master will most likely be another old man. If you're lucky, he'll want you purely for sex."

"And if he beats me? Cuts and peels back my skin like Master Kain does to his slave? Kills me like Master Pollock does with the multiple slaves he buys?"

"You can take a beating." He paused. "But if he breaks your skin, I'll break his neck. Then we will be here, reselling you again. It'll be like that until you die. The only way you'll ever escape Whitlock is in ashes."

"Why are you doing this for me?"

"I told you, it'll not be for free."

I stole a glance as we continued walking along the curved hall. "So, you'll come to me. You'll want sex even if I have a Master? What if he finds out? What if he hurts me because of it?"

The door opened to Medical, and Bram grabbed my arm, nearly dragging me into the room he was pointed to. When the door shut, he was angrier than I'd ever seen him. I was practically thrown onto the hard hospital bed, and his hand settled on my throat as his face moved in close. My injuries screamed to life as pressure built in my face.

"You ask all these questions, yet you're afraid of the wrong people. Don't fear your Master, slave. Fear the devil at your back. Fear the reflection you can't see staring back at you in the mirror. I'm everywhere. I see your every move. I've seen...*for years*. When and what I want of you, I will take. Fuck everyone. Let them try to get in my way. You belong to me when I decide the time is right. For your sake, you better hope that day never comes."

CHAPTER 5

BRAM

"Move."

The nurse nearly dropped her tray as I pushed through the door to leave my slave's room. I couldn't think through the conflicting emotions colliding inside me. Anger, jealousy...*love*. God, the love. She'd kissed me. And then to tell me she wasn't sorry? What the hell had I been thinking bringing her back to my room and delivering her myself? I should have left her with the guards. I should have steered clear. But I hadn't. If I had any weakness, it was her. The small span of time we'd spent together only proved that. This morning, when she kept staring up at me, I knew a small part of her was at least interested. But the kiss. God, that fucking kiss.

The halls blurred as I made my way back to my quarters. The moment I burst through the door, I only wanted to curse more. West was standing next to the bar, watching me as he sipped his drink. He wanted her. He wanted what was mine. If I was any friend at all, I'd hand her over to him and be done with it. I just wasn't sure I could. He'd fall in love with her even more than he probably already was. And her? She'd love him too. Then what? Would I kill him out of jealousy? Possibly.

"Get cameras on that underground entrance. And down the road. It should have been done a long time ago."

West refilled his glass and eyed me as he made me one.

"Already done. I've been told it will take a couple days, but I put a rush on it. They'll do it as fast as they can."

I nodded, taking the drink and tossing it back.

"Are you in love with her?"

The liquor burned my throat, but the lie on my tongue scorched me even more. "I'm assuming you're referring to slave twenty-four-six-ninety. The answer is no."

"Then tell me what I have to do to convince you to let me have her."

Throwing my best friend a look, I walked over to pour myself another drink. "We have rules. If I'm lenient with you, others will expect the same. I can't do that, West. She goes up for auction, and if you have the money, you have the opportunity to buy her."

"What's the starting bid?"

I downed the shot, then refilled. "Seven hundred thousand."

Silence. I turned to see West's face harden as he stared at me.

"That's a lot more than blue slaves go for."

"She's more than blue. She's beautiful. She has a fantastic body. Men will pay a lot for someone like her. Besides, I already told you. You can't afford her."

"I'll give you three million this very minute if you let me have her now."

My eyebrows rose in surprise. "You have a mortgage—a fancy little place on Mansion Hill. You have three expensive sports cars you dumbly got a loan for."

"The house is on the market. I've already gotten an offer. The cars are gone. I sold them."

"That's convenient. And *suspiciously* alarming."

West smiled. "I stay here more than anywhere. Why would I keep a house and cars if I'm not using them? Truth is, I've been thinking about buying a slave for some time now. Twenty-four-six-ninety just happened to come at the perfect moment. Nothing more. One could even call it fate."

"Fate is for fools."

He shrugged. "Maybe, but I like the sound of it. Bram, take my offer. Let me buy her. We both know she deserves better. She's not like the other slaves. Everleigh is different."

"Everleigh? Is that what you'll call her?"

"No. She will be my slave in every sense of the word. She's already trained. She's beyond gorgeous. I don't want a virgin, or to have to go through the process of training one. She's a good match for me."

"I said no."

A deep sound left West and he joined me at the bar, grabbing the decanter.

"You're a stubborn son of a bitch. You always have been. I would do this for you if you asked. Rules be damned. You're like my brother. There's nothing I wouldn't do for you. You know that."

"And the moment you gave in to my stupid request, the walls of this place would come tumbling down. Mark my words, West, it can't be done. Ask me for anything else. Ask me for a fucking one-hundred-million-dollar yacht as a belated birthday gift, and it will be yours. But do not ask this of me."

"Fine. Forget the yacht and match the price of the highest bidder so I can have her. No matter the cost."

I slammed my glass on the bar, pinning him with a look that no doubt revealed the evil inside me. What he was asking nearly killed me—killed him. It fed the jealousy and took everything I had not to wrap my hands around his neck until he convinced me he'd changed his mind. "You test my patience, friend."

"You test mine every damn day."

Heat singed the inside of my chest as he kept my stare. I couldn't continue to do this. West was right. They were a great match. "Fine. You want her so badly, come auction day, I'll do what I can to make her yours."

West let out a long exhale, his eyes closing. "I'm indebted to you. I'm here for whatever you need. And I'll pay you back. You have my word."

"Indebted. Yes, you are." *More than you know.*

A knock had me leaving without another glance his way. Things were shifting within me. I knew I loved West, but now, I had a wall up concerning him. He was somehow different in my eyes—fading from the man I had always trusted. It was ironic how things worked out that way. Anyone could have wanted my slave, and I wouldn't have held a quarter of the anger I did toward West.

"Main Master, the bodies are delivered to the holding room awaiting your instruction. Is there anything else you need?"

I took in Lyle—his short black hair and slightly crooked nose amongst handsome features. He had broad shoulders but wasn't anywhere near my height. He had to have been close to mid-forties. Choosing him was the wisest thing I could have done. I could trust him, and I would need to.

"I want you and a team of men to head to the far west wing—the part that isn't used anymore. In the very back, you will come across a door that leads to an abandoned garage and road. Scour every inch and find me something this murdering intruder may have left behind."

"Yes, Master."

He bowed his head and turned, taking off at a quick pace. I shut the door, wanting nothing but peace…and silence. I wanted to go over my slave's kiss again. *Watch it replay over and over.* What had been in her eyes when she had pulled back and looked at me? Who had she seen when she stared up at me afterward? Surely not the same man standing here now. Definitely not the one who threw her raped and bruised body onto that hospital bed and told her what a mad man he was. No, she wouldn't have expected the monster, or the secrets I divulged in those moments. I was losing it—slipping with my pent-up frustrations of not having her for myself.

"You look tired and it's getting pretty late. I'm going to take off to my room. Are you okay? You sure there isn't anything you need?"

I glanced at West, shaking my head. I couldn't speak to him right now. There was something going on with him that was throwing red flags. I had learned to trust my intuition long ago, and this had nothing to do with the jealousy I felt concerning my slave.

"See you tomorrow, Bram."

I barely heard the door as it shut behind him. I was already heading toward my computer—the one place that had been a window to my slave. I hit the buttons, pulling up Medical. She was curled on the bed, tears streaming down her cheeks. The reality of it hit as I turned up the volume to hear her soft cries.

The nurse was standing at the far side of the room, her back to twenty-four-six-ninety, but I cared nothing about her. Fascination drew me in while I watched my slave's tiny body shake. A sense of calm settled through me, and my shoulders lost their stiffness.

Happy or not, nothing mattered except for the fact that we were together now. Her sadness, I could deal with. Her absence, I could not.

The door opened, and a female doctor walked into the room wearing her designated white scrubs and holding a chart. While she read through it, she came closer to the bed. I went back and forth as I quickly let my fingers work to pull up our moment in the hall on a smaller screen.

"You have some bruising and tearing. Nothing that won't heal from rest. As for your face..." She finally looked up, her brow drawing in as she sat on the edge of the bed. Twenty-four-six-ninety pushed to sit up. "You'll need to ice it over the next few days to bring down the swelling. Do you think you can stay out of trouble in the meantime?"

"Oh…well, yes. My Master…"

More sobs.

"Her Master is dead. She's headed to Slave Row." The nurse came up from behind to address the doctor, stopping just a foot from them. "She's the one I was telling you about," she whispered.

"I see."

The women looked between each other, and my slave shifted uncomfortably.

"I didn't kill him. It was a man in a mask. They're looking for him now. I..." My slave sniffled, wiping away the tears as fear shadowed her face. It was evident the crying wasn't over. She looked worse than ever. "I just want to go home," she sobbed. "I want to wake up and know this was just a dream."

"Shhh," the doctor said, reaching for her hand. "No more crying."

The scene had me cocking my head. Why hadn't I been aware of this doctor's caring nature? Or the nurse's, for that matter. This wasn't what was best for slaves. Slaves were meant to feel like no one. They weren't supposed to get support from anyone but their Masters—if their Master willed it.

"Look at me," the doctor continued. "Everything will be okay."

"No, you don't understand. Where I'm going in Slave Row, it's full of rapists. I'm not a virgin. I've heard such bad stories. They'll get me. They'll be waiting. A guard had his hand cut off because of me. They're going to want revenge. Maybe even want to see me dead. I'm not safe. I've been assured I am, but I can't be watched at all times. They'll know when to strike, and when they do, I'm done for."

The doctor cut her eyes up to the nurse, the anxiety evident on their faces as they stared silently at each other.

"I know the man you speak of. He's down the hall." She took a deep breath. "What is your name?" the doctor whispered.

"Twenty-four-six-ninety."

"No…your real name."

More tears. "Everleigh."

"That's a beautiful name, Everleigh." Her hand lifted my slave's while her other came up to sandwich their embrace. "Listen to me, Everleigh. If men come for you, don't fight them. I know that sounds horrible, and outside of here, I wouldn't be telling you this, but this place is unlike any I've ever seen. And like you, I cannot leave. We deal how we must." She paused. "That's why I'm going to tell you not to fight. If you fight, they will hit. Rape comes with its own injuries, and I can help you with those. You may not be so lucky if they beat you again. Men can kill here and get away with it. I can't help you if you're dead. Do you understand me? Lay there. Do nothing…not until you're able to."

My slave's nod was full of something I couldn't understand.

"We never had this talk," she said lowly. "But I am here, should you need me."

The doctor stood, then glanced at the nurse, who followed. The moment the door shut, my slave opened her hand and her eyes flared. Her fists were under the blanket so fast, I didn't get a chance to see what she held.

CHAPTER 6

WEST

Greed and jealousy had the power to do things to a man even torture couldn't touch. The two were a pain mechanism all their own. They may not physically injure the body, but they destroyed and corrupted the soul.

My soul had been picked apart long ago. When you're compared to someone you know you'll never be as handsome, or rich, or powerful as your entire life, the constant envy and hate takes their toll.

I hated Bram Whitlock. He was everything I wanted to be. Even if I could have been half the man he portrayed, I would have been happy. But that wasn't the case. I wasn't born into a rich family. I wasn't handed everything I wanted. Not in the same sense. My father worked for his as the high leader. My mother, an absent drug addict I hadn't seen since I was four, while his mother was the world's biggest socialite. I used to play at their extravagant mansion when we were kids, which led Bram's father to notice how well me and his son got along. From there, I was sent to the same schools as Bram.

Where I excelled, Bram outshined me. Sports, academics, girls—he was always better in everything he tried his hand at.

And he never cared for any of it. Not even the girls. What pleased him the most was proving he was the best. Then he was done.

But now, I was going to have something he wished for. Twenty-four-six-ninety was going to be mine. He loved her. The longing in his eyes while he hid behind that screen proved that. It was desperate and pathetic. Bram had never paid so much attention to a woman before. This one, this Everleigh, was different. Even for me. It was as if I could feel their connection. His yearning became my own. It corrupted me, warping my malicious mind. But even there, he and I were similar. Neither of us were good men. He just didn't know it. To him, I was the good one. But there was no honor when I thought of the two of them together, or even her alone.

It all started with him leaving her apartment up on his screen. At first, I hadn't paid attention to the old man walking around, but then, there she was...beautiful, angelic even. Bram exploded when I'd asked about her. He didn't want to talk about it, and that was enough to more than pique my interest. He wanted her, and that made me want her more. Then, a few weeks after he took on his role as Master of Whitlock, the visits came. We'd go by their apartment often, and the way their eyes always found each other never escaped me. And his reasons for needing to visit Master Vicolette were bullshit. It was her. It was always her.

Knock. Knock.

My fist connected a third time against the metal door, and Bram opened it, his eyes still heavy with sleep.

"Got your coffee. Black with sugar, just the way you like it."

He paused, swinging the door open and taking the Styrofoam cup. "Thanks. What time is it?"

I walked in, noticing the blanket on the couch. The bastard never slept in a bed. Give him a couch or chair and he'd make do. Hell, even the floor. I never understood it with the money and luxuries he had at his disposal.

"A little after six. I take it you didn't get much sleep last night?"

"Slept fine."

He took a sip of the coffee, then put it down to head to the restroom. I waited for the door to close before I walked to his computer. One tap of the mouse and a cell came into view. Two women were sleeping on the small beds lining each side of the room. From the dark hair, I knew which one was Everleigh, but the length was gone. Her hair, it was no longer than a few inches. If she was lucky, it would come to her shoulders, but I doubted it. The sight made me curse under my breath. The routine was one I'd seen throughout my time here, but I hated that it had to be done to her. My fantasies of seeing her long hair draped around her nude body were gone.

Water turned on in the distance, and I refrained from touching anything so the screen could black out again. Within minutes, Bram was walking back out dressed in a suit that cost more than my monthly salary. And me, I was doing what I always did: waiting for his direction.

"You'll take the chopper to the office today and make an appearance."

"I went last time. You're not going?"

Bram picked up the coffee and cast at glance my way as he headed for the computer.

"No. I have stuff to take care of here. You have it under control. If there's anything that needs to be done, I trust you'll handle it."

I breathed through the anger. He didn't have anything to do here. He just wanted to watch her.

"Of course. Is there anything you need while I'm gone?"

Bram sat, his focus going between me and the screen. "No." He paused. "Actually, yes. There's a doctor in Medical. I think she's new. Dr. Cortez, I believe. Find out who she is. I don't remember approving her admittance here."

A smile tugged at my lips. "Because you didn't. I did." At his stare, I came closer. "It was a few months back. You asked me to go over the list and see who we needed for staff. She's a surgeon. I had her taken from Baltimore. Her record is outstanding, but not enough to bring notice. She didn't have much in the way of family or friends. It was an easy…kidnapping."

Bram nodded, going back to the monitor. "She gave slave twenty-four-six-ninety something last night. Some sort of weapon is my guess. I was half tempted to have it removed, but I don't think I will. The slave believes the guards will disobey my orders and try to get her back for the punishment I ordered. Let her see she has nothing to worry over. As for the doctor, I will leave it to you to punish her. This *was* your doing. She obviously hasn't been taught the ways of our world. If you're going to become part of it, even more, it's time you took these matters into your own hands."

The challenging look was one meant to show me up. Little did Bram know, I wasn't as good as he thought me to be. Truth was, he had no idea who I was inside.

"Done. I'll go see her now."

"Do that. Make it clear she's not to be encouraging these slaves. And in no way is she to give them weapons to hurt my guards."

"It won't happen again. You have my word." Bowing my head, I turned and headed to the door. With how early it was, I doubted she was in Medical, but the staff had residence not far from there. And I knew where she resided. I'd seen to the placement of her quarters myself.

I shut the door, going in the direction of the long, curved hall not far away. The guard stood erect, staring at the wall before him as I passed through the entrance. I was someone here. Someone they respected. Someone they were cautious over, which was good. They needed to fear me more than they knew. The ones I had on my side were loyal, but I knew to be careful.

After a good hundred feet, the hall intersected, and I turned, going down even farther. When I passed the next guard, I paused, looking over his face. He was young. Maybe mid-twenties. He'd want to prove himself. They always did.

"I have orders from Mr. Whitlock. We have a situation, and I need you to follow me. Call your high leader and have him send a replacement."

"Yes, Master."

"I'm no Master. Not yet. Sir will work just fine."

"Yes, Sir."

The guard radioed in, and I waited. Within minutes, three men in black uniforms approached. Although I wanted to smile, I held in the reaction at the power I felt.

"You stay," I said, pointing to a shorter man just as young as the first. "You three follow me. We have a doctor who thinks it's okay to pass weapons to slaves. Mr. Whitlock wants her dealt with accordingly." I glanced back, taking in the way their hard faces stared ahead. When we turned again and approached the door, I gestured. "Open it."

The thicker of the two took lead, not even pausing as he grabbed the knob. When it didn't turn in his hand, he brought his foot up and shot it forward. Wood cracked from the frame, and he threw his weight into the barrier, sending the door flying open. The guards rushed through, and I let them take over as I followed.

"Doctor Cortez," I said loudly, walking straight to her room. Lights were already flooding the small space and her dark hair was wild around her as she sat in the middle of the bed. Back and forth she went, staring at the guns trained on her. When she met me with panicked eyes, I lifted my hands for the guards to lower their weapons.

"What's happening?"

"Something you're probably not going to like. You were

witnessed giving something to a slave under your care. A weapon. Do you deny it?"

The fear increased as she took in the men. "I don't know what you're talking about."

"No? Perhaps I should remind you. Men," I turned, showing them my rage, "I'm sure you're all aware of what happened last night. Remind Dr. Cortez why slave twenty-four-six-ninety was brought into Medical."

There was no hesitation as the bigger guard brought back his fist and slammed it into the doctor's face repeatedly. Screaming filled the space as she tried to fight him off, but there was no use. Even slightly taller for a female, she was no match for the large guard. Fabric tore, and I placed my hands behind my back as I let all three men rip off the white slip she wore. The cries grew louder as one flipped her onto her stomach and jerked at his pants.

"To help slaves is strictly forbidden. I do believe you were given this talk when you were brought here. Yet, you provided one with a weapon to harm the same people who allow you to live. Do you think yourself irreplaceable, Dr. Cortez?"

Sobs racked her body as she clawed and yelled into the blankets. She wasn't fighting her attackers or the rape.

"I asked you a question."

"No!"

"No is correct. You are very replaceable. I thought you'd be a good fit, but I see I was wrong. You have a softness I don't have time to squash. You'll join the people you pity. Welcome to your new life, slave." I looked back at the guards. "When you're finished, throw her in Slave Row. If she gives you any trouble, kill her."

I didn't wait for their response. Turning my back, I left the small room. My whistling filled the silent halls and I let a smile come. Today was going to be a great day. And once I returned, I would visit my slave. Let someone try to stop me.

CHAPTER 7

24690

"I want to go home. I want to go home."

The mantra filled the cells for hours, and there was no stopping it. Over and over, the girl who shared a room with me cried and begged.

"I told you, this is your home now."

"No," she sobbed. "I want to go *home*."

"The sooner you accept that you no longer have home, the easier this will become. Trust me, you're only making this harder on yourself."

Bloodshot green eyes stared at me as I paced. The redhead's lip quivered, and her balled fist rose to her mouth. The desperate sound that came out had me slowing. "They put something inside me. T-They did something to my insides. I hurt."

I frowned, knowing what she was referring to. My Master talked about the changes plenty when they'd discovered the new ways. "It's a type of hysterectomy. They do it to all of us. No periods, and no pregnancy. You're lucky, and you'll be thanking the heavens when you get your Master. Besides, your procedure is new. I have the scar on my stomach to show what I went through. You got it the easy way."

"Hysterectomy? But...*I'm only eighteen!* If I get out of here, I won't be able to—"

"You're not leaving," I stressed. "It's impossible. I've been here for fourteen years. If there was a way, don't you think I would have found it?"

The crying grew louder, and I closed my eyes, trying to calm. I had no right to treat her so coldly. Truth was, I was on edge. The louder she cried, the more attention she drew from the guards.

I walked over, sitting on the edge of her bed. Her short red hair was chin length, like mine. She wasn't beautiful, but her dark green eyes made up for her common face. They were speckled with yellow, capturing attention, which might not have been a good thing.

"I'm sorry," I whispered. "I know you're scared. So am I. But I've been through this before. I know things."

The sobs died out as her attention focused. "What sort of things?"

I paused. "What's your name?"

"J-Julie."

"No," I said, shaking my head. "Your new name. It's a number." I pulled down the white shirt I wore, exposing my cleavage. The tattoo was small but couldn't be mistaken. Her lip trembled as she tugged at the collar of her own shirt.

"Twenty-six-nine-seventy-five. That is your new name."

She sobbed again, wiping back the tears as she let go of the shirt.

"You're not a virgin, are you?"

Her head did a quick shake. "What does that have to do with anything?"

"It has to do with *everything*. We're slaves of anything our Masters want. Anything. And you're in the same predicament I am."

"What do you mean? Masters? Who are these men?"

"They're the rich, the famous—the ones who can afford to buy us."

Something flashed in her eyes. Something I didn't understand. She didn't seem so afraid suddenly. She seemed intrigued.

"Our prices will be lower than most of the girls. That's not good, but it doesn't have to be bad. There are men here who are just looking for sex—for a woman to do things they maybe can't find out there. My best advice is to catch the attention of an older man. The older, the better. In my experience, they can be more gentle."

"Old?" Repulsion swept over her face. "If I'm going to be bought, I don't want some *old* man."

"You don't understand. Most of the men here are cruel. They do things to the girls you can't even imagine. Yes, some of the older ones do those things too, but in my experience, it's the younger ones who are more…out for blood. With the money they have, they aren't incapable of finding a woman on the outside world. What they want here is what they can't legally have. Do you understand? *They want to hurt you.*"

"Blood?"

Again, fear. Good.

"Some men will pay a lot of money just to slice open your skin. To *kill* you. Do you want a younger man who enjoys death, or an older, nicer one who may beat you on occasion, but takes great care of you?"

At her silence, I rolled my eyes.

"I'm trying to help you. I don't want anything bad to happen to you, and you don't know what to expect. This isn't a game. You're not going to wake up one day and have men bursting through the door to rescue you. No one is coming."

I stood to start pacing again and froze as my eyes met one of the guards. He was staring through the small window in the door. Up and down, his gaze traveled over my body. I couldn't help but jump when a hand grasped mine.

"Who is that?"

"Just a guard," I said quietly. "Don't look at him."

I turned, facing her as I stole another glance. He was still there. Still watching.

"They'll be here for me. Not you. Don't be afraid. They'll know you're still healing. They're forbidden to touch you until…after."

"Touch me?"

I took a deep breath, stealing another look. He was gone, replaced by someone else. Someone who left me shaking even more.

"Shit."

"Who's that?"

The interest in her tone had me wanting to shake her. She was so naïve—so unaware of how this place worked and how the people who resided here acted. A handsome face only meant one thing at Whitlock: pain, and possible death. The better looking, the more dangerous they were.

"That's Mr. Whitlock. This fortress belongs to him."

The door opened, and I took a deep breath as he stepped in. His stare narrowed, and guilt had me swallowing. *He knew.*

"A vast improvement, but not enough. Maybe I should have them cut your hair a little shorter."

My hand lifted on instinct, but only midway before I quickly dropped it back to my side. "If it pleases you, Master."

"Pleases me? Pleases me?" He laughed angrily. "You have no idea what would please me right now."

I stayed quiet as he circled around me.

"When I discovered your Master was dead, I knew you were going to stir up trouble. I have to say, though, I wasn't prepared for how much. Do you know how many Masters have come to me this morning inquiring about you?"

My stomach dropped. "No, Mr. Whitlock."

"Three," he growled. "Your Master's body hasn't even been

disposed of. I suspected a few, but Master Kain…I didn't expect. Do you know how much he offered for you?"

Fear left me spinning and flying to Mr. Whitlock's feet. "Don't let him have me. Anyone but him and Master Pollock."

"Eight million, slave. Eight. I get that much for virgins. But you are not pure. You're not even that beautiful. I had to ask myself, why would he want you at such a price? Before I could come to an answer, a friend of your Master arrived. Master Yahn."

I had heard about the rich banker extensively over the years. The talks about his money would go on and on for hours. Not to mention, he was one of the Main Masters…

"He is kind from what I know," I managed.

"Twelve million is what he offered when I said no. And, more than anyone, he knows better than to push me. Yet, he did. For you." Pain stung my scalp as Mr. Whitlock jerked my head back to look at him. "And do you know who has to match that price. Me! You are not worth twelve million."

Tears raced down my cheeks as he gripped even tighter. "If you think what they offer now is high, wait until auction night. You may break records. What I want to know is why? What did you do while you were under your Master's care? Did you lead them on? Did you *fuck* them behind your Master's back? Why you?"

"I don't know, I swear. I did nothing." And I hadn't. I stayed as inconspicuous as possible. "You said you would have to match them. Why?"

He let go, staring down at me with more hate than I'd ever seen from anyone.

"You don't worry about that. Nothing is marked in stone, and your future here becomes more aggravating by the day. Men, *the doctor*…I may have you killed and spare everyone the grief you bring us."

My face shot to the ground as nausea beckoned. *He did know.* I could go to the White Room if he chose to send me.

"That's right, hide yourself, little mouse. Retreat into the submissive shell you are. I should put you over my knee and beat your ass black and blue. You drive me mad."

To glare up like I wanted would no doubt land me a beating I couldn't afford. *Little mouse.* My breathing turned heavy while I let my short hair cover my angry expression.

"Stand."

Slowly, I rose, keeping my focus a few feet ahead. I saw nothing, felt nothing but the deadening of the fury I'd held only moments ago. It wasn't safe to embrace such emotions. The more I let them fester, the braver I became.

"If you could pick one Master out of everyone you know, who would it be?"

I did look up then. "Will my choice matter?"

"No. I asked you a question. I want it answered. Who?"

I knew no one good enough to stake my future with. Anyone could act kind, but behind these walls, their true secrets came out. And there were things darker than someone taking a blade to another's skin. The things I had heard gave me nightmares—dreams so vivid and disturbing, I could almost feel my meat being cut from my bones in small increments over time.

"I don't know. Master Yahn, perhaps?"

"That old bastard? Why?"

"He's not that old," I braved.

Mr. Whitlock moved more from my side to come stand before me. "He's damn near sixty."

"He's probably safe," I whispered.

"He is not," Bram said, only inches from my face. "He's had one slave throughout his twenty years here. Have you ever seen her?"

I shook my head. "No."

"Nor will you. She's mummified, lying on his bed. Beaten to

death after one of his episodes. He sleeps with her every night, kisses her good morning, and sings to her when he thinks no one is watching."

Horror had my stare rising to his.

"You are safe with no one. No one, slave. So, I ask you again, which Master would you choose?"

"Mr. Harper was interested." I swallowed hard, knowing he was the last person I should have brought attention to. I wanted him the most, but Bram shouldn't know that. "Should I fear him?"

"You fear everyone. Have you not learned that? We all have secrets. His may be the darkest of them all."

"Really? How do you think?"

"*Slave*," he growled. "You ask too many damn questions."

"Then…I choose you."

Silence.

"You said there was a price for helping me. Pay it. Make me yours if you're going to take me whenever you want anyway. There's no use selling me if that's your plan."

"I will *not* make you my slave."

"You said I brought grief. If you sell me, and then come to me, my Master *will* find out. Imagine the chaos that would cause. He'd kill me. If that's what you want, take that scalpel from under my pillow and end this now. I don't wish to die at the hands of a mad man murderous with jealous rage."

Bram's finger slid along my cheek, tucking a piece of hair behind my ear. The act was opposite of the reactions he'd displayed at my proposition.

"To die from jealous rage." He laughed under his breath. "I'm afraid you may not have a choice either way."

CHAPTER 8

BRAM

Make her my slave…

Did she even know what she was asking? She feared the men within these walls but had no idea I was the worst of them all for her. Love didn't tame monsters like me. The stupid fucking emotion only intensified it. I couldn't do it. I couldn't become like everyone else here. To give in was a sentence I would never recover from. I'd like it too much to even try. And then, there were my suspicions. Fuck, if they weren't growing by the hour. No. She wasn't safe with me.

"If I don't have a choice, what does it matter? If you don't want me as your slave, but still want me, put me somewhere only you have access. Or do us both a favor. *Don't come to me at all.*"

My hand struck her face before she had the chance to continue. The words, the act of striking her…my blood was fucking boiling. Worse, the lust was unbearable. "You forget who you're talking to. I'll come to you whenever I damn well please. Maybe," I said, grabbing her throat, "maybe I'll take you right now. Does your new little friend want to watch while I make you scream?"

"P-Please."

The plea came out strained as I applied pressure.

"Please, what?"

"Please, Master."

I let go, forcing her to the floor. I should have gone. Left before I fucked her. Dammit, if I could have only made my feet work. My mind was racing, already calculating ways to ruin everything I had tried so hard to avoid.

"What will you do with me?"

I looked down, taking in her worry. She wasn't trying to stand or move away. She knew her place and the reason I put her there. It only made me want her even more.

"Master, please. I beg you to tell me."

"You talk too much, but you know that. Stand. You're to follow me. If you say one more word…"

My order had her scrambling to her feet. Her head went down, and silence followed as the door opened and I stalked down the hallway. With each step, the darkness within me grew. To want something so much, to know nothing but that gut-wrenching torture and face it every day, had taken its toll. I wouldn't have twenty-four-six-ninety as my slave, but I would have her before anyone else did.

"Faster."

Footsteps padded behind me, her presence growing stronger the closer she got. My adrenaline left my pulse vibrating over every inch of my body. Questions and doubt tried to push through, but my battle was long lost. If my suspicions didn't amount to anything, she would belong to West soon. That ownership, I couldn't come between. I wouldn't. So, why was I doing this now?

I pulled out my keys, unlocking and throwing open my door. The fear clouding my slave's face was all I needed to latch onto her arm and pull her inside. The fog that took over was one I could barely fight. My lips crushed into hers, and her weight in my arms was nothing as I took us into my bedroom.

The bed bounced under our weight, and I ground my hard cock between her legs, kissing her harder. Heaven, sweetness, the feel of her tongue as it hesitantly met mine, left my body moving into her small frame even more. Had she ever been kissed? *Really kissed?* I didn't think so.

"Master?"

The heavy pants drove me forward to press into her lips again. I didn't care about her hesitation. My body lifted enough to jerk the dress to her hips, and in a swift tug, I brought her panties down. She lifted her legs to help me remove them, and in one tiny moment of our eyes connecting, the world I had known disappeared. Everything was gone. Time ceased to exist, leaving me lost within her depths. Forever seemed to pass within seconds.

No words left my slave as she widened her legs beneath me. It was consent in the purest form, but was it one she wanted? She was too well trained to fight. She knew better, and me? I wouldn't know the truth unless I felt for myself.

My head lowered to her neck, and it took everything I had to trail my fingers up her thigh. If she didn't want me, it would hurt. But if she did…in the end, it may have hurt worse. She'd become more mine—more than she ever had been.

A small sound was followed by a deep inhale as I cupped her pussy. What my fingers met twisted my stomach into a million pieces. She was so wet. So ready for me. It was a relief and the end all at once. We couldn't fight this need. No matter how hard we had tried over the years, we couldn't escape. And I knew she felt it too. The looks, the beatings she'd taken for them. I may have scared the hell out of her, but we were doomed to this desire.

My finger inched inside her channel, and I cursed myself for not being able to wait. Hadn't she been through enough? If I was going to do this, shouldn't I at least let her enjoy it? She wouldn't. Not really. The pain would bring me happiness, but it was going to cause her discomfort. The man I'd become over the years didn't care. Her opinion or wellbeing didn't matter. She was a slave. The part she'd won over worried about her reaction —her feelings.

The volume of her moans increased, drowning out my worries. I sucked against her neck, easing another finger inside. At her gasp, I pushed deeper. My thrusts became faster at the haze engulfing me. My cock ached. I was tired of drawing this out. I couldn't make love to her. I couldn't show too much emotion. Yet, I was. More than I should have.

Withdrawing my fingers, I pushed up enough to jerk off my jacket and shirt. When I removed my pants, my slave's stare cut up to mine. She was filled with such terror, it only pushed me over the edge of excitement. She scrambled higher onto the bed, but barely made it there before my weight collided with hers. Her fight was automatic. Even with the training and beatings she'd undergone, fear won.

"Don't hurt me. Don't—"

My mouth found hers again, and I didn't force my cock into her like I should have—like the Master of this place *would* have. Instead, I slipped my tongue back into her mouth, teasing, coaxing her to open and accept me. Minutes went by while I let her trust build. When I pulled the top of the thin dress down past her breasts and rolled her nipple between my fingers, she gave herself to me even more. Her body softened, and within minutes, her hips began to rock beneath me.

Leisurely, I slid down her chest, sucking against one of her hard nubs. The whimper that followed came from so deep within her throat, I felt it through every inch of my cock. Her breasts weren't very big, but enough for me to squeeze against the soft flesh while I tugged at her nipple. Faster, she moved, pulling at my arms, trying to bring me up.

"Relax."

My demand had her heavy lids rising. Wetness enveloped the

head of the cock as I slowly pushed forward, letting her adjust to my large size. She was so small under me. So frail and breakable. God, I *could* break her. I wanted to. I wanted to be rough and unrelenting. To have my way with her like I had fantasized. No matter what I wanted, the actions weren't coming. I stayed cautious. My mind kept saying, *next time*. Next time, she'd be healed. She'd be ready to take something that brutal.

"Mmmm. Yes." Twenty-four-six-ninety's mouth flew open, and she lifted her head as I withdrew and surged in deeper. I was maybe halfway, and her wet grip was killing me. I needed more. Wanted more.

"Fuck. Kiss me, slave."

She didn't need an order to ravage my mouth. The spirit inside I had witnessed before returned. She threw herself forward, wrapping her arms around my neck and her legs around my waist. The invitation was more than I could handle. My cock buried inside her, and I drank in her screams, holding still.

"Did I hurt you?"

"Y-Yes, Master."

"Good. It wouldn't have been right if I didn't at least once."

Tears escaped. Such beautiful tears.

I pushed to rest on my knees, gently withdrawing while watching the pain flicker and leave her face. When I reached the head of my cock, I began to move back in deep, keeping the thrusts agonizingly drawn out, rubbing over her clit to soak in her reactions. It wasn't until she was arching and reaching back for me that I lowered to move against her.

"More, Master. More. Yes."

Nails tore into my back as she clawed into my skin. The stinging had me going faster. Harder.

I bit against her neck, and she grew louder in her demands of me…and I let her. I began fucking her right. Fucking her like I wanted. My fingers buried in her hair on both sides of her head, and I gripped hard, slamming into her with everything I had. The screams and spasms that shook her body were the purest, most powerful drug I'd ever experienced. It sank its hooks into my obsession and doused the emotion with something new—something so strong, it was all I could feel.

"You like this. Tell me you like it."

"I do."

My toes pushed into the mattress as I drove myself into her mercilessly. The suction on my own neck, the raking against my back…it was ecstasy. The more pain she inflicted, the harder it became to withhold my release. It had been so long since I had been with a woman, and my slave wasn't just anyone; she was all I had ever wanted. Years of restraint were coming down to this moment, and it was more than I could handle.

"I'm coming back for you later tonight. In the morning." I slowed, grinding my hips into her inner-most thighs. "I'm going to fuck you so much, your new Master will never come close to giving you what I do. I'm going to ruin you for him, slave. He may be attractive. He may treat you well. But you will *never* want him like you want me. I feel you. I see you," I whispered in her ear. "I've got you."

The screams that came with her orgasm triggered my own. Wave after wave, I shot my release into her, and with each one, I lost myself even more.

CHAPTER 9

WEST

"You look like you're in a better mood than before I left."

I took the drink Bram handed me, confused by the slight grin permanently etched into his face.

"Do I? Must be the scotch." He lifted his glass, downing another shot. In the five minutes I'd been in his living room, he'd tossed back at least two a minute. It was nonstop. It wasn't right. *He wasn't right.*

"What happened? Because something did, and it was either really good or really, really bad."

Still, the grin was there.

"Both? It's nothing. Tell me what happened at the office."

I shrugged, sipping the liquor. "Nothing of importance. Things are fine without us. Our lawyers are the best. I guess that's the perk of owning and not working the actual cases."

"I'll drink to that." Bram refilled his glass, downing it in one drink.

"How's Everleigh? Have you checked on her today?"

The grin melted into a glare. "She's twenty-four-six-ninety.

She is not Everleigh. I don't understand why you keep calling her that."

"Because it's easier than saying some long fucking number. When I'm with you, I want to say her name. When she's with me, I will call her slave and do away with the stupid number altogether."

"I don't want to hear her name."

I stepped to the side, following Bram as he tried to turn away.

"Why is that? Does it make her too real for you?"

"Of course not," he snapped. "She's a slave. She's always been and will always be owned. She's nothing."

My lids lowered, studying him as he turned and grabbed the decanter. As if Bram had second thoughts, he placed it down with the glass and walked into the kitchen, grabbing a bottled water.

"What's on your agenda? It's getting late."

"Late?" I looked at my watch. "It's barely after nine."

He shrugged, collapsing onto the couch. "It's late, and I'm tired."

"If that's the case, I guess I'll revisit Everleigh. I'm sure she's awake. She was when I left and seemed to enjoy our conversation."

Bram's face turned serious as his legs dropped to the floor. He sat up, and I missed nothing as his anger resurfaced.

"She's not just some guest you can go hang out with. She's a slave, and she is for sale. Just because I said I would help you get her does not give you free reign to see her whenever you like."

"But *you* can? Her roommate mentioned you going to their room today."

"This is my place!" The bottle crackled in Bram's fist as he stood to hover over me. At my six-foot height, he was still a good three inches taller. "I've let you continue to stay in this life. I have partnered my business with you and given you everything you have ever asked for. You're like my brother. *Do not* push me further than is safe, my friend. It would be unwise of you. Stay away from her. You are not to see her again until after she's yours. You've been warned."

I laughed under my breath, shaking my head. "Warned? Are you threatening me?"

"You should know by now I don't make threats. I'm giving you something when I don't have to. Follow my orders, or I put an end to it all."

I stepped back, holding in my hate and the other million things I wanted to say. "I apologize for upsetting you and stepping out of line. I won't bother you anymore tonight."

Bram's breathing was heavy as his stare followed me to the door. When I shut the barrier between us, I let my bitterness take over my expression. Who was he to tell me I couldn't see her? I did *everything* for him.

I walked two doors down and threw open my door. A smirk had me nearly exploding.

"What the fuck are you doing here? Have you lost your damn mind?"

I shut the door, watching Eli stand from my couch. The guard shrugged, lifting his beer. "My shift was over and I thought we could have some drinks before I head to the barracks and crash."

"Drinks? I had you do me a favor and you come here for drinks?" I glanced to where I knew the camera was located. "Pretty stupid, don't you think?"

"Nah. You have to have friends here or you'll go crazy. Grab a beer. I put them in the fridge. Sit with me."

I waved the offer away but grabbed the chair to bring it closer. "This is dangerous. I know you're smarter than this. What is it?"

Eli sat back down, gulping a few pulls before resting back. "No bad intentions. Friends. That's it. You're about to become one of the Masters. It's good to have friends in high places.

Besides, a lot of them hang out with the guards. We're all one here. Money on the outside doesn't matter. There's nothing dividing us inside these walls."

He was wrong, but I wasn't focused on that. My guilt was making me uneasy. Not that I regretted having Everleigh's Master killed. Even if Bram did find out, I didn't think he'd kill me over it. Maybe never let me leave here again, but I didn't care about that. This place had always been home.

"Okay." I stood, walking over to grab a beer. "Friends. Turn on the TV. Find us something to watch."

A smile stretched across his face, and he grabbed the remote off the end table. When I returned to take my seat, a football game was on. I didn't watch sports, but I didn't mind them.

"I used to play pro. Bet you didn't know that."

"I didn't. What happened?"

He took another drink. "Shoulder injury. Just didn't have it anymore."

"How did you end up here?"

A smile exposed white teeth as he glanced over to me. He was good-looking for a man. Tanned skin, wide shoulders. Thinner lips, but wide eyes. I couldn't deny he was handsome, but the darkness in him was all too evident in his look.

"I worked some security jobs after I stopped playing ball. My size made it easy. My past made me likable. I made a lot of friends. Guess you could say I made the right ones."

"Sounds like it to me."

"I like it here. Sure as hell beats out there. Free food, no rent, girls whenever I want them."

"Consensually?" I threw him a look, and he laughed.

"Always. Mr. Whitlock doesn't mind either way, but I've never had to take a girl against her will. So long as I stay away from the virgins, it's all good. It's really all about Slave Row. God, I love Slave Row."

"My slave's there," I said, tipping my can toward him. "Keep your hands off twenty-four-six-ninety."

"No worries, West. I can call you that, right?" At my shrug, he continued. "No one is going to touch your slave. Mr. Whitlock has made sure of it."

"Billy's hand," I said lowly.

"Well, yeah. But also, his threat. Hell, today he threatened to have a guard's eyes gouged from his head if he didn't stop looking through the window at your slave. The man scares the shit out of ninety percent of us."

"But not you," I said, smiling.

"Not me."

His mirrored expression had me downing my beer. A real friend. It was ever better than won-over guards, than paying them off or manipulating them. It was free. More loyal.

"No!" Eli's hands shot up at the TV, and I turned to take in the game. Bram's threats sank into the background, and I tried not to think about how it would be another few weeks before I would be able to see Everleigh. With Bram always watching, I couldn't even consider it.

"When was the last time you went to a real game?"

Eli's eyes shot over to mine. "Hell, I haven't been in a stadium since I played in one."

"We should go. Pick a game, no matter where it is, and you and I will make a week of it."

"You're joking."

"I'm not. I need a break from here. Can you find someone to cover your shifts?"

He shook his head. "I'm not supposed to leave."

"Bram won't mind. Let me take care of it."

And I would. I had a feeling my friend was dying to get rid of me. Just as he had been tonight. Let him grovel in his heartbreak. I wasn't going to be at the brunt of his anger. I'd stay away as much as I could until the auction. And when I returned, Everleigh would be mine.

CHAPTER 10

24690

With every step, every pull of my muscles, my body screamed through the soreness. Bram had stayed true to his word, retrieving me the first night and the next morning. He was insatiable, continuously returning at odd times throughout the day. It wasn't that I had to care about my roommate anymore. She was removed shortly after his first nightly visit, but it was the guards I worried about. They were looking at me differently. I didn't like it.

"Faster, slave."

I clasped my hands as I picked up the pace behind Bram. It had been five days since our first sexual encounter, and even now, I couldn't process what was happening. What did I feel for him? There was something. There always had been. Sure, he scared me, but I couldn't dismiss the times I'd seen his tenderness. He'd helped me more than once over the years. Even now, I prayed he was saving me from some disaster only he knew was coming.

"Slave."

The growled threat had me practically running to stay close. I didn't like these constant visits. There were eyes everywhere.

Every door we passed housed Masters. Every entrance into a new hall presented a guard. I had to say something…but what? *Sorry, Mr. Whitlock, I can't see you anymore?* I couldn't do that. He wouldn't listen even if I did. And did I want to stop seeing him?

No.

Bram's quarters came into view, and I kept my head down as we neared the entrance. The moment he had the lock undone, he swept me inside and pulled me up to straddle him. The hunger that met my lips, my tongue, was one I couldn't help but return. Damn this situation and the bastard he portrayed himself to be. In these moments, I saw the real him—the one he tried so hard to hide away.

"Did they do as I instructed?"

"You know they did," I said between kisses. "I know you watched. I know you smell it on me."

"Of course I *watched*. Do you think I trust those bastards in the shower room with you?"

Fingers wove through my hair, pulling my head back as Bram bit and sucked against the side of my neck. My back arched, and I blindly pulled, loosening his tie. He let go, and I dove back for his mouth, barely getting to taste him before I broke away, gasping. Two fingers slid in deep, nearly taking my breath away. A moan poured out as I went back to slide my tongue against his.

The grip around my waist tightened while he thrust in a slow pace. In all the times my old Master had my body, it had never been like this. Not even close. There was no passion or lust. I knew my duty, and I'd tried to make him happy by doing it. Here…Bram was introducing me to a world of sensations I'd never experienced before.

"I knew the scent would be a good match for your skin. I could already smell you all over my bed…on me. Now, I'm going to smell this new you in its place. It's stronger and will last longer. You'll be here even when you're not. And the same will go for you. From now on, you wear this. Every day. Even if you aren't expecting me. This is me on you—with you. You'll never be alone."

I drew back, seeing his brow crease. Whatever he was thinking, he wouldn't say.

"Just wear it," he growled.

A smile wanted to come at the withdraw of his tenderness, but I knew better than to make it obvious. He was trying to fight what he felt so hard.

"I'll wear it every day."

The fingers that had stilled inside me slowly began to move again. I rested my cheek against his, bringing my other hand up to cup his rough cheek. The combination of my arousal combined with the stubble electrified the pleasure. He hadn't shaved today. Or yesterday, for that matter. I loved the darkening on his cheeks and how rugged it made him look. *And the feel.* God, I'd felt it everywhere only hours ago.

"I will wear it every day, and I will think of you—of this right here," I moaned, rocking my hips. "Will you think of these moments when you think of me?"

The thrusting increased as he bit into my shoulder. Instead of answering, he lowered us to the bed and pulled my dress off almost instantly. Without anything underneath, like instructed, I was already ready for him.

"So smooth." His fingertips rubbed over my shaved folds, circling around to dip back into my entrance. As the thrusts continued, he jerked at the buttons of his shirt, removing it. I watched, half eager to help, half savoring every inch of his exposed skin. His body was like nothing I'd ever seen. The hard muscle of his chest and shoulders, down to his defined abs, left me tracing the lines and dips long after we finished. It also usually led to him having me again before returning me to my cell.

I bit my bottom lip, gripping the comforter as he rotated his shoulder to push even deeper. My legs spread wide on instinct, and I rocked down to meet him. His eyes darted from where he thrust, to my face, and the sound that left him made me even more impatient. He was always watching my every expression.

"Master?"

"No." He gave a hard shake, denying my need for him as I reached out. It was followed by his other hand rising so his thumb could tease my clit. It didn't take long before my head went back and forth. I was on fire. He always seemed to manage that.

"Do you see how wet you get when I touch you?" He leaned down, kissing and nipping at my knee. When he continued to move his lips up my thigh, the answer wouldn't stop coming.

"Yes…yes…"

He paused, looking up, and smiled. The beauty of the man I was suddenly staring at left me in awe. It was as if I was looking at a complete stranger—one I couldn't help but want to gravitate toward.

"Yes, you see, or yes, you want to me continue?"

"Both," I forced out. "Don't stop."

The smile disappeared as he went back to kissing, and the sadness that came with that was an odd emotion. I was beginning to more than like Bram. I wasn't sure what I felt, but I knew it was something I'd never gone through before. When we were together, I was swept away, but alone…I was scared of these feelings. I missed him more than I should have. And the trust, the connection I felt to a man I feared before this, rattled me. I was so confused.

Suction replaced his thumb, and my head shot up as pleasure exploded through me. Faster, I moved underneath him. With his digits still working magic inside me, I knew it wasn't going to be long before my orgasm came. He talked about teaching me to control the need, but I had no idea how I was supposed to do that. I'd only just learned what it was to have an orgasm. My Master never lasted long enough. To stop what was coming seemed impossible.

"Master. *Master*."

"Mm-mmm"

I jumped at the vibrations that nearly triggered me. But he didn't stop humming. My legs jerked wildly, and I screamed as my release surged through me. I knew I was going to get punished, but I couldn't help it. *He did it on purpose.*

"I think you're incapable of following orders. Do you do it just to spite me?"

Bram removed his fingers, only to replace them with his tongue.

"No, Master. I tried to tell you. I—"

My words were cut off as he pressed his fingertips over the top of my slit. The motion of back and forth left my legs pushing down into the bed.

"Keep going," he said, lifting his head. "I didn't tell you to stop."

"I…" Faster, his hand moved over the sensitive nerves, stalling my train of thought. "I…told you. I'm trying to last longer. Or…get better."

Was that what I was trying to say? I didn't even know. His head was up again, resting against the inside of my knee while he watched me. If I didn't know better, I'd assume he was amused, but it was hard to tell with how closed off he tried to keep himself.

"Will you kiss me now?"

"Kiss you? Did I not just kiss you enough?"

"Not there. On my lips."

"Slaves shouldn't get kissed like that."

No hardness came to his features, just the same soft look as he stared at me.

"So, don't kiss me. Let me kiss you."

His lips tugged back on one side as he rose, settling his weight on top of me.

"Kiss away, slave, but don't expect me to return your affection. I'm not so easily swayed."

I smiled, grabbing his cheeks and sliding my tongue over the separation of his mouth. My legs locked around his waist, and I moved against him while my teeth pulled at his bottom lip. A deep exhale left him, and he opened for me. I took my time, letting my tongue sweep along his. He didn't kiss me back. Instead, he gave me the time to do as I pleased. When I added suction and sucked against his tongue, he dove forward, unable to restrain any longer.

My fingers slid through his hair, tightening like his always did to mine. There was power in my grasp I couldn't get enough of. My thighs tightened around his waist, and I broke from his mouth, still holding on. Deep breaths left us, and there was something I'd never seen before in Bram's eyes—enthrallment? Yes. I pulled him back to me, kissing him hard, mirroring his actions. I was flipped onto my stomach so fast, the room spun in a blur. Bram jerked against the clasp of his pants, pushing them down at a fast pace.

Whack! Whack!

The fire that flared over my ass had a yelp exploding from my mouth.

"Your bravery grows. You get too comfortable taking control."

"You like it," I countered.

Whack!

Tears burned my eyes, but I didn't care. I slid my knees to my stomach, keeping my head down so my ass would be in the air the way he liked. But I never broke eye contact, and Bram didn't either.

"You like it," I said again, my voice quieter. "Admit it."

Whack!

I cringed through the pain and anger quickly flooded me. The top of my body lifted so I was on all fours. Bram's head cocked to the side, but I couldn't keep myself from turning and crawling toward him. The power I'd experienced was still there, still luring me into a personality I'd never been allowed to test out. Temptation was all too sweet, especially when I knew how much my Master wanted it.

I moved in, brushing my lips back over his. Fingers pushed through my hair, gripping tightly as he held me even with his face. His eyes pierced mine, so full of dominance, my inner self wanted to scramble to get away. But I didn't. I didn't so much as blink.

"Lay down," I whispered, trying to move back to his lips. "Let me be on top this time. Let me pleasure you the way I want to."

For seconds, he searched my face. When my palm settled over his chest and I applied pressure, he didn't fight me. The hold on my hair eased, disappearing as he let go and lay on his back, his eyes cautious. I didn't push my luck anywhere else. I lowered, tracing my tongue over the head of his cock, letting the connection of our eyes hold. Bram's chest rose while his breathing became labored. My lips encased the tip as my tongue swirled around the bottom side of his length. The moan that left him fed into that addicting feeling. *That power.*

Inch by inch, I took him into my mouth, licking, sucking, stroking. I put everything I had into trying to make it feel amazing for him. The more ragged his breaths became, the more I knew it was working. My Master's fingers were back in my hair, but not as a form of control. His hand followed me down repeatedly. When I withdrew and straddled his cock, Bram was the stranger again. He was beautiful.

Thickness stretched my channel, and I eased down, taking him within me. His hands rose, but before he could place them on my hips like he had intended, I interlaced our fingers, holding them between us as I began to move against him. The pained expression, the longing…he couldn't hide what he felt in his moment. *In our moment.*

I rotated my hips, moaning as I took all of him deep. Bram jerked against our connection, sitting as he did so. His arms were suddenly around me, working me up and down on his cock as I wrapped my arms around his neck and kissed him. The passion we shared left me euphoric. Everything disappeared but the two of us. We kept it slow, increased our speed, went back to leisurely, taking our time. Hours seemed to pass, and I never wanted our moment to end.

Sweat covered our bodies, but I didn't care. I continued sucking against the salty juncture of Bram's neck. Another orgasm was on the verge of coming, and I could feel him swelling inside me.

"You'll stay with me tonight. You'll sleep with me so I can hold you like this. I don't ever want to let you go."

And with those words, I let myself shatter. My body shook with spasms and my heart swelled to heights I'd never imagined. True to his word, I became ruined for anyone else. I wasn't a slave in our moment. *I was his.*

CHAPTER 11

BRAM

Had I loved her before when she wasn't mine? The amount didn't seem comparable to what I felt now. Twenty-four-six-ninety left me enchanted with her presence. I couldn't imagine being without her. And soon, I would. Soon, she might belong to West, and he'd have this part of her. He'd love her, just as I did. And she would come to love him too. Who wouldn't? West was gentler than I was. He wouldn't talk down to her. He'd make her feel like a queen, not a slave.

I blinked through the heaviness of my lids, staring at her sleeping face. Such peace for someone who had been through real hell. The bruising was fading, but I saw no discoloration when I looked at her. Only the beauty I had witnessed from the beginning. God, I loved her. I loved her more than what was fathomable. How was I going to release her to another man? I knew I should have never taken her this way. What had I been thinking?

As if my slave could feel my eyes on her, she stirred, reaching up to hold my neck. My arms were still wrapped around her. I doubted they'd ever left her during our few hours of sleep.

And the sleep...*fuck*. I'd never slept so deeply. Her love worked miracles on the man I had been.

I leaned forward, brushing my lips over hers. Light blue was almost lavender as she peered up at me for the smallest moment. Sleep took her again, and I almost wanted to kiss her harder so she'd wake. But if I did that, we'd be up, and I didn't want this to end. I never wanted it to end.

The grip on my neck tightened as she snuggled into my chest. How could a heart feel so much emotion? The vastness seemed to spread infinitely within me. But with it was a sinking weight of pain to come—pain I wasn't prepared for. *Pain I couldn't begin to comprehend.* If I thought I had loved her before, if the sadness of not having her was that strong, this might literally kill me.

A yawn came from her mouth and she blinked, staring up at me. My hand came to rest on the back of her head as I pulled her closer.

"Go back to sleep. I forbid you to wake. Not yet."

A small laugh echoed around us, feeding the love. She threw her leg over my hip, squeezing me tight before silence once again took over. Minutes passed, and her breathing lightened. She was sleeping again, and I was content to live the rest of my days just like this. But I wouldn't. *Couldn't.* This may have been heaven, but the time would come when my true colors broke through. I'd ruin what we'd shared and destroy her. I knew it, just as I knew what I was feeling was nothing more than an illusion. Love did that to people. It gave them a glimpse of the sweetest dream, only to show them what a fool they'd been to trust it. I wouldn't do that to either of us. This, I could hold to during the hard times. I couldn't hold a corpse unless I wanted to become Master Yahn.

No, I wouldn't be like him. Today, I'd say goodbye to my slave. It had to be done. West would be back any day now, and the last thing I needed was him knowing about us. It was better this way.

"Up. Go shower."

I broke away, practically dumping her on the bed. Twenty-four-six-ninety stretched and sat up. She didn't test my patience. Crawling from the bed, she stiffened, walking into the bathroom. I knew she was hurting. I'd known it when I went back for her the day before. I couldn't help it. I couldn't control this obsessive need to have her with me.

The water to the sink came on, and I knew she was brushing her teeth. And fuck if I didn't have a toothbrush for her resting in my holder. I'd had it there since day two, when I practically dragged her from bed at five in the morning. I made her shower and get ready here. Then I fucked her and took her back, only to get her a few hours later. I should have just kept her here. I would have gotten to spend more time with her than the stolen hours where I'd broken down throughout the days.

When the water turned off and the shower started, I opened the door, taking my spot in front of the sink. My eyes lifted to the reflection of her nude body under the spray. The glass shower gave me the perfect view—a view I was never going to forget.

"Will you come back for me later?"

I shoved the toothbrush in my mouth, refusing to answer. When I was done, only then did I lean against the counter and give her my attention.

"No. I will not come for you anymore."

Her head spun to me, and she reached out, wiping over the glass where it was starting to fog. The wideness of her eyes, the shock she held in them, was damn near crippling.

"Ever?"

I shook my head, swallowing hard. "West will more than likely win the bid on you. I'll cover the amount, but no one will know that. He's to have you."

Her head jerked back and forth as she continued to stare at me.

"It's for the best. He'll be a good Master."

Again, she silently said no with her head.

"It has to be this way, slave. It *will* be this way."

"But I chose you. You asked me, and I told you who I wanted."

My teeth clenched as my chest felt as though it had caved in. "The choice is not yours. You have no choice. You are no one. How many times do I have to tell you that?"

The door to the shower flew open and water dripped from her body as she stomped toward me.

"My Master told me who I am. I am Everleigh Davenport, daughter of the former billionaire, Henry Davenport, CEO and owner of Northway Airlines. I am not no one. I could have been *someone.* I was someone! Your father and that bastard of an owner I had took everything from me. *I demand a say.* You owe me that!"

Instinct brought my hand back, but for the life of me, love wouldn't let me strike. She was right, and the truth was something I'd locked away from the beginning. I didn't want to look at her like a human being. I wasn't raised to. This fortress and the responsibilities had been pounded into me since I was too young to know the difference. My father's fists were a constant reminder of what was and wasn't supposed to be. Whitlock was my responsibility, and if I brought it crumbling down, I was a dead man. The men behind these walls had money and power—more power than me on the outside world. I was trapped with this curse, and there was nothing I could do about it. Nothing I *would* do about it. Whitlock was here to stay. Even if I did end this, the men wouldn't stop. They wouldn't do away with their crimes. They could possibly become out of control. Here, there was a system. Rules. Keep the monsters in a cage and they couldn't bite the children. They couldn't wreak havoc on society.

I made it that. I stopped the pedophilia. I did what I could to clean up this place to the best of my abilities.

"Clean off that soap and get your ass dressed. If you ever speak to me that way again, I *will* have you whipped."

A sob escaped and she threw me a glare before spinning back to the shower. My pulse hammered. I was torn. Fuck, she wanted me, and I wanted her more than anything. It just couldn't be. I wouldn't be the one who broke her completely. West would be a perfect match for her. He'd fix the mess I'd created. Hell, he'd had her Master killed to have her. I knew that. Although it pissed me off, could I blame him? He'd gone to her apartment with me plenty of times. He had seen the beatings. He took care of it. I still didn't trust him and planned to look into it even more, but he would protect her.

I turned back to the sink, ignoring what I had discovered as I began to wash my face and shave. By the time I finished, Everleigh stood dressed behind me, waiting. I stole glances in the mirror. She wasn't looking at me. Her head was down and her hands were clasped behind her. I took my time, regardless of the fact that I should have been rushing her back.

"You should probably know I love you and will never love anyone else. You wanted to ruin me. Congratulations. You succeeded. Since I will not see you again until the auction, I ask that you spare both of us from having to pretend this didn't exist and not place me with your friend. I want a different Master. One you're never around. I don't care which one it is. Anyone but Mr. Harper."

"Stop being dramatic. It's not fitting for you."

Her eyes jerked up to mine and there was a calmness there that didn't sit right with me.

"What you have done is far worse than what any other Master can do. You showed me hope. Love. What did you think you were doing by messing with my emotions? Slave or not, I have feelings. And you don't care about that, Mr. Whitlock. I'm done with anything involving you. I'm done," she said, trailing off.

I wiped my face, unable to stop the fury that came with the fear. *Done.* I'd seen her ultimately done. It had drenched my clothing and body as I'd held her in my arms. She was just a girl then, but she was capable of suicide. I'd saved her then, and I couldn't now. Not short of putting her in a padded room.

"You say you're done. Do you plan to kill yourself?"

Her eyes lifted again. No tears. Nothing. She was more stoic than ever.

"No."

"Then what do mean? How do you plan to live out your days here?"

Silence.

"I asked you a question, slave. Answer it."

"I am *no* slave. Not to any Master who buys me, and sure as hell not to you. The moment the winning bidder takes me is the moment I flip the roles. You can doubt me all you want, but I will not kneel to any man a moment longer. Let them beat me. Let them kill me. I will go down as Everleigh Davenport, and no one will take that away from me. Don't believe me?" She closed the distance between us. "Have me whipped. See if I break."

I did slap her then. I couldn't stop myself. She was serious, and I had created this. My fear was coming true, but not in the way I'd imagined.

Dark hair covered her face from the impact but fell back as she straightened to glare into my eyes. She didn't say a word, but she didn't have to. I knew that look. It was mine. She wouldn't be beaten at this game.

CHAPTER 12

WEST

"What do you mean I can't have her?"

I looked at Bram incredulously, despite trying to hide the shock. I'd been back for three days and we had talked twice, but it hadn't been for long, and it hadn't been over anything but work. He kept himself locked in his apartment, barely speaking to anyone at all.

"She's not stable. She won't be a good match for you."

"I beg your pardon? She's a *great* match for me. We got along perfectly when I last spoke to her. You don't think I can control her?"

He gave a quick shake of his head, throwing back another scotch. "She's changed since then. She's becoming rebellious and refuses to obey another Master. I believe her."

My eyes narrowed as I came closer. "She's mistaken. Anyone can be put in their place. I can do that to her. I can make her my slave."

The skepticism on his face left me reeling, but I didn't fall into the temptation to argue. Instead, I took another route. "Let me see her. Let me assess her. If you're right, I won't argue. I'll take another slave."

Bram's brow creased. "All right. You can see her, but don't get your hopes up. She's not going to bend to you. She challenges the guards. She looks down her nose at them. It's taking everything in me to convince them not to beat her. I don't want her black and blue before the auction. Dammit," he cursed under his breath, pouring more alcohol into the glass. "Damn, slave. If I didn't…if I didn't feel something for what she's been through, I'd be done with her. But she has been through a lot. She's just going through something. She'll come around when her new Master gets ahold of her."

I knew he was more talking to himself than me.

"You're right. Give me some time. I'm going to see what I can do. I'll return shortly."

I left without looking back, my feet carrying me through the halls like a man on a mission. And I was. I wasn't going to let Everleigh screw this up for me. I was too close to having her. Too close to having the one woman Bram loved.

My nod to the guard was returned, and more of the white walls blurred by. By the time I came into Slave Row, I heard her voice all the way down the hall. My fists clenched and I picked up the pace. Her door was open, and a guard stood a foot inside, his face deep red as he glared at her. Food was splattered across his chest, and I almost couldn't believe what I was seeing.

Everleigh's short hair was a mess, and her white dress was wrinkled and stained with what I assumed to be old food, but it was the look in her eyes—the hate—that had me coming to a stop.

"What the hell is going on here?"

"Twenty-four-six-ninety refuses to eat. *Again.* Mr. Whitlock told us to make sure she doesn't miss another meal. She has barely eaten in two days. This," he said, gesturing to his chest, "was her response when I told her to eat."

I turned to her, letting my eyebrow raise in disapproval.

"Did you do that?"

"I did."

"Why?"

She grew quiet, losing some of her stiffness as she looked down.

"Why did you do that, slave?"

The anger returned as her stare shot up to mine.

"I am no slave. I am Everleigh Davenport. My father had more money than you do. My status in the outside world would have made me famous—more famous than any of the so-called Masters who have to buy women down here. Sick fucks. All of you. I hate you. I hate all of you!"

I was on her so fast, I could hardly remember moving. I spun her, locking my arm around her neck and flexing my bicep to limit her breathing. Everleigh went wild, thrashing and clawing at my suit jacket. The more she fought, the tighter I held. A good few minutes went by before she began to calm. I leaned in closer, inhaling the rich, exotic scent of her skin. It drew me in, intoxicating me.

"I don't doubt what you say, but that isn't who you are. You are owned. You are a slave. That life doesn't exist anymore. Only this," I said, spinning us to show her the small cell. "Your days here can be a nightmare, or you can swallow your pride and get happiness out of your upcoming match. I want to be your Master," I hissed in her ear. "Don't be a fool and damn yourself to years of torture. I will take care of you. I will treat you better than any slave in this fortress. I will love you," I whispered, keeping my voice down. "Let me love you, Everleigh. I know who you are. Only I can give you the kind of love you deserve."

A whimper echoed in the room, and a sob quickly followed. Weight pulled at my arms as her legs gave out and cries left her. My grip eased, and I spun her to face me. Before I could prepare, her arms latched around my neck and she pulled me close, crushing her lips into mine. And me…I kissed her with every ounce of lust I harbored inside.

Blindly, my hand waved out to the guard as I continued. My fingers dug into her lower back, and the moment the door shut, she broke away, peering up at me with bloodshot eyes.

"Do you promise?"

She didn't elaborate, but she didn't have to. I knew she wanted my word that I would love her. That I would treat her well.

"I promise. When I'm your Master, I'll give you the outside world right here. I'll show you things you could never imagine. *I'll make you happy.* All you have to do is what I ask. If you can obey my wishes, there will never be a better match."

Seconds stretched out while she stared at me.

"I know I'm not supposed to have demands, but I have one request."

My head tilted, but I nodded.

"You are to never leave me alone with, or give my body to, Mr. Whitlock. If I never have to see him again, I would be even happier."

I paused, having no doubts Bram was listening to every word we spoke. I refrained from smiling, ignoring why'd she'd request that to begin with.

"Bram is my best friend. You will see him, and probably a lot. But if makes you feel safer as my slave, I promise not to leave you alone with him. You damn well have my word that I will not share you with him or anyone else. That's not my style. When something belongs to me, it's mine. *Only mine.*"

"Thank you. Then I accept you as my Master if you should win the auction."

A grin tugged at my lips, and I made a path with my fingers down her cheek.

"I hate to see you this way. You're better than this. I want you showered and fed. You will not refuse this time. Do you understand me?"

I kept my tone gentle, and it was enough to have her nodding in agreement.

"Good girl. Give me a minute. I'll have everything set up and return when you're finished. There's something I have to take care of, but I will return. We need to talk." I looked at the door. "Guard!" The door swung open, and I led Everleigh forward. "Have her showered and bring her the meal I ordered for myself."

"Yes, Mr. Harper."

Everleigh stayed quiet as she walked out into the hall. The man followed, and I glanced toward where I knew the camera was located. Let Bram see I had won. Let him see my happiness over it. He wouldn't deny me Everleigh. I knew him too well for that. He loved her. It was me or something worse—he wouldn't damn her when she clearly wanted me too.

Whistling, I continued my walk back to Bram's. The minute I opened his door, I wasn't faced with the brokenhearted man I thought I'd see. In fact, he was nowhere to be found. Did he even witness what had happened?

Anger sparked while I headed toward his bedroom. Bram stood with his back to me, his shoulders hunched as he looked down at something on his dresser.

"Any luck?"

A curse threatened to come, and maybe would have had I not suddenly noticed how deep his breathing was. And his fingers, they were pushed into the wood, as if he were trying to control himself. *The kiss.* That had to have been what had set him off the most. "Yes. She's agreed to be my slave. She seemed to take to the idea once I calmed her down. I have them showering and feeding her now."

Bram nodded, still not turning around. "It's settled then. Twenty-four-six-ninety will be yours if things work out. I'm moving up the auction to tomorrow night. Let everyone know."

I smiled, already stepping back. "I'll make the announcement right away."

Before I could turn to leave, Bram continued.

"The tour starts tonight. There's…" He turned, sweeping passed me as he went to the computer. I followed, knowing he was in work mode now. There was a ritual, and with Bram, everything had to be perfect.

He began pushing buttons, but before the address could load, a red blinking light flashed in the corner of the monitor and alarms sounded in the room. He growled, his fingers working faster. Screens began to pop up, and one moved to the front. It was a camera and the picture was black.

"Which is it?" I asked lowly. My stomach was suddenly in knots as he pushed from his chair and flung his drawer open. The large knife he pulled out was one I'd seen him use more times than I could count.

"Shower room."

CHAPTER 13

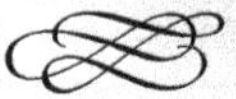

24690

"I think someone needs to be put back in her place. You get a little dick from the Main Master and think you run this place? You think you run us?"

I stayed against the stone shower wall, putting distance between me and the two guards as I countered their steps.

"Oh, it wasn't little," I said, bracing myself to run. "Far from it. Don't let jealousy consume you and get yourselves killed."

"No one is going to kill us. No cameras, slut. We'll be out of here before they even know what happened."

"You're a fool," I spat. "He's going to know. I bet Bram is on his way right this very second."

My pulse exploded inside me, but I wouldn't cower to them. I didn't feel like a slave anymore. And I wouldn't be one to West Harper. Not in the way slaves here were treated. But was it enough? I may have told Bram I didn't want him, but I missed my Master. I just couldn't have him. West was the closest I'd get.

"Get over here." One of the guards lunged, and I barely escaped. A scream tore from my mouth as I tried sprinting to the exit. The other guard was on me before I made it halfway through the room. We hit the tile floor hard, and I cried out as the surface burned into my arm and side. Instinct had my arms and legs kicking and clawing as he tried to pin me down with his weight.

The first hit sent lights flashing behind my eyes. My sight wavered, but I swung anyway.

"Grab her arms! I want this bitch standing when I teach her a lesson."

"No!"

I was jerked back, but not enough. My foot drew up, and I slammed my heel into the guard's cock as he tried to stand. He rolled to the side, yelling and groaning, and I didn't hesitate to use the guard's grip and my wet body to slide toward the other one and kick at him. His connection broke and he went to throw himself toward me when he went rigid. Brown eyes flew open wide and he edged back, bringing up his hands.

Looming just behind me, I turned and caught sight of a Bram I'd only seen once. It was the day he killed those guards in my Master's old apartment. He was beyond furious. He was murderous.

"West, get her out of here. She doesn't need to see this."

More guards pounded into the room. West yanked a towel down from the hook and pulled me up, wrapping it around me. The men crowded behind Bram, and I was pulled from the room so fast, I nearly fell. The moment West had me in the hall, yells echoed all around me. West didn't seem to care as he ran his hands over my arms.

"Are you hurt? Son of a bitch," he said deeply.

His fingers grasped my jaw, angling my face. I could see his predicament as he shifted to head to the shower room but came back to me.

"Bram's going to make them pay for what they did. They'll be dead for this. No one hurts what's mine and gets away with it." His hands cupped both sides of my face as he made me meet his stare. "Do you hear me? No one is going to hurt you again.

No one. I don't care who they are. I'll kill them. I'll kill *whoever* you want."

My eyes left his, going to Bram's bloody face and body as he emerged from the open doorway. Our gaze met, and I couldn't stop the ache in my chest as he looked at my cheek, then moved back to my stare. I wanted nothing more than to throw myself into his arms. Why did he have to pull away and discard me like I was no one to him? I knew he felt something. He'd been a different person in our moments alone.

His jaw tightened, and the bloody knife swung at his side. Breaking our contact, he looked to West.

"Get her ready for the tour. I'll make the announcement."

"Tour?" I knew what he meant, but the tour wasn't scheduled until the night before the auction.

Bram ignored me as he headed in the opposite direction. West turned me, and I followed him down the hall into my room. The moment the door closed, he led me to the bed and sat down next to me.

"What's happening? Tour, I thought…?"

At my confusion, he moved closer, grasping my hands.

"Bram moved up the auction. It'll be tomorrow night."

"Tomorrow?"

"Yes." He smiled. "You don't have to be afraid anymore. Soon, you'll be moving into my quarters, and you'll never have to worry about anyone attacking or trying to rape you again. You'll be safe with me."

At the caress he made down my finger, I tried to force a smile, but it wouldn't come. *Tomorrow?* My mind was spinning, trying to figure out what was happening. Was Bram so quick to push me onto West? Obviously. He'd never cared. It had all been a lie. The tenderness, the looks, the smiles. I'd somehow convinced myself he cared, but what did I know? He couldn't if he had intentions of going through with this. I'd hoped he would come to his senses. That he'd come back and tell me I was going to be his whether I liked it or not. And wasn't that truly what I wanted—him to force this on us? It was why I had kissed West. Why I had told him yes. I was so wrong.

"Let me get your clothes."

"I'll be in the blue this time."

My words had him turning back to face me. I hadn't meant to say them out loud, but the realization suddenly scared me. I hadn't had time to prepare, and I needed to.

"It doesn't matter. You'll be okay. You're strong. Just stay quiet tonight and tomorrow. Pretend you know nothing about this deal, and rest assured, when the auction is over, you'll be leaving with me."

"Do you know the count?"

A few seconds passed. "Total? The whites rest at eighty-three. The blue…two. You and the redhead. There was three, but the doctor didn't make it. I was told she passed away in her cell last night. Your old roommate will be the only other."

"The doctor?"

West stiffened a little. "Giving slaves weapons is not allowed. She was demoted to slave. The transition and punishment wasn't easy for her.

My head lowered. *Bram.*

Footsteps disappeared in the distance, and minutes went by while I stayed lost in my thoughts. When the door finally reopened, it was a guard who placed my outfit inside.

"Where's Mr. Harper?"

"Business."

The door shut behind him, and I stood, walking over to grab the dress. It was paired with a long, bright blue, silk chiffon scarf. My fingers ran over the soft, transparent material, and I cringed at the symbolism. From the tour to the auction, anytime I left this room, I was going to have to wear it. Everyone would know. The target already on my back was about to grow a million times larger. For those who didn't know who or what I was, they would soon enough.

Grabbing the matching dress, I slid it over my head, though it did nothing to cover my body. Aside from giving my curves a blue sheen, it was as if I were walking around nude. And walking we would do. The tour covered the city center located directly in the middle of the fortress. We were allowed there without our Masters, so long as we had permission from them. The small shops, the food store...for as nice as it sounded, it was anything but. I never went alone. I wasn't allowed to without my old Master, but the others wouldn't know the horrors a simple stroll could hold. The worst Masters lurked there. They didn't care if a slave was owned. If we were alone, we were fair game.

My breath was ragged as I placed the scarf over my shoulders and awaited my departure. There was still time before I had to lift it, and the last thing I wanted was to be any more a part of this tradition.

I moved over, grabbing the lotion Bram had bought me. In slow strokes, I rubbed it over my legs, arms, and chest. Memories of us together returned, and I let them. His arms and kiss were so real. My lips tingled at the phantom pressure, and tears clouded in my eyes. I grabbed the matching perfume and pumped, letting the fragrance take me further away.

"Twenty-four-six-ninety?"

I turned at the female voice. A dark-skinned woman with long curly hair came forward. Her head was down, but she moved at a quick pace. I knew immediately she was owned. Everyone here was either slave, Master, medical, or guard. Even the attendants were slaves. From her draping gown, her station was obvious.

"Yes. That's me."

"I'm slave Jenkins. I wanted to introduce myself before our appointment tomorrow."

"I'm sorry, our appointment?"

Her eyes rose and I nearly gasped at the green color. They were practically glowing they were so bright. She was older than me, maybe close to fifty. She was one of the most beautiful women I had ever seen. It took me a minute to process what she was saying.

"Your makeup, hair, and application. You're in the blue. I'll be doing all three."

I shuddered at the mention of the application. The oil was meant to calm us, but it did more than that. My old Master said it was a drug. It left us turned on and ready for sex for when the auction was over. Even the virgins were oiled up. I could hardly remember my auction night, but I knew now I hadn't been in my right mind.

"Of course. I didn't wear makeup last time. I forgot only the blue does."

"Yes. I'll be here to accompany you early. You and the other girl will be paired together, closer to the auction room. It shouldn't take me too long to get you both ready." She lowered her head again, stepping back, but paused before turning. "The best of luck on your tour."

My lips separated, but she left before I could utter a word. It wasn't minutes later that my door reopened. Bram's eyes met mine, and I lifted the scarf to fit over my head, keeping my stare directed at the floor. I didn't wait for him to tell me to come forward. He did the tours. He laid down the laws and struck the fear of God into us.

"The blue is at the end of the line. The girls are already lined up. I will leave you there and take my place at the front."

"Yes, Main Master."

He stopped and pushed a finger under my chin. Although my head rose, my eyes didn't.

"Look at me, slave."

Still, I refused.

"You can be mad at me all you want, but it changes nothing. West is a good match for you. Better than me."

I jerked my head to the side, turning to glare at him. "How do you know what is best for me?"

His face was angry as he met my stare. "I know what is best for everyone. That is my job. Trust me when I say you'd despise being mine. I'd break you worse than anyone ever could. I'd hurt you, and you would come to hate me."

The last was said softer, but it did nothing to douse my pain.

"Hurt me…? Too late. Nothing you could do would hurt me more than you already have. Are we ready?"

Bram's hand hovered closer but balled into a fist at the last second. He turned, eating up the hallway in his furious departure. Two halls later, we approached a long line of girls. He waited at the end, not even looking at me as I took my place. The redheaded roommate I used to have turned and glanced back. The yellow and black webbed under her left eye was fading, but it was evident she'd been introduced to the hell of Slave Row. The tears that welled at my apologetic expression didn't fall down her cheeks. Maybe she was already slightly broken. I wouldn't know since we weren't allowed to speak.

"Listen up, slaves! This is your tour. You will pay attention, or you will wish you had."

Bram walked toward the front, and she quickly reached back. I took her hand, holding tight and stepping in as our Main Master continued.

"Tomorrow, you will be auctioned off, and I am here to tell you where you are allowed to go. City Center is yours. If your Master permits it, you can shop and attend the shows, but you will do so at your own risk. You, alone, are responsible for your well-being there. If you don't want to get beat or raped, go with your Master. If your Master refuses to accompany you, weigh the risk very carefully."

We began to walk, and I stayed close. A guard was farther

back, but he wasn't in a position to help me if I needed it. He wouldn't get to us fast enough. And he wasn't meant to. The men would taunt us. They would try to scare us. What happened would only be a small dose of our reality.

Light flooded the space as the walls opened to reveal a large open area that seemed to go on forever. I couldn't stop my gasp as my eyes squinted and raked over the wonder before me. There was grass around the center, stretching around the circle, and a mall of multiple shops in the middle. People buzzed around in the distance, some even laying out on blankets in the grass. But I didn't care for any of that. My stare lifted, taking in the massive fortress built along the rock stretching up high above. Some of the stone rooms protruded farther than others, and there looked to be six floors. Above the white stone walls of Whitlock, brown rock led to the circular opening above. The blue sky had me stopping in amazement. We were in a mountain, plain and simple. I knew it to be a fact. I also knew there was nothingness for hundreds of miles around us. At least, that was what my old Master had told me.

"Move."

The guard's voice had me walking again, but I wasn't the only one gaping. Julie's hand shook in mine, her eyes darting all over as reality, no doubt, began to sink in. If she thought there was hope before, surely that was disappearing now.

"What is this?" She sniffled, wiping her cheek quickly with her free hand.

"Whitlock," I whispered. "Hell."

I turned to look at the clusters of buildings in the middle of the lush, green grass. As pretty as it all was, I was all too aware of the illusion it cast. But I couldn't deny the lure. Especially after all the white walls and confinement. Here, we had freedom. Scenic beauty. We could be alone to shop and buy things. I'd wanted to go in the past, but my Master only brought me a handful of times. He didn't trust the others any more than I did. *I was a risk.* A light in the dark for the evil looking for a new doll to play with. Coming hadn't been worth it. It still wasn't.

Bram's hand went to the railing guarding the second floor and he stared off into the distance. Silence filled the area as we all came to a stop and waited.

"The shops have the best of everything. For the ones granted the right to live, this doesn't have to be a bad life for you. The world is not over because you have become a slave. Listen to your Masters, obey their every want and desire, and you may have the smallest chance at finding freedom."

He glanced back to me before turning to continue walking, and it wasn't long before we got to a flight of black iron stairs. As I waited my turn, I couldn't ignore the two Masters approaching. My hand squeezed tighter to Julie's, and her head swung toward where I was looking. Seconds stretched out, and still, the whites went down the stairs.

"Don't fight them," I whispered.

"What do we have here?" An older balding man threw an evil grin toward a taller Master. He seemed more my age, which was younger than normal. Regardless, there was no hiding the sadistic look on his face as he sized me up.

"Fuck, I don't know, Harris, but I sure want to find out." His finger trailed up my arm as the older man rounded us, moving closer to Julie. My eyes lowered to the field ahead and I met Bram's intense gaze. He was watching every move the men made.

"Looks like you're in need of a new Master. I could use a slave like you," he said, stepping in closer. "I bet you have all sorts of talents hidden up your sleeve. Do you like pain?" His touch rose, moving across my chest while I tried to stay still. To fight would land me in the White Room for sure—especially attacking the Master so publicly. "How's that mouth of yours work?"

"I say we get them and make them use their mouths on each

other. Do you like the taste of pussy, Red? I do. Why don't you spread your legs so I can taste yours?"

Julie whimpered and she squeezed my hand tighter as he fondled her breast.

"Why don't you be a good girl and get on your knees for me?" The boy's hand settled on my shoulder, pushing down, and I tried to ignore the need to strike him. "Come on. Down you go."

Harder, he pushed, until I didn't have a choice but to lower. I glanced back to Bram, only to find him gone.

"Open your mouth. I want to see how wide you can stretch it. I'm not so sure my cock will fit."

Fingers shoved into my mouth, spreading my cheeks. I clenched my fists, fighting to urge to bite or gag as he pushed them deeper. Julie's cry stole my attention, and she jumped as the other Master trailed his hand up the back of her thigh.

"Have you paid for that?"

At Bram's voice, my head jerked over, dislodging the Master's fingers. The knife at the man's throat had my eyes widening.

"No, Main Master."

"That right. If you had, I'd have the money sitting in my account. Which I do not. Until you buy, keep your hands off what is mine. You can look. You can speak to it. You do not touch what I own."

"Understood, Mr. Whitlock."

"Get up," Bram growled out to me.

I didn't hesitate to push to my feet and follow him to the stairs. The whites were halfway down, and Julie and I clung to each other as we took our place in the middle of the staircase.

"I was so scared," she whispered. "I don't want him as my Master. *I want to go home*."

"I know. I wish you could."

Silence drifted between us as I took the steps. When I got to the grass, it was the only happiness I harbored. Memories of a time that didn't seem real played before me. A yard. A swing set. Me swinging while a man I knew as my father pushed me. We were laughing…and joyful. The flashes were so dulled, I wasn't sure whether they were real or I had somehow invented them in some desperate hope that my life had held more than this. It was heartbreaking and comforting at the same time. It drove me forward. As the cool earth connected against the bottom of my feet, it took everything I had not to bend down to touch it. The color of the grass, the unfamiliarity of it, called to me.

"I will not lie about the dangers this place holds. Some of you have already gotten a taste of what disobedience will get you. It's no different than what will happen with your new Master. He has every right to do what he pleases with you. He can beat you, rape you, cut you, burn you, or kill you. It will be his choice. As for out here, your safety belongs to him and yourself. I urge you to be careful. If you think to try to escape or stand up to anyone of authority, I promise you will not like what happens. You may even die because of it. Unless you have a suicide wish, don't."

The line began to move again, and my fingers broke from Julie's. She glanced back, and I bit my bottom lip. Before I could stop myself, I scooped my hand to trail along the short blades of grass. They were so soft, I couldn't help but smile. Footsteps pounded up behind me, and I tensed, straightening myself. Within seconds, the guard had me by the back of the neck.

"What do you think you're doing?" A hand forced mine open, searching my palm.

My eyes rose to a guard I'd never seen before. He was young, maybe thirty, with dark skin and even darker eyes.

"I wanted to feel."

"Feel what?"

"What is going on here?"

The slaves were all staring. Bram's massive form came

swiftly in our direction, and I wanted to hide at once again drawing attention.

"She..." The guard paused. "She bent down. I thought she was grabbing something from the ground."

"Slave?" Embarrassment sent heat to my cheeks. "I asked for your side. What were you doing?"

"She said she wanted to feel."

"Feel what?"

The growl had me wiggling out of the guard's loosened grasp. "The grass. I..."

"You've never felt grass before?"

"Of course I have. Just not since I've been here."

Bram's stare darted to the guard, and he waved him away before his attention came back to me.

"Dammit. Make it quick."

He meant to sound angry, but I heard the softening of his words. His hand flicked toward me, and I bent my knees, lowering to run my fingers back through the soft blades. I quickly stood.

"Thank you."

"Fucking grass."

His head shook as he yelled for the slaves to turn back around. We started to walk again, and Julie's hand reached back to me. She seemed so in need of contact.

I slid the tips of my fingers along hers and she bent them toward her, holding me as we moved along. The buildings grew closer, as did the crowd. The number of people made me nervous. There were slaves and a few Masters present. Most of the slaves wore long, loose dresses with matching veils covering the majority of their face. Others wore scarves like ours. There were even a few who had nothing on at all to hide who they were.

I swallowed hard, stepping into Julie as we neared. A group of men laughed in the distance, and my eyes glanced over only long enough to count how many. *Five.* Some were strangers, but I didn't miss Master Pollock at the end. He bought more slaves than any of them. At least a good seven to last him the six weeks before the next auction. Most didn't live but a few days, and it was a blessing. Only months back, he'd tortured a slave for almost three weeks before he finally killed her. My old Master said he'd heard the body was unrecognizable by the time he had dumped it outside his door for the guards to collect. I wasn't supposed to go around him. *Ever.* Not even open the door if he showed up. My Master didn't have to tell me twice. The man terrified me.

"Clothing, collectibles, home décor, food—whatever you need, you will find it here. At the end, there's a movie theater. I suggest you not attend without your Master. Veteran slaves are allowed to work there or in the shops, but again, only if their Master allows it. For those who live long enough, remember that."

I leaned toward Julie, whispering in her ear. "Have you ever been to one?"

"A movie theater? You're joking, right?"

"No. I think I went a few times as a kid, but I don't remember. I was pretty young. My parents were gone a lot."

"I went a few weeks ago. The movie sucked. The popcorn was good, though."

"I like popcorn."

She glanced back, smiling. "Me too."

"Slave!"

Bram's voice had me jumping.

"Are you socializing in the middle of my tour?"

My head quickly shook.

"Are you lying to me? I clearly saw you talking and smiling. What is so funny that you feel the need to laugh while I'm talking about your safety?"

I glanced at Julie, then paused as I looked back at Bram.

"I like popcorn."

All he could do was stare at me. One minute, he was slightly shaking his head. The next, he had my bicep in his grasp and was pulling me out of the line.

"Radio for Mr. Harper and tell him to come down to City Center."

Farther, I was pulled away from the others. Bram spun me to him, grabbing my throat as he jerked me close. Where the others may have believed he was hurting me, he added no pressure. If anything, it was a comfort. How many times had he held my throat while kissing me? So many. Was he going to now? I only hoped. So much so, I had to ask.

Licking my lips, I tilted my head back even more to look into his eyes.

"Will you kiss me in front of everyone?"

"Don't be ridiculous. What I should be doing is beating you to prove a point."

"What would you beat me with? Your fist? Something else?"

Bram's eyes flickered before closing for a few seconds.

"I would beat you so hard with my cock, but I'd much rather shove it down your throat so you stop talking back with your smartass mouth."

"Can you still feel my tongue licking around you? Can you feel me sucking you deeper?"

Fingers tightened, and his face grew closer. "Watch it, slave. You don't know what kind of fire you're playing with. You'd be smart to stay hating me. You're safe there." He swallowed hard, moving in even more. "You're wearing what I got you. I can smell it everywhere I go. Do you do it intentionally? Are you trying to make me lose my fucking mind?"

"I like it. It smells good on me."

"Liar."

"So are you. You're doing this. There's still time. Put an end to me being in this stupid auction. You don't want me going to West Harper. *You can't.*"

My voice cracked, and Bram's eyebrows drew in. Something swept over his face, but I couldn't read what it was.

"He hasn't given me a reason to deny the request. Yet. You will go to him. I'm a man of my word. I already told him yes."

"But you don't want him to have me. Tell me you don't want that."

"*I want you alive*. Happy. You won't have that with me. Especially if I… You won't be safe. Leave it at that."

Motion blurred in the far background from my peripheral. My time was running out.

"I *would* be happy with you. I would be a good slave. I wouldn't give you reason to be angry. Tell him no. Tell him you want me."

The grip loosened, and Bram dropped his hand to step back. "I can't."

Tears burned my eyes, blurring his saddened face. Within seconds, West was jogging up.

"What happened? What's wrong?"

Bram wouldn't look at me as he focused on his best friend. "Take her back to Slave Row before I have her whipped in front of everyone. She keeps interrupting my damn tour."

West took a deep breath and slid his palm under my arm. Bram was already walking back to the front of the line as West locked on my bicep, turning me, and I suddenly didn't want to go. The grip was light. Barely existent compared to Bram's touch. I hated it. I was beginning to become very familiar with that emotion.

"Come, slave. You don't want to anger him anymore."

"*He angers me*."

"What happened?"

We passed the guard, and West took his time as he led me to the stairs.

"I haven't touched grass since…before. I bent down to feel, and the guard thought I was picking something up from the ground. It caused a big scene."

"What else?"

The slight smile on West's face led me to continue.

"There's a slave—my old roommate. You've met her. Her name was Julie before she was brought here. Anyway, Mr. Whitlock was talking about the movie theater and I asked her if she'd ever been to one. I haven't since I was a little girl, and I really don't remember."

"Wait." West pulled us to a stop. "Your Master never took you to a movie?"

I shook my head, looking down. "City Center isn't to be trusted. There are men there who would taunt him. We stayed inside most of the time."

"You were with an old man. I will take you. And often. We will shop and see the shows. And the concerts. Did you know Master Blaze plays here a lot? He's very famous on the outside."

"He's the rock star?"

"Yes."

"He's come to see my old Master before, but I never met him."

"I'll introduce you. This place really isn't so bad if you know the right people."

Fear had me stealing glances at him as we walked up the stairs, but I couldn't deny the intrigue. Could he really keep me safe? Given what I could see of his body, I would think so. He wasn't as wide or tall as Bram, but he was still muscular looking. I scanned over his light brown hair and brown eyes, going lower. I could see how men may fear him. He was a good foot taller than me. Taller than most men here. And wider.

"You're sizing me up." He smiled. "What do you see? Do you think I'm attractive? Can I protect you?"

"I believe so." He paused, and I wanted to bite off my own tongue. "I think you're very attractive as well."

"Good. You're going to love me as your Master. I promise."

"May I ask you some questions, Mr. Harper?"

"Ask me anything."

"All right. It has to do with you as a person…here. Do you like to cut away women's skin?"

His head reared back. "That wasn't what I was expecting. But no, I don't."

"Do you like to beat women?"

We entered the open hall, and he glanced into the distance at City Center. "No. I don't enjoy it at all. Would I beat you if you weren't listening? Yes. It would have to be done. It doesn't mean I would enjoy it."

I twisted my lips, letting more questions filter in.

"Master Harbone once told stories to my old Master about sticking weird things inside his slave. Do you plan to do that to me?"

West jerked to a stop and turned me to face him. "What kind of weird things? Toys?"

"Food. Objects. His foot once."

He shook his head and slowly continued us on. "Food and feet, no. Toys, you will use in front of me, yes."

"What kind of toys?"

"Did your old Master make you use toys? Dildos, vibrators?"

"No. Never."

"Hmmm. You will with me, and there's nothing wrong with that, so don't think there is. What else?"

"He once peed on his slave. I heard him say so. You're not going to—"

A loud laugh echoed through the halls. "Your innocence is shockingly refreshing. No, I will not urinate on you, nor will feces be involved at any point of our relationship."

"Will you choke me during sex?"

The smile melted from West's face, and we slowed in our walk again.

"That I may do, and you may come close to passing out from it. You have nothing to fear, though. I won't hurt you."

Some of my relief washed away. This man had secrets; I could feel it. There was something about him I just couldn't trust. And I still didn't forget what Bram had said about him possibly holding darkness. What was he hiding? I didn't expect him to be honest with me about everything tonight. Some things I wouldn't discover until the time came—a time I prayed didn't happen.

CHAPTER 14

BRAM

I like popcorn.

The damn phrase would not get out of my head. It was why I was eating it by the handful. The reason I had a full bag in my goddamn hand headed to Slave Row. I was spoiling the damn girl when I should have been beating the ever-living hell out of her.

No. It was all a lie wrapped in a pretty little excuse. I wanted to see her. Heaven help me, I needed to smell her again. To fuck her until this suffocating feeling of losing her was gone. What was I doing? I needed to turn around right this minute and head back to my apartment. Tomorrow was a big day. Twenty-four-six-ninety needed her rest.

Everleigh.

Fuck…me… I had called her that. Not to her face, but in my dreams. There, in my private little space, she was Everleigh, my slave. I'd woken up pleading to her. Begging her to come back. She kept running away—running back to something or someone I didn't know. But it wasn't her running; it was me.

"Master."

The guard nodded in respect, and I handed over my half-eaten bag of popcorn as I passed. He smiled, taking it, and followed me down the rest of the way to her door. As I held my slave's bag, my pulse increased. The keys jingled in the guard's hand as he opened the door. Everleigh sat up in bed, staring at me, confused. I kept quiet as I stepped in and shut the door.

"Popcorn?"

"What are you doing here, Main Master?"

I walked to the bed, sitting on the edge as I handed her the bag.

"This has to be done before tomorrow. I doubt we'll talk much afterward, and you need to know." My hand pushed into the top of her bag, grabbing a handful as I forced myself to say it.

"I like you."

Still, she sat there staring at me. One by one, she popped them into her mouth, and I couldn't stand waiting for her response. Not that it mattered. My feelings meant nothing.

"You like me, but we still won't talk much after tomorrow."

It wasn't a question. She was stating what I had said, and I couldn't stand how this wasn't easy.

"I like you, but that doesn't matter." I paused, taking more popcorn. "West is a good man. He'll—"

"Will you stop, already? I know he's a good man. *Or he appears to be a good man.* I don't like him for some reason, but that isn't relevant. None of that changes what is right."

"And what is that? My overprotectiveness? My temper? My jealousy? I've killed for you, slave. I've killed for you more times than I've ever killed for anyone else. More times than you even know about. If I could do that to someone determined to hurt you, what will I eventually do to you? And before you say nothing, think again. You've never seen the side of me I hide. You have no idea how much I'd love to hurt you. What you caught a glimpse of was the man who has spent years longing to have you. What you didn't see was the beast lurking in the shadows. He's there, and he wants to see you bleed. Don't give him the opportunity. Don't do that to me."

"Bleed how? What do you want to do to me?"

My forearms came to rest on my thighs while I stared at the ground. To speak the horrors out loud only gave them life, but she had to know.

"Short of sleeping with your mummified corpse in my bed, probably every horrible thing you've ever heard that goes on here. Although…" I laughed in disgusting disbelief, "if I did end up killing you, I can see how I wouldn't want anyone to take you away. Maybe it's the reason I haven't rid Master Yahn of his former slave. Call me sick, but I've seen everything there is. Nothing gets to me anymore."

"So…you'd beat me? Try to kill or torture me? You'd want to cut me?"

I glanced over, unable to take the way she was studying me. The unease had me pushing back on the bed to rest against the wall.

"Maybe. I don't know." I swallowed through the sickness I felt over myself. "Kill you, that I can't say. But hurt you? Yes. And I'd do more than just cut you. I'd mark my ownership all over your body. Whether it be actual cuts, bruising, scars, I don't know. Maybe all. *Those* may eventually kill you. If I got a taste for it, I think the action would become more routine. Maybe you wouldn't even be recognizable after a while."

I paused, seeing all the demented things flash before me. "Dammit, slave, I'd fuck you covered in your own blood then bathe in it if it didn't mean I'd lose you. That's my dilemma. I've wanted you so much and for too long, nothing is impossible."

Silence.

"What would you cut into me? What would it look like—your name, numbers, just cuts?"

I snapped my head to her, my lips tightening at her even

asking such a stupid question. She should have been repulsed. She should have been begging me to leave.

"I don't know. I haven't given it serious thought. I won't. If I did…"

I looked away as she shifted on the bed. I couldn't do this. It was a mistake to think I could come down here and talk sense into her.

"I'm not normal. I've never been. At least…not after I came here. I wish I was som—" I hissed, jerking my hand from the mattress. A bead of blood surfaced over the top, and a deep rumble vibrated my throat. "What do you think you're doing?"

"Making my mark first," she said, holding the scalpel. "Are you going to be a baby about it or do I get to continue?"

"You've lost your damn mind. We're not *marking* each other. You belong to another."

"And if I didn't belong to someone else?" She bit her lip, rolling on her knees to lean toward me on all fours. "If I were yours, would you let me mark you? I'd let you mark me."

"Stop it."

"Would you carve in Bram? Whitlock? Mine? Tell me, Master. No. Show me."

I flew from the bed, ready to attack her. "You don't know what you're doing."

A smile tugged at her mouth, and she reached up, sliding the thin straps of her night dress over her shoulders. The material caught on her nipples before pooling in her lap. As I watched her raise the scalpel, my hands started to shake.

"Maybe it's just the blood you like, not so much the cutting." She pushed the tip of the tiny blade into her chest. Once. Twice. The third time, she gasped, and my legs were moving on their own. Fascination drew me forward. Streams of blood raced over her breasts toward her stomach, and I couldn't turn away. I couldn't stop myself from crawling back onto the bed.

Everleigh's chest rose and fell faster, and I could see her fear.

She trusted cutting herself, but me…that was an entirely different story. She didn't know me well enough.

"You like it."

I tore my eyes from the crimson stains. I didn't give my answer. It wouldn't come even if I wanted it to. My hand shot forward, gripping the back of her hair to pull her into my mouth. As if I were afraid this would stop, my other hand came out at exactly the same time. Warm wetness had my palm gliding over her chest while I made my way up to her throat.

Her small sound of pain got trapped in my mouth, but it didn't stop her tongue from meeting mine with such need, it made my head spin. Up and down I went, letting her blood coat my fingers. I smeared the substance over her breasts and back up to her throat. The essence of her blood, of her life, took over my senses. My cock was so hard, I couldn't fight the one thing I had fantasized about more than just fucking her. This—this was what I wanted. What I craved and dreamed about.

"Why do you do this to me, slave?"

I broke away, undoing my belt and the clasp of my slacks. In a hard tug, I brought her up to straddle me and had her sliding down my cock before she could answer. The sight that met me as she leaned back and moaned through the rough invasion made everything but her fade out. Her lips were parted, and her eyes closed. My fingers were imprinted on the side of her throat, symbolizing something so vast, so great, I couldn't move as she slid further down my length. *Blood.* I'd killed for her. I'd always kill for her. No one else would ever be for me. Slave twenty-four-six-ninety was the one for me, whether I wanted to admit it to myself or not. She'd come this far in trying to prove she wanted me, and it was me pulling away. I always had out of fear. But here was a taste, so vividly before me…and she wasn't dead or completely mutilated. *Yet.*

My hand gripped the side of her neck as I pulled her back to my mouth. She was riding me now, taking control of my fantasy as she brought my other hand back to her chest. When her fingers slid through the tips of mine, she let us glide higher. And then…me. The wetness of her blood smeared over my cheek and chin. I moaned louder than I ever had, lost to the spell she was casting.

Faster, she rode my cock, and words fell from my lips. "Everleigh. Everleigh."

No. This couldn't be right. This whole situation was wrong, and it was going to be my undoing. It would be Whitlock's undoing. Without her, I had control. With her, I clearly had none.

"No." My head shook hard, but her fingers were already shooting up to grip my hair. She held tight, meeting my eyes with a force that all but tried to put me in my place. She was the slave, not me. Yet, she was no slave right now.

"You want me. You want this."

Deeper, she took me. The movement of her hips was so perfect, it was almost impossible to fight the fog I floated in. Anger—the true Bram—somehow broke through, and red blinded me. I growled at my own fear of her dominance, spinning and slamming her on the small bed so I was on top. *She had to see. She had to know how far I would go.*

One of my hands locked on her throat while the other slid over her nose and mouth. I fucked her mercilessly, pounding into her as the suction from her breathing pulled against my palm. She was trying to scream, or maybe she was. I didn't know. The blood…she was covered in it, and so were my hands. I was gone. I wasn't the chained beast anymore. She had unleashed me, and with the freedom, I wanted her to see the consequences.

"Do you like your Master now? Is this what you want your life to be?"

I removed my hand, allowing her to gasp through the panic the loss of oxygen had caused. Her head was rolling. She had been on the verge of passing out. Brutally, I slapped her, continuing to thrust—continuing to slam into her as if her small body could take it.

"Speak! Is this what you want?"

I slapped her again. Once. Twice. My hand fitted back over her nose and mouth, cries muffling under my weight. She tried to turn her head back and forth, but I didn't allow her air. I pushed my fingers into her face tighter, lowering and meeting her eyes as I came to a stop.

"This is what happens when you play with real fire, slave. You don't just get burned, you get fucking disintegrated. I hope you learned your lesson. Tempt me again, and you may not live through the day. If I had my way, you wouldn't live through tonight. As it is, I made a promise to my friend—one I don't know if I can fulfill now." I let go, and she inhaled deeply, sobbing as she tried to catch her breath. "Tomorrow, you'll be sold to someone. If you so much as look my way again, it better be because you have a death wish."

I pulled my cock out of her and pushed to stand. Cries shook her, and she curled onto her side, burying half her face in the blanket.

"Coward," she whispered, her voice scratchy. "Coward!"

I fastened my slacks and belt, feeling sick—feeling like I had made the biggest mistake of my life. Deep inside, I had wanted to end this. I wanted her not to be able to love me. And I'd succeeded. Coward. For her love, perhaps I was.

CHAPTER 15

WEST

I couldn't stop pacing. I couldn't stop running my fingers through my hair. To say I was a nervous wreck was an understatement. There was so much riding on this auction—on making Everleigh mine.

"Drink," Bram snapped. "You act like you're getting married. She's just a damn slave."

I took the glass he offered and downed it in one gulp. "It's bigger than marriage. There's no divorce, and this purchase costs money. Lots of money. I don't know how I'm ever going to repay you."

Bram glanced over but went back to staring mindlessly at the floor.

"You'll give me what you can, when you have it."

"You said Master Yahn offered you twelve million. *Twelve.* I offered you three. I have it, sitting in my bank, with enough left for me to feel comfortable after I pay you. But do you know how long it's going to take me to clear this debt? Never. Because come tonight, I know twelve is going to be a fucking speck of dirt in the actual cost. It'll soar, and I don't have that kind of money. Everyone knows it. I'll bid higher and higher, and they'll know the truth."

Bram's eyes rose, and he nodded. "That's why I'm going to have to give you a cap. If it goes over twenty, you stop. I will not match anything over that price. I can't afford the kind of trouble that would stir."

"So, I'll lose her?"

My stomach dropped and the nervousness rose. Had I thought I had this in the bag? That Everleigh was mine? She wasn't. Not yet, and maybe never.

"You'll lose her," Bram confirmed. "I'm sorry."

He turned, refilling his glass, and all I could do was gaze at him while my mind blurred. I had to have her. I had to. I had changed everything around in my life so I could finally have something Bram never would. Now this… *No.*

"She doesn't deserve to go to any of them. She deserves to be with me. To be happy."

My voice was low, but Bram heard every word. He looked over, sighing. "If this place wasn't my responsibility, I'd give you every cent I owned so the two of you could be happy."

"Would you?"

"Of course I would. West," he paused, his brow creasing, "there's something I need to tell you. A lot, actually. You and I, we're in need of a serious talk."

Knocking had his gaze going between me and the door. The pained expression only lasted a moment before he shot forward to swing the barrier open.

"Master, everything's ready. You can take your place."

He nodded, turning back to me.

"What were you going to say?"

"Nothing. It's nothing. Look at me. I can't think because of you." He laughed. "I'm sure you're worried for nothing. I can't see her going over fifteen. You should be fine at a twenty cap. You can tell them you got an inheritance. It'll all work out fine.

You'll have twenty-four-six-ninety, she'll have you, and I'm sure the match will be flawless."

Grabbing his suit jacket from the back of the chair, he slid it over his broad shoulders. I finished the rest of my drink, then snatched up my own. I felt sick. Everything rode on this auction. Everything. It had to go my way.

I glanced at my watch, then buttoned the jacket before following him out. My mind raced, and I knew what I had to do.

"I'll see you down there. I need to go back to my quarters. I forgot something."

Bram looked over his shoulder, and I didn't miss the way his eyes narrowed suspiciously before he leaned over, whispering to his high leader. Instead of worrying over it, I focused on what I knew. He didn't want me to have her. He did, but he wanted her for himself. He loved her. If it weren't for his responsibility and the rules here, he'd be the one bidding. Luckily, the law prevented that from happening. That only left one person in my way.

Staying true to my word, I grabbed my phone and headed toward my apartment. Eli answered on the first ring.

"Main Master would have my ass if he knew I had my phone on me while I was on duty."

"Good thing you don't give a shit. Listen, I need a favor."

"Another one?"

I pushed through my door, closing my eyes at the anger. "Master Yahn. I want him dead."

A laugh echoed through the line. "How am I supposed to manage that? I'm stuck on guard outside The Cradle. I can't leave. If I do, he'll see it on the cameras and I'm dead. I don't mind dying, but I ain't doing it because of stupidity."

"*He has to die.* He's the only one who will outbid me. I can't let that happen."

There was a pause on the other end, and Eli's breaths were the only thing that let me know he was still there.

"Listen, there might be another way. You can't go to our barracks because that would be suspicious, but maybe I could run there real quick."

"For what?"

"Poison. I confiscated some a while back from a slave. Her Master kept getting sick and became suspicious. I kept it after he murdered her. You don't have to kill Master Yahn, but you *can* make him miss the auction."

A smile stretched across my face. "Of course. Perfect. Where will you put it?"

"I'll be on break soon. While I'm eating dinner, you can come see me. After all, it's auction night. You'll want to pass some time talking with a friend to drown out the nervousness."

"You're a fucking genius."

"I know. Give me fifteen minutes, then head my way. I'll see you soon."

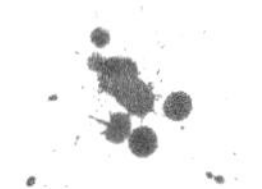

The auction room was packed, the richest sitting at the top of the circular room. Their luxury booths were doused in red velvet and gold chairs. Matching curtains hung from the top to close them off if they wished not to be seen. Waiters delivered drinks of their choice, and slaves held trays filled with the finest delicacies. The room was a buzz of voices. Everyone wore their expensive suits, and the slaves attending with their Masters looked more suited for the red carpet than a selling of humans to the highest bidder.

I nodded to Bram, who was a few feet away. He was speaking with a few Masters in the center of the room, and although he appeared invested in the conversation, I knew he didn't want to be there.

A girl in deep burgundy chiffon, the required color for attendees, swept by with her tray, and I waved her away. Food wasn't what I wanted. I gestured over to a boy, grabbing a glass of champagne as my eyes rose to the upper level. Master Yahn was already in his lavish booth. The slaves weren't present yet, but it wouldn't be long before they started *the march*. The process would begin in maybe a half hour, but I was in no rush. The poison was already in the right hands, ready for Master Yahn's cup when the time came.

"Mr. Harper."

The loud voice had me turning. I smiled and held out my free hand to one of the Main Masters—Bram's second.

"Master Kunken. Pleasure to see you here tonight. In the market for a new slave already?"

He let out a laugh, his large belly shaking as our hands embraced. The need to draw back from touching him was automatic. Lord only knew the last time he'd been elbow deep in body parts as he prepared his newest meal. "I'm on the fence. We'll see if one catches my eye."

"There are a few you might be interested in. There's quite the selection this time."

"What about you? Any grab your attention?"

I tilted my head tilted, shrugging. "You can say that."

"Well, now. I knew we'd win you over. I better take my seat. My detail tells me the march will start soon."

"Yes. It won't be long now. Happy bidding."

I turned, heading for Bram as the Masters he had been speaking to walked away.

"How you doing?"

He threw me a look, adjusting his tie as he glanced around. "I could be better. It's not looking good for you, West."

"What do you mean?"

"Word has gotten around about twenty-four-six-ninety. I know what they're after."

I paused in surprise. "What's that?"

Bram placed his hand in the middle of my back as he led me toward the small stage in the middle of the large room. "Apparently, her Master left her everything. She's filthy rich. Men are willing to pay a hell of a lot of money to get her inheritance. And it's all under the table, so to speak. Master Vicolette made sure of that. What I want to know is why I haven't been contacted yet. I'm sure it's coming."

"*Fuck*," I growled out. "What did you tell them?"

"I pretended to know something. It would have been stupid not to. I said I was aware of everything concerning slave twenty-four-six-ninety, and that the details were disclosed. I wouldn't admit, nor deny it. Dammit. I didn't expect this." Bram wiped the sweat from his brow as he continued to take in the people crowding in. "Money turns us into animals. Although it may not sway some, others see her as an investment. They'll be willing to spend a fortune if they think they're getting a return."

"So, you think Master Yahn knew this?"

"Definitely. Supposedly, he and her old Master have the same lawyer. Of course, it's outside our firm. Otherwise, I would have been prepared. Now, I'm left with this mess." Bram paused. "He's not the only one who knows. Word is out, but there's one person who may have Yahn beat. The Master wants her badly enough. He told me himself not minutes ago."

"Who?"

Bram glanced to the right, and I followed his stare. "Master O'Farrell?"

"That's right."

"Great. Just what I need." Once again, my stomach twisted. "He's a fucking actor. He's too high profile. How does he plan to get access to her funds?"

"From what I was told, he'll be able to with the way it was

set up. Master Vicolette wanted her taken care of. He said enough to me while asking for legal advice a while back. The only thing in our favor is it's nothing more than a rumor as of right now. They may not want to risk the money without knowing the truth." He paused as a guard signaled. "Go to your booth, West. It's time. Let this night start so it can be over with already."

Over…it was only beginning. The news should have made me fear losing Everleigh even more, but it didn't. I'd have her *and* her money, even if I had to kill everyone in my path to make it so.

CHAPTER 16

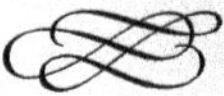

24690

Who was the woman before me? The one who's dark hair was twisted back elegantly? The one who's face was done in the most amazing shades? She looked like a version of me, but I didn't know her. She was beyond beautiful. She was to die for. Or maybe it was the drugs pumping through my system that had me ready to fuck myself.

A long sigh left me as I continued to stare into the mirror. Fingers tracing down my neck had me looking up. I met Julie's eyes, and she lowered next to my face to stare back at my reflection.

"I think this is the happiest I've ever been in my entire life. I feel so good. Maybe this isn't such a bad thing."

I didn't return her smile or enthusiasm. Even drugs couldn't numb out the reality of what I knew would happen once we started our march.

"I keep thinking about what you said. There will be famous people here. *Famous.* I wonder who? Do you think I've heard of them?"

"I don't know. Have you heard of Rob Blaze? He's a Master here."

Julie's eyes went wide, but the expression was delayed. Her drugs were starting to kick in. "Rob Blaze? No way."

"You don't want him as a Master."

"Fuck if I don't. Rob Blaze! He can do whatever he wants to me. I don't care. I want him to pick me. I *adore* him."

My head shook at her naivety. Why were looks or fame so important to people? And Julie wasn't the only one. They all were. Everyone was so ready to bleed for love. They wouldn't be staring up at their Masters with adoration when they began peeling back their skin.

"Up!"

My pulse jumped, hitting with the force of a cannon. It faded out as everything began to blur back together. Julie was calming too. We were turning into zombies with each second that passed, and I was happy for it. I knew what was coming. I knew how we were about to be paraded before everyone and sampled like a fucking buffet. Well, the virgins wouldn't have it as bad, but none of us escaped the greedy grip of the sadistic rich.

Julie's hand came back and I took it as we headed through the door. Instinct had me jerking to a stop at the sight. Virgins stood in line for as far as I could see. The truth was sickening. In a sea of white silk chiffon, I was the beacon screaming for notice to the monsters. I was the cheap, the impure—the expendable.

"Julie."

She was going to have it so much worse. For some odd reason, Masters wanted me, but her…

"Julie," I said louder, pulling her to face me.

"Slave," a male voice yelled. "Get in formation."

"Julie, please, listen to me. Keep your head down. Don't…" I trailed off as I tried to put thoughts together. I was fading into haziness…and my fear was disappearing.

The line began to move, and I knew I had to keep saying something, but the more worked up I became, the stronger the drug pulled me under. My head swayed, and I blinked rapidly through the vertigo. A hand clamped on my shoulder and stayed there as we headed toward the large opening ahead.

Voices grew louder, and clapping became deafening as we poured into the brightly lit center. The open space before the stage began to fill up as each slave stood, making a long row. When it reached the end, another row began. Being the last slave, I stood at the opening, watching in a fog as men began to come down the aisles.

"Come, slave. Try to be steady."

I reached for Julie as her fingers broke away and she began walking. Back and forth, I went from her to the man holding to me. Whatever I meant to tell her escaped my mind as I stayed focused on eyes that stared at me as if they held every world secret. "You're kinder than the others." I looked up at the familiar guard. "I know…you."

He laughed under his breath. "You do. I'm the high leader, Lyle."

"Yes," I barely managed to get out. "I remember. I'm…not well."

"I know. Mr. Whitlock made sure you'd be taken care of tonight. Your oil is special. Stronger than the others."

Blinking began to feel like a chore. Lyle pulled me along, though I couldn't comprehend how I was walking. We neared the stage, and I looked up, catching Bram's worried expression. He was studying my every move, but I could barely lean my head back to look at him.

"I'm going to leave you for a little bit, slave. Stand here and be as still as possible. Whatever anyone does, ignore it."

I tried to speak, but nothing left my mouth. He stepped back, and it was as if I'd only blinked before men were all around me. In me. My head jerked hard, and I looked down to see a younger man's hand between my legs. Instinct screamed for me to run, but I couldn't. I wasn't even sure how I was managing to stand.

"Fuck, she's tight. Mmmm. Let's see what's under her dress."

My shoulder drew back while more hands removed my scarf and the straps of my dress. I could feel myself breathing faster—so fast, I was sure I was going to pass out. Screams echoed around the room, and I tried to turn, to do something, but the hands wouldn't let me. They were pulling at my nipples and forcing themselves inside me.

"What's the matter, slave? Remember me?" Deep laughter left my head swaying back as I took in Master Pollock's face. "There we go. Yeah, you remember. You scared?" His teeth snapped at me, and a sound escaped my mouth. I managed to sidestep away, or maybe I was being pulled? "You're so terrified of what I can do to you. Wait until you see what I make you do to yourself. You're going to be begging me to kill you."

Pressure on my arm jolted me in the opposite direction as heated voices blended in with the rest of buzzing.

"Master?" The word left my mouth without warning, and it didn't stop. My bottom lip trembled as I searched around me for a familiar face. "Master? Master?"

"Hold her still, dammit."

Fingers dug into my thighs so roughly, my entire body lurched from the pain. The action elicited a scream so deep from within, drugged or not, I was suddenly thrashing against them. A man buried his face in my most intimate area, and I screamed even louder for my Master as he sucked and pushed his tongue inside me.

"Enough! This is an auction, not a free for all. You are men, not animals—act like it! The next person who gets out of line will have their right to bid revoked!"

An arm was suddenly around my waist, pulling me back from the crowd. I couldn't stop the sobs that left me as he turned me into his chest. A black chest. A uniform.

"It's okay. Shhh," the voice whispered. "Did you not hear Mr. Whitlock? Back! One at a time." The voice lowered again as he came up next to my ear. "Almost done. Stand tall, slave. Don't let them see your fear."

Lyle righted me, and I tried to stop the sobs, but I couldn't. I had no control over them or the one word that kept slipping past my lips.

"Master!" Racking tears shook me, and the room blurred as I looked around, lost. "Master? Master!"

"Jesus." A man shoved through the others, picking up my clothes from the ground before rushing up to me. The anger on his face was evident, but it didn't scare me. *I knew him. I was safe with him.*

"Mr. Harper?" More sobs came as he took his position behind me, next to the guard. Their hands settled on each bicep, holding me up, and I swallowed back the need to vomit. A man walked forward, and I closed my eyes as his hands ran down my body, caressing and poking into the sides of my stomach. When they forced my thighs apart, my body trembled uncontrollably. Fingers stretched me wide, and I jerked my head toward West, trying my hardest to bury my face into him so I could disappear from what was happening.

"Next!" Mr. Harper's voice boomed from behind me, carrying authority and rage. Each man touched, some even sliding their fingers inside me. Numbness may have been a veil over my emotions and actions, but the hate and violation couldn't be desensitized. With each Master, it grew, festering.

I brushed away the strands of hair that had escaped, and sniffled. The tears were long gone. My back stayed straight, and I tried my hardest to memorize each face that came forward. Some I knew; others I didn't. Regardless, I'd remember...if it was the last thing I did.

"The time has come. Slaves, leave us. High Leader."

All but the first who had come in began to file out. Lyle's hold disappeared, and I waited as Mr. Harper helped me dress before excusing himself. My head turned, and I stared back to where Bram and the guard were talking, projecting the betrayal and rage I felt toward him. He was looking at me, but his stoic expression revealed nothing with how foggy my mind still was.

Lyle returned, grasping my arm. "Let's go, slave."

My legs felt like lead as I began walking. My steps staggered, but my limbs were working a little better. I broke into the aisle, meeting the eyes of a man who'd ran his hands over my body. He was younger and unbelievably attractive, which only made me hate him more.

"Who is that?" I asked, glimpsing up to Lyle.

"That's Master O'Farrell. He's a big actor. If I were a betting man, my money would be on him winning the bid on you."

My fists clenched as I lifted my head higher, breaking the connection with the Master. "Why him?"

"You're worth a fortune and they all know it. Why do you think they behaved the way they did?"

I tripped at his words, stumbling before Lyle's grip caught me.

"What do you mean? Worth a fortune. How?"

He paused, looking around before leading me a little farther down. "Main Master just informed me your old Master left you an inheritance. Your new Master will have control over the funds."

"Will I…have access?" I rushed out.

He nodded. "Possibly."

"If I do, will you help me when the time comes? Will you help me escape?"

The surprise on his face only lasted seconds before he hardened his expression. "I'm loyal to my Master. Don't ever ask me or anyone else that again, or you'll leave me no choice but to report you for bribery. You know the cost for that." His face lost the anger as he paused, leading me farther back. "Luckily for you, I don't think you'll have to worry about that. Mr. Whitlock wanted me to pass along a message. One I think you're going to be thanking him for later. Prepare yourself. He wants you up next. He wants this over with."

CHAPTER 17

BRAM

Nervousness, sickness—nothing compared to the sensations manifesting in every part of me. This was so wrong. Selling my slave? *My* slave. No one else's. She didn't deserve this. Yet, I'd put her in a fucking mob of vicious predators ready to eat her alive. What the fuck kind of person was I?

"Next up." I gripped the podium tighter. "Twenty-four-six-ninety."

Blue chiffon molded to my slave's body, and with every sway of her hips, she grew stronger. Braver. My jaw tightened, and I met her stare despite the need to turn away. This was wrong. I could feel it in my gut. With each step closer, I saw it. Not just her fear…*my fear*, reflecting back at me through her stare. It hit me head on, latching on so strongly, I couldn't stop my mind from racing.

Blue eyes lined with black eyeliner became almost hidden behind her narrowed gaze. Then…her lips quivered. The action sliced right through my heart, nearly dropping me on the spot. I was speechless as she took her place on the slightly lower level before me. What was happening to me? What had she done? I didn't know this man who felt so much love for a person, who overflowed with so much emotion. This man couldn't be me. It wasn't fathomable.

I looked at her paper, staring at the starting bid. Seven hundred thousand. How much was my slave worth to me? Fuck, she was priceless.

"Bidding starts at seven hundred thousand."

Before I could finish, multiple lights on the front of the booths lit up. I paused, not wanting to go any higher. Not wanting to continue.

"Do I hear eight hundred—"

I spun in a circle, taking in all the booths with red glowing circles. My eyes darted to West, and I forced the words to continue. All the while, my mind raced, scheming. Taking in what I knew. *What I hid.*

"Do I hear nine…?"

The last wasn't even necessary with how fast they were hitting their buttons. I glanced back to West, dropping my eyes. He was worried, and he had every right to be. Tonight, she wouldn't be his—or ever.

"Do I hear one million? Two—three—ten—? Up and up, it climbed. With each million, the lights began to decrease, but my anxiety didn't. Sweat soaked through my shirt, and I pulled at my tie. Four lights remained. Four.

"Do I hear—"

"Twenty-five million!"

My heart all but stopped as I met Master O'Farrell's stare. He was standing, as if he'd all but won.

"Thirty million!"

Heads turned in the direction of Master Yahn's men. He was gone, but two of his guards remained.

I glanced up at West, meeting the rage he displayed. Satisfaction surged, but I held it inside, refusing to let it show on my face. All he got from me was a sympathetic look—one he tossed aside from the glare he cast back.

“Thirty-two million.”

Master O’Farrell jerked at his tie, and I knew it was over for him. I’d been doing this long enough to recognize a hanged man when I saw one.

“Fifty million!”

Gasps rang out as Everleigh’s voice echoed through the room. It took everything I had to hold in my smile. Silence took over quickly as she turned to face me. “I will bid fifty million for my freedom.”

“There is no freedom, slave.” I hesitated, looking around at the Masters’ greedy faces. What was happening was unheard of. There were no rules for this. It was all up to me, and I’d known that when I gave the order. “For fifty million, I will give you your choice of a Master. Nothing more. You will still be a slave.” My eyes rose. “Unless someone outbids you. Fifty million. Going once? Going twice?”

I brought the gavel down before anyone had a chance to dispute or react. She had an inheritance, and it was supposedly a lot, but there was no proof. Either way, I didn’t care. My heart was racing as relief filled me.

“Choose a Master for yourself, slave. There is no changing your mind after this decision.”

“Can I choose myself? May I be allowed to be a Mistress? I will stay here for life, but I wish to be responsible for my own life. I am *no one’s* slave.”

My heart dropped to my toes at the unexpected request. She was meant to choose me. To trap me in front of everyone, yet she hadn’t. The shock and surprise were enough to leave me swallowing back the hurt.

“You *have* the money,” I said, shrugging. “I will grant your request. You will take residence in one of our empty apartments. We will go over the details after the auction.” I gestured to Lyle and leaned down as he approached from the lower level. “Take her to my apartment. Have her wait for me there. Stand guard outside and make sure she's protected."

"Yes, Main Master."

West was already standing. I nodded for the next slave to be brought out but kept my eyes on my supposed best friend. I hated how he was going after her. I had to figure out a way to fix these mistakes I'd made…with them both. My slave wasn't twenty-four-six-ninety anymore. She was Mistress Davenport, *but she was still mine*. And my best friend wasn't as careful as he thought.

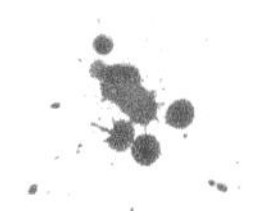

"Next up. Twenty-six-nine-seventy-five."

My eyes stayed on the paper before me, my brow drawing in as I studied the details of the slave. She was a blue. I barely recalled the redhead I'd removed from the cell she had been sharing with my slave. I'd been so wrapped up in Everleigh, I hadn't given her much thought.

Confusion had me looking down. *Eighteen, non-virgin, wealthy family.* Why she was here didn't make sense. We specialized in virgins. Rarely did we get one who wasn't, unless they were previous slaves. And definitely not the wealthy. That was asking for trouble.

The veil eased from her head, resting around her shoulders as she stood taller. She didn't seem afraid, though she should have been.

"Starting bid is two hundred thousand."

Lights lit up throughout the room, and I increased the number. It was average, going two to fifty thousand at a time. By the time it got close to six hundred thousand, only two lights battled over the girl.

"Do I hear seven hundred thousand?"

I kept my attention mainly on the paper, glancing up every few seconds. I was tired, yet amped to get back to my slave. What was she doing? Was she even still awake? It was late. Hours had gone by since she'd left.

"Six hundred and eighty thousand going once. Twice. Sold." I brought the gavel down, watching as an older man stood. One who was all too familiar—one of my Main Masters.

"Uncle Percival?" Her head shook with confusion, but it quickly faded to something more—something so full of fear, I recognized the secrets she must have held. But if he'd done anything sexual to her in the past, she had a lot more to worry about down here. Master Kunken ate his slaves. And he rarely kept them for long. Getting her only meant he was about to do away with the one he had now.

"N-No. No!"

The girl's voice cracked. One minute, she was sobbing, and the next, screaming and trying to run. The guard had her before she could get more than a few feet away. She was going wild in her hysterics, clawing at everyone who tried to get their hands on her. I looked at the Main Master, seeing his excitement. It sickened me. Somehow, he'd gotten to my scouts. I could lay into his ass and even fine him, but my hands were tied unless I wanted to stir more trouble.

"That wraps up tonight's auction. Feel free to stick around for the after party."

I barreled down the steps, heading in the opposite direction of everyone else. Where I should have felt guilt or shame at everything I'd done tonight, I didn't. The noise died out, and within minutes, I was approaching my door, already forgetting about the auction. Lyle still stood there, watching as I walked up.

"I take it everything's okay."

"Yes, Master. The…excuse me. Mistress Davenport and Mr. Harper are inside waiting for you."

"Thank you. Go to Headquarters. I'll be there shortly. We need to talk."

He gave a nod, and I pushed through the door, easing it closed as I spotted Everleigh asleep on my couch. West stood from the chair, holding the decanter and a glass. When my eyebrow rose, he shrugged. He was drunk. Beyond drunk. That was clear in the way he swayed to the bar.

"How long has she been out?"

"An hour or so. Took everything she had to stay awake as long as she did. She was pretty drugged up."

"My doing," I said, grabbing a glass. "I was trying to spare her what I knew was coming. Although…I never expected that. I've never seen the men act that way. Fucking savages."

"Men do unthinkable things when they want something badly enough."

I paused, taking the decanter from him and pouring my drink. My anger sparked as I let what I knew filter through. Him have Everleigh…? Never. "Do you want to elaborate?"

"Not particularly."

"But there is something to elaborate on?"

West collapsed into the chair, sipping on his drink. "I wanted her. I wanted her to be mine."

"I know."

"No, *my friend*, I don't think you do. Bram…" He sighed, closing his eyes for a few moments. "I wanted her, and now I can't have her like I wanted."

"Nothing about tonight turned out as expected."

"No. It did not."

I tossed back the first shot, refilling another.

"What will happen to her now?"

Back and forth, I looked between the two of them. Everleigh's beauty had me stopping and staring as I answered.

"I'll put her in the empty apartment between ours. Mistress or not, she won't be safe. She'll never be safe here. It'll be up to us to watch over her. Not that I think she's going to let us. Damn woman is the most stubborn person I've ever met. For a slave, she was beginning to have one hell of a mouth on her. I fear that's only going to get worse now."

"You shouldn't have granted her independence, Bram. You should have made her choose a Master."

"She wouldn't have chosen you, West."

"And what makes you think that?"

He sat up in his chair, and I shook my head at the truth echoing in my mind. "She would have chosen me. She said so the night before the auction. She may be mad at me now, but had I forced her, it would have been me she picked in front of everyone."

"But she told me she wanted me to keep her away from you."

"Like I said, she's mad at me. Why do you think that is?"

West closed his eyes and breathed out heavily through his nose.

"I'm not stupid. I know you've been fucking her. But…"

I stayed quiet, watching his expression. At my silence, his eyes opened.

"You were going to buy her for me, but you were fucking her the entire time. And you won her over just to spite me."

An angry laugh left me. "It's not always about you. Besides, you didn't own her yet. And it wouldn't have continued if she had become yours. I told her that."

"Sometimes I don't understand you, Bram." He pushed from the chair, stumbling as he slammed his glass on my desk. "You didn't touch her until you knew I wanted her. I've done everything you've ever asked. Why take this away from me? *Why?*"

I stayed quiet, glimpsing the real West as he began to circle around me. "Fine. Don't answer. Will you have her now? Will you make her your slave, but leave her status as Mistress intact?"

"We both know she's not safe living under my roof. Not with how I am." *Not with my keeper plotting against me.*

For seconds, West studied me, the mask he wore so often sliding into place as he smiled.

"You're right. She wouldn't be, and you're too smart to put her in danger, even from yourself. She'll be with me. She'll choose me."

CHAPTER 18

WEST

I wasn't sure who was hurting more, me or Everleigh. I groaned, rolling to sit up from where I had apparently passed out on Bram's floor. I could barely remember anything from last night. Everleigh's eyes were swollen with sleep, and she held her head, wincing in what looked to be pain. The humming and banging from the kitchen had me wanting to throw something at Bram.

"You both look like shit. Coffee?"

I pushed to stand, swaying from the alcohol still in my system. I didn't speak as I walked over and threw back another shot of scotch. The burn and taste had me forcing down the fiery liquid. Another groan left me, and I mirrored Everleigh as I reached for my head.

"I wasn't dreaming? I'm free?"

Bram glanced over, pouring a cup. "I wouldn't say free. You're a Mistress as of this moment, but you're far from free."

"Not having a Master is being free. The location makes no difference."

If she only knew how wrong she was. She'd been away from the outside world for so long, she had no idea.

Bram walked over, handing her the coffee and sitting next to her with his own. I headed for the kitchen, making myself one as I stole glances of them.

"I've already emailed your old Master's attorney. I should be hearing back from him soon. Until I do, you're under my and West's care. I have seen no proof that you have inherited any money, and if you did, I think I would have been the first to know. If I find out this is some rumor and bears no truth…" he trailed off, and my pulse quickened as I headed for the living room.

"I won't go back to Slave Row, will I? Tell me you won't auction me again."

He glanced over at me, and I pulled the chair to sit closer.

"No. You will go to the Master of my choosing. No auction, just placement."

A rugged breath left her, and she frowned as she stared into the cup. "And if I did inherit this money? What then?"

"You are your own Mistress. You will move to the apartment between mine and West's, and we will watch over you. You can do as you wish down here, but that's the extent of it. You will not have the freedom to leave. *Ever.*"

Silence filled the room while she sipped her coffee. When her head rose, she turned to look at me.

"I never got to say thank you for what you did for me last night. You protected me against those Masters." She swallowed hard, wiping away tears before they fell. "Thank you. That meant more to me than you know. They were…"

"Monsters," I supplied for her. "They were out of control, and you didn't deserve to have to go through that. I only did what I felt was right."

"Thank you. You didn't have to." She glanced over to Bram. "And you, for stepping in as well. I've seen them do worse at the auctions, although…that was pretty bad from what I can remember."

"One of the worst. And don't thank me. You don't mean it, you're just saying what is ingrained in you. I saw the way you looked at me last night. You were ready to get on that stage and attack me for what I was forcing on you."

Her eyes tore from his as she stared down at her cup. "You do what you must. You didn't ask for this. I remember your father." She glanced over at him. "But you're not him. The differences you've made since becoming Master are more noticeable than you know."

Bram tensed but stayed silent as he seemed to go into his thoughts.

"Mistress Davenport." I smiled. "I hope you don't mind me calling you that. Or would you prefer Everleigh?"

"Oh." Her eyes blinked, and within seconds, her face lost some of the stress it harbored. "I don't know. Everleigh is nice."

"Okay, Everleigh. I think you're in need of a new wardrobe. What do you say to going shopping this morning?"

Her head quickly shook. "I don't have any money."

"Maybe, maybe not. Allow me to treat you either way. If this inheritance doesn't exist, I would still like to have you as my slave. Nothing has changed there." I glanced between her and Bram, seeing the tension so clearly between them. "You may choose Bram, but he has made it more than obvious he will not have you. I, on the other hand, would be more than honored. I could make you happy, Everleigh."

She stared at her coffee, only looking up when Bram pushed from the sofa and stomped back to the kitchen. The confliction she held as she watched him didn't feed the anger like I thought it would. I didn't see longing; I saw something else. I just couldn't put my finger on it. If she still wanted him, she was doing one hell of a job hiding it.

"If this inheritance is real, then I will pay you back. If not, and I have to choose a Master..." Her jaw tightened as she stared at the floor. "I will choose you, Mr. Harper. I believe you have my best interest at heart, and that is what's important. You will make a great Master. I would be lucky to have you."

Bram's hand froze mid-pour, and I held in my smile as I focused on Everleigh. "You've made the right choice, but let's not think about that right now. Why don't you take a shower and I'll go home to do the same? I can come back to take you shopping when you're ready."

"That sounds like fun."

Apprehension was etched in her smile. I headed for the kitchen, placing the cup on the counter next to my friend. Bram turned, and I knew he was angry, but he stayed silent as he walked past me.

"I'll have clothes brought over for you to wear. Go ahead and shower."

He nodded toward his room, and she stood, heading toward me to place her cup down. She stayed quiet and obedient at his order as she disappeared. I didn't head back to the living room until I heard the bathroom door close. The moment it did, Bram's face drew in with rage.

"You may be set on having her, and she may agree, but the decision is still *mine*. I will place Everleigh with who I feel is the best choice for her. Me, *not you*. Whitlock belongs to me. I run this fucking place. No one else."

"Of course. I didn't mean to overstep my position, but I do recall you saying you didn't want her. That makes me the obvious best choice. You have to know that. No one is going to treat her better."

"That might be so, but I will be the one giving the word if the time comes."

Bram glared only a second more before heading toward his desk and picking up the phone. I didn't excuse myself. I was done being the nice guy for now. Let him think what he wanted. If the decision was made to where she needed a Master, it *would* be me.

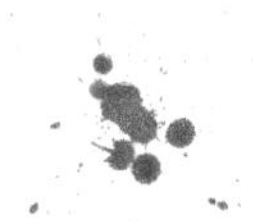

"That looks lovely on you. Fit for a Mistress, indeed."

Everleigh's smile couldn't be contained as she looked into the full-length mirrors. The long, black dress was fitted at the top, baring her shoulders but covering her arms. It was loose at the waist but molded to her curvy hips and thighs. Her back was completely exposed, and her smile slipped as she turned to look at it.

"I don't know. I love it, but it's not safe."

"Sure it is." I came closer, reaching to the side where she'd placed her pale pink scarf on a chair. I picked up the silk, waving it as my head shook. "This is in the past. Mistress or slave, you will not hide a moment longer. No one is going to hurt you anymore. You don't have to cover yourself. The more you cower behind material, the more you become a target. Hold your head high. Don't let them think you're scared of what they can do. You have authority now in their eyes. They'd be fools to try anything—especially with me by your side," I said, smiling. "You're a new person. Prove it to them."

Everleigh nodded, pressing her lips together. "You're right."

"Of course I am. You'll get the dress, and the other clothes you liked. The matching shoes too."

"That's too much," she rushed out, turning around. "Mr. Harper, I know you mean well, but—"

"West," I corrected. "And I mean better than well. We can still be friends. *We can be more*. We can be whatever you wish. All we have is time."

Silence filled the room as she stepped down and came toward me. "You know about me and Bram? About…"

My hand rose, not allowing her to continue. Hate bubbled

deep within, but I kept the soft look on my face. "I know enough, and I don't care. Bram is content in his ways. He will never take a slave. What he does here is his duty, and his duty is his love. He may have felt feelings toward you, and perhaps he still does, but he won't make you happy. If anything, given what he's told me, he wants nothing more than to hurt you. Maybe badly. Don't you think you've been through enough pain? Don't you want happiness? Freedom, in a sense?"

"Yes," she breathed out. "But—"

"But nothing. Stick with me. I know how to treat a woman, and I know what happiness is. It's right around the corner of this shop."

Confusion masked her face, turning into a grin as she took my arm and followed me out. As I paid at the counter, she looked around nervously. The caress and push of my finger under her chin had her smiling and standing straighter.

Bags littered my free hand as I held out my other. She took it again without hesitation, and the pride I felt at having her on my arm was incomparable. I may have been attracted to her because of the lure she had on Bram, but I had it toward her too. Her beauty made it easy for me to forget about anything but her.

I led us around the shop, weaving through the crowd already thickening in City Center. Looks were cast our way, and I didn't miss the way the regular Masters damn near gawked at Everleigh's new appearance.

"Pick your flavor, Mistress. But not vanilla, because that would be boring."

Everleigh laughed, leaning over the glass window of the ice cream cart to view the flavors.

"Is that one good?"

She pointed, and I squinted as I took in blue drizzled throughout vanilla. "The birthday cake flavor? You've never tried it?"

"My old Master didn't allow me to have sweets. His diet was *very* strict."

"Then you're going to have to get some. Two of the birthday cake," I said, turning back to her. "Speaking of birthdays, when is yours?"

"Oh." Her tone wavered, and her voice dropped. The moment her head went down, I knew she was upset. "November. But I don't celebrate it. I refuse. That's when I was taken. On my tenth birthday. My parents were throwing me a party. It was at this big amusement park. I…I didn't even make it to the part where I got to eat cake or open presents. We were running from ride to ride at the time. That was when I saw it. This beautiful pony. I broke away from my friends thinking maybe it was my gift. I had asked for one, and even though my father said no, I still hoped it was my surprise. It was the most beautiful white pony. Like it was out of some story my nana would read me." She blinked hard, shaking her head. "A man took me then. I don't like birthdays. I don't even know why I chose this ice cream."

I took the cones, frowning. "I'm sorry for what happened to you. I truly am. But this…" I said, lifting the cone, "this doesn't have to be about that horrible day. This right here is the best tasting ice cream you will probably ever eat. Aside from hot fudge, because I'll be honest, nothing really beats that."

She smiled, taking the cone. I didn't even have to lift my arm for her to wrap her hand around my bicep. My heart swelled, and it only grew as she moaned at the first lick. Her eyes shot to me; her smile radiant.

"To happiness, West."

"To happiness."

CHAPTER 19

24690

"What do you mean he's unavailable? I've left three messages. Do you know who this is?"

Bram paused, tapping his pen repeatedly as he glared down at his desk.

"Yes, this is Bram Whitlock. I have an urgent matter to discuss, and I expect him to call me back at his earliest convenience. Like *now*."

He hung up the phone, letting a deep sound escape as he pushed to stand from his desk. "Due to personal circumstances, he's apparently unavailable to everyone. I'm sure he'll get back to me soon." Bram's anger melted away as he stole another glance in my direction. He crossed his arms and began to pace, once again looking over. "You look great, by the way. I didn't get to tell you earlier when you came in because I was on the phone, but I like it. The dress, I mean. A little…risqué to wear here, but whatever you're comfortable with."

"West seems to think it'll be okay. He says I need to prove to them I am no longer a slave."

"Perhaps, but you saw how they reacted last night. It'll take a long time, if ever, to view you as anything other than what you've been."

I grew silent as my fears resurfaced.

"He's right, though, in a way," Bram continued. "You have to be strong if you're ever going to make it clear to them you will not be intimidated. I'm not so sure that's the way, though."

"What would you suggest?"

His eyebrow rose and a smile tugged at his mouth as he continued his path back and forth.

"You look like arm candy—just another slave to a rich Master. There's nothing wrong with that. There is an elegance about the dress, despite the sexiness. If it were me, I'd suggest slacks and a turtleneck. With the right accessories, you'd look dominant—powerful without having to flaunt what you have. They all know what lies beneath that dress. *They've seen it. Felt it.* Don't remind them of what they lust for. Cover yourself, Everleigh. You're beautiful no matter what you wear."

His words wrapped around my heart, despite trying not to let them affect me as strongly as they did. I was afraid to feel anything more for Bram. After the auction and what he'd done to me in my cell, I wanted to hate him. He had tried proving a point to me, but he went about it the wrong way. I knew the darkness he harbored, but I also saw how we were when we were together. He hadn't tried to hurt me then, not that he probably hadn't thought about. Just because he had urges didn't mean he couldn't sate them in other ways.

"I've upset you."

I glanced up, immediately lowering my eyes back to the floor as I tried to think.

"No, you're right. I was hesitant about the dress, but I won't deny liking it. I'll wear what I feel, and if it turns out I do have an inheritance and I am a Mistress, I'll portray myself as you suggested."

"And if you're not. If you're a slave?"

"I've told you my views on that. I will not be a slave to any man. But…if I'm to play that role, Mr. Harper will be swayed by what I like."

Bram's jaw flexed repeatedly as he came to a stop and looked at me. "And if I say no to the two of you?"

"Why would you? You were going to match Mr. Harper's bid so I could be his. You *wanted* me to go to him."

"Maybe I've changed my mind."

My mouth went to open, but I hesitated. My heart was beginning to race, and it was so hard to fight the anger and betrayal. I'd known him long enough to understand his bad side. It wasn't like I didn't think he was incapable. The risks with a man like Bram were expected for my previous station. It made me relate to his personality where others might not have grasped it. And I loved him. I couldn't deny that.

"Who would you put me with then?"

"I don't know yet. I'm still thinking it over."

Moments passed while he kept looking at me. Finally, Bram came to sit on the edge of the couch. "I know I said I wouldn't have you, but maybe if—"

I gave a hard shake as fear nearly closed my throat. It wasn't that I was afraid of what he could do to my body, but more my emotional wellbeing. And that was only the beginning. I couldn't flip the roles on him. I knew that like I knew I had to be very honest, despite what that meant.

Anger set hard into his features. "You're not even going to let me finish what I was going to say?"

Again, my head shook.

"Tough shit. You're still technically a slave, and I'll tell you whatever the hell I want. If you don't have money to buy your freedom, I'll keep your ass next door and have my way with you whenever I see fit." He pushed to stand, glaring over to me as he began to pace again. The anger didn't last long before his expression softened into worry.

"That came out wrong."

"No, I don't think it could have come out any more truthful. You'd use me as your whore when you know it's your love and my freedom I want. As a slave, I'm not supposed to request or want such things. As it turns out, I may not be a slave for much longer, so I'll say whatever I want."

"Watch it."

"Or what? You're going to punish me for being honest with you?"

He stalked forward, jerking me to stand. "I'll punish you for your smart mouth. I'll punish you because I can. Mistress, slave, do you think it makes a difference to me? You're still mine, regardless of your status. You don't believe me, push me. Taunt me. I will bend you over my knee so fast, you'll be screaming for me to stop. And I bet we already know what will come from your mouth during your pleas." His palm pushed into my lower back, bringing me in until my body was tightly against his. "Say it, Everleigh. *Slave. Who's your Master*?"

I jerked against him, but his grip trapped my arms against his chest.

"Tell me. Let me hear you say it."

His tone softened, his fingers digging into my bare back while his other hand slid to lace through my hair.

"God, you're so fucking beautiful. You drive me insane. What I wouldn't do to tear this dress off you and—"

The door opened, but Bram didn't break away as West stepped in. I jerked again, and only then did his hands drop. The expression Mr. Harper held was enough to leave me shaking. The air felt heavy between all of us, and I hated being at the root of it.

"Did you forget how to knock?" Bram's rage cut to West, only to disappear as he turned his back to us and walked over to the bar.

"Must have slipped my mind. I won't forget next time." He

turned to me, dismissing Bram. "Movie starts in two hours. I thought I would give you time to get ready. I got this for you."

He walked over, holding up a bag. "Slaves don't wear makeup. Although I don't believe you need it, I figured you'd want to make it known you were free to do as you pleased with your face. That is, if you decide you want to. They're all natural colors, so it's only an enhancement, but a statement nonetheless."

"Thank—"

"She's not going. She's already made her *statement* for the day. She's still a slave to me until I get the news of her inheritance."

West's eyes met mine, and I lowered my head.

"Perhaps I should return to Slave Row until you get the news."

"Bram." West turned from me, walking closer to him. "Everleigh has done nothing wrong. Don't take your frustrations out on her. She's innocent in all of this. If you're angry at me for interrupting, fine, but don't punish her for it."

The drink disappeared as Bram poured the contents into his mouth. When he put the glass down, he turned his attention to his friend.

"You're right. I apologize…to both of you. This situation, the last few weeks, it's all been stressful, to say the least."

"Agreed." West glanced between me and Bram. "Why don't we all go see the movie? We can take a break from roles, status, *feelings*, and just have fun."

Skepticism flashed on Bram's face, but something registered as he studied his friend. After a few seconds, he exhaled, nodding. "I think we sometimes forget ourselves. I know I do. A night away from responsibilities would be nice."

"It's settled. I have some things to take care of at the office, but I'll come back in an hour or so. I'll let you both get ready."

He headed for the door, stopping when he grabbed the knob. "I'll be sure to knock next time."

With that, he was gone. I stood, biting my tongue from asking permission to change. Bram may have still looked at me as a slave, but if I asked, I gave him power, and he wouldn't get that from me. Not as a slave. That was over for me.

The phone rang, and I turned, heading for the room.

"Where are you going?"

I paused in my advance to his bedroom. "To get ready."

There was no anger as he picked up the receiver. More… contemplation as he began to talk and write something down. His answers were short, revealing nothing of what the conversation was about. After a few more moments of silence, he hung up and followed me, pausing at the entrance. His mouth opened, only to shut. I wasn't sure what he was thinking. "You can dress in the bathroom. I'll take the bedroom."

I looked at the suit he wore, trying to make the best of the situation. Trying anything to move us past this awkward point of instability into more of what I wanted. I wouldn't let things play out this way. I refused.

"What, are you going to change your tie?" The suit was black. The only color I'd ever seen him wear in all my years as a slave.

Bram paused for what had to have been a good minute as he stared at me. He blinked through my words, catching my teasing. "I have more than just suits. I'm not working tonight, remember?"

"Are they going to be black too?"

A smile broke out on his face. Just like before when I'd seen it, this was real. *It was beautiful.*

"Black is authority. As it happens, I do have other colors. Would you like me to wear something special for you? I could do that. There's almost nothing I wouldn't do for you, Everleigh."

He bit his bottom lip, reaching to grip the tip of my index finger. The small traces of his thumb went back and forth, so small yet powerful in their significance. I stood there, unable to breathe as he brought my finger to his lips. Time left me, and what could have only lasted a second burned into my brain as he disappeared into the room.

Almost nothing he wouldn't do... I was about to test exactly what that meant.

CHAPTER 20

BRAM

"It's black."

My eyes rose from my reflection in the mirror to settle on Everleigh who was standing outside the bathroom door. She had done as I'd suggested earlier and wore a pair of black slacks with a white blouse. I swallowed through the awe, turning slowly to face her. With the makeup on and her chin-length hair pulled back from her face, she looked like a completely different person. And she was beyond words. Beautiful or stunning didn't hold a candle to my mind's interpretation.

"What?"

"It's black," she said, gesturing.

I glanced down at the fitted, long-sleeve shirt. "It's gray. Dark gray, but gray."

Her lips pursed as she headed to my closet. There was caution in each step she took, but she braved my possible wrath to invade my personal space. Hangers sounded as she slid over my clothes. I stepped into the doorway, leaning against the frame as I watched.

"This. Wear this one."

My eyebrow rose at the white V-neck t-shirt.

"I sleep in that."

"Then this."

She grabbed a light blue polo from the back, holding it in my direction. I hadn't even been aware the shirt existed, much less where the hell I'd gotten it from. I would have never chosen something like that. Something so…informal. I was already wearing jeans. That was bad enough. The Master of this place couldn't go parading around like a commoner. My father imprinted how we were supposed to project power. This girly shirt wasn't going to project shit.

"Fine."

I grabbed it, not missing the smile on Everleigh's face. I'd have to buy more clothes. Ones more my style, but different colors. Maybe then she'd see I was at least trying.

I hesitated from taking the shirt off the hanger. What exactly did I want her to see? I wanted her, but I knew the cost. She mentioned wanting my love. God, I never thought this day would come.

The hanger fell to the floor, and I pulled off my shirt, letting it fall as well. Invisible pressure seemed to push against my back, and I turned, seeing Everleigh standing a few feet away. She was watching me. But it was more than that.

I faced her, and there was no denying the beast that roared through. *Lust.* The crux of my conundrum. There was little good in me. God knew it. Just as he knew the odds were not in my favor for catching a break from the crisis that was my very existence.

But those eyes and the way they looked at me…I could almost forget the knife in my back.

"I think you're beautiful too," she whispered. "And I think a part of you loves me. Show me. Don't use me as a *slave*. End this tonight. Make me yours in the true sense."

"You don't know what you're asking."

"I do! We both know there's no one else for either of us.

Admit your feelings, Bram. Not to me, but yourself. You know you couldn't bear me going to another Master, and I've seen the real you. I choose that you, no matter what that means. If it's death, so be it. I love you. Show me you love me too. Not with words, but actions."

The shirt balled in my fist while I fought everything I knew was wrong. She'd never go to a Master because she was no slave. I'd just learned that from the lawyer. Everything was left to her, and if I didn't keep her safe, all hell would break loose.

Years of convincing myself this couldn't happen collapsed around me as I closed the distance between us and pulled her into my arms. "You want me, fine. But don't you dare say I didn't warn you. You have no idea what you're walking into—the risk. And not just from me." So many emotions stirred. Confessions were on the tip of my tongue before I managed to stop myself. She couldn't know. Not yet. "*You're mine.* That's final, as of right now. I don't know how this is going to work out, but it's done. I'll speak to West after the movie. I don't want to ruin our date." I jerked her back by her hair, making her face me —*the real me.* "When I let go, you start walking away, little mouse. *Fast.* You may not like what comes if you don't."

"This is going to work." She reached up, gripping the back of my neck, and I let her pull me down so she could kiss me. The fire within raged, tapping into the forbidden I'd kept hidden for so long. "I fear nothing being with you. Only being without you." Lips pressed into mine once more, but she didn't push me. She broke away at my unresponsiveness and it took everything I had to let her go. The moment my hands were down, she looked like she wanted to say more, but I saw the moment she decided not to. Without a word, she turned, leaving the room. And I cursed, jerking the damn ugly shirt over my head. My cock was throbbing, and my heart was bleeding from the continual daggers of truth I kept forcing through it. But fuck if I was going to lose her. She had ruined the old me. I was no longer bulletproof from emotion. The day I'd kissed her and made her mine was the day I condemned myself to a future I couldn't run from. She had me, and I had her. There was no escaping that anymore.

I grabbed my black book of poems and headed for the living room. Everleigh was on the couch, watching me. I sat at my desk, flipping through the pages as I put my focus into the dark words. Dark words that came from me. From my soul. I always escaped here when things were complicated and read over my purest thoughts.

To look up and see my muse sitting across the room was something I could hardly handle. So much confusion. So much love and desperation intertwined. Betrayal, rage, secrets. There was nothing I missed. *Nothing.* It was about to peak. Ready or not, I knew one thing for sure: she'd be protected.

Time ticked by as I let the possibilities of the future engulf me. I placed the book down and messed with my computer. Between West walking through the door and the damn collar of the shirt I kept pulling at, I couldn't take it anymore. I stood, heading into my room. Again, I looked in the mirror, turning from side to side, shaking my head through the aggravation. The blue shirt hit the floor at my toss, and I reached down, grabbing the gray one I'd had on to begin with. Before I could completely pull it over my head, a throat cleared behind me. I jerked it down, looking over my shoulder.

"Not a word. Not a *single* word."

"It looked good on you."

I glanced at West and the polo he wore. "Of course you liked it. I bet it was yours."

"Actually, it was. I think I left it here one of the nights I came in drunk from the outside."

The memory returned and my mouth twisted in recognition. "That's right. The Cavender case."

"Yes," he said, pointing. "The fucking Cavender case. A damn nightmare."

I pulled at the hem, moving up to fix my watch. "I don't want to talk about work right now. I have enough shit on my mind. Are we going?"

"Are you going to cheer up? I want to have fun and watch a movie. You're not going to be grumpy the entire time, are you?" At my look, he sighed. "Fine. But don't ruin this for Everleigh. She hasn't seen a movie since before her time here. I want it to be a night she never forgets."

I kept quiet, replaying his expression in my mind as we headed for the door. We weren't a few steps out before he moved in closer to her.

"What are we going to see?" Everleigh hesitantly looked at me as West offered his arm. At my slight nod, she took it.

"It's a romantic comedy." My groan had him throwing me a look, but he continued. "It's supposed to be breaking all sorts of records. I think you'll like. It'll be a good reintroduction to movies for you."

"What else is playing?" I asked, stepping forward to meet their pace. I couldn't help but look down as Everleigh wrapped her arm around mine too. There was obvious pause from West as he cleared his throat, but I didn't care. Soon, she and I would be like this all the time, and he was just going to have to accept that.

"Action, I believe. Gun fights, car chases. Probably not a good first movie."

"Probably not." I looked down at her hold again, focusing on the fluttering in my stomach. It was nothing. Just a grip to my forearm. But to me, to what I knew was coming, it was everything—a beginning that was sure to rock Whitlock like nothing before.

"I want to watch the action movie."

"Of course you do," I mumbled.

"It might be too much of a shock, Everleigh. You haven't been to the outside world in a very long time. I'm just not sure it's a good idea."

I rolled my eyes at West. "She said she wants the action movie. Hasn't she been through hell? What's a few car chases and gun fights? The slave pulled a fucking knife out of her Master's eye to fight off rapists and fought off more guards in the shower room. She won that fight, by the way. Do I even need to mention last night? She's tough as shit. If she wants to watch the damn action movie, she can watch it."

"What the hell, Bram?"

"What, *West*? I'm just saying, there's no point in sheltering her. She's experienced more horror than a cheesy Hollywood flick. If you really want to protect her, don't convince her to watch Howard the Duck. *That* one will give her nightmares."

"I had no idea what the movie was about when I said we should watch it. What does it matter? It was like *ten years ago*."

"Last movie I saw, and it was for the best. You have the worst taste ever."

West shook his head, growing angrier. "That's the only movie I've ever tried to get you to watch, and I thought it sucked too. Don't blame me."

"Can we watch it?"

"No."

Me and West answered at the same time, smiling as Everleigh's shoulders bumped back and forth between us intentionally. Her face was beaming with happiness. It was enough to erase my foul mood. To see her smile…it was suddenly the only thing that mattered. Not jealousy or West's secret intentions. *Her.*

"I will find a way to get this movie and we will all watch it," she said, staring ahead. "I wanted revenge on the two of you, and you just gave me the perfect weapon."

I groaned, still smiling. When West mirrored me and our eyes met, I could feel the atmosphere shift. In our moment, it was us again—the best friends. The kids who weren't corrupted by blood, rape, and death. There was a lightness for that second.

Peace. How had we allowed ourselves to lose that? We used to be so close. Now, everything was legal business, slaves of Whitlock, and schemes.

"You know, I could rent it," West said, leading us down the stairs to City Center. "We could watch it tonight when we get back. It won't be too late."

"I *knew* you liked it," I teased.

Everleigh burst out laughing, and West and I couldn't help but follow. Though I may have acted happy, I couldn't shake the way my skin crawled at the softening expressions my friend gave me. Like he missed me. Missed us. If West was good enough to confuse me after what I already knew, he was better than I gave him credit for—which was a dangerous mistake on my part.

CHAPTER 21

WEST

"Three things of popcorn, three large drinks, and candy. Lots of candy. One of each."

As Bram went over the order with the clerk, I smiled at Everleigh. Bram couldn't believe she hadn't tried any of the sweets and was quickly making up for what she'd lacked in the past. And me, I was soaking it in—watching every little move my best friend made. Moments like that were important. You had to pay attention and memorize the details if you were going to grow as a person. If you were going to remember an unforgettable night…

"Anything else? Cotton candy? West, you want anything specific?"

"No, I'm good. I think we have enough to last a lifetime."

"Or at least the other movie tonight. Two movies in one night." He shook his head, still smiling. "I haven't watched one in years, and now, two. Why haven't we watched more movies?"

My smile faded as I took in his question. It stirred something in me, almost making me wonder if the plans I'd set into motion were the right ones. Here I was trying to fool him, yet he was fucking with my head. Or was he? Was he pretending like me? I wasn't sure anymore.

"I don't know. Work?" I said, shrugging. "We've been so busy since we got out of school. Hell, even before then. I can't remember the last time we just relaxed. It's always been something. One dilemma after another. And they've gotten tougher each time, haven't they? More challenging or time crucial? Is it just me?"

Bram handed over my drink and shook his head. "No, you're right. Every time, every year, it grows tougher. I used to think it couldn't get harder than it was, but it did. It always does. What do you think would have happened if we would have just walked away? Just put up our hands and said, 'fuck it, we quit'?"

My smile was completely gone as I let his question simmer. "I don't know. That's not us. We've never ran from anything."

"Nope." Bram grabbed the bag holding all the candy and handed Everleigh her drink. "We never run. We never call it quits. Duty is who we are. It's what we were bred to take on."

We. Not he.

My brow creased with confliction. He had been born and bred to take over Whitlock, not me. Yet, he put us as one. The significance meant more to me than I wanted to admit. I'd always thought Bram kept me at his side because I was just another duty, a routine ingrained in him. But what he'd just said hadn't sounded like that. *Brothers.* We had always said we were. I'd just never really believed it.

We weaved through the crowd, handing the attendant our tickets as we broke into the hallway. Darkness engulfed us as Bram held open the first door for me and Everleigh. Goosebumps tightened my skin, and there was nothing I could do to stop it. Perhaps I wrong? Or…maybe I needed more time? *He needed more time?*

"We should do this more often," Bram said, letting the door

close behind us. "Maybe once a week? Every Saturday night or something? That's when new movies come out, right?"

"I don't know," I mumbled. "I can find out."

Lower and lower, my voice dropped. My mind was racing, my pulse damn near exploding at the force.

"West, you okay?"

Bram came to a stop short of the turn leading to the theater. His face was illuminated by the previews on the screen, and everything felt so surreal. My legs wouldn't walk any farther. *They couldn't.* They were meant for this exact spot—all my life, all these years.

"West?"

I glanced at Everleigh's concerned face, forcing myself to breathe.

"I'm suddenly not feeling so well."

"Even in the dim light, you look pale as shit. Here, let me help you." Bram took my drink and put it on the ground as he wrapped his arm around mine to keep me steady. We broke for the doors and light enveloped us once again as we made it into the hallway. But the light held no sense of hope for me. I gestured toward the bathroom, forcing my weight in that direction, still unable to speak.

"Hold on," Bram whispered to me. "Everleigh, stay. You, guard," Bram called out. "Watch her. Don't let anyone near her." He turned back to me, wrapping his other arm around my back as he walked us faster. "It's okay. Are you going to be sick?"

"I think so." And maybe I was right. Even though excitement pumped through my veins, I couldn't dismiss the sickness coming with it. I knew it would fade. It was only a matter of time before I looked back at this day with relief and not regret. It was just going to take time.

Bram pushed open the bathroom door, and the moment the room opened, I was jerked at the impact of him being caught off guard. I spun to the side, catching myself before I fell. The stabs were so fast, I barely righted myself before Bram's legs buckled.

"Cut off my hand, you son of a bitch! How do you like that!"

Eli met my eyes, letting his arms slide out from where he had Bram restrained, dropping him. I didn't wait. So many emotions rolled through me, I lunged forward, grabbing Billy's blond hair and twisting his neck hard. He thought he'd be helping us, and he had. But not like he assumed.

"You were just in here using the bathroom. Get the guard by Everleigh and tell him to ring the alarm. The Master's been attacked. Take her back to Bram's. I'll meet the both of you there. Don't let her out of your sight for any reason."

"Got it."

"And, Eli?"

He turned in his fast retreat.

"Touch her in any way, I'll kill you."

He laughed. "Are you going to get me to do it myself?"

"Don't underestimate me. I have no one to hide from now. Meet Whitlock's new Master…*me*."

"You son of a…*bitch*." Bram groaned as he tried to roll to his side. But he couldn't. He was fighting to even breathe. "I'll…k-kill you."

Blood soaked through his gray shirt and crimson sprayed from his mouth as he began to cough. I felt nothing anymore. No guilt or remorse. Nothing but the need to end this as soon as possible.

"Kill me? You can't even move. Sleep sweet, dear brother. I'll take good care of her for you. I promise."

My leg came back, and I kicked Bram in the side of the head as hard as I could. No more pain. No anger. No more possible fear of death for him. Peace. I'd given him a gift. Luckily, he gave me more.

"Go," I growled to Eli.

Within seconds, the guard burst through, but not before

Everleigh. How she'd managed to make her way around Eli was beyond me. All I knew was that scream. It pulled me from staring into Bram's unconscious face as I kneeled over his body. It sent the hair on my arms standing and my rage boiling.

"Get her out of here!"

"Bram! No!" She was a foot from reaching us when Eli's arm wrapped around her waist, pulling her back. The guard was still yelling into his radio as he slid to a stop at Billy's body. Screams echoed everywhere, amped by the tile walls surrounding us. Harder, Everleigh fought, scratching and trying to claw at Eli. The pure determination on her face to make it to Bram was like nothing I'd ever seen.

"The high leader is in the field. He's calling the surgeon now." The guard lowered, letting his hand hover over Bram's chest as he pushed the button to speak again. "Three stab wounds in vicinity of the chest. One seems to be right around the heart. Maybe over it. That's all I can see right now."

Within moments, more guards rushed in. The high leader was almost right behind him, panting as he pushed the others back and began ripping off his gear to remove his shirt.

"You, you, and you. Help carry him as I apply pressure. The chopper will be here shortly."

"Chopper?"

I stood as he moved me out of the way and took his place next to Bram.

"That's right."

"What's wrong with the hospital here?" I asked. "They can get to him sooner. *They can help him.*"

The moment I met the leader's eyes, I knew something was off. He knew things—things I couldn't begin to guess.

"Mr. Whitlock warned me this might happen. He's to be taken out of here and moved to a civilian hospital."

"Civilian hospital? Which one?"

His eyes shot up to mine as he pushed the shirt onto the wounds.

"That's for only me to know."

I swallowed past the guilt as the guards lifted Bram and began rushing him out. The scene blurred, but I followed through the large gathering crowd until we were heading outside. It wasn't long before the spotlight from the helicopter flooded the green grass. It lowered, and I didn't stop running behind them until the door came open and a woman I knew all too well faced me. Those eyes, they'd stared at me with more terror than I'd ever been confronted with, and at the time, I had loved it.

But how was this possible?

"You! Jarett!" The high leader's voice was barely audible as he pointed to one of the guards. "Take lead. I'll contact you when I can."

And just like that, the door closed, and only moments later, the light turned brighter as the chopper rose into the sky. I couldn't move as I watched it disappear out of Whitlock.

I'd overlooked more than I should have. If Bram had suspected something and gone to lengths to secure the woman surgeon, Dr. Cortez, when I was told she was dead…what else had he known?

"Sir, I need a word with you. Can you tell me what happened?"

The temporary high leader… I didn't know him. Not personally. I'd seen his face plenty of times, but we had never spoken.

"I wasn't feeling well. Bram was helping me into the restroom when some guy…I think he was a former guard, just started stabbing him. I fell at the initial attack. By the time I stood, Bram was dropping to the ground and…" I took a ragged breath. "I barely remember lunging forward. I jumped the attacker, and in our struggle, managed to break his neck."

"And that's it?"

"No." I shook my head. "There was another guy in there

when this happened. A friend of mine, actually. I yelled for him to get help. I'm not sure when I yelled it—if it was while I was fighting off the former guard or after. I can't really remember." I paused. "Do we have to do this now? My best friend was just fucking stabbed in front of me. The Mistress we were with had to witness the aftermath. I need to get to her."

I didn't wait for permission. I took off toward the stairs at a fast pace, half jogging, half walking. The moment I burst through Bram's door, Everleigh flew toward me.

"What happened? Where is he?"

"Shhh. Calm down. It's okay. They airlifted him to a hospital."

"What happened? Was he…? He wasn't…"

Sobs left her as she pushed her short hair back from her face, and all I could do was what I had wanted from the beginning. I pulled her into my arms, holding tight as I tried to soothe her.

"I don't know. I don't know anything right now. I'm sure they'll update us the moment they know something."

I glanced toward Eli, his gaze moving from me to the computer. He wanted me to delete the footage, and I had every intention to do just that as soon as I calmed Everleigh.

"It was B-Billy. I saw him dead on the ground. He did this, and it's all my f-fault. If anything happens to Bram, I…"

"It was not your fault. No. Shhh. Come."

I led her to Bram's room, jerking back the blankets as I forced her to sit on the edge. "I'm going to get you a drink and I want you to try to stop crying so hard. You'll go into shock if you don't try to relax. Do not move. Do not get up. *Stay.*"

The authority in my tone had her brow creasing, but she nodded as I headed for the door. I shut it behind me, pointing to the decanter as I walked toward the computer.

"Pour her a drink." I pulled a pill from my pocket. "And put this in it. She'll be out in no time."

Eli grabbed the pill, breaking it open as I hit the button to wake the computer. The lock screen appeared, and I quickly let my fingers type in the letters.

Password denied.

"What the fuck?" Again, I typed.

Password denied.

My eyes shot to Eli.

"What is it?" He was stirring the drink as he walked over.

Again, I typed it in.

Password denied.

CHAPTER 22

24690

"I said it doesn't matter. I'll take care of it."

West's raised voice had me focusing to hear more, but nothing was said. The door opened and he walked in, carrying a glass of amber liquid.

"Drink this. It's going to make you feel better."

"I don't want it. I'll be—"

"*Drink.*"

The anger in his voice had me reaching for the glass despite not wanting to. I took a sip, cringing at the fiery bitterness.

"Nope. Not good enough. Drink it all."

"All?"

He nodded, and I looked at the amount. It was a third of the way full, and I knew I wasn't going to like the effects or taste. Regardless, I braced myself and took a huge swallow. The immediate need to spit it out was overwhelming, yet I managed to swallow it down. My body jerked through the vile flavor, and I swallowed the rest, nearly gagging.

"Good girl."

A smile stretched across West's face, but it was anything but nice. It didn't look normal. It looked evil. The sight triggered the former slave within me, making her want to cringe back in fear.

"I'm proud of you. I tell you to do something and you do it. You're going to be such a good slave."

"I'm not a slave anymore."

"Yes, you are." He took the glass, placing it on the table. "You have no inheritance, Everleigh. The note is on Bram's desk. You're still a slave. And with him injured, possibly dead, that makes you *my* slave."

The coldness had my lips parting. Another sob came at how unfeeling he suddenly was. I couldn't believe it. It was like looking at a complete stranger.

"Bram's not going to die."

"Oh, but I think he is. He was stabbed three times in the chest. Not many people live after that. I'm sorry, slave. I don't think he's going to make it."

"He will make it," I argued. "He can't die. He *won't* die."

"I hope you're right. Here, lay back and get some sleep. Maybe by the time you wake up we'll hear some news."

My hand lifted to knock his away from me, but something was different. My arm was heavier than normal. I rotated my shoulders, feeling my body began to sway.

"What did you do?"

"It's just a relaxer. You're very upset. This will calm you."

Fingers pulled at the buttons of my blouse, and I somehow managed to push his arm away. The slap to my cheek wasn't hard, but I gasped, trying to keep myself upright.

"That was a warning. Raise your hand to me again, and I promise it will be the last time. I have a feeling we are going to have a very intense first few days."

"Bram won't…allow…for this."

My head fell back, rolling to the side. West barely caught me before I hit the mattress. My shirt was jerked free and the bra followed. Once I was stripped completely, I could barely stay awake to feel the covers pulled over my body.

"Bram gave me permission to have you long ago. Face it. You're mine."

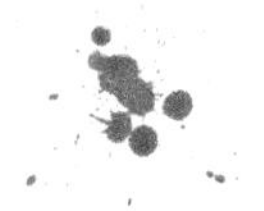

"Everleigh. Everleigh."

"Hmmm?" Colors blurred, blinding me as I tried to force my eyes open. I was so tired. Too tired to wake up for a voice I didn't care to place.

"*Slave!*"

Like an alarm clock, the title ingrained in me had my eyes flying open. A face distorted before me, and my eyes rolled as my lids began to close. No matter how hard I tried, I couldn't fight the pull of sleep. At least, not physically. Mentally, I knew there was a reason to be awake. There was something important. Someone...

"Slave, I have bad news. You have to wake up. It's about Bram."

"B-Bram?"

The name came out stuttering as my thick tongue almost choked me. My entire mouth was bone dry, and I felt sick.

"That's right. Open your eyes. Here, let me help you sit."

My body swayed, feeling as though I were falling to the side, but it stopped as soon as I was sitting. Light broke through again, and I blinked a few times. West's features took a few moments to focus. When they did, I somehow found my voice.

"What about Bram?"

He handed me a glass of water, and I took a sip as he stared at me solemnly.

"He just got out of surgery. He's alive, but they don't think he'll make it another couple hours."

My chest tightened and my lip trembled as a small sound left my mouth.

"Oh, slave. I'm sorry. I know how upset you must be."

Slave. Yes, to him, I was still a slave. I didn't have an inheritance. And soon, I might not have Bram. If that was the case, I didn't have time to be stubborn.

"May I please ask you something?" The title got caught in my throat and I cried, hating to even think about saying it. "C-Can I please ask…Master?"

A slight grin appeared, and he nodded, reaching up to move back the hair falling in front of my eye. "Ask anything of me, slave."

"Will you take me to see him? I want to say…goodbye." I did sob then. It tore from me with a power that left me hunching over and curling into myself. I had no power over the agony serrating my heart. We'd been so close to being together. For the first time in my life, I almost felt happiness. Like something good was finally going to happen to me. He tried to scare me with how he was, but I'd already seen, and I wasn't afraid. I loved him, and I knew he loved me.

"I wish I could take you to him. I really do. I'd give anything to see him myself, but it's impossible. For one, they won't tell me what hospital he's at. And two, I have no one to contact. The high leader is relaying the messages, but it's one way. All the information is coming from him, and I have no return number."

"But…why would he not give you the number? You were Bram's best friend. Why can't we see him? His attacker is dead. W-We deserve to say goodbye."

Louder, my voice grew, and there was nothing I could do to stop the hysterics. Bram, on the verge of death? It didn't seem possible, but I'd seen him. He was covered in blood. And his eyes, they'd been closed. It wasn't some nightmare. It had been real. I'd seen it, just as I had seen my first Master. Both stabbed, laying on the floor.

I wiped the tears as West patted my back. Red lights caught my attention, and I took in the numbers on the clock, confused.

"Is it day or night?"

"What?"

I sniffled as pieces of the night before filtered in. I remembered Bram, but then…the drink.

"It's day. Why do you ask?"

"It's three? Three in the afternoon?"

The concern melted from his face as he pulled back and sat up straighter.

"You were very upset last night. I just helped you sleep."

"*You drugged me.*"

He gave a quick shake of his head. "It wasn't like that. I did it for your benefit. And see, I told you we'd probably know something when you woke up. Although, I learned this an hour ago, and I'm guessing Bram got out of surgery way before that. It's possible he's already dead."

My breath hitched in my throat, and he rolled his eyes as he pushed to stand.

"I told you this was going to happen. Last night, I told you he might not make it. I saw his wounds, slave. There's no way he'd survive that. Besides, that's the reality of life in this place. No one can be trusted. You know that better than anyone."

To argue with a man I was quickly becoming disgusted with was not going to help me. I had to think of a way to learn more about Bram.

"May I take a shower, please?"

"Make it quick. The Masters are stirring. They're requesting a meeting, and you'll be attending."

"Me?"

I pushed back the covers to stand.

"As my slave, of course. They're all going to have to see at some point. What better time than when they face the new Master of this place?"

I shook my head through the sickening in my stomach.

"If Bram dies," he bit out, "who do you think is left to rule? *Me.* I am the closest kin he has concerning Whitlock. Everything goes to me."

"Did you kill him?"

The words left me before I could take them back. Something didn't seem right. He was too cold. Too uncaring over a man he claimed to be his best friend.

Fingers bit into my bicep as he jerked me close. "If I ever hear that question from your mouth again, I'll cut out your tongue. Get in the fucking shower."

The slight shove almost had me falling. My legs were heavy and shaking as I fought to catch myself. I could still feel the drug coursing through me, leaving me groggy and delayed. It did nothing for the horror I suddenly felt concerning the situation.

Jittery, I reached to turn on the water. Before I could so much as draw back, West barged through the door.

"You'll wear this makeup, and I want your bangs pulled back from your face. Today, things begin to change. When I become Master of Whitlock, we bring back the old ways. *But better.* This place will be thriving more than it ever has."

He glanced over, but I had nothing to say. Nothing to think. I was shocked to the core, staring at a man I didn't even know. Bram wasn't even dead, yet West was acting like this was a done deal.

Cautiously, I got in, watching him through the glass. Panic ran rampant inside me. Trust was gone concerning Mr. Harper. He scared the slave still inside. She knew these men. Knew what they were capable of. Hadn't I told Bram I didn't like West? There was always something about him that bothered me, I just hadn't been able to put my finger on it. Now, I knew. *She had known all along.*

Again, my new Master returned, placing jewelry next to the white, form-fitting dress he'd hung by the counter. He went to leave, pausing as he reached forward and picked up Bram's razor. When he turned to me, I fought not to cower.

"Until I can get you into Medical to have them laser the rest, shave everything. Every day. You'll keep it that way from now on. If you don't, I'll make sure you don't forget."

He walked over, pulling the glass door open. My fingers fumbled over the handle, and I almost dropped it. Back and forth, his head shook as he took in the dark strip just above the juncture of my legs.

"I don't mind it so much, truthfully, but Bram would have seen you like this. I want a new version of you. *One he didn't fuck.* Shave it all off."

The door slammed shut, and I jumped at the impact. How did it go from one of the best days of my life to the worst in just a matter of hours?

Tears stung my eyes, but I pushed away the need to break down. There were bigger happening, much bigger than myself. West wanted to bring back the old ways, and I knew enough to fear the possibility of that happening. I had to reach the high leader. He had to know what was going on. Until Bram was gone, the guards needed to step up and take control. If not for my sake, then for the children and every slave here. If West had his way, the moment Bram took his last breath, he'd open The Cradle. He'd bring back the trials, public executions, stoning, and public rape. It wouldn't just be a nightmare. All the sins of hell would come to Whitlock, and we'd all burn with them.

CHAPTER 23

WEST

"You find out everything you can on what Bram knew. The high leader mentioned he suspected something would happen, and the evidence shows as much. From the changed password to the surgeon being alive after I was told she was dead, to a plan to get him away from here if he was injured…it doesn't look good. I want to know if it was me he suspected." I loosened my tie as I glanced down the hall to the loveseat where I had Everleigh sitting. "And find me someone who can hack into that fucking system. The guy who does it for Bram is suddenly nowhere to be found. There's no telling if Bram gave someone else the password. If he did, I want that shit erased before they get in."

"If they haven't already." Eli crossed his arms, peering down the other side of the hall that led to the meeting room.

The Main Masters would be here soon, and while I was excited to display my new authority, I was agitated I'd been taken away from trying to break the password myself. I didn't like there being proof of my involvement in Bram's attack. *What if he lived…*? No, it was impossible.

"There's been no other word on his condition?"

Eli gave a quick shake at my question, still keeping his attention down the hall. “If there has, no one’s told me. Not that they would. The whispers are all but quiet right now. No one trusts anyone. Especially after the high leader gave his replacement, Jarrett, the order to kill anyone who sways from Mr. Whitlock. As long as the Master lives, I don’t think anyone will talk.”

“Dammit. I still can’t believe that motherfucker told me he’d get back to me with an appointment time. Me, taking an appointment from a temporary high leader. Fucking unheard of.”

“He’s cautious around everyone right now. The less that gets out, the easier the situation is to manage. To them, Bram’s life may still be in jeopardy. Or maybe he’s already dead and they’re trying to maintain control until they can slip in a replacement. There’s no telling.”

“I’m the replacement,” I snapped. “*Me.* I was the closest thing to family concerning the Whitlock name.”

“Maybe it’s not blood they’re wanting anymore. Maybe one of the Main Masters will take over.”

“Why, because they have money? *I have money.*”

Eli glanced at Everleigh. “How much was it?”

“Enough to be a Main Master. No wonder Bram didn’t mention it before the movie. The bastard probably wanted to keep it for himself. Well, it’s mine now. It’s enough to give me just as much right to take over this place. Thing is, I’m in with the Whitlocks’, and that makes me the rightful heir.”

“I guess we’ll see.”

Voices broke through in the far distance, just in time for a group of men to walk around the corner and come into view. I snapped my fingers, and Everleigh stood, coming to stand behind me. The closer the men got, the more their stare focused on her.

“What’s this?”

Offense filled Master Leone’s tone, and he turned to me with the anger I expected.

"This is my slave. What does it look like?"

"She's supposed to be a Mistress. Why is she your slave?"

I reached over, turning the knob and swinging the meeting door open. The men filed in, taking their seats as I took Bram's. Their hesitancy was one I wasn't going to take. I snapped my fingers again, and Everleigh rushed to my side as I sat down. When I pointed to the ground, she glanced at the other men, slowly easing to kneel at my side.

"Everleigh is my slave because Mr. Whitlock willed it. She proved not be a fitting Mistress, so he stripped her of the rank. It's that simple. She needed a Master, and I needed a slave."

"How convenient." One of Master Yahn's eyebrows rose. "And her inheritance?"

"Is now mine."

Everleigh's head shot up and anger met me as she rose to her feet. "You lied to me. You said I didn't have an inheritance."

I stood, angling my chair away as I towered over her. "You don't. I do. You are a slave."

"But Bram—"

Whack!

Her head spun to the side at my slap.

"That's Mr. Whitlock to you. Don't you forget it."

"*Mr. Whitlock* didn't strip me of my rank, you did! *Mr. Whitlock* also made it clear not an hour before his attack he was keeping me for himself. *He loved me,* and the last person he wanted to have me was you." She spun to the table, wiping her escaping tears as she faced the main members. "I have money, and status. Don't let this man take it away. Mr. Whitlock is *not* dead, and he's not going to die. You have to stop Mr. Harper from overstepping on what is not rightfully his. You—"

"Oh, slave. You just don't learn." My fingers buried in her hair while my other hand latched to her throat. I jerked her eyes inches from mine, and every ounce of hate and rage collided inside me at her words. At Bram's claim on her I knew nothing about.

Her weight grew heavier as I squeezed, and fear had her trying to jerk and fight in my hold. "Do you really think these men are going to let you have a status you don't deserve? You came here a slave. You will die here a slave. No one cares about what *you* want, or even what happens to you." I gave her a hard shake. "Do you hear me? No one cares about you! You are nothing more than what I decide to make of you."

Whack!

"Back on your knees."

Everleigh collapsed to the ground, coughing and trying to catch her breath. The nearly silent crying that followed was enough to grate my nerves. I grabbed my chair, looking from it to her. I couldn't have this emotional slave distracting the Main Masters with sobs and claims she said I didn't deserve. I may have asserted my real personality to gain their respect, but it wasn't enough. If they were going to take my lead, I had to show them who I truly was. *The real me.*

"Enough."

My fingers went back to her hair as I dragged her to the door. Her legs kicked behind her, trying to gain purchase, but I didn't allow her. Eli looked at me for direction and opened the glass barrier at my nod.

"We'll be fine in here. Watch her outside. I can't listen to that shit anymore. If the tears don't stop in two minutes, give her another reason to cry. If she doesn't stop after that, hit her again. She'll learn."

Everleigh was fighting to stand when Eli snatched her up and shut them outside. The instant silence had me taking a deep breath as I turned around.

"Sorry about that. Where were we?" The men looked at each other while I pulled out a cigar and lit it. "If no one remembers, we can start with our current dilemma. Our Master,

Mr. Whitlock, is in critical condition at an unknown hospital. I'm told he's getting the best care possible and had a long surgery overnight. He pulled through, but it doesn't appear hopeful. Due to the circumstances and my relationship with Mr. Whitlock, I've taken on his responsibilities until we know how he fares."

"How exactly did that go down?" Master Yahn's fingers steepled on the table as he stared at me suspiciously. "You were there when he was attacked, weren't you, Mr. Harper?"

"Master Harper," I corrected. "And yes, I was. Mr. Whitlock was helping me," I said, glaring. "I had suddenly become ill. It was odd and came out of nowhere. He was helping me to the restroom when a former guard attacked us. He stabbed Mr. Whitlock in the chest three times before I could recover enough to break his fucking neck."

Some of the men shifted as they looked between us, but I never broke my gaze from Master Yahn.

"Interesting you mention that Master Harper. You see, I too recently fell ill like that. Did you go get checked out at Medical?"

"No. Why would I? My best friend had just been stabbed. I could deal with the sickness. What I can't deal with is not being able to be there for my family. He's barely hanging on, and I can't even see how he's doing. I can't call or get updates. You're the Main Masters. One of you has to know how to get ahold of the high leader."

Heads shook all around the table. Five men, all holding their positions due to money and their power in the outside world. Alone, they were dangerous. Together, bound into one force by Whitlock, they were equivalent to God. We could make anything possible, anyone or any*thing* disappear. Their force and influence was pivotal. And they all claimed to know nothing about Lyle.

"I would hate to think any of you are lying to me. Mr. Whitlock's life could depend on this. How are we to know what kind of care he's really in? None of you, with all your connections, don't know how to find your Master?"

Again, they shook their heads.

"All right." I tightened my jaw repeatedly. "Let's talk worst case scenario. If Mr. Whitlock doesn't make it, we're going to need a new Master. It'll have to be a smooth transition. If there's any debate or argument, all hell is going to break loose, and we all know we can't afford that."

"Let me guess. You think you're the person we should look to?" Again, Master Yahn taunted me.

"It makes the most the sense. I was Mr. Whitlock's partner in the outside world, and his right-hand man here at Whitlock. I shadowed him. I fucking grew up with him. *I'm family*. He's my brother, and I know I can pick up where he left off."

"What if we don't all like the way things run here?" Master Kunken, Bram's second, leaned forward, placing his forearms on the desk.

"I won't lie," I said, tilting my head as my plans barreled through. "There will be some changes if I become the Main Master. Some that might be to some of your liking. More…*the old way*. I don't want to go into too much detail now. I don't want to disrespect Bram. That's not my intention here today. But for who takes his position, this has to be discussed."

Master Leone's fingers tapped along the desk as he took in the men around him. "Banker, trust fund baby, Senator, analyst, and me, Oil Tycoon. With Master Kunken's political background, he'd be my pick out of all of us, but let's face it, he doesn't have the time. Neither does Master Barclane, the analyst. That leaves me, Master Kain, and Master Yahn. No, to both. You, though, are here all the time anyway. You grew up within these walls with Master Whitlock. *You* have my vote."

Silence lasted until Master Kain pushed his chair back. "I may have the time being the trust fund baby, but I don't fucking want it. I'm only here for the fun. You won't get any argument from me. Master Harper for my vote," he mumbled.

"Well, I think I could do the job better than anyone. I'm rich. I'm successful. I own banks. I have the time."

"No offense, Master Yahn, but no." Master Kunken gave a shake of his head and pushed his chair out too. "It has to be majority, and the majority has pretty much already agreed." He looked at me. "I'm late for lunch. Being second in command, I'd like to be contacted with an update of the Main Master when you get it. If you'll all excuse me."

Nodding, he left the room without so much as a backwards glance. It broke formality, but this wasn't formal. Besides, I had his vote. I had most of their votes. That's all I cared about.

CHAPTER 24

24690

"Please, come in."

West widened the door, waving in Jarrett, the temporary high leader. The guard looked around the living room, then glanced at me before coming to stand a few feet inside.

"What's the news? How's our Main Master? How's Bram?"

The emotion lacing West's voice seemed genuine, but I knew better. He wasn't concerned over Bram's condition. All he wanted was to take his place.

"Mr. Whitlock hangs on, but it's not good. They've had to bring him back twice so far. He hasn't woken up. The high leader says the doctors don't believe he will."

My fists clenched as fire burned the backs of my eyes. "Can we not see him?"

West surprisingly stayed quiet as he waited for the guard's response.

"I wasn't told where they are. I don't believe so, no."

I glanced at West but braved my next question anyway. "Will you please tell Lyle I would like to speak with him when he calls you again?"

"*Slave*." The threat was clear in West's voice. Regardless, I turned back to the guard.

"I beg you. Please tell him I need to speak with him. That it's urgent."

West's death glare was enough to cause the slave in me to shake. I knew it wasn't going to be good when we were alone again, but I needed help. I needed someone on my side.

The guard kept quiet as he turned his attention to my new Master. "Is there anything you'd like me to relay to the high leader?"

"I want to see Bram. I *have* to see him. He's the only family I have left. If the high leader doesn't allow that, at least tell him I'd like to speak with him personally."

"I'll relay your message the next time he calls."

"Can I not call him myself? Do you not have the number?"

"No. For security purposes, no one does."

West nodded, licking his lips. "What of the surgeon who accompanied Bram to the hospital? Where is she? She's a liability outside these walls."

"I have no idea, Master Harper. I wasn't made aware of her whereabouts. I'm sure our high leader has everything under control."

"You're right. Of course."

"If that's all, I should be getting back."

"Thank you for the update," West said, his tone sincere. "Please, pass along my requests when you get the chance. I want to see my brother. He needs me there."

The guard nodded, then glanced back at me before leaving Bram's apartment. The moment the door closed, I eased to my feet. Fear engulfed me—and for good reason. West was already heading forward, pure malice lining his features as he matched my steps toward the bedroom door. I had nowhere to go. Nowhere to hide.

"Lyle? You and the high leader are on a first name basis?

Why is that, slave? What have you done? Did you fuck him too?"

"No." My head shook as I passed the threshold to Bram's bedroom. Without thinking, I grabbed the door, trying to slam it closed. The weight that crashed into it sent me stumbling back. I spun, rushing for the bathroom when West's arms hooked around my waist. I screamed, kicking and twisting my body as he wrestled me down on the bed. The first hit connected harder than any of the others. A high-pitched noise rung in my ears as he hit me with the back of his hand again.

"After the meeting you, I'd thought you would have learned." *Whack!* "Do I need to beat you harder? Do I need to pound it into your head to keep your mouth shut unless it is me who is speaking to you?"

"N-No! No! Master, please."

Fingers squeezed into my throbbing face, blood streaming from my nose. The metallic flavor exploded over my tongue as I swallowed, struggling to catch my breath. West smiled, lowering to run his tongue over the blood racing down my cheek. A sob left me as I cringed at his nearness.

"That's better, slave. Tell me who owns you again."

A whimper came, and for the life of me, I couldn't answer.

More of West's weight pressed into me as he licked the warmth trailing down my face again. Kisses moved over the throbbing flesh, and I clutched to the comforter, trying to imagine I was anywhere but on Bram's bed with West on top of me.

"Did Bram fuck you good? Did you like it? Hmmm?" His fingers pushed back in, turning my face as his lips moved to my ear. The tugs against my earlobe had me trying to shake my head to get him away.

"Slave, you wouldn't be lying to me, would you? I think you liked it. I think you begged him for more. And I bet he gave it. How was it? Did he fuck you hard? Use you like the whore you are? Or was he slow and passionate? Did his love manage to seep through his pitch-black soul? He loved you, you know? He's loved you for years. There were times he'd sit here all day and night just watching you. I couldn't make him leave. The look on his face as he stared at the screen…I knew he adored you. He'd smile and sometimes laugh. But there was always that darkness. Always that greed and lust shining through his eyes. You were his obsession. And it didn't take long for me to figure out why after watching you myself."

His arm shifted, pulling up the side of my dress. Instinct had me wanting to swing, even at knowing he'd hit me again. My fist rose, only for West's other hand to shoot up, pinning it down.

"Don't be stupid. I know you want him, but aren't you going to at least give me a chance? You chose me once as your Master. I can make you like this. You could come to enjoy what we share." He gripped my wrist tighter. "All you have to do is see your place. Be my slave in every sense, and I will treat you like a queen. I do have feelings for you. Our match could be a good one."

Higher, his fingers traveled up my thigh. The hold on my hand eased, and I squeezed my eyes shut as he buried his face in my neck. The brush of his lips had my fingers balling into fists. I knew the slave in me should have returned, that I should have just let this pedestal Bram placed me on crumble beneath me. Go back to no status—no rights. But I couldn't accept this fall. Bram didn't want me with West. He'd wanted me for himself.

"Stop."

Where I expected him to hit me again, a laugh vibrated my lower throat. He lifted, smiling down at me. "I was hoping you'd resist. It's going to make this relationship so much better. Compliant is boring." His hand rose, and I braced. The loud knocking had him pausing. Within seconds, boots stomped against the floor. West was barely lifting off me when Jarett appeared in the doorway. He looked between us, letting no expression show as he motioned for me.

"You must come."

I scrambled the rest of the way out from under West, nearly falling as I bound from the bottom of the bed.

"She's my slave. Where do you think it is you're taking her?"

The man peered toward West, but his arm came out to me.

"The high leader is on the phone. He wishes to speak with her."

"And me? What about me? I asked to speak with him as well."

The guard steadied me, keeping his hand on my bicep. "I'll transfer him to this line when she's finished."

"And then you'll bring her back."

West wasn't asking. He came closer, and with his advance, I moved more into the guard's side.

"I will do as I'm instructed from the high leader. If he wishes her back in your care, I will return her."

I was turned, and I couldn't keep in the tears as they rolled down my cheeks. Relief nearly had me collapsing. Three guards moved in behind us as we left Bram's apartment at a swift pace. No one spoke through the maze of curved halls. When I walked into a long, open area, the temporary high leader broke away from the other guards and shuffled us into a big office. He sat me in one of the two chairs before a large oak desk and kneeled before me.

A box of tissues rested on the corner, and he grabbed one, wiping the blood still coming from my nose. When he patted my lip, I jerked back at the pain. His mouth twisted, and he shook his head, standing.

"You're not like the others," I said lowly.

He grabbed the phone, pausing, then lifted the receiver. "I have her."

My whole body trembled as I reached out and placed the phone to my ear. "High Leader." I swallowed hard. "Lyle…?"

"How are you holding up, Mistress?"

I sobbed, wiping the tears the moment they fell. "Not good. How's Mr. Whitlock? Please tell me he's okay."

My voice cracked, and there was hesitation on his end.

"I'm afraid it's not good, but that's not why I'm calling. I had specific orders if something like this happened, and in all the commotion and chaos, I'm afraid I failed on your end. You were meant to go into holding. Mr. Whitlock wanted you protected if something were to happen to him. I'm sorry about anything you may have endured in the meantime. *Did* anything happen? How are you?"

I grabbed another tissue, sniffling through the new tears. "Fine. Just a few beatings to haze me back into being a slave. It could be a lot worse."

"Things are about to get really bad. You have to know that. But you'll be safe from here on out."

I nodded, letting out a pent-up breath. "Please tell me more about Mr. Whitlock. Has he woken up at all? Said anything? I don't trust Mr. Harper," I rushed out. "He wants Whitlock. He's said so."

Silence. "Mr. Whitlock suspected, but that doesn't matter. The worst has happened, and now we must let things play out. Mr. Harper may be responsible, or he may not. Time will reveal all. For now, we go by our Master's instructions and what happens, happens. If the Main Master wakes up and wishes you to know, I will inform you."

"Thank you, High Leader."

"Lyle. And, Mistress, head up. Stay strong. When I get back, you will have your status again. That's where he left you, and I will see his wishes through."

A sad grin tugged at my mouth, and I handed the phone back to Jarrett.

"Sir." He paused, looking over at me. "Busted lip. Her nose is still bleeding a little. I believe he was in the process of rape when I entered. Yes, sir. Right away."

The guard hit a button on the phone, hanging it up.

"I just transferred him to Mr. Harper. I'm afraid he's not going to be happy at what our high leader has to say, but you have nothing to be afraid of. You're to stay in a safe room so we can monitor you."

"Here?" I glanced toward the door, flashbacks of the guards attacking me in the shower room flooding in. "Some don't like me. I—"

"Will not be harmed. I give you my word. You'll not be staying here. There's a room for you in The Cradle. You'll be protected at all times. We have two guards posted at the main door. If anyone so much as touches you, the person or persons involved will die. They know this. They know who you are to our Main Master. They won't touch you."

"Who I am to him? Did he say?"

The guard stood from behind the desk.

"You were in his instructions. He made them in the early hours after the auction. I was here when he personally delivered them to the high leader. You were to be a Mistress. He…had plans for the two of you I believe. The high leader didn't elaborate, but it was clear you were Mr. Whitlock's. No one else's, unless he gave the word. I was told to tell you that in the event of something happening and the Master didn't make it, everything of his was to be yours. Except Whitlock. That was to go to Mr. Harper upon his innocence."

"Even if…" the guard hesitated, his eyebrows drawing in. "Say our Main Master passes and for some reason you are to go to another…like Mr. Harper, if he becomes Master. Unlike your previous owner, your funds are not to be obtainable by him or anyone else. Only you. There's power in that if you know how to use it. It's all about wealth here. If—"

"I don't care about the money," I snapped. "If something happens to Mr. Whitlock, Mistress or not, Mr. Harper *will* take me. And he will have the right being Master of Whitlock. Money will do nothing to save me in that situation. His intentions for me are not good. Neither are his intentions for Whitlock. He plans to revert to the old ways. What about the children?"

The guard's eyes dropped. "You have a lot to learn, Mistress. You see an end. I'm here to tell you it's not. Not concerning you. As for the old ways or the children…if the time comes, it will be out of our hands. He has the right to change whatever he likes. I pray that isn't the case, but the Master's word is law. Our hands will be tied.

CHAPTER 25

WEST

"No! Did you see that? What the fuck!"

Cheers and yells echoed from the walls of my apartment, but I wasn't celebrating or even watching the game. Six guards were crowded into my space, and although I'd been working to connect with them more by the day, tonight I couldn't focus. All I could think about was how Bram was still outsmarting me even while clinging to life.

Four days I'd been without my slave, and it was driving me crazy. I'd come so close to having her as mine, and the minute I thought I had everything in the bag, she was taken from me. Again. By Bram. *Again.*

I downed the rest of my beer, unsure of how many I'd had. Enough to know I was far from sober.

"Come on!" Eli crushed a can in his hand, standing. "You want another?"

"Keep 'em coming." I tossed my empty beer, not caring if any spilled. Eli caught it, walking swiftly into the kitchen. I leaned my head back and closed my eyes as I felt her body under mine. *I could still taste her blood, feeding me. Urging me to spill more*. I didn't want to think about how Bram wasn't dead yet. Or if he'd truly woken up or not. From what the high leader said only an hour ago, he'd supposedly gotten worse. It put me at ease, letting my mind drift to Everleigh even more.

"Head's up!"

My lids were heavy as I forced them open. I barely caught the can Eli tossed to me. Coldness splattered across my face as I opened it, and I looked down at the drawstring waistband of my sweatpants. They were wet from the overflow, but I didn't care. I laughed, drinking down even more.

"Give me one of those slices." I pointed to the guard sitting in a chair closest to the open pizza box. I felt like I was in college again, but it was good to raise the morale of the men I wanted on my side, and they seemed to enjoy this.

Knock. Knock.

"Ay-oh!"

Eli's voice was loud as he jumped up, springing to the door. He shook the other guard's hand as the guy came in.

"West, this is Abbot. Abbot, West."

I brought up my hand, pausing as I noticed the pizza in one and beer in the other. "Nice to meet you, Abbot. Grab a beer and take a seat. Pizza's right there," I said, using the hand holding the slice to point.

"Thanks, Mr. Harper."

"West. No one is working."

He smiled, grabbing a slice as Eli sat back down. "Thank God for that. Long night."

I sat up straighter, glancing to Eli. I knew my guy invited this one over for a reason. He'd mentioned his suspicions earlier, but we still weren't sure.

"Hopefully nothing too bad happened."

"Nah. Boring as hell. There's only so much I can take of crying little kids. Although, I guess it wasn't so bad tonight."

My pulse jumped and I took another drink. "Does she keep them occupied?"

He hesitated in taking a bite, looking from me to the men around the room. We all stared, and I knew he probably felt trapped. "Yeah. She's good with them. She's got that whole motherly thing going on."

I smiled, tearing into my pizza angrily. So, she was being kept in The Cradle. I was permitted there. Anyone could go. They might not have her where I'd be able to see her, but knowing I wasn't forbidden helped ease the lack of control spiraling inside.

"Relax, Abbot. Grab a beer. No one is going to hurt your Mistress or say you told us anything. I'm not worried about my slave. When Bram returns, everyone's going to see she's mine. He's already given her to me. The high leader and everyone else will know that soon enough."

The guard's shoulders relaxed as he headed for the kitchen, and I went back to watching the game. Time passed, and I wasn't the only one drunk by the time the men started filing out.

"Don't let him fall down the damn stairs on your way back to the barracks."

Patrick laughed at me, raising the beer in his hand as he held Benson steady. Had this become my life? Most would enjoy it, but not me. I wasn't naturally a social person…more one-track minded. And still, she plagued my thoughts. It was stealing every ounce of focus I could manage. And the only thing I could come up with was I'd win her over. I'd put her in her place, but I'd make it good. She'd bend, and then the damn guards would get off my back. I also couldn't deny, in my drunken state, that I wanted her to want me. She'd wanted Bram. Why not me?

I put down the can, swaying as I stood. Eli was passed out in the chair, and I kicked his foot as I approached.

"Couch."

"What time is it?"

I looked at the clock, yawning. "Almost one. Guys just left. I'm headed to bed." The door swung open, stopping me in my tracks. Where I expected to see one of the guards coming back to get something they forgot, the face didn't register right away.

"Ah, Jarrett. Surely I'm not in trouble for giving the guys a few beers."

He swallowed hard, pulling off the uniformed ballcap he wore. "I'm sorry, Mr. Harper. I've come with grave news. I'm afraid our Main Master has passed. The high leader asks that you leave for Chicago first thing in the morning. You are to approve the funeral arrangement Mr. Whitlock had in place."

"Passed?"

"My condolences…Master."

I swayed as the blood seemed to rush from my head. I'd known this day might come, but now that it was here, I felt overwhelmed with emotion. And not just from excitement or shock, but sadness. I had loved Bram to an extent. We used to be close. I'd seen that again the day I had him killed. Now, I was feeling his chapter in my life end.

"Thank you." I blinked, and it took me a few moments to register. "Master?" I whispered, looking up.

"Mr. Whitlock made it known in his instructions. You are our new Master."

My hand pressed against the wall as I forced myself to stand taller. The high leader hadn't mentioned that in our conversation. Although I knew I had the support of the other Masters in charge, I didn't think Bram would just so readily hand it over. *I'd had his blessing all along.*

"Of course. Please have the chopper ready for me at eight. Have Mistress Davenport and her things ready. She loved Bram. She deserves to see him one last time."

"But…"

"Do it! Enough of this. She will go. I can more than handle her if she gets out of line. Have her ready and at my door come eight o'clock."

"Yes, Master."

The guard eased from the door, and I walked over, locking it behind him. When I turned and glanced up at Eli, he had a big smile on his face. "And so it begins. Welcome, new Master of Whitlock."

A laugh burst from his mouth, and I couldn't keep the smile from mine.

"You'll come and stay by my side. You'll help me keep my slave in line, and when the time is right, I will be welcoming you as my new high leader."

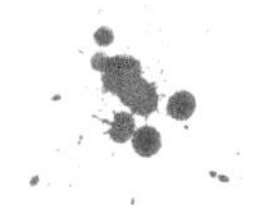

"Will you go?"

Everleigh stood at my front door talking to Jarrett. He glanced over at me and shook his head.

"No. I must stay here. You'll be fine. Remember what I said. Stay by our new Main Master's side. The outside world can be a scary place. He will take good care of you."

Blue eyes peeked over at me, and she nodded. "I will. Thank you for everything."

"Of course. Safe travels, Main Master, Mistress." Bowing his head, he turned, and his men took off. I brought my attention to my slave, frowning as I took her hand. She didn't fight, flinch, or try to pull away. I was surprised when she actually stepped in closer, letting me lead her down the hall toward the stairs. Eli was following behind, but I paid him no attention as I looked over at Everleigh. She was in a black dress with a high neckline. Her arms were bare except for a pair of black silk gloves that reached past her elbows, and she was carrying a purse. Even though I saw her wearing it in the dressing room when I bought it, the impact was enough to nearly take my breath away.

"I'm sorry," I said softly. She turned her head to me but didn't speak. "I know you loved him and you're going to miss him. The way I've treated you, trying to bend you to my will was wrong. I see that now. I thought if I treated you more like Bram, I could make you fall for me too. I feel horrible. I can't replace him. I'll never be able to. All I can ask is that you give me another chance. We can start over. I can make this up to you."

The glimmer of tears building in her eyes nearly spilled over. Everleigh's head lifted higher, and she took in a deep breath before speaking.

"May I have time to think on your request? I've been told there's a possibility my title as Mistress is unbreakable, but I've been thinking over how my life will play out if I'm…alone." Tighter, she gripped my hand. "I've seen the real Mr. Harper. The one you changed into after Bram's murder was not who you are. If I can have the old West back, I may be the one offering you a proposal."

"Me? What sort of proposal?"

"I'm not ready to divulge the details yet. I'm still thinking it over. Can I have a few days?"

"Two days. I've been told the funeral preparations are already in order. I'm to approve them. They have Bram's funeral set for the day after tomorrow. That night, you will either have an answer or propose something of your own. We will go from there."

"All right."

The lack of "Main Master" at the end had me clenching my teeth, but I ignored it as we walked down the stairs and headed for the chopper in the middle of the field. Resistance pulled against my hand, and I looked back at Everleigh's frightened face.

"It'll be okay. I've got you."

The gushing wind as we neared made my words almost inaudible. She leaned into my side as I wrapped my arm around her and rushed forward. With her heels, she fought to maintain a decent speed, but I didn't show agitation. I helped her into the cabin, leading her to the white leather sofa as Eli shut the door behind him. He was in his black uniform, on duty as my bodyguard. I hadn't noticed his gun out until he placed it in his holster and sat in the recliner closest to the door.

"I don't like this," he said under his breath. "I have a bad feeling. I trust no one."

I threw him a look, but the chopper lifting had Everleigh squeezing my hand in a death grip. It stole my focus, and I smiled, loving her innocence—innocence I secretly craved to destroy.

"Calm. It'll be okay. We have a good two and a half hours before we make it to Chicago. It's best to relax now."

"So long? But why would they take…Mr. Whitlock so far away?"

"You can call him Bram. It's okay. I was wrong before when I hit you. I don't mind. And Chicago is unexpected. Cheyenne would have been the closest hospital, but Bram had an amazing surgeon and staff on board. Anything the doctors in Cheyenne would have been able to do, she and her team probably did better. He was in great hands with her. They could risk the flight. Especially since no one would have expected Chicago. If there were indeed more people out to end his life, they would have never found him."

Her head lowered as she nodded.

"Plus, Bram had a soft spot for Chicago. We opened our first practice there. It makes sense to me why he'd go back."

"I see." A confused looked swept over her face as her head snapped up. "Cheyenne? We're in Wyoming?"

My back straightened as I glanced over to see Eli's raised eyebrow. "You must never tell the location to anyone, Everleigh. No one. It holds a sentence punishable by death."

"I won't tell." She looked over, scanning my face. "I didn't tell you thank you for letting me come to say goodbye. You didn't have to bring me. I'm grateful."

"Well, you're welcome. I knew how much he meant to you. If this gives you closure, I'm happy to take the risk. And it is a risk. Bram was high profile. His family name is very well known throughout the world. You'll keep your head down and be at my side the entire time. When we get to Chicago, I'll buy you a ring, and you will wear it. If anyone asks, you're my wife. It'll make things easier."

"Your wife? I'm not worthy to have a title like that. Not even in a lie."

I laughed, unable to stop the wheels in my head from turning. Wouldn't that be the ultimate fuck you to Bram? Make Everleigh my real wife, but treat her as my slave? Degrade the definition of what our vows really meant? Sure, I could just treat her as a slave and have her that way, but to *really* have her, both in our world and the outside world? Even Bram would have never gone that far.

"What if we did it? Not under your real name, but under another. Everleigh, look at me."

I cupped her face, turning her to look at me. Tears were already trailing down her face. She looked terrified, like a cornered animal.

"I know you have this proposal you're thinking over but hear me out. What if we did get married before we went back? No one will love you more than me. This time, things will be different. I will run Whitlock, and you will be by my side...as my wife. *Not my slave*. I mean it. We can start over. We can do this right."

Full lips parted as she stared at me wide-eyed. "You don't mean that."

"I do. I heard you were at The Cradle while you were away from me." Manipulation had my heart racing and adrenaline soaring. "Did you like the kids there? I could give you one of them. You could be a wife and a mother. I can make dreams you never imagined come true. Would you like that?"

A ragged breath left her as she glanced over at Eli, only to come back to me.

"I…I…" Still, the broken breaths left her.

"This is too big for you to grasp right now. I forget sometimes how sheltered you've been. You've probably never imagined this being possible. Take the two days and think over it. I will buy you a ring, and you can see how things will be when we're married. For me, my role as a husband starts now."

I brought up our joined hands, kissing her knuckles. She was still thinking. I could see it in her eyes as she went back to looking at her lap. Time passed while Eli flipped on the television. The movie that began had the hair on my arms standing. The title displayed, and Everleigh's face shot to mine.

"Coincidence," I mumbled. "Nothing more."

But that damn duck movie left me uneasy. What were the odds of that one film playing over any other DVD?

Fascination had Everleigh moving to the front of the sofa, and I settled for watching her reactions to the movie. Flashes of Bram's face plagued me. The memories I had of us groaning through the movie kept repeating. Our smiles. Our laughs. *The day I had him stabbed.*

"ETA: five minutes."

The pilot's voice echoed through the cabin, and I couldn't have been more relieved.

“Remember, you’re not Everleigh anymore. Just Lee. Lee Harper.”

Dark hair bounced around her chin as she nodded.

“Lee Harper. It sounds good.”

“It could be real. *Everleigh Harper*. I think it sounds perfect.” I leaned forward, brushing my lips over hers, trying my best to push away suspicions over Bram. I saw the damage he’d undergone. I knew he was dead. Soon enough, I’d see it for myself.

CHAPTER 26

24690

I was going to be sick.

Diamonds sparkled as I rotated my hand back and forth over the glass display case. This wasn't happening. I had meant to play the role of submissive slave long enough to see Bram. After all, West didn't have to bring me, but he had. During our time here, I meant to be compliant so he wouldn't have any reason to send me back or keep me away. Now, I was in over my head. What happened if I said no? What he was offering was any slave's dream—my dream. But not with him. Any hope of happiness for me was gone. I was mourning—aching for someone I would never see alive again. This wasn't happening. I still couldn't believe it was true.

West grabbed my hand and smiled down at me. "What do you think? Do you like it?"

"It's beautiful. Beyond beautiful. I don't know what to say. It's too much," I whispered, leaning in.

"Too much for you?" He turned the mirror on the case to reflect us. "Do you see yourself? Nothing is too much for you. Especially if you marry me." He turned me to face him. "You don't trust me. You might even hate me. I don't blame you after my behavior. I'm just asking you to try to forget about the person you saw. He won't exist if you decide to be mine. Just this West, right here."

I looked back at the ring, wanting to cry. I didn't want to marry him. I didn't want to be in the same room as him. I wanted Bram. I wanted this nightmare to end.

"We'll take it."

West's voice had me looking up. He grabbed the matching band and slid it on. Within moments, the jeweler came back, handing him a piece of paper to sign. It was as simple as that. I didn't understand how things worked. We'd taken a car to get here, and it was worse than the helicopter. The fast movement of the surrounding vehicles, the blur of colors racing by, had me closing my eyes more than half the ride. I was a nervous wreck, and all I wanted to do was get back to the penthouse where we'd landed. How was I going to pretend if I couldn't even think straight?

"Eli."

At West's gesture, the guard disappeared out the front doors, and as soon as the long car drove up, we headed out.

"Ride in the front. Watch *everything*."

Anxiety drew in West's features as our door opened and he helped me in. Something was off.

"What's wrong?"

He turned from looking out the back window and pegged me with a nervous stare. "I'm sure it's nothing. You can just never be too cautious. This place isn't safe, Everleigh. That's why it's so important to stay by my side. Believe nothing anyone tells you up here. You probably don't remember much from your youth, but things have changed since then. People live to lie. They'll do everything in their power to trap you for their own means. You look rich and have money. Trust no one."

I turned my head to look behind us and my stomach twisted

at what he was implying. Was it so unsafe here? Surely it couldn't be worse than Whitlock. But what if it was?

"I won't talk to anyone."

"No one. Especially if they try to get you alone. If they so much as imply anything like that, you tell me. Even if it is a guard or someone you think you know. I'm the only one you trust."

"I'll tell you."

West pushed his fingers into my hair, gently leading me to his lips. I could have pulled back. My soul screamed to. But I couldn't ruin this yet. Not if I wanted to see Bram. Until we got back to Whitlock, I had to try my best to play by his rules.

"You look beautiful. The bruising isn't too bad on your cheek, and your lip is already healing. The makeup hides it well. No one will even notice." At my slight withdrawal, West pushed his lips back into mine. "You never have to worry about me doing that to you again. I won't. You have my word."

"But you enjoyed it." I did pull back then, unable to control the words as the car jerked to slow. My heart raced as I tried to adjust to the motions of the vehicle.

"I won't lie. I did like it. But maybe not as you think."

"What do you mean?"

He twisted his mouth, grabbing my hips to sit me on his lap.

"It wasn't the hitting I enjoy, wife. It was the fight. The struggle of you trying to break free. I wouldn't have raped you, although I did like you to believe I was going to. It's what builds me up. I am generally a nice man. You see the way I act now. You've known me for years before seeing that side of me. A man has to have a certain darkness in him to feel…validated. Unless you're a man, you won't understand this. Growing up at Whitlock, I guess it just sort of rubbed off on me. You have to at least understand, as a child, I was molded to this place. It wasn't easy witnessing the things I did. Or doing the things I was forced to do."

"You were forced to do things?"

He nodded. "Bram and I both. Did you know we were made to torture and kill disobedient slaves before we were thirteen? Bram's father wanted us…prepared for what we'd have to face some day. We were beaten very badly, on many occasions. The things we were made to do…I will never tell you about. I don't believe you could handle it. Just know, what we became was not something we were born to be. We coped the best we could. Now, all I want is what I was groomed to. Have a pretty little wife, and maybe down the road, a kid or two. Is it so bad for me to want happiness after the hell I've had to live? You know hell. You know torture and pain. Why is it so wrong to try to erase the past and start over?"

"There's nothing wrong with wanting that." *If it were the truth.* I didn't trust anything West said. What did bother me was the insight into these men's lives. Into Bram's. It explained so much. It made my heart bleed in my chest even more. "I'm sorry for what happened to both of you. We were on opposite sides, trapped in the world of Whitlock. We both experienced horrors that will never leave us. At least now you can make a difference. You can make it better than ever."

West frowned as he turned to look out the window. I knew he didn't want to make it better. He wanted the old ways back. He'd said so himself. That only told me one thing: he was more evil than good. There was no hope for him, or a marriage for us, or for me to even survive long matched to him. It would only take one mental snap and he could kill me if he wanted. Or worse…I would kill him. I had to figure something out. Every path I had before me held a chance of backfiring. I was running out of time.

Minutes passed while I tried to calm the anxieties of the sights around us. When the car pulled into the circle drive of a large building, West placed me on the seat next to him.

"Time to eat, Lee. Remember, stay close. Keep your head up,

but your eyes off anyone's face. Do exactly what I tell you. Don't do anything to upset me."

"I won't."

He nodded as the door was swung open. I let him help me out, sliding my fingers through his as he initiated the hold. The guard stayed behind us, constantly taking in the surroundings as we strolled through the entrance. The large room had me gasping at the grandeur. The ceiling looked like a picture I'd seen in a book of a cathedral. There was gold and glass aligning the walls. Everything was sparkling. I tilted my head back at the large chandelier, then righted myself at the tug on my hand.

We turned left, heading into an even larger room filled with just as much splendor. I barely noticed the woman behind the podium as we came to a stop.

"Reservation for West Harper."

"We've been expecting you, Mr. Harper. Right this way."

As we weaved through the tables, I kept my gaze ahead, not daring to look at anyone at the tables. I didn't even want to be here. For as long as I could remember, all I wanted to do was escape Whitlock. Now that I was here, I didn't know what to expect. I kept waiting for someone to attack us. I'd been on guard for so long, it was hard to relax.

"Sit."

West pulled out a chair, and I obeyed, letting him push me in. When he sat across from me, Eli took his position standing against the wall not a foot behind us. His hand grasped his wrist at his waist as he scanned the surroundings. It only added to my apprehension. What was happening if our guard was so cautious? Who was going to hurt us?

"Can I start you out with a drink?"

West scanned over the menu, then placed it down after a brief glimpse. "A bottle of your best red."

The waiter nodded, rushing away.

"Red?"

"Wine, wife."

"Oh." I picked up the menu, looking over the selection. I didn't recognize a single thing. I felt so out of place. Sweat began to cover my chest and it was getting hard to breathe. My body swayed, and I gripped the table to try to stop the unbalance.

"This is too much for you. You're terrified right now. Look at your hands. You're trembling. Eli, bring her chair over here."

My palms pressed against the white tablecloth as I stood. As much as I hated West, he was all I knew. There was a comfort in that for the slave who needed familiarity. There was also anger over needing him at all.

Ringing filled the space as I sat. West reached into his pocket, pulling out his phone. "Hello?" He paused, his brow creasing. "I see. We're getting lunch now. We'll meet you there in an hour." Hanging up the phone, he peered over at me as he placed it back in his suit jacket. "That was the high leader. They've moved up the viewing."

"Viewing?"

"Yes. There was meant to be a viewing tonight for his closest friends and family members. Seems the time has been moved up and they're having it sooner than expected."

Nausea hit hard, and I tried to slow my breaths. I thought I would have two days to prepare myself before seeing Bram's dead body. Now, it was only an hour away. Could I do this? I knew I had to, but if my heart was aching now, how much worse was it going to get when faced with the reality that the man I loved was never coming back?

CHAPTER 27

WEST

Where Everleigh couldn't eat, I had consumed the best meal of my life. Taking one last drink of wine, I placed the empty glass on the table and leaned back. Life was great. More than great. Soon, I'd see Bram dead for myself, and I could get back to Whitlock. To what was mine.

I grabbed Everleigh's hand as I stood and basked in the ease at which she let me lead her. Maybe she was a little intoxicated as well? Hell, she'd had two glasses of wine to my five. For someone who never indulged, she had to be feeling *something*. Was she leaning into me? I smiled realizing she was. She was probably having trouble walking. My day just kept getting better.

"Mr. Harper?"

I slowed at my name. Not quite placing the voice, I scanned the room with a fuzzy mind. It took a moment to place Mr. Barber, who was now waving at me. He was a former associate, and not one I really cared for.

"Mr. Barber." I walked us over and reached out to shake his hand as he stayed seated. The sad expression on his face was one I would have loved to knock off.

"I heard about Mr. Whitlock's passing. My condolences. He was a great man. Very charitable, just like his mother."

Was he? I forced a similar look of grief, nodding. "Yes, his passing was most unfortunate. I'm not sure what I'm going to do without him." I trailed off, hopefully appearing a lot more lost than I felt—which was technically more drunk by the minute.

"I'm so sorry. The two of you were inseparable. I don't think there was a time when I didn't see you together. It's been a while…three, four years. But I remember. You two…" he trailed off, his grief evident as he swallowed and cleared his throat. Bram had liked Mr. Barber. I'd never understood why. They were closer than I was with the associate.

"Will you be at the funeral on Saturday morning?"

"I will. I definitely will."

"I'm sorry." I shook my head as I pulled Everleigh's buried form out from where she was hiding at my side. Her body had been stuck to mine, and she was trembling so badly, I wasn't sure how she was standing. "This is my wife, Lee. Lee, this is Mr. Barber." I leaned in next to her ear. "Shake his hand and tell him hello."

Everleigh's hand came out, trembling worse than her body. Mr. Barber didn't seem to notice as he reached forward to grasp her fingers.

"I wasn't aware you'd gotten married. Congratulations to the both of you."

"Thank you," I said, smiling and pulling her in close again. My arm wrapped around her shoulders, hugging her body to mine. "You'll have to excuse my wife. She's taking Bram's death extremely hard. They were very close. He actually introduced us."

Mr. Barber looked at her, his face turning sad once more. "I understand. I'm *so* sorry for your loss, Mrs. Harper. Please know I'm here if either of you need anything. Anything at all. Bram was loved by so many. He was one of the kindest men I knew."

Confusion once again seeped in. I knew Bram had donated to some charities. It had been part of his duties, but had he been so *kind*? Sure, people loved him. He knew how to play the part of happy socialite, but had it made all the difference? He was an asshole. A coldhearted bastard most of the time. He ran an underground fortress full of slaves, rape, and murder. No one knew Bram. Not like I did.

Fingers dug into my suit jacket, bringing me back. "Yes. Well, if you'll excuse us. We have to be going. It was a pleasure seeing you here, Mr. Barber."

I reached out, shaking the man's hand. By the time I got Everleigh into the car, I damn near had to pry her off me.

"What is the matter with you?"

A sob exploded from her mouth as her eyes scanned the cars and busy sidewalks. She was panting, trying to leave my arms to get down to the floorboard. Eli paused in shutting the door, crawling in to sit farther down instead.

"Everleigh," I growled. "Sit up."

"Yelling won't help. She's having a panic attack. Like… PTSD or something. It's too much for her. She's…" Eli tilted his head, watching while she buried her face in her hands. "Pop her up with something. Did you bring anything?"

"Yeah," I snapped. "I carry a fucking pharmacy around in my pocket. Of course I didn't bring anything."

"I just," she tried to catch her breath. "I need air. Quiet. Alone. I'll…be okay."

"We're in the car in the middle of traffic. Quiet and alone isn't coming for a while, so you better get yourself together. We have to go to the viewing, remember? We only have a short window. They're not doing this again. It's now or never."

Everleigh wrestled out of my arms, scrambling to the side seat to lay down. Her arm came up and she covered her face in the crook of her elbow. The deep breaths still left her, but she seemed to be better away from me.

"I kept waiting," she said, shakily. "I thought he would try to h-hurt us. I don't like this place."

I smirked at Eli. I'd wanted her to fear being on the outside, and I had succeeded.

"We're lucky he didn't. He was closer to Bram than he was me. I have no idea what kind of man he is. But that's why we have Eli. He'll protect us. Won't you, Eli?"

Rolling his eyes, he pursed his lips as he continued to stare at her. "Yeah. Definitely." He paused. "Mistress, may I ask you a question?"

My lips pulled back slightly at his address, but I stayed quiet as I studied my guard. Everleigh's arm lifted, and she wiped away the tears as she sat.

"Of course. What is it?"

"Are the stories true? About you and The Cradle?"

Dark hair swayed as she shook her head. "I'm not sure I understand. What stories?"

He glanced at me. I could still see his anger toward something, and I didn't like it.

"Is it true you brought all the children into one room and slept with them there, so you could protect them?"

Her cheeks reddened as she peeked over at me. "Some were afraid. I feared they had valid reason. I wanted to make sure every single one was safe."

"You would have died to protect them?"

"Without hesitation. They don't deserve this life. They're innocent. I know no more have been brought in since Bram took over from his father a few years ago. The ones there are from before. But if we could help them—if we could do *something*… The youngest isn't even five. She's been there since she was only weeks old. The oldest, only twelve. They don't have to know this life. It's not too late to set them free."

"*Free*?" I shook my head. "We can't set them free. They were taken. Kidnapped. You're asking me to release a good twenty kids into the world. Do you not think the police aren't going to wonder why so many suddenly reappeared? It's too risky."

"There are fourteen. And it doesn't have to be all at once. We can set two or three free at a time, spanning the release of all over a year or so. You can put them anywhere. Far from their home, but in the hands of someone who can help them and get them back to where they belong. *The parents need their children.* Have they all not suffered enough?"

Still, my head shook. We needed them for foundation—for the first auction I planned to host a few weeks from now. It would be an introduction back into the old ways. I couldn't lose the one thing I had that would make a statement.

"We could do it," Eli said quietly. "We could set them free. I could be in charge of it. I'd personally make sure they were delivered into the right hands."

"You too? Have we not talked about this?"

His jaw tightened as he clasped his hands at his knees. "And I told you I didn't like the idea of it. I am capable of anything. *Anything*. But I don't do kids—not the selling, not the sick shit that happens to them. I don't support it, and you know that."

"And I told you you wouldn't have to be a part it."

Eli kept his head down, remaining silent as he stared at the ground. I knew he was thinking, and I hated that Everleigh had one up on me concerning the damn kids.

"We'll talk more about it later. There may be something we can do with the younger ones, but the older ones, I won't budge. They know too much. They're not going anywhere."

CHAPTER 28

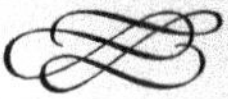

24690

The silence that met us as we walked into the funeral home was so thick, I didn't think anyone was even here. It wasn't until the high leader appeared from a pair of double doors in the back that my anxiety spiked. This was real. Too real. I wasn't sure I could go any further.

"Main Master." His head bowed and tears made the room blur as West practically pulled me toward him. To hear him call West that when I'd spent the last few years knowing Bram in that position was a slap in the face. I was starting to awaken to the nightmare that was my life, and the truth was too much to bear.

"High Leader."

West glanced around the room, shaking his head. Tears pooled in his eyes, and my lids narrowed in anger. He didn't care that Bram was dead. Not like I did. I'd heard the coldness he harbored. I knew his plans and how he was going to destroy everything Bram had worked so hard for.

"If you'll come this way. The viewing is almost over. You made it just in time. They're about to close off the room from anymore guests."

Lyle turned, and we followed him into an elaborate room.

Chairs were on both sides of the long aisle and a few people were already sitting. Guards surrounded the back of the casket, and one was even leaning over the top, bowing his head.

Wetness slid down my cheeks, and I sniffled to hold in the sob on the verge of leaving me. The closer we got, the harder it was to continue. I wanted to collapse to the floor—to curl in on myself and never move again.

"He fought hard in his last moments. When they turned off the machines, I wasn't sure he was going to go." The high leader sucked in a shuddering breath, and a whimper left my lips. Bram's face came into view, and I reached out, grabbing Lyle's forearm so I wouldn't fall. I knew West had me, but I was reaching for trust—for loyalty—as I held our high leader.

"Shhh," West whispered. "It's okay."

But it wasn't. He was really there. Really dead.

"Allow me to take care of her while you say your goodbyes."

Lyle reached for me, and West hesitated before nodding. The high leader led me to the side and West walked the few feet ahead. The guard stepped over, going back into position at the foot of the closed casket. I could only see Bram from the chest up, and I wanted to open the entire thing and crawl inside with him. I didn't want him to leave me. There was nothing left. Nothing but the children. They were the only reason I wasn't grabbing the guard's gun and joining the man who had my heart.

The grip on my shoulder eased me around. Lyle's handsome features were so full of emotion, it fed mine.

"I loved him," I whispered. "This isn't real. It can't be. Bram's not dead."

"I'm sorry. I know this is hard for you, but I have something…something I think Mr. Whitlock would have wanted you to have. I had it brought in shortly after the accident so I could read it to him. I used to see him with the book quite often. I think you should read it too."

The high leader gestured with his head and another guard

walked forward, handing me a black hardcover book. One I'd seen before…the same day he'd been stabbed.

"When you get lonely, or times are hard, I want you to go somewhere where you're alone and read this." He glanced at West before coming back to me. "There's a particular poem he enjoyed in the middle. I marked the page for you. Read it and have hope. Hope, above all things." His finger lifted, pushing under my chin to lift my head higher. "Stay strong, Mistress. Don't let them see your fear."

The words had my lips parting. He'd said the same thing to me at the auction. My head was spinning. It all felt like a dream. I nodded, squeezing the book to my chest.

"Come say goodbye."

As he led me to Bram's casket, I couldn't stop the tears from coming again. The high leader let go, leaving me as he called West over.

"B-Bram?" Hesitantly, I reached forward, leaning in close. My free hand cupped his smooth cheek, and my chest shook as I lowered to rest my forehead against his. "I want to stay with you," I whispered. "I don't want to leave. Come back. Come back and I will be the perfect slave to you, I promise. Don't leave me." I breathed in deep, still smelling his aftershave. How many times had I breathed him into me, wishing I could keep him there forever? I savored every moment when we were alone. God, I couldn't do this without him. "Come back. I…*I love you.* I should have told you that. You should have at least known. You were afraid of hurting me, but you loved me. I know you did. We were going to make things work. We were going to be happy."

My fingers brushed back the short hair, gripping for the smallest moment before I lifted, pressing my lips into his. A hand settled on the middle of my back, and I stiffened, raising to stand. West met my stare with nothing—no emotion whatsoever.

"We should go. They're closing."

I turned back to Bram. What would they do if I begged to

stay? If I climbed inside with him and refused to get out. I wanted to. I wanted to hold him and shut my eyes and never wake up again.

West looped his arm in mine, and I brought the book back to my chest, allowing him to lead me away. With each step, a hollowness edged in. *The children.* They were my only concern now. I'd set them free—consequences be damned.

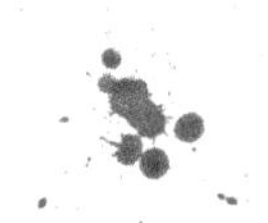

"What is that?"

My eyes opened and I curled more into a fetal position as I brought the book deeper into my chest. I kept waiting for the opportunity to read it, but West was always there. Always talking to me every few minutes.

"Poems. The high leader thought I might like to have it."

"Bram's book?" West reached over the bed, pulling it from my hands. He shuffled through the pages, then handed it back to me.

"What does he expect you to do with a book of old poems?"

"I don't know," I said quietly. "My guess is read it."

West cocked his head to the side as his eyes narrowed. "I hope my wife hasn't decided to get an attitude toward me."

I swallowed through my raw throat. My eyes ached from crying so much, and it was almost impossible to swallow. I didn't have the strength to fight with West right now. All I wanted was to be alone.

"Of course not. I'm sorry if it sounded that way. I'm tired."

"You're upset. You need to bathe and relax. Come."

I didn't say anything or move as I met his stare. It was a clear sign to him that I didn't want to, but he didn't seem to care as he took the book from my hands and swept me into his arms. When he placed me on my feet outside the large tub, my hand shot out to stop the advance of his.

"I have two days to decide."

"You do. But I'm not expecting an answer right now. I'm trying to help the woman I care about. She's grieving and shouldn't be alone."

He turned me, unzipping the dress. Rage hammered inside, looking for a reason to escape. I held it in while he stepped away and grabbed a long lighter. One by one, he lit the candles surrounding the bathtub. When the lights went out, he started the water. Still, I stood and watched his every move.

"I won't touch you again. Undress and get in."

He moved to the counter, unscrewing a canister and shaking what looked like salt into the water. A light, relaxing smell filled the air, and he went back, pouring liquid into the stream. The bubbles were automatic. I let the dress drop and climbed in. Again, something poured in the water, but I was too tired to argue. The smell lured me to lay back and I closed my eyes as the bubbles rose. When the water stirred, my lids shot open. West was sitting on the edge, still dressed. His sleeves were rolled up and he was dipping a large sponge into the water. His eyes met mine and he leaned over, turning off the water. It was full now, even though it had only seemed like seconds had passed.

He didn't speak as he dipped the sponge again and brought it to my chest. Instinct had me grabbing his wrist hard before I could stop myself. My anger was still there, buzzing in my head while I fought to think.

"No, no. Close your eyes. You're safe right now."

But it was a lie. I was never safe with West. Never.

Darkness took over, and it wasn't long before I yawned. Warmth rushed over my shoulders as the sponge took its time sliding over my arms, chest, and stomach. When West lifted one of my legs to rest on the edge of the tub, I could barely think about how wrong it was. I blinked, taking in the tingling of my skin. Faster, my mind raced. There was a familiarity here. Too much familiarity…and fear.

The click in my brain left me fighting to move my limbs. Water splashed, but my control wasn't my own. Words were a jumbled mess on my tongue, and the only thing that came were sounds.

"Calm, slave. I'm only washing you. *Feel*."

He didn't leave me a choice as my body sunk back into the comfortable state. This time was different than before. At the auction, I'd at least been able to walk, even if I couldn't figure out how I was doing it. But now, it was almost impossible to move. Even in my moment of fighting, I was aware how my arms and legs were barely moving.

"There we go," he whispered, pulling my knee closer toward him—spreading my legs wider.

The foamy square went back and forth over my inner thigh until West dipped even lower. Sensations exploded as he let his fingers trace over my folds. My body jerked, but I still could barely move—only feel, like he wanted.

"You know, I have to admit. Listening to you talk to Bram, I was pretty jealous. Enraged, actually. But then I thought, what do I have to be envious over? He's dead, and I have you. At least to an extent. And I have Whitlock. I have everything I've always wanted. And my plans for you, they're not entirely dishonorable. I'm going to give you a chance to love me like you loved him. I'm going to treat you well. Ultimately, though, it will be up to you how things play out. You may be angry at me for what I'm doing right now, but you'll come to see how it was for the best. To experience me like I want you to, I can't have your innocent little mind working up reasons why not to give me a chance. You have to see the other side of me. The one you keep pushing away."

His fingers rose higher, rubbing over the top of my slit. The sponge floated to the top of the water, and I blinked heavily as ecstasy soared inside me. It shouldn't have been like this. I didn't want it to be, but my body cared not for the little denials that managed to seep through my mind.

"Feels good, doesn't it?" He bit his lip, reaching down to ease his finger inside me. "I can feel it too. It's in the water. Soaking into our skin. Fuck, I'm going to make it good for you. You're going to love this."

The thrusts only lasted a few more moments before he drew back and pushed down the drain. Pressure pulled against me from the water, but I felt like I was flying. Like I was being sucked toward some unmovable force.

West didn't grab a towel. He reached down, sweeping me back into his arms as he took us to the bed. He grabbed the book, tossing it to the floor as he lay me on top of the comforter. Despite being unable to move, he reached to the ends of the bed, pulling up cuffs. Panic broke through the fog, but all I could do was stare as he stretched out my arms and legs, restraining me. I knew I should have been fighting—screaming for help, but it was impossible. And my body still wanted something else. Something more.

Deep breaths left me as he jerked at his clothes, removing them. Like a man possessed, his eyes held mine. He lowered to the foot of the bed, and kiss by kiss, worked his way up my inner leg. Each brush of his lips sent my skin burning with even more fire. My stomach was so tight, a cry involuntarily left me. The sound had West smiling as he glanced up from where he hovered between my legs.

"What is it you want? This?" His tongue traveled the length of my slit, pushing between my folds as he flicked over my clit. "Or maybe this?"

A cry tore free at the pressure of his tongue invading my entrance. My head somehow managed to shoot back and forth, and I took a deep breath. The drug gave off a rolling sensation as the effects slammed back into me.

"Fuck, you're so hot and wet." He sucked against my folds, going back to thrust his tongue inside. My eyes closed and the feeling numbed for only a moment before kicking into something a million times stronger. I was shaking. I knew that much. And screaming? God, I was having an orgasm… The thought was enough to make sickness fester. But it didn't last.

He continued to suck and lick, and with every sweep of his tongue, he built me even more.

"I could do this every night. I think I'd like that. And I know you would." He rose, sliding his fingers inside me as he moved to kiss up my stomach. When teeth tugged at my nipple, my body arched, trembling and jerking again. But this time, my orgasm was more powerful. And I had no control or even warning.

Tears raced down the sides of my face, but sobs didn't come. Only the deep inhales and exhales as he rubbed along the inside of my channel. Suction drew my nipple into his mouth and the vibrations from his moan ignited a humming so strong, even my teeth vibrated. I gasped, hating how I was beginning to rock against him.

"You want me. God, I knew you'd want me."

He rose higher, a grin forming as he stared. Softly, his lips brushed against mine, and the cringe came naturally. It reflected my mind, and I held to hope. But it didn't last as he began to stretch me with his cock.

"Yes. This," he whispered against me. "This is how things will be between us. I like this side of you: quiet, unmoving. Someday, I will tell you why. Someday, you will know more of my secrets."

A jolt locked my body as he slammed forward. Pain hit sharp but faded just as fast. The oil was feeding me false emotions.

False sensations. His cock began to feel good. Almost as if it were meant to be inside me.

With each inch, each thrust of his long length, the oil burned hotter. My fear faded, as did my nonconsensual mindset. Everything vanished but the pleasure, and I knew in that moment the drug had me. I wasn't Everleigh anymore. I was no one but a dead slave while still alive.

CHAPTER 29

WEST

Could I get any happier? I didn't think so. Bram was almost in the ground, and my slave was pretty much mine. I had everything a man could dream of.

"Mr. Harper, my condolences. I'm so very sorry for your loss."

I shook the older woman's hand, having no idea who she was. Hell, I barely knew anyone who'd attended Bram's funeral. Some of the Masters came, and all our associates, but as for the others…I didn't have a clue. Not that I cared. I shook their hands and said thank you. They moved to Everleigh, saying the same. She was a damn mess again. I'd barely been able to keep her under control during the service. She was crying harder than anyone. Her body shook against mine as I held her close, and in appearance, it looked good, but it was driving me crazy. Good thing was, I knew how to make it better when we left. I'd bathe her again. And again. Every day.

"My condolences, Mr. Harper. Mrs. Harper."

"Thank you," I said, already looking to the next person. Everleigh sobbed, and I glance over as her hand broke from my arm. She turned, walking back to Bram's grave. I frowned, shaking the couples' hands, but continuing to turn back to look at her. The high leader was heading in her direction, and I relaxed, going through the motions. He'd make sure she didn't do anything stupid. Not that I thought she would. With each hour that passed, she grew quieter. More unresponsive. I should have worried, but I didn't. I preferred her silence. It meant less work on my end.

"Mr. Harper."

I nodded, grasping the hand of a younger man. The line was coming to a close, and I couldn't wait to get back to the penthouse. In truth, it was Bram's…or now, my slave's. I wouldn't think about how he left the bitch everything. *Even his money.* Not right now. Come tonight, I'd make her my wife. It may not be officially legit, but no one would know the difference. Everything of his would become mine. It may have seemed impossible from the paperwork, but I was no fool. I'd figure out a way.

I went through the rest of the handshakes, nodding to the last person. Cars were already driving away, and the cemetery was clearing out. I headed toward the closed casket, crouching to place my hand on Everleigh's back as I arrived.

"It's time to go, wife."

Her head shook. "I don't want to leave. I'm not leaving."

My eyes went to the high leader's, and he frowned.

"Come, Mistress," Lyle coaxed. "Mr. Whitlock wouldn't want to see you so upset."

Bram? What the fuck about me? She was meant to be *my* slave. These guards standing out here shouldn't have been seeing her moping over a dead man. She had me!

"Everleigh." My tone was deeper. When my arm grasped her bicep to help her stand, she turned, letting out a scream so high pitched and forceful, I froze in surprise. Her body launched toward me, knocking me on my back as her fists slammed down toward my face and chest.

"Rapist! You sick, vile—I hate you! I hate you!"

I rolled her over, pinning her arms as I looked around at the men gathering closer.

"*You push me*. You don't want to do to that."

Blood swept over my tongue, and I stood, jerking her to her feet. I wasn't two steps in before the high leader rushed up. "I'll accompany you back to the penthouse."

"You will not," I exploded, continuing on. She fought me the entire way to the limo, screaming and cursing as she tried to break free. The moment I had her in the car, my hand locked around her throat, and I slammed her on the seat. I pushed my weight into her as hard as I could, squeezing around her neck as her face turned a deep red.

"Rapist? You think what I did to you was rape? Oh, slave. You want rape, I will show you rape. You'll be hanging onto life by a thread. And I'll bring you back and do it all over again. I will make you *beg* for death."

I let go, pushing back to sit. Coughing shook her chest, but she didn't join me. She stayed in the fetal position, panting while she cried and fought to breathe. Within seconds, the car began to move.

Had I thought I'd had this under control? Had I thought I could pretend to be the man I'd been my entire life so I could make her fall in love with me? No. Perhaps I knew things would go to shit before we ever returned to Whitlock. Maybe it was even why I'd brought her in the first place. I needed a cold dose of what my subconscious already knew. I'd never have Everleigh. Not how I wanted. But I could have her money, the appearance of her as my wife, and her body. That was good enough for me. I didn't need her heart. Bram could keep it. It was probably just as cold as his dead body anyway.

"Tonight, you'll sign a paper saying we're married. You will sign it, or I will slaughter every one of those children you intend to protect. If you so much as hesitate in moving the pen to paper,

I will make you help, make you slice open their little bodies while they beg you to stop. Do you hear me?"

Slowly, she sat. The hate was like nothing I'd ever been faced with before. My fist clenched through the need to hit her, but I held still. I couldn't do that yet. Not until we were back at Whitlock. There was no telling whether I'd run into anyone before I left, and I couldn't have them suspecting I abused my wife. I still had my business and status on the outside world I needed to maintain. Especially if I was going to make a name for myself like the Whitlocks' had.

"I will sign your paper and hand myself to you freely…after I see every one of those children gone from that wretched place."

I laughed. "You don't give the orders, slave. I'll kill them all."

Everleigh came at me so fast, I barely had time to catch her hand as she stabbed something into the top of my chest. I ripped back her wrist, seeing it was the letter opener from the penthouse desk.

"Bitch!"

Pain flared, but I knew she hadn't hit deep. I dove forward, flipping her over to her stomach and tearing up the dress as I threw myself on top of her. Just knowing what I was about to do sent my adrenaline racing. My cock got so hard while I pulled at my belt. She was struggling but couldn't break free with my hand planted on the center of her back.

"You want to kill me? You hate me so much?"

Whack! Whack! Whack!

A scream echoed from me spanking her ass as I continued to undo my pants.

"You have no idea. I *will* kill you. So help me, I will. The slave has found a backbone somewhere deep inside that pretty little body. You keep fighting and hating me. I'll keep making you scream. It'll be a wonderful marriage."

I spit into my hand, stroking down my cock for only a moment before I jerked her hips up. With one hand, I held the top of her body down. With the other, I spread her ass, looking at what I knew was going to be mine. Fuck, it was beautiful. So much so, I clenched my teeth, imagining the way it would feel. Two of my fingers pushed into her entrance, slamming in hard. Her cries were like the sweetest melody. They drifted around me, exhilarating me while I rubbed the wetness over her back entrance. Back and forth I went—pussy, ass, pussy, ass. My thrusts became fierce as I plunged them into her hard and deep. When I moved her juices back to her ass again, I buried my fingers in as far as they would go. Watching her stretch. Feeling the unbearable tightness squeeze against me. Everleigh's body locked up and she gasped so deep, she choked as she fought for breath.

"No! No!"

I didn't coat my fingers in saliva this time. Impatience and sick pleasure had me spitting directly on her back entrance while I rubbed it into her. When I added more to my cock, she twisted and almost broke free from under my hand. I didn't wait. In one swift motion, I slammed into her ass with everything I had. The pitch that filled the interior was like nothing I'd ever heard before—half agony, half pleading for help. It said everything she couldn't, and it made my sadist soar.

My arms wrapped around her chest in a bear hug, keeping her captive as I forced myself farther into her. The strain around my thickness had me grinding my teeth through the pleasure and pain. I saw everything, yet nothing. What I was doing was like a dream—one I could have had over and over and never gotten enough of.

I withdrew, slamming and burying myself into her just as violently. Everleigh gagged, still trying to scream, but I didn't care. I loved our moment more than anything in the world.

"How's this for a rapist? For a husband? Oh, Everleigh, how

I adore you. Cry for me a little louder, baby. Don't get quiet. Don't stop fighting."

I thrust at a steady pace, not going deep, but more teasing. I didn't ever want it to end, but the pleasure of my cruelty was too much. Cum shot from my cock, and for seconds, I still couldn't break away. To savor the moment was easy. The sobs were temporarily gone. She was barely even moving, and the blood that met me as I looked down to fasten my pants had me smiling.

"You have one minute to get up to the seat or I'll have Eli do this to you again when we get to the penthouse."

The smell of vomit had me rolling down the window, only just realizing she'd actually gotten sick.

"Now! One minute."

Everleigh pushed her torso up, but her shaky arms gave out. Her eyes appeared dilated as she clawed at the floor toward the seat. And her teeth, they were chattering. I stared, fascinated, as her legs barely moved. They trailed behind, gaining strength with each second that passed. Nails tore at the leather, and her ankles turned out as she slithered up beside me. Small sounds fell from her lips, but she didn't say a word as she sat angled on her side. Tears weren't even streaming anymore. It made me frown as I continued to stare at her.

"It didn't have to be like that. Hate me all you want, you're the one responsible for everything that happens to you."

Nothing.

I reached up, pushing against the tear in my suit jacket. Blood was soaked around it, and I cursed as the scene replayed. There was no way I was going to be able to hide what had happened. And I didn't have to look behind me to know I was being followed by more than one car. The guards would want to escort us into the room. They'd want to do a sweep of the place before I even entered. I shouldn't have cared what they thought, but the cautious attorney and new Master in me did. Some of the guards had a soft spot for Everleigh. I didn't understand it, but I didn't have to. It was a fact I'd be stupid to ignore. Until I made my mark, set my leadership in stone, I couldn't afford to lose any of the ones who might have been loyal to Bram.

"Let me fix your dress."

I reached forward, pausing as she flinched at my approach. I continued, inching forward to ease her dress down. When she cried out at me trying to lift her, I jerked her into my lap. Fuck it. I'd carry her inside. Except, my leg was already becoming saturated in blood. I could see the wetness glistening against the black leather seat.

"Look what you've done. Could this not have waited until we got home? What was so important with staying at that fucking grave?"

I brushed her hair back, getting more pissed at how pale she was. Grabbing my phone, I hit Eli's number, and he answered almost immediately.

"You're in the car with Lyle, correct?"

"Yes." There was a pause in his answer.

"Everleigh's not well. I need you to have them pass us and get to the penthouse as fast as they can. I want it swept before I arrive. Make something up. Say I told you the alarm went off or something. I don't give a shit. Get in and out as fast as possible."

The line disconnected without so much as a word. One SUV passed, and then two more. I took a deep breath, pulling Everleigh more into my chest. I hated how the need to apologize was there, and with it, came the need to hurt her more. Just a few more hours and I wouldn't have to worry about anything. I'd be home free.

CHAPTER 30

24690

"Deep breath."

My hand shot to West's shoulder as he stood from the limo. The need to cry out beckoned, but I suffocated it back. We'd entered from the parking garage instead of the front like we usually did. It was dim and barren as we approached the elevator. But it wouldn't have mattered anyway. No one could help me.

I tensed through the pain at his shifting, taking slow, deep breaths as I stared around in a daze. There were no thoughts. No grief or fear as I floated in the security of myself. Silent, I was safe. Silent, I didn't exist.

A ding echoed in the distance. Or maybe it wasn't so far away.

The light brightened inside the enclosed space, and I gazed at the buttons as they lit up. West kept moving us back and forth. He couldn't stay still. He reached up, pushing my head to rest on his shoulder, and I let him. I didn't fight to lift it or even care it was him I was laying on.

A jolt fluttered in my stomach, and he swept through the doors the moment they opened. His pace was fast and heavy, and he didn't slow as he stalked between a few guards standing outside the open door.

"We've checked the residence, Master Harper. Nothing seems out of sorts."

"Great. Leave us, High Leader."

"I have something to discuss with you, if you can spare a few minutes."

Lyle's voice had us turning back to face him.

"Make it fast. What is it?"

He cleared his throat. Although my face was buried in West's neck, I knew he was approaching by the sound of boots getting closer.

"Mr. Whitlock left behind instructions he wanted me to go over with you. If you'd like, one of the guards can put her to bed and we can handle business in another room."

"Absolutely not. Can't you see she isn't feeling well? I'm not leaving my soon-to-be-wife when she is sick."

Silence.

"I wasn't aware you were intending to marry Mistress Davenport. Has she consented to this?"

"Of course she has. Haven't you, honey? You were just upset earlier. Tell them."

His chin brushed against my forehead, and I blinked my heavy lids as I lifted to face the high leader. Before I could so much as speak, a light blinded me.

"She's in shock," Lyle said, lowering the flashlight. "I'll call the doctor."

"You will do no such thing. It's grief. She's devastated—nothing more. I have medication. She'll be sleeping in no time. You're all dismissed."

Lyle seemed to pay no attention to West as he reached out toward me. Before he could touch my burning throat, West stepped back.

"What do you think you're doing? Did you not hear my order? I said dismissed!"

"I heard you, but I don't take orders from you, Master Harper. If you would have followed me and listened to Mr. Whitlock's instructions, you would know this. I am assigned to Mistress Davenport. *Not you.* She is under my care from here on out, and abuse of her person is not something I will tolerate. If you'll hand her over, I'll assess her myself."

"We're all going to die," I whispered. "The children will bleed."

"Give her to me," Lyle said forcefully, moving toward us.

Grrth.

Warmth splattered across my face as I stared into the high leader's bulging eyes. Then, he was falling. Was I falling? No. I lifted my stare, coming face to face with the bloody blade of a knife—Eli's knife. He'd used it to slit the high leader's throat. Guards were rushing over, but no one was doing anything.

"I believe your Main Master gave an order. Out!"

Dark uniforms hesitated while they looked at each other, but they filed out, shutting the door behind them. Eli turned to us, raising an eyebrow. "Now what the fuck is going on? What's wrong with you?" he asked me.

"Turn on the shower, dammit."

The order had Eli turning to leave us. We followed behind, but at a slower pace. Emotion was gone, singed and scorched so far within me, I wondered if I could live in the blissful sense of nothingness forever.

West stood me up, then snapped for his guard to come over.

"Unzip her, then grab her so I can get her undressed."

Cool air brushed against my back as the dress opened and dropped to the ground. Pain had my body seizing as he spun me around. Stars danced before me, and I clawed at his chest through the burning.

"What…the fuck?" He stared at the crimson on his hand,

then returned his gaze to my body as he scanned me over. “Where’s the blood coming from?” Holding my shoulder, he moved to the side. Gently, he pulled at my panties, lowering them. I could see the tear on the side seam as he let them drop. “Son of bitch. You…raped her?”

“Give me a break,” West cut in. “Like you’ve never raped a woman.”

“I never *have* raped a woman. Haven’t needed to. I told you that. Just because I don’t mind killing, doesn’t mean I’m capable of everything.” He reached out to my back, unfastening my bra, and the action had my shoulders jerking. I lifted my leg to step toward the shower, barely able to stand from the amount of agony zapping through me.

“Well, Mr. Holier Than Shit, the bitch deserved it. She fucking stabbed me in the chest with a letter opener. She wanted a rapist, so I gave her one. She’ll learn to keep her fucking mouth shut.”

Eli held me as he let me take one step, then another. When I stopped, he lifted, carrying me the rest of the way. He eased me to the seat, and I automatically moved to rest my weight on one side. I could see West in my peripheral, but I didn’t feel the need to look over. I was beginning to feel again, and I didn’t like it. My emotions were all over the place, and I didn’t want to experience what I’d gone through. I didn’t want to feel anything at all.

“I don’t think it needs stitches,” West said, more to himself. “Get me some butterfly Band-Aids. Those will work.”

“He’s going to kill the children.” Eli jerked to a stop, and I slowly turned to look at him through the glass. “He’s going to make me cut them open all because he wants me to marry him and I don’t want to. Does that sound like a man to you? I’m going to rape him like he did me, then I’m going to kill him.”

Each word was spoken at a leisurely pace, reflecting my state of mind. Control over what I said was gone. Luckily, I was still numb enough not to care.

"You fucking cunt."

West only got two steps before Eli had him around the waist.

"She's in shock. She doesn't know what she's saying. She probably won't even remember this. Let it go. Come shower in the other bathroom. I'll get you the bandages."

Color disappeared from the corner of my eye as I stared ahead. Water rushed over me, and time passed. When motion pulled me from my thoughts, I only then realized I was crying.

"I'm to get you out and put you to bed. Master Harper is cooling down in the study."

I grabbed the bar, struggling as I stood and straightened. The glass door opened, and Eli's lips twisted.

"Did you wash yourself? You need to clean yourself with soap. It's going to hurt, but it has to be done." He turned to the side, facing away from me as he waited. I reached for the bottle, trying to wash as fast as I could. The stinging was like nothing I had ever felt before. My hands came up, and I noticed the bleeding had subsided.

I finished rinsing myself off. The moment the water stopped, Eli had the robe ready. He helped me put it on and let me take my time as I fought to walk. When I finally reached the bed, he helped me climb in, then covered me. I wanted to hate him as much as West. He'd killed Lyle. But I could barely feel anything. All I knew was he'd kept West away from me. He cared about the children. That was the only thing keeping me from attacking him too.

"Get some rest. People will be here soon. Master Harper will return to you after that. I'd suggest you do as he says and not put up a fight."

"The marriage," I mumbled.

He nodded and stepped back. "Sign the fucking papers. It's only signatures. A slave has no use for money anyway."

"I'm not a slave. I'm a Mistress."

"No, you're a slave. You will always be a slave at Whitlock.

Nothing will change that. Not even marriage. Accept and make the best of it. That's all you can do."

"And if I refuse?"

His jaw flexed as he sat on the edge of the bed. "Then you're the stupidest woman I've ever met. Think of those children. Do they not need you? Accept your role, and I will do what I can to convince him to let you have visitation. Spend your days there, away from him. Do your duty to *them*. I've seen things you can't imagine in The Cradle. They need you. I need you," he said, dropping his voice. "My little sister is in there. We do what we must. *We can do something*."

My lips separated and my eyes jerked to the open entrance of the room. "Kill him. Kill West right now and we will leave this place and release them."

"You think it's that easy? There are guards who are loyal to the Master. I couldn't get through them with Bram leading, but I'm hoping I can with West."

"Bram? Did…you? Did he?"

Whatever my expression said had his hand slapping over my mouth. "I did what I had to. And I will continue to do so. That means you too. Don't give me a reason to hurt you. I told you about my sister hoping you would help. Don't make me regret it."

I knocked his hand away, slapping his face with every ounce of power I had. "Don't you threaten me. If you want my help, from now on, *you answer to me*."

CHAPTER 31

WEST

"What the hell is taking so long?"

I stormed into my room, seeing Eli hesitate as he handed Bram's book to Everleigh. She was sitting up in bed, her eyes still swollen from all the crying. I only paused for a moment before surging forward. I half expected her to cower at my nearing presence, but she didn't. She grabbed the book, drawing it closer to her chest. She stayed silent as I stepped past Eli and ripped it from her hands.

"This is mine now. It's part of your punishment from your outburst at the funeral. When I feel you've learned your lesson, maybe I'll give it back."

She stayed quiet, moving her stare to her now clasped hands resting in her lap.

"What, no argument?"

"No, Master."

Eli retreated, heading to stand at the threshold of the door. I didn't pay him much attention as I turned back to Everleigh. Back and forth, my mind went. The man I was battled the man who had schemed to get as far as he'd come. I wanted my slave's love, but the true me wanted to hurt her for knowing she'd never give it to me. There was no going back now. What I had done couldn't be erased. And she wouldn't forget.

I tossed the book down on the end table and sat next to her. She didn't try to move away from me, when, again, I'd assumed she would.

"I won't apologize for what I did. Your allegation, your behavior…I was trying so hard to be a good husband, and you ruined it. Rape? Did I not take my time to make you feel good? Did you not enjoy it? If I recall, you were begging me for more. We both know you were."

Shaking rocked her shoulders, and she sniffled, lifting her head high as she looked at me. Still, she stayed silent. And still, the tears came.

"You think I'm making excuses. That I raped you our first time because I used the oil. Put that aside for a moment. I already told you why I did it. Ask yourself this. Did you enjoy it? Are you casting your anger toward me because you feel as though you've betrayed the man you love?" I paused as her brow creased through her thoughts. "Bram is dead. If he were alive and this had happened, maybe your anger would be warranted. But you don't have to feel guilty for feeling something for me. Let him go. Stop putting up these walls toward me and see the opportunity before you. It all rides on you. All I asked was that you were a good slave. Are you incapable? Is it so hard to put aside your pride, or these feelings you think are love, and give me a fucking chance? Everleigh, I'm trying with you. Why can't you attempt to try for me?"

Eli shifted, breaking my focus. Annoyance sank in, but I brought my attention back to my slave—my wife, within the hour.

"Fine. Don't talk. How's this going to play out? Are you going to fight me when the judge and lawyer get here? Should I be expecting you to make a scene?"

Her head shook. "No, Master."

"Are you sure?"

"Yes, Master."

I grew quiet as thoughts took me. Mindlessly, I looked around, grabbing the damn book she kept holding onto like a lifeline. Opening it, I saw Bram's name scribbled on the first page. I turned more pages, coming to the first poem. Glancing over at my slave, I cleared my throat before reading aloud.

The Devil and His Keeper

Walls cannot buffer this hell we call home.
Embedded amongst all that pulsates of perversion,
is a place made of stone.
He and I sing the true melody of love.
Can you hear the beautiful tune
as we whisper from above?
I hum it so sweetly,
a harmonic little tune.
You grasp it desperately,
like you long for the moon.
He hears my song,
he whispers to death,
the alluring lyrics flow
while I take my last breath.
You sway amid the words,
drawing us closer.
We fight for your love,
I want her, I choose her.
I'll save you, he sings.
Enslave you, I whisper.
And around we go.
Bleeding anew,
battling for love,
killing for you...

I slammed the book closed and flipped it around in a complete circle so I could look for the title or author. Nothing. I glanced over to Everleigh's engrossed, yet shocked expression.

Again, I opened the book. I wasn't sure why I wanted to continue. Although I read the words, all I could hear was Bram's voice in my head…and see how it related to *us*. I didn't want to hear more, but there he was, worming his way into my life once again. And I kept taking it.

Unseen

Amongst a throne, behind stone walls,
the emptiness will not evade me.
But there is one,
one girl, one sun.
If only she could save me.
Broken bones bend to the beat of my heart, falling.
Love is death.
Bump-bump.
Can you hear the drums calling?
Louder it projects,
luring you in.
Close your eyes and see me, I say,
tugging and shredding at your heart as I grin.
I am the shadow over your shoulder.
Look up.
There I am.
Do you feel yourself growing colder?
Let the devil love you,
the shadow projects delusions.
Imagine what that sort of love is capable of.
I'm the macabre,
Master of illusions.

"What the hell is this shit?" I turned to the very first page, flipping through them again. Did Bram write this? No…he couldn't have. Bram couldn't write.

"I think it's beautiful."

Pursing my lips, I glanced at Everleigh.

"It's depressing and morbid. Why would you ever want to read this?"

"I like it," she said quietly.

"You and Bram both, obviously. I don't see the appeal."

I placed the book down, still unable to shake the way my skin was tightening with goosebumps. It was too close. Too similar to his mindset. *To her.*

"Thank you for reading to me. You didn't have to, but you did."

Her attitude has me looking over, confused. "How are you feeling?"

Her gaze jerked down and all softness from her face disappeared into nothingness. "I'm fine."

"I don't think you are. I…" My hand settled next to her as I turned more in her direction. "I think I hurt you badly. Not just your body, but here," I said, placing my finger against her temple. "And here," I said, moving my touch over her heart. "You either hate me, or you're going to. I never wanted that. I never wanted it to be this way. Yet, I did. I want both. I can't help the way I am."

"It's my fault. You're right. The way I acted was…inexcusable. Forgive me."

"Spoken like a true slave. I bet in your mind you're wishing you had that envelope opener again."

Her head quickly shook. "I should be dead right now. What you did…that was letting me off lightly. I'm grateful to be alive—for your mercy."

The speck of guilt eased. She was right. I could have had her killed for attacking me. Maybe, in her mind, she truly believed what I had done was just. After all, she'd been a slave long enough to know the difference between right or wrong.

"Master, may I ask you something?"

"Of course."

Everleigh shifted, wincing as she managed to inch a little closer. "I'm sorry if my question upsets you, but I have to ask. You plan to marry me tonight. Me, a disobedient, horrible slave. You've been trying to have me since my old Master was killed. You're very handsome. You could probably have any woman in this outside world, or any slave at Whitlock bowing to worship you. Why me?"

"Wife…" The question stirred my true self just as much as the man I pretended to be. "You have no idea how the outside world works. Sure, there are women I could have, but they would never satisfy me. Even if they could, they're not you. You're beautiful. Unlike any woman I've ever seen. As for your disobedience, you will learn."

"Will you rape me like you did again?"

The fear in her blue depths called out to me. I licked my lips, unable to resist leaning in to brush my lips over hers. "I can only hope. If you're a good slave, then you'll have nothing to fear."

CHAPTER 32

24690

It took everything I had to hold in my hate for the man before me. Letter opener? No. The new emotions boiling inside me wouldn't let him off so easily. I wanted to make him suffer—make him pay for the pain he'd caused. Someday, I would. But not yet. Right now, I had bigger things on my mind.

"Lift your arms."

I obeyed West, leaning forward as I slipped my hands through the thin straps of the white, silk dress. It was plain. But in its simplicity, it was beautiful. The top was moderately high, but the back was completely bare. It was a trend I was beginning to notice with West.

"Stunning. More than stunning."

He shook his head and stepped back, reaching to the dresser for a black box. The necklace that appeared as he lifted the lid was dripping with diamonds. I couldn't stop the gasp that left me as my eyes shot up to his.

"Turn."

I did, and pain shot through my body. I tensed at the soreness. Every move was a reminder of my rape, and every reminder grounded me even more. It fed my innermost thoughts and desires. I'd always known what I would do if I were put in this situation, and I had no plan to back out now.

"We may not have an actual wedding, but I will have fond memories of this night. The significance means more to me than you know." The necklace was put around my neck, and I couldn't stop my hand from reaching up to the sudden weight of it. When he spun me to face him, he took a step back, smiling. "Perfect." He turned his head, looking at the door. "What do you think, Eli?"

The guard nodded but didn't smile.

"You're a lucky man. Damn lucky. Prettiest bride I've ever seen, and that's the truth."

"Thank you. You're both too kind."

West grabbed my hand, leading me to the large mirror.

"We're not being kind. We're being honest. Look at you." He stepped up behind me, reaching around to trail his fingers down my necklace. They made a path over the diamonds before traveling between my cleavage. When he flattened his palm against my stomach and drew my body into his, I breathed through the need to attack. "Do you see?" he said lowly, next to my ear. "You are what men's dreams are made of. And now I have you, and no one else ever will."

"Thank you, Master."

A knock had Eli heading past us through the glass French doors of our room. He kept his hand by his weapon, looking through the peephole before grabbing the knob to open it.

"It's time." West turned me toward him, studying my face as he continued. "Don't ruin our night. Sign the papers. No matter what you see on there that may anger you, sign everything."

"You're my Master. I will sign."

"Not for long. Soon, I will be your husband." Again, he

smiled, leading me at a slow pace toward the living area where Eli had escorted a man and a woman. The moment I took in the man's face, my entire body trembled with the fury. I knew him. He was a Master at Whitlock. He'd touched and groped all over my body during the auction.

"Judge Vickery. Thank you for coming."

"Pleasure is mine. So, married, huh?"

West drew me in closer, laughing as brought us a step forward. "Look at her. Do you blame me?"

Slowly, the judged raked his stare down my body. It made me sick. Harder, I breathed, trying to push away the violence brewing within. Is this what I had become? Bram once said I'd been hidden from the horrors of Whitlock for too long. I knew he had been telling the truth, but never once did I see myself turning into one of them. And wasn't I? I craved to spill their blood—to massacre their bodies and end their lives for what they'd done to me.

"I don't blame you at all."

He looked over to the woman. She had to have been the lawyer. I didn't recognize her as a slave, but she wouldn't be since she was here.

"We'll do the paperwork first, then I'll give a short ceremony. If the two of you will come over here."

The judge took a file from the woman and pulled out a stack of papers. My heart pounded, but I cared not about what was in there. It didn't matter. Fighting wouldn't save me. The money I knew West wanted wasn't going to save me. I'd never be accepted as a Mistress in Whitlock. I'd never stand a chance alone.

"Mr. Harper, you can look over these and see if they're satisfactory."

For minutes, West scanned the pages. When he grabbed the pen and started signing, there was the biggest smile on his face.

What I wouldn't have done to sew his mouth shut so he could never smile again.

"Your turn."

I took the pen, not even looking at the content. Signature after signature, I scribbled the name printed below the line. It wasn't mine—Everleigh Davenport. But Everleigh Vicolette. My former name.

West's eyes burned into me, and I didn't miss the way he began stroking up and down my back as I leaned forward, scribbling the signature of a name I wished I'd never held.

"Excellent." The Master's voice was deep with happiness as I stood. "If the two of you will hold hands and face each other, we'll begin."

I glanced toward Eli as he watched on. Even though my body was twitchy with the need to run, to be sick right here between West and our clasped hands, I looked up into his eyes, keeping my true emotions hidden.

"Dearly beloved, we gather here today to join West Harper and Everleigh Vicolette in holy matrimony. Although their relationship brief, their love is apparently strong."

The words faded out as stared up in a daze. I wouldn't be a part of this. Of these lies consisting of things I didn't want.

"Do you, West, take Everleigh to be your wedded wife? To live together in holy matrimony? Do you promise to love, comfort, and honor her, for better or worse? Richer or poorer? In sickness and in health, and forsaking all others, be faithful to only her, until death?"

West's features drew in and he paused, seeming to take in the vows. "I do."

"And do you, Everleigh, take West to be your wedded husband? To live together in holy matrimony? Do you promise to love, comfort, and honor him, for better or worse? Richer or poorer? In sickness and in health, and forsaking all others, be faithful to only him, until death?"

Never. "I do."

West smiled, not even waiting for the judge before he wrapped his hand around the back of my neck and pulled me in, pressing his lips against mine.

"Okay then," the judge laughed. "I now pronounce you man and wife."

"Wife," he breathed out, breaking away. "*My* wife. Thank you, Judge. I won't forget this."

"It was an honor. I'll leave the two of you to enjoy your wedding night. I'll see you soon."

The men locked eyes, and West was still smiling as he nodded. I knew what went back and forth between them in that silent moment. They meant at Whitlock, and I dreaded the thought of seeing the judge again. No, I wouldn't. I'd avoid any and all Masters. I may have been married to West, but I had plans of my own. If he wanted a wife, a compliant and loving slave, I'd give him one. I'd make him believe I was the best thing to happen to him. And in the process, my hold on him would grow. I'd do what I told Bram and flip the roles as much as I could.

The moment West shut the door behind them, he turned to me, his smile dropping.

"You didn't like him."

It wasn't a question, but a statement as he stared into my depths.

"I recall him being one of the Masters who was particularly rough the night of the auction."

Recognition seemed to sink in, and he nodded. "As my wedding present to you, two nights from now, he will be no more. Just let him take care of the paperwork first." His lips pressed into mine, loving, coaxing, as if he'd never held me down and raped me in the most brutal way.

"I won't forget this," I breathed out, meeting his lips again as he pulled me into his body.

Despite my need to draw back, I forced myself to kiss him back. To *really* kiss him back. In our moment, I could still hear Bram's poems humming through my mind. When I got the chance, I'd try to read more. I'd try to see what the high leader felt was so important for me to know.

CHAPTER 33

WEST

I still couldn't believe it. One good rape and my slave had turned completely around? She was even loving, snuggling up next to me when we'd gone to sleep. The papers… she signed without so much as a pause. I'd been anxious to get back to Whitlock, but after the ease of our union, I suddenly wasn't in such a rush.

A yawn came from Everleigh and she winced, jolting awake. Her stare came to mine, and where I expected the old slave to return, she smiled, wrapping her arm around my chest. Mine came up, pulling her closer. I couldn't speak. Couldn't think of what to say. I was married…to Bram's dream girl. And she was here, holding me—the Master of Whitlock.

"Are you hungry?"

"Starving."

"You haven't eaten much in the last few days. I'll order breakfast while you get ready." I paused in breaking away from her. "Do you need me to help you?"

Softness, almost adoration, eased into her features. "I'm not sure." She eased to a sitting position, closing her eyes for a few seconds. When she scooted to the bed and stood, she shook her head. "I think I'll be okay."

Each step she took to the restroom was small. The closer she got, the better her pace became. I reached for the phone, hitting Eli's number.

"Breakfast."

"No good morning?"

I sat up, stretching. "Good morning. Get me and my wife some breakfast and make it good. Do you know what my slave likes to eat?"

"How the hell would I know?"

"Because you're supposed to be my new high leader. You need to know this shit. One of everything."

I hung up the phone and headed to the other bathroom. Pain webbed out in my shoulder, and I groaned through the annoyance. It didn't take me long to go through my routine and get dressed. When I came back into the room, Everleigh was trying to fasten the strap of her heel.

"Let me get that."

I walked over, crouching before her. She remained quiet as I buckled the straps and pulled the slacks down over her ankles.

"Thank you." Her mouth closed as she peered down at me. "Master?"

"Husband," I corrected, standing. "Master in the bedroom. Husband all other times." I pulled her in close, unable to resist the happiness filling every inch of me.

"Husband," she said, placing another kiss on my lips. "I like that. I like you this way." Another kiss. A knock had anything else she meant to say dying off as her attention went to the door. It was enough to sour my mood. I wanted her affection. Needed it.

"That must be breakfast. Come in!"

The door opened and Eli pushed a cart inside. It was obvious his mood was just as bad as mine suddenly was.

"One of everything. Just like you asked." He took the lids off the platters, then turned to my wife as he pulled a notepad from his pocket. "Apparently, it's my job to know your favorite foods for future reference. Let's start with breakfast."

"Can it wait until after we eat?" I snapped.

His lids narrowed as he glared.

"It's okay, husband. Really, I don't mind." Her smiled dropped completely as she faced him. "Yogurt: strawberry. A banana, a slice of toast with the butter on the side, and one small bowl of oatmeal with brown sugar. Cranberry juice, not orange, and a glass of water. For lunch, I will take one of three things. The first: grilled chicken salad. No tomatoes, with ranch dressing. The second: steak, cooked medium—not rare, and definitely not overdone. It is not to be over six ounces, and there will be double the vegetables, which will be a mix of broccoli and carrots. Not asparagus, not potatoes. The third: grilled chicken and vegetables. The same as before—broccoli and carrots. And not over six ounces of meat for that either. Dinner, the same as lunch."

Eli's stare came to me, but my attention went back to Everleigh as she threw me the sweetest smile. "How was that? Worthy of a Master's wife?"

I didn't think about the possible pain I would put her through. I pulled her to me, crushing my lips to hers. The way her body softened into mine as she wrapped her arms around my neck swept me away even more. I didn't mind her directness toward the guards, just not me. It was actually perfect for Whitlock if I wanted to make my mark.

"If there is nothing else, I'll take my leave."

The irritation in his voice had me breaking away to look at Eli. "Do you have a problem with my wife's authority toward you?"

"Of course not. Mistress Harper only responded with what you asked of me."

"So, it's me you have a problem with?"

"Not a problem. Just don't forget who your friends are."

He glanced at Everleigh before turning to head for the door. When it shut, I turned back to my wife, pressing my lips into hers again. "Let's eat. Then we'll go home. I'm going to have them reopen Ol' Master Whitlock's wing. We're going to have the best of everything. I'm going to make sure of it."

A soft cry left Everleigh's lips, and her fingers clawed into the table as she sat down. I reached for her hand, refusing to apologize, but still letting her know I was here. Her eyes opened and she took a deep breath.

"I'm sorry. I wasn't thinking to be careful. You were saying, Ol' Master Whitlock's wing? I thought that place was haunted."

I laughed, giving her hand a squeeze as I sat and began making my plate. She quickly followed my lead.

"There are no such thing as ghosts. Besides, even if there were, the bastard can kiss my ass. He was the biggest asshole I ever knew…but I admired parts of him. He was a powerful man. I wanted power like that someday."

"And now, you have it."

I joined in on her smile, baffled by her change. It was like night and day. Whatever I'd done with that rape worked.

"And now I have it," I repeated. "Are you sad to be going back? I know you didn't like this place, but it has to be better than looking at the white walls of Whitlock."

"Whitlock makes me feel safe. Everything out here is so open. Things are constantly moving, and that makes me anxious. Cars and helicopters, I don't like them. I like Whitlock. I like feeling confined. That's where I belong."

"Are you sure?"

Her head tilted. "What are you asking, husband?"

"Nothing. I'll be coming to the outside on occasion. Probably not here, but Denver, Los Angeles, Reno, New York. I go all over. I just wasn't sure how you felt about traveling with me."

"Sounds overwhelming." She grinned. "I would come if you wanted me to, but I won't deny that it makes me nervous."

"We'll see what happens." I grabbed my coffee and added sugar while Everleigh sampled the fruit. I ate light, just watching. There was something I couldn't put my finger on. She was a slave. I'd obviously sent her reverting into that status after the rape. Why else would she be so compliant to give me everything? And this new mood of hers. She said she was grateful I didn't kill her, which was why she was this way, but was it the truth?

"Are you going to try to run before we leave for Whitlock?"

Everleigh paused mid-chew, slowly swallowing. "Why would I run? That leaves me stranded here. I don't want to be here."

"Maybe that's just what you want me to think. Maybe you'll leave so you can try to find some of your distant family."

"And put them in danger? I'd have every Master in Whitlock after me. No thank you. I'm content exactly where I am."

I nodded, frowning even more. If she wasn't planning to escape, what was it? She had stabbed me. There was hate in her then, and it hadn't suddenly vanished. Unless…maybe the rape screwed her up in the head enough to make her see she was in the wrong.

"Are you going to try to kill me?"

Again, she paused. "And go to a new Master? One who will peel back my skin, or slowly burn me alive? No. I would be lying if I said I didn't have contempt toward you. I am still very upset and angry at what you did to me. But I deserved it. I see that now. I'm lucky to have a Master…" She grew quiet. "A *husband* who wants to take such good care of me. And you're not mean all the time. I saw my mistake, and I'm grateful you chose me."

I stayed quiet, drinking coffee.

"It's the children then. You're doing this for them."

Her hands came down on the table as she leaned more toward me. "They weigh heavily on my mind, but my behavior is not based around them. Yes, I'm worried about their safety. I don't want them apart of Whitlock. But you're the Master. You know how I feel and what I'd like to happen. It doesn't change that the decision is ultimately up to you. I'm your wife now—something I never thought I'd be to anyone. You have no idea what that means to me. I've been *blessed*, and for that, I am devoted to you."

"I appreciate that, but you have to know, I won't be releasing them. I can't. If Whitlock is going to thrive, it has to be done. I've watched the decline in funds since Bram took over. His way just wasn't working. He tried to clean it up. He tried to make things better, but it was only a matter of time before it fell around us. I mean, look at how empty Whitlock is. It never used to be like this. Men like the Masters there, they don't just pay for slaves. They pay for murder, pedophilia, all the stuff that would have them arrested here. That's what Whitlock is about. And that's the way I will make it again."

Everleigh's eyes lowered, and I grabbed a slice of bacon, tearing into it.

"Don't pout. I don't like pouting. It's just the facts, and it's best to move on. I won't be swayed. Why don't you focus on something else? Interior design. You can look through colors, fabrics, and all that wifely stuff and fix up our new wing just the way you want it."

Her eyes eased up, and her head lifted. "You would let me fix our place anyway I wanted? Me?"

"With the exception of pink. No pink. Or yellow, for that matter. Unless it's more gold. Other than that, yes."

A smile appeared and comfort within me grew. *Simple.* I'd give her something to do, and she'd stay out of my business. Married life wouldn't be so bad, and Whitlock would once again reign supreme for the men who wanted to pay a fortune for their sins.

CHAPTER 34

24690

"This isn't good. This shouldn't be happening."

My words came out rushed as I glanced up to Eli, who was standing at my side. We were a few feet away from West as he continued his speech about the *new* Whitlock. The stage we stood on was centered in the middle of the field at City Center and Master and slaves could be seen for as far as the green stretched out. I could already feel the energy of the large crowd shifting as our new leader's statements darkened into ones these men could have only dreamed about.

"For too long you have been denied what you pay for. It never used to be this way. The Whitlocks started this place generations ago to cater to what we *really* wanted. What we needed! Now, we begin again. With me, the old ways will return. To start my reign, I will hold the most elaborate, most sought after, auction in years. The Cradle will be opened, and from here on out, will thrive."

Cheers roared in scattered locations, making the unease seep into my bones. I jerked my gaze to Eli and couldn't stop the panicked breaths from leaving.

"Before we go into that more, let me ask you this. Does your slave have a problem taking orders? Have you been wanting to teach them a lesson—one they'll never forget?" West's hand shot up and a guard a few feet away jerked a large white sheet free. "I give you our stocks. Lock them in. Remind them who the Master is. I guarantee they won't think twice about disobeying you again. Whip them. Beat them. Rape them in front of everyone. Let whoever comes along rape them. They're *your* slave. Shouldn't you be able to discipline them however you want?" He turned, glancing behind him, and I couldn't follow his stare. I already knew what was there.

"This," he said, his arm rising toward the gallows, "is what used to be our foundation for entertainment. No more White Room private deaths. Trial and public execution. To make things interesting…and entertaining," he said, smiling, "we'll bring back The Wheel. Who remembers The Wheel?"

Again, cheers echoed around. But it wasn't from the slaves. Their horrified expressions couldn't be hidden as they stared on. It was a like a hit in the gut as I watched, terrified for them.

"With a spin of the wheel, their death will be chosen. Guillotine, the rack, impalement, rat torture, the tub, the breast ripper. You name it, we've got it. I've even added in two of my favorites. Maybe there's more than one Master who needs to be rid of their slave? Let's all be friends. Let's have some fun. Ever heard of the republican marriage? Let's tie them together and torture them as one. Drown them or set them on fire. Your imagination is limitless. Maybe you can throw them in the tub and watch them get eaten away over the weeks by maggots and pests. Whatever you like. Or, if you're not ready to be done with your slave, you can always silence the mouthy ones. Remember our tongue ripper? Haven't heard of it? Ask around. It's the long-term answer to all your problems. And me, your new Main Master, is here to help however I can."

"The auction! Tell us about the auction!" someone yelled.

"Wife." West motioned me over, and for the life of me, I

couldn't move. It took Eli's hand pressing into my lower back to get me walking toward the front of the stage. Once I got to his side, he turned me to face the crowd. "Let me officially introduce all of you to my wife. That's right, *wife*. The option was never available to you before, but that's all about to change. Maybe you're not into killing off slaves like others. Maybe you love your little pet. Marry her or him. You won't be able to leave with them outside these walls, but they'll be yours in a way they've never been before. I cater to all our needs. Including The Cradle. For more information on our auction, I hand over the reins to my wife."

I quickly shook my head.

"Tell them what I told you earlier." West's voice was slow, yet full of authority…anger.

I swallowed hard, facing the crowd. Silence was damn near deafening as they waited.

"The…" I glanced over at West as he nodded. "The auction will be held in four w-weeks. It will only be for those in The Cradle." My eyes burned as I turned to West, begging him with my stare. When his head tilted down for me to continue, I took a deep breath. "It will be for all ages. Fourteen children ranging from f-five years old to twelve."

My voice cracked, and I did everything I could to keep the tears in. West made it to my side, kissing my cheek as he picked up where I left off. I heard nothing more. All I could see was the faces of the children I'd spent time with. Their eyes. Their smiles. And now, the man I was married to was hellbent on destroying their lives.

"I leave you all with what we have out so far. The stocks are for your personal use. Use them as you wish. We have one set up now, but there will be a total of eight before the day is out. If you wish for The Wheel and want to skip the White Room, put in a request with our high leader, Eli. We'll prepare everyone for the show. Have a good one."

The moment West's hand rose to wave, the Masters went wild. I didn't hesitate to follow him off the stage. I wanted out of there. Slaves were already screaming, and I could hear multiple arguments brewing in the distance.

"Shall we escort you to your quarters, Master?"

Although I heard the guard's voice, it was West's growl that drew me from looking at the chaos of a fighting slave being pulled toward the stocks. She was screaming, slashing her hands toward anyone she could grasp onto.

"I'll be going to Master Kunken's quarters. Follow behind but stay outside and wait for us." West turned to me, speaking angrily under his breath. "He's the Main Master under me, and he wasn't even here. That's unacceptable. I want to know what was so fucking important he couldn't show his support."

West guided me forward, his irritation making his pace almost impossible to keep up with. I was practically running at his side.

"Husband, please." I fought not to fall from the damn heels he'd made me wear. Understanding seemed to dawn and he came to a stop. The battle was obvious in his features as he gazed at me. Rage—restraint. Restrain won.

"I'm sorry. I wasn't thinking. Here I am, dragging you behind me like a slave. Forgive me." He leaned forward, pressing his lips to mine. "I'm upset. I shouldn't be taking it out on you."

"I just didn't want to fall and embarrass you. I can try to keep up, but maybe at a slower pace?"

He smiled, wrapping his arms around my waist as he eased me into him. "The only way you'd hit the ground is if I put you there. I'd never let you fall."

Heat engulfed my cheeks as my hate for him ignited. "Thank you, husband."

"Of course. Now, come. We'll meet with Master Kunken,

and maybe you can visit with your slave friend, Red, while we go over business. If, of course, he permits."

"Red?"

"Yes. The red-haired girl."

Julie!

"Oh, yes. Thank you. I would love to visit her."

"Don't get your hopes up. He may not want her socializing with someone of your…independence," he said, moving into my ear and tugging against it. "Let's get this over with. I want you. I want to bathe you like before."

My lids blinked slowly, the dread all too real. "If it pleases you."

"It would please me, immensely."

Fingers dug into my lower back for only a moment before he pulled away, holding my hand as we began to walk again. When we came to a door, I couldn't help the eagerness that began to push away the fear of what lay ahead. I held to visiting Julie like a lifeline. Like it was the only thing in the world that mattered. She could be my happiness—my friend in a time where no one was to be trusted.

West's knocking was answered almost immediately. At the smell that met us, my head jerked back.

"Master Harper. Please, come in. Master Kunken thought you might come."

The shorter man stepped back, opening the barrier for us to enter. From the stench, to the Master's guard before us, I didn't want to continue.

"Thank you." West nodded, leading us deeper into the metallic aroma. My apprehension only increased as I was faced with Julie. She was sitting at a table in the dining room, eating a large plate of fruit. Grapes and watermelon were like a mountain, piled high before her. She looked sick as she forced herself to swallow and wipe the juice from her mouth. A grin appeared but faded just as fast. Her eye was nearly swollen shut and her cheek was massively bruised with a slight laceration across it. My heart sank as I held West's arm tighter.

"Master. What can I do for you?"

A large man rounded the corner of the kitchen, coming into view. Blood covered his arms, up to his elbows, and the smell filling the apartment was suddenly clear. He wiped his hands down the nearly saturated apron, and I could tell by his tone he wasn't happy. All hope of talking to Julie faded as he got closer.

"I sent word that you were to attend my announcement. You're the highest of my Main Masters, you should have been there."

"My man took notes and relayed them to me just seconds before you arrived." He paused. "My position would have said I supported you, but I'm afraid my attendance would have done more harm than good. I'm glad I decided not to go."

"Why is that? If I remember correctly, I had your vote. I mentioned bringing back the old ways and you were intrigued."

He nodded, glancing over at me before turning back to West. "You did, but I assumed it was only for The Cradle. This… brutality you evoke. It doesn't benefit me. I was here through Old Man Whitlock's reign. This place wasn't safe. Not even with the Masters having their own personal guards. And you plan to make it like that again. *But worse.* You'll turn this place into a bloodbath of carnage and slaughter before it's over. And it's your right. Maybe some men like public pandemonium, but it will never work. Not here. When you break down barriers and make death public, you ignite a beast in every man. Animals don't get along very well when you introduce them to a feast of food and sins. It will never be enough. They'll want more—more blood, more torture, more punishments. You'll make hunters of us all. They'll find ways to use this against their enemies. And they will destroy this place. Probably you with it. You should have kept the majority of Bram's laws and just opened the damn Cradle. That would have been the best option."

West stiffened beside me. "His laws held us back. These men —you—pay good money to do as you please here. Just because you don't like your business to be public doesn't mean everyone feels the same. Every Master has a right to what they pay for."

"They pay for the laws currently set. They knew what they were getting under Bram's rule, and they were content with that. What you offer now will be your undoing. I'm telling you they would have been just as gratified had they not known the difference. And for the ones who did, they had adjusted to the change. Now, you set the monsters free from their luxurious little cells. I hope you're ready for the repercussions that will follow."

"We'll be able to handle the outcome. I don't fear their savagery. There's beauty in barbarism. You just have to know how to flow with the ferocity or else you may drown. I won't let Whitlock sink with the added violence. I plan to make it prosper more than it ever has."

Master Kunken shook his head, snapping his fingers angrily. Julie scattered from the chair, nearly falling over herself as she slid to her knees at his feet.

"You think you know what these men are capable of because you got a small taste of it growing up. But you have never led them. You've never seen the true depths of their evil. Old Man Whitlock sheltered you boys more than you know."

The Master gestured with his fingers, cracking the guard into action. He walked toward the older man, handing him a large, jagged knife. Julie let out a whimper, shifting below. I could see her need to run. The terror on her face left my nails clawing into West's jacket as I tried to make myself stay still.

"Not all men share the same sins, Master Harper. Exposing the darkest will eventually smother out any light that remains within these stone walls. Can you lead if all you have is the pitch-black void that surrounds you? Will it eat you alive? Consume you as well?"

Plump fingers buried into Julie's hair, and her cry left me

trying to take a step closer. But it was impossible. West had already taken his arm from mine and held me around the shoulders, so I was stuck at his side. The guard rushed over with a metal tub, and Julie's body tried to shoot up to stand, but his hold of her hair had her legs and hips moving off to the side while she tugged and screamed in his grip.

"Uncle, please! Uncle!"

Master Kunken didn't stay a word as he stared my husband down. He jerked Julie to stand straight and wrapped his arm around her forehead. The slice of the blade cut across her throat from ear to ear while blood gushed in a fountain of deep, red crimson. The clink of the stream splashing into the metal below had sobs coming from me before I could stop them. Movement blurred in the distance, but I saw nothing but the life leaving Julie's eyes as her body spasmed in his arms. And maybe I saw my own dying a little too. A minute of hope for finding a friend—a lifetime of heartache for even thinking it was possible.

"I've loved my niece since she was a toddler bouncing on my knee. I watched her grow. Fucked her before she was out of junior high. Some things should not be made for public entertainment, Main Master. Death is a special lover. It is to be cherished. Savored between killer and victim. What you're doing, I do not condone." He gave Julie's lifeless body a hard shake, moving them to the side as a scraping sound drew me from the girl's stoic face. The guard dropped two hooks just over the tub and instinct had me yanking against West's hold. But he wouldn't let me go. And he wouldn't let me turn into him to hide from the gruesome sight before me.

"Watch," he growled in my ear. "You are the Master's wife. You will not balk from intimidation."

"Intimidation?" Master Kunken repeated. "I offer no such thing. This is beauty in its purest form. I'm not trying to prove a point to you. I'm merely showing you what will soon litter our once semi-peaceful circle. You offer a massacre to these men.

The buzzards will be seen from miles away at the amount of blood they'll soon spill. Better take that into account, Master Harper."

The guard rushed over, tying a loop around each of Julie's feet. He helped Master Kunken lift her limp body upside down onto two separate hooks a good three feet apart. The popping as they forced the hook behind each of her Achilles tendons left me lightheaded. When they began cutting off her clothes, I couldn't stop myself from looking up to West.

"Please," I mouthed. "I can't watch anymore…"

The hard expression only increased as he held my gaze. When his eyes narrowed, my stomach roiled with the need to be sick. I knew that look. He planned to make me pay for not being strong.

"I'll be sure to have a group of guards ready to shoot the majority down. The others will…what did you say? Something about a feast of food and sins? Sounds fitting for the scavengers. They can help with the torture."

"What an evil mind you have, Master Harper."

"Some would think so. I know Everleigh does. She seems to be having a problem adjusting to our ways. *To mine.* Maybe if you allowed her to take the lead in helping you prepare your… dinner, it would help her accept the role she's been given as the Main Master's wife."

"W-What? Oh, God. Please. Please don't make me—"

West's hand clamped over my mouth, but he kissed my forehead so lovingly. "This is to be expected of your status," he said softly. "You will not cower to death. You will not stir or cringe at the sight of blood or gore. Skinning and gutting your friend will be good for you. Attachments to anyone or anything is useless. Let this be a lesson, *wife*."

CHAPTER 35

WEST

The internal smile wouldn't leave me as I kissed Everleigh's forehead. Tighter, she gripped me, and I couldn't get enough of it. Her body trembled and each little shake hummed through me like a magnifier to the sadist within.

"Let go," I whispered. "It'll be okay. Just follow Master Kunken's orders."

"But…" She swallowed hard, gazing up with terrified eyes.

"Let. Go." I pried her hands from my lapels, where they had risen in her fear. I could see my slave changing the longer I projected my authority. The walls inside her were lifting. The little signs started out with her fists unclenching. Then her shoulders widening. She was either going into shock or numbing out. But I cared not of her mental stability. It was pleasing me to see her squirm. To see her so afraid. "That's my girl. Shhh. *Do it.* Stand tall, turn, and obey Master Kunken."

Dark hair rubbed against my jaw as Everleigh's gaze went from the Master to the girl's strung up body. Her arms dropped to her sides, and in slow steps, she broke away from me and walked forward. A weird sense of pride began to make my heart beat faster. This was Bram's sweet Everleigh. The love of his life. And she was mine to destroy or love in any way I saw fit.

Master Kunken pointed. "Take her hand and place it in the loop of rope hanging down from her ankle. We want her arms, and legs, spread."

Shaking took over my wife's chest, but no sounds left her as she obeyed and lifted Julie's wrist. Once she had it in the rope, the guard pulled down on the knot, tightening the hemp to the dead girl's wrist.

"Now, I want you to rub your hands down her leg toward her head. Like a massage. Can you do that, Mistress?"

A ragged breath left Everleigh, but she didn't so much as glance or address the Master. Her hands rose and she turned her face away from the body, staring at the wall while rubbing her way from the top of the calf to her upper thigh. The color drained from her face, but she stayed erect, going through the motions as the minutes went by. When she reached for Julie's arm and began doing the same thing, the Master threw me an approving smile. She didn't have to be told, which he seemed to like.

"Very good. Now we're going to pump the stomach. This will remove more of the blood. Give me your hand and we'll begin."

Bloodshot blue eyes turned to stare at me, and she held my gaze as her hand came out robotically before her. Master Kunken flattened his palm over hers and placed it against the lower part of the girl's stomach, pushing in with enough force to have him holding the small of her back so the body wouldn't rock. Blood gushed from the mouth and wound at Julie's neck, making plopping sounds as it rippled the thickening dark liquid.

Lower, Everleigh's lids dropped. It was as though she was glaring, but something told me she wasn't here. Over and over, the Master pressed, lowering toward her head. When he pulled back, he grabbed the knife from his guard, crouching.

"Now, we remove the head," he said, looking up at her and

drawing her attention. "I'd let you do this part, but I'm afraid you're not going to have the strength to twist it free."

Silence.

Everleigh swayed as he sawed through. When his fingers weaved through the saturated hair and he began to jerk and twist, I wasn't even sure my wife noticed. She was still looking down. But…devoid of everything, like a statue.

The crack of bone sounded, and blood ran down in a stream as he passed it to the guard.

"Now comes the fun part," he said, grabbing a smaller knife. "Although, perhaps this is where we should say goodbye, Mistress."

"Mrs. Harper," I corrected. "And she's fine. She can go a little while longer. Can't you, wife?"

Everleigh blinked hard, looking between me and the Master. "I can go longer."

Her hand extended with the monotone words and my heart raced faster. I took a step closer as Master Kunken walked around the body to stand behind Everleigh. He started the skinning himself, peeling back the layers until he got it level with her face. When she took the knife, his hand molded around hers, moving the blade in slow slicing motions while he worked the skin toward the knee. More and more muscle became exposed, and minutes passed as Everleigh's breathing increased and decreased.

"You're doing wonderful," he said, moving their hands toward the dead girl's inner thigh. "You have a very steady hand. Perhaps…you'd like to come over and help me from now on?"

The softening of the Master's tone had all fascination leaving me. I took in his position and closeness, suddenly seeing the intimacy he was experiencing. The jealousy inside me raged as I came even closer.

"You're done," I ground out. "It's time to go."

A grin appeared, and Master Kunken went to remove the

knife from her hand. Her grip was so tight around the small handle, he had to force her fingers open. She didn't seem to want to let go of the weapon. When Everleigh turned, I knew she was gone. Her face was pale, and her pupils were huge. Where it would have worried most people, it didn't bother me. I'd seen her like this before—after the rape.

"Come, wife. It's time I get you back home so you can relax."

Seconds went by before she came forward.

"There we go." I placed her hand around my bicep. "You did great. I'm very proud of you." I kissed her head, glaring at the Master. "Next time I say to be somewhere, obey. You're my second. *Act like it.* I don't give a shit whether you approve or not. You miss anything else and I'll kick you from the board so fast, it'll make your head spin. I don't give a shit about old policies. I'm the Main Master now, and I make the rules."

I led Everleigh out, letting my guards who waited outside shut the door behind us. Blood still covered her hands. Her fingers kept twitching against my arm as we headed down the hall. I couldn't stop stealing glances at them, or my wife. *She'd done it.* She proved to be worthy and so much more.

"Slave."

Blue eyes shot up at the address. I knew that's where her mindset was. Had I called her my wife, or by her name, the act would have been drawn out. Right now, she wasn't Everleigh. She was no one. A shell.

"Yes, husband?"

"Do you want me?"

She blinked slowly, and a muscle in her cheek jerked. "If it pleases you."

"Don't give me that generic response. I asked you a question. Do you want me?"

"I…I…" Everleigh heaved, grabbing her stomach as she spun to brace herself on the white wall. Blood smeared, and her fingers scraped down the length as she continued to head toward our apartment. "You…know…I do," she managed. "I'm just… unwell right now."

Deep breaths left her as I swept her into my arms roughly and stomped toward our door.

"And you were doing so well handling your lesson. I see it's catching up to you."

"I…skinned…" She gagged, and I cursed under my breath.

"Get over it. It happened, and you did beautifully. Your mind is just weak. We'll fix that, though. You'll be better than ever by the time I finish with you."

Our door was opened, and I headed straight for the bathroom. The sound of the water hitting the bottom of the tub sent Everleigh flailing in my arms.

"I don't want t-to. I don't want—"

"*Enough*. You will bathe, and you will relax."

For the first time, sobs left her. Her fist swung in my direction, and I grasped her wrist, expecting it. I spun her, trapping her arms against my body. At the restraint, her legs went wild, kicking while she screamed. I barely managed to get to the oil before I heard the hard sound of boots rushing in my direction. Eli burst through the door, pausing at my glare.

"Well? What is it?" I snapped.

In jerky movements, his stare went from Everleigh to me. "You're…needed."

"Where?"

Again, he hesitated. "City Center. You're going to want to see this."

CHAPTER 36

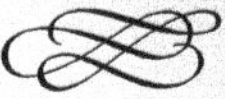

24690

Eli saved me once, but I knew it wasn't going to be long before West returned. When he did, he'd want to continue. He'd want to rape me while I was drugged. I couldn't let that happen. To have me sober was bad enough, but under the influence while I couldn't move was something I refused to endure again. That was why I'd showered as fast as I could while he was gone. If I could offer an excuse, it was better than nothing.

My mind drifted into the haze of what I could only assume was insanity. My actions, my thoughts, raced. Focusing didn't last long. I couldn't stop shaking. Every time flashes of what I'd done surfaced, the sickness I felt was overwhelming. I had helped prepare Julie. I had cut and peeled down the skin of a girl who had trusted me probably more than anyone here. My brain wouldn't accept what I was becoming. *I* couldn't accept it.

Faster, I paced the length of our living area.

What was I going to do? If I killed West, I'd go to the White Room to await my death in City Center. If I managed to somehow do it without bringing suspicion to myself, I'd go to

Slave Row to be sold again. My next owner could be Master Kunken. And then I'd be Julie…

I pressed my hand pressed against, nausea roiling through me until I nearly became ill.

Get over it. It happened, and you did beautifully. Your mind is just weak. West's words came floating in out of nowhere. He was right. Where I had moments of strength, I had moments of weakness—crippling moments that stole away reality. They left me here, fighting through this fog until my wits returned. I didn't like it. I wanted to be stronger. To have nothing affect me so West couldn't find ways to hurt me anymore. *I wanted the blurring to stop from the corner of my vision. It kept stealing my attention.* It was like someone was there, even though no one was.

Clips of me and the temporary high leader's conversations surfaced. He'd talked of games, of control, when I'd spent time in The Cradle. Even though I knew the significance, I couldn't process it in the moment. All I felt was anger at the way my life was turning out. Anger and hatred toward West for the things he'd done. It ruled me in the moment…and tempted me to do things I shouldn't.

A darkness had me jerking my head to the side. I froze at West standing in the doorway. I hadn't even heard it open; I was so lost within myself.

"Who am I looking at, my wife, or the fragile, little slave?"

I stood taller, keeping my eyes on his as I walked forward. "Your wife. I must apologize for my behavior. You were right. My mind is weak. Forgive me."

The door shut at his push. The glare he cast followed me as he walked over to the bar and poured himself a drink. When he shrugged his jacket off, the blood splattered across his button-up shirt caused my entire body to twitch. I tried to push my reactions away as I licked my lips, braving moving closer.

"What happened down there?"

"Games." He paused, throwing back the shot. The annoyance disappeared as he placed down the empty glass. "The Masters have quite the affinity for violence. They've taken to this change with open arms. Their imagination surpasses anything I could have hoped. It seems one of the Masters here is a professional fighter. He's taught his slave some of his skills." He laughed, shaking his head at whatever he was thinking. "Apparently, he told another Master his slave could kick the Master's ass. It started as a joke, but long story short, the crowd went wild and began to instigate the situation with yells and remarks. The Master didn't take well to that and hit the girl. He broke her nose, but the moment Master Max gave the command, the girl demolished him. It was outstanding. Like nothing I've ever seen."

My stare dropped back down to his shirt.

"Did you…?"

"Fight her?"

"Yes," I said, taking in the pleasure on his face.

"No. After she won, a bigger fight broke out. One between the men who placed bets. It appears they weren't clear on the rules. I took care of it." Lust masked West's face as he closed the distance between us, stopping to tower over me. "You see, wife, most of the men down here are dying to release the storm that churns inside them. I've seen this for years. They didn't have to physically fight to settle this, but that was their first reaction. The rage is who we are. It's a living thing, seething within and begging to be set free. I gave them that. We build, we erupt, and there, we thrive. It's the steps. Just like fighting, drinking, and fucking. Now, take off your clothes."

I didn't argue or focus on my need for revenge. I grabbed the straps to the loose dress and drew them over my shoulders, letting the material drift to my feet. West followed my action, ripping off his shirt and bringing his hand toward me. Cuts and dried blood crusted over a few of his knuckles. He groped my breast, rolling my nipple between his thumb and index finger as he massaged. When he gripped harder, I cried out, grabbing his wrist.

"If you ever fucking fight me like you did before, I will treat you like the slave you were portraying. My wife listens. She obeys. When I tell her to get in the damn bathtub, she goes." He spun me, dragging me to the sofa. Roughly, he pushed his hand on my back, bending me over the arm of the couch. "When I tell her I want to fuck her, what does she say?"

A million words whispered through my mind—a million manipulations.

"Don't go easy," I said, looking back at him.

A smile exploded across his face, and his body lowered against mine. "You don't have to worry about that. Maybe I'll tear you apart." Suction tugged at the dip of my neck and shoulder, and I braced as his fingers rubbed over my slit. My eyes immediately closed, and I drew far back into my memories. So far away, I could almost hear Bram's moans surrounding me.

"Fuck yes. I knew you'd bounce back fast. I knew the woman I've seen over the last few days was stronger than some broken slave crying over a little blood."

I barely heard West's words. His fingers were pushing into me, moving faster as his arm locked under my chin. I didn't grab at the hold. I didn't even want to acknowledge the fear spiking at the action. Let him choke me. Let him do whatever he wanted. Here, I had control. I could fight if it came down to it. More than I could the oil. But even though I could, I wouldn't. Not if I wanted more power over him. And I could do it. I could rule him. Instinct told me it was possible.

"More," I moaned.

My plea was demanding, and he took the bait almost instantly.

West's arm tightened as his fingers disappeared from inside

me. When his cock pressed against my entrance, my teeth clenched through the hate of my situation—of him—*of myself.*

"God…dammit!"

I screamed right along with his words, feeling my legs kick out as he plunged into me. His arm was like a metal collar around my neck. It was heavy against my throat, fastening around me like it was locking me in, promising a lifetime of no escape from the slave in my core. With each brutal thrust, it secured even more, cutting off my air. My hands shot up, and I intentionally let my nails bite into his skin.

"More. More!" I thrashed in his hold, feeling like the mad woman I was becoming. I could barely catch my breath as he slammed into me, over and over. I didn't think. I let my nails tear down his arm with all my rage. Tears flowed from my eyes while I fought, and the chuckling behind me was anything but amused. His arm dropped from my neck so fast, I wasn't prepared for the grip that ripped into my hair, forcing my head down even more. If I had thought he was going hard before, I had no clue what he was capable of.

"You're feistier than I gave you credit for. How much can you take before you go back on your 'more'?"

"I'll take what you give."

West pushed into my back, harder, pulling my head more toward him. He was arching me so far, my hands shot out before me, and I bucked to break his hold. When I drew my knee up and planted it in the leather, it took everything in me to wiggle free beneath him. His hands scrambled, catching my hips, and he yanked me back, surging deep into my channel. Maybe he saw it as a game, but I didn't. I truly wanted to best him in any way I could. The pure fact that I could get loose was enough to keep me from truly attacking him.

"Jesus. Get the fuck up here, wife." West let go, grabbing my shoulder to pull me up so I was back against him. The moment his chest connected, he wrapped his arms tightly around me, hugging onto me as he slowed his pace. It was almost passionate—loving. "Kiss me."

My head angled, and his lips met mine with a hunger almost impossible to fake. Deeper, he thrust into me, grinding his hips into my ass. I gasped, breaking away long enough to take in oxygen from the pain. His hand brought me back to him, and his tongue pushed into my mouth while he held me there. I could feel him swelling inside me, getting thicker as he got closer. Cries left me, and he drank them in as he nearly crushed me with his arms.

"I could learn to love this," he said lowly, moaning next to my ear. "*Love you.*"

CHAPTER 37

WEST

My poor little pretender posing as my loving pet—my faithful wife. The way she lightly snored and rested against my chest. The way she talked in her sleep. I glared at the ceiling, trying to get control over the need to snap her neck and throw her off me.

"B…ram?"

"What?" My jaw clenched. I should have left it alone, ignored who she subconsciously called to. For the life of me, I couldn't. I needed the violence. I needed to hurt her more than beating her pussy up. If she was calling to him, I didn't have her yet. And hadn't I thought maybe I was getting close?

A moan had her snuggling deeper into me. My fist clenched as what I had said to her came back to haunt me. Had I whispered I could love her? Had I spoken that lie? Lie…maybe not entirely. I wanted to trust her so I could unleash some of this fury. Anyone could close themselves off to emotion. But to love a person…it made you more of everything. More of a leader…*more of a killer.* Hadn't Bram told me that once?

What sounded like a soft giggle tore into my heart. I rolled her on her back, putting my weight on top of her as I fit myself between her legs. Everleigh's eyes blinked heavily, and there was a hesitation before she seemed to force a smile on her face.

"Good dreams?"

The grin turned genuine as she moved into my forearm, snuggling her face back into me.

"I don't know. I really can't remember."

"No? That's too bad. You sleep so sweet. I bet you're just as beautiful when you scream. Let's find out. Be sure to cry out for Bram again. Maybe he'll come rescue you."

Everleigh's eyes flew open, and her attention jerked to me. I ripped the pillow out from behind her head and slammed it over her face. Muffled screams were automatic. Nails clawed into my arms and her legs went wild, pressing into the bed as she tried to twist herself free. But it was impossible with the hold I had on her face.

"Bram? Bram?" I yelled out loudly. "Where are you? My wife needs your help." I waited out the time, then lifted the pillow, letting her gasp for breath when I noticed her movements slowing. "That's who you want, right? Bram? Not me? Maybe I should call to him again."

"No! N—"

The end was cut off as I pushed the pillow back over her face. At her lack of fighting, my rage eased into anger. I took a calming breath, holding a few more seconds before I removed it once again. Her intake of air was loud. My hands shot down over her shoulders, trapping her from moving.

"I had such a good day planned for us, and now you've ruined it. *You're mine.* This," I said, tapping against her temple, "belongs to me. If you don't get Bram out of your head, I'll smother him out. Do you understand me?"

"I didn't know," she rushed out. "I...yes."

"Good."

I went to crawl off her when she reached up, gripping my bicep. My pause had her palm cautiously rising to settle on the side of my throat. My eyes narrowed, but she continued to slide her grip around to the back of my neck. Pressure tried to pull me down, and although I fought her for the slightest moment, I couldn't stop myself from lowering.

"Smother him from me. Make it stop."

Tears clouded her eyes as she led my mouth to hers. The kiss was firm, but full of something that left my mind twirling. I wanted to believe she was telling the truth. There were moments where she seemed to try to please me. To feel something for me. *She tried…*

"Do you choose me?"

I lifted enough to meet her stare. Disbelief flickered but softened out as she gazed up.

"It's always been you."

"No." I gave a hard shake, dislodging her hand. "You picked him. Your scene at his grave…"

"You saw me grieve over a man who spent years protecting me. Killing for me. We shared something, yes. I won't deny that. He protected me when no one else had. I held to that until I realized that was exactly what you'd been doing too. You have, haven't you?"

Confusion and truths left me silent. I could tell her yes, I had Master Vicolette killed. I could tell her a lot of things, but I kept quiet.

"Get dressed. I'm going to make coffee."

I pushed from the bed, grabbing my pajama bottoms to slide on. The frame creaked behind me as she obeyed. She was good at that. She listened to me, even when she didn't want to. Just like in the case of her slave friend. What she'd done had to prove something. She may have fought the bath, but she'd helped skin a slave because I'd told her to. This Bram thing, it would pass.

Water in the distance had my attention leaving the coffee pot. She had started the shower. Although there was a need to go and push her further, to wait for her to get out and oil her up so I could have my way with her, I ignored it. There was too much to do. And maybe I wasn't entirely in the mood to have her so unresponsive. She had passion when we'd been together. Angry passion. It had worked a magic I wasn't even aware of. I liked her fight. More than I thought I would.

I pressed the start button, then turned and headed back to the room. A slight sound from the closet had my eyes narrowing. I looked between the bathroom and back to the closet. Each step was quiet as I neared. When I peeked inside, Everleigh was shuffling through my clothes.

"What are you doing?"

She jumped, spinning to face me. "I…"

"I asked you a question. Are you looking for something?"

A blush crept up to her cheeks and she nodded. "I am. You said you had plans for us today. That it was going to be a good day. Since we've been back and you've taken the position of Main Master, there's an appearance you must uphold. I only wanted to assess your wardrobe so I could do my best to match you and look good by your side. Your ties…the colors are vast. I was thinking it wouldn't be hard for me to find something if you told me what it is you planned to wear."

"Match me?" I looked from her to the expensive suits lining my closet. Ones I never thought about wasting money on before. *Yes, she did try to please me*. "Well, I'll wear this one. Red tie. If I recall, you have a red dress. It's very modest yet fitting in stature. Wear that. We'll match."

She bit against her bottom lip, smiling for only a second before she leaned in, pushing to her tiptoes to kiss my cheek. "Thank you, husband." And like that, she was gone.

My eyebrows drew in and I glanced around the space, taking in all the shoes and clothes. There wasn't anything else she could have been looking for here. Clothes…? I had to get used to this. She may have been a slave, but she was still a woman. Still groomed to please in all ways.

I grabbed the suit, walking to place it on the bed. Humming left me even more conflicted, and I pushed the pajama bottoms down, heading in the direction of the bathroom. Everleigh was just stepping into the shower as I walked through the door. She paused, holding the door ajar as she raked her gaze over my body. It was full of lust, and with the look she threw me, all I could do was stand there like a fool.

“Are you coming?” At the lick of her lips, I was lost—heading in her direction without so much as a thought of the earlier anger.

CHAPTER 38

24690

"I don't care what you have to do as high leader, I need you with me more. There's no clue how far West will go if he snaps again. Smothering me with a pillow..." A growl left my lips as I glared at Eli. "There has to be a way to get the Masters to come around. To see me as something *more* than a slave."

"They won't. They once saw you as a Mistress, but West ruined with the way he treated you in the meeting room. They may use the term because of your marriage to their Main Master, but if he ended up dead, you'd be back in Slave Row, or worse. We both know that." Eli glanced across the large dining room on the first level. West was finishing up his conversation, laughing at something Master Leone was saying. Just the look on his face made it almost impossible to hold in my desperation to be rid of him.

"I have to figure something out. This can't continue." I spoke more to myself, but Eli nodded in my peripheral.

Breakfast in the downstairs restaurant was supposed to go better than it had. Slaves weren't allowed inside the doors of the

Master's private dining area, yet here I was, and still, I couldn't help but feel like an outcast. *Unworthy to be within these walls.* They didn't want me here. The disapproving glances, the sneers when they thought no one was looking…I was still a slave to them.

"I have to get back. West will wonder what's taking me so long. Stay close."

"When will we talk more about our plans?"

I paused, glancing over my shoulder, trying to ignore the dark shadows beginning to plague me. "First, find that driver. We'll go from there." I kept my head high, making sure to meet the eye of every Master who looked my way. It was a dangerous game, but one I wouldn't bend on.

"Husband." I threw him a smile as I took the arm he offered.

"Master Harper was just telling me about your little playdate with Master Kunken. I hear you helped him skin his niece. Surely that can't be true."

My stomach rolled, and I fought the lightheadedness. Anger was my only weapon and strength. I clung to it like an anchor, praying it didn't drown me by mistake. "It's true. I'm tougher than I look. Blood doesn't bother me. I'm not really sure much does anymore."

His eyebrows drew in as he held my gaze. "Big difference from the sobbing girl kneeling at her Master's feet."

"Watch it," West cut in.

"That sobbing *girl* had lessons to learn. She was taught them well. As you can see, the slave is gone. Who you're faced with now is your Master's *wife*." I smiled as West kissed my head.

"A big change, for sure." Master Leone nodded. "It was great having breakfast with the two of you. I look forward to the dinners when your wing is finished."

"A few more weeks," West assured. "We'll see you then."

He gave a nod to the Master, then turned us toward the door.

The smile he sported was long gone and his change made me nervous as I let him lead me. The moment we were out of the doors, it wasn't long before footsteps began to follow us. I knew it was Eli and the other two guards who were a constant presence. They weren't to leave my husband's side. It was a plus for me, concerning Eli, but he and I still had trouble speaking over our plan for the children. If Eli was near, so was West.

"I wish I would have thought about making you my wife before I put you in the place of a slave. Nothing that can't be erased over time, though. You did well standing up to him. Assertive without insult."

"Thank you. I want them to view me as your wife. I'm trying very hard to change their minds."

He glanced down. "We'll work on it. Just keep it up. Don't let them talk down to you. If they do, tell me. I'll take care of it."

"Thank you."

Although I wanted to smile at the calculation my mind conjured, I stared ahead. There was no point in doing anything rash. Time was my friend concerning West and the Masters. Only question was, could I last long enough? West was two different people. If he didn't end up killing me, I feared what I was capable of if pushed far enough. I could ruin everything.

"Where to now, husband?"

"The wing, of course. I want to check on the progress of the cleaning and redecoration. I was impressed with the notes you gave—"

Yelling broke out around us, echoing from the walls as it blasted from the guards' radios.

"We have a situation down here in room five-twenty-nine! All available guards. I repeat, all available guards please report."

"What the hell is going on?" West stepped us in closer as he looked to his high leader. Eli's radio went off before he had a chance to say anything.

"High Leader, come in."

"Talk to me."

The guard was breathless as a loud scream broke through. "Sir, he's fucking lost it. The Master, sir. Fuck-ing shit. You have to see this. I think we're going to have to take him down."

"Take down a Master? Is he serious?" West's voice boomed from next to me. He was running and dragging me behind before he got a response. The speed at which he went, I knew I couldn't keep up. Not like this. I ripped my hand free, kicking off the stilettos before he could yell at me like he was going to. His mouth opened, and I sprinted back toward him, grabbing his hand as he led us even faster through the halls.

Yells came back over the radio. I sucked in air as we sped down the stairs and headed to the first floor. The maze continued, but it wasn't long before I heard the guards shouting.

"Put it down! We don't want to have to hurt you!"

A female's screams grew as West dragged me closer. Some of the guards outside the doors lowered their guns at our approach, but they didn't appear to want to. Their weapons stayed trained toward the entrance, their eyes nervously darting between us and whoever was inside.

"What the hell is going on here?"

They parted as West stomped toward the door. The moment my mind could grasp what I was seeing, I couldn't help but squeeze against West's palm. The once white carpet was almost entirely saturated in blood. The bodies of two men and a woman were spread throughout the space, mangled and decapitated. From their clothing, I knew at least one of them was a Master. He wasn't wearing a suit, but from the large gold watch around the wrist, he had money. His large bicep was covered in tattoos and rested where his head would have been. The way his broken fingers were protruding out in odd directions told me the decapitation probably came long after the torture.

"Put down the machete, Master Gilpner, and no one is going

to hurt you." West let go of my hand, stepping more into the room, and I felt myself follow. I couldn't stop looking at the scene. Looking at the woman's dismembered head. Her face was all but mush. Where her nose once sat was now flattened and unrecognizable. Swollenness and dark bruising encircled eyes peppered with broken blood vessels. I wasn't sure on her ethnicity. There was so much bruising. So many lacerations on her face, the blood smeared across it made it hard to tell. But still, she stared right at me from behind drooping lids. All I could see was me staring at myself. That could have been me. *That could be me.*

"What Master Max did was wrong. He shouldn't have had his slave embarrass you the way she did. I understand that. But what's done is done. You've gotten your revenge. You don't have to make this harder than it is. Put down the machete and let's go for a walk to cool off."

The hand that held the large knife rose, but the man didn't speak. He didn't even seem like he was in the room with us while he paced and grunted.

"Master Gilpner. Put down the machete. Let's go."

West took another step forward, but I barely noticed as movement darted in my peripheral. I narrowed my eyes, staring between the bedroom door and kitchen. *Had that been real this time?* My mind was suddenly spinning. I wasn't sure.

"Put…it down," West said, his voice angrier.

"Mistress, you need to step back." Eli's voice registered, but the moment I went to face him, a whimper stopped me. My head jerked back to the area between the two rooms, and I inched further into the living room to try to see.

"There's…someone." I paused, glancing at West, then Eli. They both had their attention on the Master. He was watching me, pointing the large blade in my direction. And he was moving, circling the room wide, trying to make his way around West.

"You see no one," he said slowly. "*You see no one.*"

"That's right. She doesn't see a thing. Put the weapon down. Let's go on that walk." West moved more in my direction, and the guards quickly surrounded him on the far side of the living room. Their guns were still drawn as they waited. Cold metal from the door connected with my arm and Eli stayed by my side at the entrance.

More whimpering, turning into light sobbing. The Master blinked rapidly, growing more agitated as it continued to get louder.

"He made a fool of me. Do you know who I am?"

"Yes, Master Gilpner," West assured. "You're a very important man. He deserved what you did. You're not in trouble. Put down the weapon. I'd hate for one of my men to have to shoot you because of something you might do in the heat of the moment."

"No one will ever look at me the same here again. They laugh at me now! They laugh!"

"They won't be anymore. You showed them. You shut them up with what you did. Now, put down the *fucking* machete."

West's irritation grew with each response, but I was confused by his words. Was he really going to let this Master off? Allow him to get away with the murder of another Master and slave? That wasn't the law. Bram wouldn't have done that.

I craned my neck to the side, trying to peer more into the open kitchen area. With the way the cabinets were, they were hiding whoever was crouched down behind them. What scared me even more was the cries didn't sound like a woman, or even a man. They were younger. Not childlike, but not adult either.

"There's someone back there. Do you hear them?" Eli glanced over at my whisper, nodding. "Well, the man is getting closer. He's got a big knife. What if…?" West glanced over his shoulder at me, glaring. I knew he couldn't hear what I was saying, but he didn't want me talking either.

"I think it's a kid," I mouthed.

"We're running out of time, Master Gilpner. Come with me. I'll have this mess cleaned up before we return, and we'll pretend this never happened."

"I don't want to leave. I'm not leaving!"

West's jaw tightened as his lids lowered with rage. "Then you'll allow me to have this mess cleaned up. Without that," he growled, pointing at the machete. "I need Master Max's body. Do you know what I'm going to have to do to cover up his death? He's a fucking celebrity! Do you think his disappearance isn't going to make headlines? Do you know how much money you're going to be paying to make up for this? Your humiliation and revenge just cost you. Don't let this happen again. That's your warning. Do whatever the fuck you want with your slave, but you touch another Master, and you won't be leaving Whitlock alive."

West spun, heading for the door, when a girl darted around the corner. I couldn't think, couldn't process what I was seeing as my mind tried to grasp the sight. She didn't have hair, and her face was so drawn in, she looked like a skeleton. Even her arms and legs were like bones. It all registered, even her young age, but nothing affected me more than the look on her face. I knew that fear. I had lived that fear in my first years here. She was more than terrified. And she was past the point of desperation.

Arms locked around West's waist, and his whole body jolted in surprise. He hadn't seen her coming.

"P-Please, Master. Please."

"Jesus! Fucking…" West pried the arms from around his waist, but they glued themselves around his legs as the slave hugged him for dear life. The man was already coming forward, murder in his eyes. He was going to take her back, and West would give the girl to him. I knew that like I knew I needed air to breathe. I didn't think. I grabbed Eli's gun and pointed it at the man. To hesitate would have been useless. It wouldn't have gotten me anywhere. My finger snapped back once. Twice. And I couldn't stop.

Bam! Bam! Bam! Bam! Bam! Bam!

Weight crashed into my side hard, but I only saw one thing: blood…a dead corpse falling to the ground.

CHAPTER 39

WEST

"You have got to be kidding me!"

My voice roared through the room as I stared at my wife holding the gun. Everything kept happening so damn fast. I couldn't focus for a second. First, the starved girl clinging to me. Then, the shots. My mind was a spinning mess of clusterfuck.

"Did you not just hear me tell him what a fucking mess I was going to have over Master Max? Then you decide to bring on more by killing another Master? Wife!"

Eli jerked the gun from her hand, easing from where he had her pinned to the door. Had I been able to remove the girl from my legs, I would have throttled Everleigh. As it were, the damn child was stronger than she looked. She latched like cement around me.

"Get off!"

"Please, come here. Don't be afraid. I'll help you."

The soft coo of my wife's voice grated my ears. Any other time, it wouldn't have bothered me, but now…now I had two dead Masters and a room full of witnesses.

Pressure and weight disappeared as the girl let go and rushed to Everleigh's waiting arms.

"I know you're very angry with me for what I did. I know I deserve to be punished. But I beg you, allow me to take her to Medical first. She's not well. I know the role of slaves here, but this…" Everleigh held the girl tighter, cradling the slave's head in her chest and almost appearing to cover the girl's ears with her hand. "Husband, I beg your mercy. Not for me, but for her. She's just a child. Barely a teenager, if that. She shouldn't even be here."

"This has been her life since she was old enough to walk," I yelled. "This was all she knew, and you took it from her. I can't sell her. Look at her!" I shook my head at the disgust festering in me. "This is what's going to happen, *wife*. You are going to let go of that slave, she is going to the White Room for a peaceful death, and you will be lashed five times for inflicting death on a Master."

"W-What?"

Her voice cracked, but I wouldn't look at her through the rage I felt. "Eli, take her to the apartment. You," I said, pointing to another guard, "take that one to the White Room and put it out of its misery."

"No. No!" Everleigh thrashed in Eli's arms as he tried to pry her away from the little girl. Both began screaming, infuriating me even more. "I beg you! Send *me* to the White Room. Send me! Don't hurt her, please! Please!"

"Get them out of here! And someone call for clean-up. Both Masters' bodies go to holding. Burn the dead slave."

Farther away the screams sounded, and with the distance, came a calming. Even an enjoyment. My wife would be upset after the lashing. *After what I'd done.* She'd need to calm. I knew how to calm her. And when I oiled her up, she'd break a little more. But come morning, she would see. She'd know not to cross me. The consequences of what she had done would be a lesson. One her little slave mind would detect. And there, she'd learn.

A sigh left my mouth as I turned, taking in the butchery and death around me. What a fucking mess. Some people couldn't take humiliation. I should have known Master Gilpner would have wanted revenge. Appearances were everything here. More so than the outside world. Here, no one had to hide who they were. There were no restraints. No consequences. That had to change. This was a lesson for me too.

Two guards shifted off to the side, waiting for clean-up to arrive. I shook my head, heading past them. *Everleigh*. Damn woman was so unreadable. So unstable in her passion for the youth. Enough to have shot a Master. It blew my mind, but should it have? She helped skin her only friend alive. What was pulling a trigger? Maybe it wasn't the significance of her actions, but to whom. I kept putting her in the role of a slave, but the more violence she seemed to experience, the less obedient she was becoming.

I headed down the hall, taking in the mass of bloody boot prints tracked along the white floors. The farther I got, the more they lightened. I liked the color. The more white I saw from these halls, the angrier it made me. All my life here, I'd had to endure the white maze leading me through this stone fortress. I would have them paint the walls. I'd do away with the white once and for all. Whitlock would become mine in every sense of the word.

I took the stairs two at a time, quickening my pace as I got closer to my room. The evil in me churned, brewing deep, heating my stomach and warping my thoughts until I was pushing through my door. Eli stood over Everleigh's sitting frame. She was perched on the edge of the sofa, glaring at him. When her head snapped to me, she held no more tears. No more sadness over the slave girl she'd offered to trade places with.

"You think you can go around killing off Masters? You think you can show me up in front of my guards?"

She jumped to her feet, barely staying balanced before my hand gripped around her throat. I held firmly, but I didn't squeeze, no matter how much I wanted to.

"My weakness won again. I apologize, husband. I deserve my punishment. You were right to end her life. She's better off that way. She deserves peace."

I paused, feeling my anger ignite in the lack of fight she was giving me.

"What you did cannot be so easily erased in my mind. Or theirs! They follow my lead. I give the orders. I kill people if it has to be done. Not you. Never you! You are meant to be by my side—strong, obedient. You don't overstep me," I yelled in her face, squeezing my hand tighter.

"You're right." Tears rolled down her cheeks, and she reached up with both hands to clutch around my wrist. "I don't know what's happening to me. I try to be who you want. Who you need. But she…the slave keeps coming back. Punish me. Show me who I'm to be."

Her head turned and lowered. At my loosened grip, she kissed my fingers, sobbing worse as she held my hand. The action, her pleas…they fucked with my head even more, softening the sadist in me. Making him want to punish her, but not to the point of breaking her like I dreamed.

"Take off your clothes and stand at the foot of the bed. Place your hands on the mattress and keep your head down. Don't you dare look up or move. I'll be in there shortly."

Wetness slid over my fingertips as Everleigh snuggled her face into my hand. The action only lasted seconds before she pulled back and left me alone with Eli. The moment the door shut, I cut my gaze over to him.

"How the hell did she get your gun away from you? Her?

She's a woman, barely over five feet tall, who can't weigh more than a sack of fucking potatoes."

"She took me by surprise. I was watching the damn Master, who, by the way, kept getting closer to you. How was I to know he wasn't going to attack you?"

"It would have been hard to protect me without your damn gun! Ridiculous. My wife shoots a Master against my orders and shows up my high leader by disarming him. Maybe I should give the fucking title of Master over to her. She seems to be wearing the pants around here."

Eli shrugged, leaning against the wall. "It might be interesting to see the roles reversed. How do you think she'd do?"

"Not funny. You think things are bad now. If she were suddenly placed in my role, Whitlock would go to shit faster than you could blink. There'd be no order. No one would listen to her."

"Women have ruled kingdoms before. If she took control, the guards would follow her." He paused, cutting his stare up. "I would."

"You'd follow her over me?" I stepped closer, closing the distance between us.

"You said if she ruled here. You said nothing about your role. I'm just saying, if she got the position, I'd serve her."

"Watch it, Eli. You're treading in very deep water right now without any idea what's lurking below. If you turn your back on me, if you so much as look at her the wrong way, I'll gouge out your eyes and make you eat them. What comes after that, you couldn't even imagine."

He smiled, pushing from the wall. Our faces were so close, seeing anything but his eyes was almost impossible.

"I once told you not to forget your friends. *I am your friend,* West. But don't you dare threaten me again. You forget the bait that treads the water is usually the hook that kills the prey. Remember that."

Weight hit my shoulder as Eli stepped around me and headed for the bedroom.

"What the hell do you think you're doing?"

"You threatened her in front of my guards. You said she's owed five lashings. That offense isn't between a husband and a wife, but between the high leader and the person, you, as Main Master, punished. If you want to keep things running smoothly, you'll go by the laws we're all sworn to protect. Unless you plan to change those too?" Reaching up to his radio, he called in two names. Before I could so much as argue, the door opened and the men came marching in. Eli opened the door, pausing as he turned to the men. "Stay." His attention went back inside. "Panties on, Mrs. Harper."

He pulled the door shut, but I wasn't having it. I walked forward, slamming my hand into the barrier. The crash against the wall had Everleigh jumping, but she didn't move as I continued to the closet, grabbing the flogger from the top.

"If the high leader wishes to give you an extra five, so be it. These are from your husband."

Everleigh held the panties in her fist and spun back to the bed, gripping the comforter tightly. I jerked to a stop, my hand already reared back. The leather strands slid against each other, and I struck forward with a force I knew was enough to break her skin.

Whack! Whack! Whack!

"Who do you take orders from!"

Nails clawed into the cover as she fought to catch her breath. When she inhaled, it was so deep and broken by sobs, it stirred all parts of me. Blood poured from her lacerated skin, running in streams down her back as her legs fought not to give out.

"Answer me!"

"You, husband. I t-take o-orders from you."

"That's fucking right. You better remember that."

Whack! Whack! Whack! I paused, rearing back and hitting

her across the ass to make seven. When I turned to face Eli, the rage on his face gave me even more pleasure.

"High Leader. Your turn." I bowed my head just the slightest amount as I offered the flogger. Everleigh tried to push to stand straight again but collapsed to the floor as her body shook with heavy cries. She kept jerking through the pain shooting through at her movements.

Eli walked forward, lowering to crouch beside her. "Shhh. We're finished here. Stand and thank your husband for the punishment." He eased her to her feet while she tried to stay steady. When he let go, she turned, throwing herself forward and falling into my arms.

"I'm s-sorry. I'm…so…s-sorry."

I smiled, raising my eyebrow to Eli. "You are forgiven, wife. You know better than to let it happen again." I brought my palm up to rest on the back of her neck while I held the other at her lower back for stability. The warm wetness left me hard. There was nothing I could do to stop my arousal. "Leave," I ground out to Eli. "I do believe my wife is in need of a relaxing bath. Aren't you, love?"

The crying turned heart breaking at her slow nods. "Yes."

Hatred met me as Eli narrowed his eyes and stepped back. I knew the look. I'd done it so often with Bram, the extent of the rage he held for me couldn't be mistaken.

CHAPTER 40

24690

"You are so beautiful." Fingers trailed over my healing back, caressing the wounds I knew would scar. My eyes blinked slowly. It was becoming routine to wake up this way. Every morning for almost a week, I'd heard the same thing. Heard the same wooing tone of his voice as he kissed around and over his marks. "Lay with me, wife. Hold me."

West was already rolling me to face him—pulling me into his arms as he kissed my forehead, nose, then lips. My hand settled on his bare side, sliding to dangle behind him so I wasn't necessarily having to put intimacy into my action. I was sick with hate. Sick with having to pretend I wasn't confused by what was happening to me from his affection. Maybe I was just getting ill in general.

"What would you like to do today? Whatever you want."

My eyes rose at his loving behavior. It had been this way since he'd given me the lashes. Since I'd given in and let him use the oil on me afterward. Limp and semi-unconscious, he had placed me on my stomach and had sex with my marred body. And for three nights, I had let it continue without a fight. Then, it stopped. Maybe he'd gotten his fill of the oil and decided he liked my responsiveness more. Or maybe it was losing its excitement. I didn't want to know. I was past the point of caring how he used me. To fight would have just been punishing myself. But was it really punishing anymore?

"You've been very good," he continued. "You name it, and we'll do it. Or maybe you'd like me to buy you something? How about jewelry? Or new clothes and shoes?"

I shook my head, staying quiet. Let him think I was sad or upset. That seemed to make him caring toward me for some odd reason. Not that I wanted him so nice. It was messing with me. Ruining me.

"You have too many clothes, anyway. How about…" He paused, getting quiet while he stroked his finger down the back of my shoulder. "How about a picnic and some ice cream later?"

"In City Center? With all the rape and torture going on down there?"

His brow drew in at my words. "You're right. That won't work."

"Just hold me," I breathed out. "I don't want anything. I don't feel so well."

Silence stretched while I stayed tucked away in the safe place inside my head. I could almost believe I was in Bram's arms. That he was holding me and this was just a dream. *Bram…* "Popcorn."

"What's that?"

West pulled back to look at me as I blinked through the memory that had suddenly swept through. "I want some popcorn. I love popcorn. Can I have some?"

"This early?"

"Is it okay?"

He paused, but laughed, pulling me back in. "Of course. I'll get up and make coffee. Eli can go pick some up."

"Thank you." Maybe it was a small fuck you to West—to

myself for feeling like I was betraying Bram with the unwanted emotions. But I had to have it.

I kissed West's chest, staying in my wifely role. When he pulled back the covers to stand and leave the room, I eased from the bed and dropped to the ground to look underneath. I'd searched endlessly for Bram's black book and I couldn't find it anywhere. West came close to catching me once, and I blamed it on the matching outfits, but I wouldn't let this go. I had to find where he hid it. I had to see what Lyle felt was so important for me to read. It ate at me. Every minute. Every day. It was driving me crazy…or perhaps I had already lost it. I couldn't think about that. I wouldn't.

I squinted through the dimness, wanting to scream as I was met with nothing. Lightheadedness hit, and I held the bed as I stood. The book couldn't be in the apartment. There was no way. Where in the hell was he keeping it?

Over and over, the question repeated in my mind as I went through my morning routine. By the time I managed to dress, I could barely think at all. The fog was getting worse.

"For my wife."

West held out a bag and the smell and memories drew me in. I took two steps when the smile melted from his face. He brought the bag back into his chest and reached in, grabbing a handful. My pulse spiked, nearly making me drop from the adrenaline. Had I told him about the popcorn with Bram? No. I had to stop worrying. He didn't know.

"Come here."

Fear and guilt begged me to run. To cower and brace myself for a beating or rape like I'd never experienced. My desperation for the smallest part of Bram, for reigniting the devotion to only him, sent me forward.

"Open your mouth."

My fists clenched as I waited for him to slam my mouth full of popcorn. To make me choke to death on it for once again putting Bram before him. But was I anymore? The fact that I felt uncomfortable for this weird attraction told me something wasn't right. The lashing hadn't just scarred my body. With the tearing of my skin, West had somehow imprinted himself deep inside me. Where I should have detested him more, something wasn't allowing me to. My fear? My slave? I didn't know.

My hold to Bram's love led me forward. I was ready to take the abuse for my loyalty and prepared myself. Instead of anger, West reached back in and pulled out a single piece. I didn't dare close my eyes until the taste registered on my tongue. My lips eased over the tips of West's fingers and flashes blinded me. Flashes of hunger and fascination. Of Bram.

"That's good," I said, savoring the taste and memories.

"Perfect. Take another."

And I did. Despite my lack of appetite, I let him feed me. Minutes went by, West and Bram twisting in my mind. They merged as one, stroking down my face between bites. Smiling down at me. It was so real, when West spoke, Bram didn't disappear right away. It was *his* voice I heard. *His* eyes that suddenly burned into me, screaming of anger and betrayal. It made me blink hard and jump back.

"Are you okay?"

My hand shot up to my head, and I grabbed West's forearm while the room seemed to tilt.

"Yes. I'm just dizzy."

"Dizzy? Come. Sit on the bed."

Each step sent my heart racing faster. The floor seemed to move beneath my feet and a cry left my mouth as ringing pierced my ears. I knew West was talking, but it was so far away. So distant. Even as I tried to focus, I knew I wasn't in the room anymore. I was gone. Disappearing.

Pressure tapped against my cheek, and West was suddenly inches away. "Everleigh, wake up. Come on. Open your eyes.

Fuck," he growled, pulling me into his arms. "Something's not right."

Tears slipped free, and my arms locked around my enemy's neck. Fear had me grasping to the one person I should have avoided at all costs. Yet, I couldn't.

"I'm scared. I…" The room blurred, and the next thing I knew, white was all I saw. White ceiling, white walls. And…" I blinked heavily, taking in Eli's worried expression not inches behind West. We were still walking, and I was wet—soaking wet and shaking. "What's happening?"

"Shhh. I'm taking you to Medical." West pulled me in closer, but I wiggled in his arms. I knew what would be coming from my suddenly caring husband if I didn't fight this.

"Let me walk. I am not weak."

"Don't be ridiculous."

"Please. I want to walk."

Something flashed in his eyes as he slowed. Without saying a word, he came to a stop and lowered me to the ground. My legs were wobbly as I tried to fight whatever was happening. Sickness, some sort of weird insanity episode? Both? I wasn't sure, but I would not go down like this. I would not be the slave he and everyone else thought I was.

My body trembled, and an odd spasm had me twitching. I clung around West's waist as he wrapped me in close and helped me walk. The halls seemed to stretch on forever as I tried to stay awake and moving. As we branched off to turn onto a new one, pressure on my back had me glancing behind us. At the very end of the hall stood the one person who seemed to trigger my episode. *Bram.* He was gone so fast, I wasn't sure I'd seen him at all. He moved just like the shadows. There and gone.

Had he been angry at me? Had he been glaring like before?

"Whoa. Whoa. Okay, you're done." West barely caught me as I hit the floor. My mouth was open and all I could do was take deep breaths as I reached out to an empty hall. It had been so real. It had been him. But it hadn't. Just like he hadn't been West in the room.

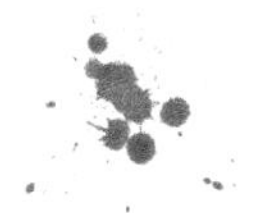

"We've been in here for over three hours. Rest. That's what you're suggesting? Do you not see my wife!"

The doctor shifted uncomfortably as he looked between me and West. "Master Harper, you declined my suggestion of medication. I believe your wife is experiencing Post Traumatic Stress Disorder. If she isn't put on something, these episodes could continue. *Will* probably continue. Since there's not a therapist in Whitlock, which I would have also suggested, rest is the best thing I can come up with. Low stress. She needs to be kept out of situations that may trigger her anxiety, although…you said she was eating when this happened." He paused, his brow creasing as he seemed lost on what else to say.

"She doesn't need medication because this is not PTSD. For one, her mind is stronger than that. For two, she's fucking sick. Look at her! What about poison? Did you check her for fucking poison?"

"We ran the blood work. We did a CT scan. We've done every test in the book. Everything came back as normal. I'm sorry, Master Harper. Perhaps you'd like another opinion?"

"What I would like is for you to get the hell out of this room and recheck your fucking results."

The doctor didn't hesitate to rush through the door. The moment he was gone, West closed his eyes, running his fingers through his hair. I couldn't stop shaking as I held the cover up to my neck. I was so cold. So sleepy. So nauseous. My mind kept going over Bram. I knew he couldn't have been there, but I wanted him to be, despite seeming mad. I wanted to escape the black hole sucking me down—*West.* Even now, there was an odd sense that I needed his presence close.

"I'm sorry for being weak. I don't know what's wrong with me."

Before he could reply, the door reopened. The doctor hesitantly walked over to the bed, studying me as he pulled out a digital thermometer and placed it in my ear. With the click, he pulled it back just as fast.

"Forgive me. I…it appears I missed some of the results that weren't in yet. The strand is surprising, but—"

"What is it?" West growled.

"The flu, Master. It looks like she's getting the flu. That's the only test that came back positive. It was just setting in, so her fever hadn't even kicked in when you arrived. I'm sorry, but I also stand by what I said before. She's not just ill with a virus, she clearly has symptoms of Post Traumatic—"

"One more word about that and I swear you'll never speak again. Tell me how to make her better."

"It'll have to run its course. I suggest lots of fluids and—"

"Let me guess, rest?" West shook his head, walking to the bed. "We're leaving. If she gets worse, we'll be back. I suggest you not be the doctor on call if that happens."

He scooped me into his arms, covering me with the sheet as he headed for the door. The vertigo of the fast movement had my eyes nearly rolling as he swept us through. Nurses buzzed around the station toward the back in their blue uniforms and my head swayed as we passed a patient's room. Color blurred on the glass window and my hand shot to West's chest as Bram's figure flashed in the reflection. I tried to turn my head to look behind us, but when I managed to finally see over West's shoulder, he wasn't there.

“Hang on, baby. We’re going home. Everything’s going to be okay.”

I buried my face in his chest, trying to push away what I knew was becoming true. Flu or not, my mind was broken. What I had seen, what had been done to me, and what I had done somehow made a permanent stain on my mind. And the horrors weren’t over. They’d never end…

CHAPTER 41

WEST

"No. No…West?"

My eyes opened as I rolled over and turned on the lamp. I hadn't been sleeping well, if at all. Hell, I hadn't slept good in days. With Everleigh's flu came nightmares almost all throughout the night and day. Normally, I would have been pissed at the lack of sleep, but I couldn't ignore the one thing that set my mind at ease: it was always me she called. Not Bram. *Me.* And that meant she was becoming mine, just like I had wanted.

"Shhh. It's okay, baby. I'm here."

I brushed back her dampened hair, pausing as she jumped at my touch. Almost immediately, her eyes flew open. There was hesitation before she launched herself into my arms. Sobs tore from her mouth as her nails pushed into my back. And she held so tightly. I knew she didn't want to, but she couldn't fight what she was beginning to feel.

"I was so a-afraid."

"Of what? Do you remember what this one was about?" I continued to stroke her hair as I pulled back enough to look into her face—a face that was quickly becoming more dear to me.

More…there weren't words, just emotions. When I looked at Everleigh, it was like my mind blanked out and all I wanted to do was continue to stare. I fed off the racing of my heart. Off how she managed to make my mind stop focusing on everything but her. How something so insignificant could be so vital didn't make sense. *Love—violent, beautiful, corrupt love.*

"He's trying to take me away from you. I don't know who he is. It's so dark, but he's dragging me deeper into the darkness, jerking and pulling at me. His voice…he's whispering threats. He wants to hurt me," she sobbed, letting her forehead fall back into my chest.

"No one will ever take you away. Look at me." I angled her head back. Her skin was still paler than normal, but I could tell she was feeling better than the previous night. The brightness of her blue eyes had me pausing before I could even think to continue. "No one is going to take you away from me. I don't care who they are. If anyone even *thinks* it, they're dead. Do you understand me?"

"I don't want to leave here. Leave…you. I've seen this before. The morning my old Master died. *And then he died.* I'm scared. He's going to take me. I know he is."

"No. Shhh. You're safe with me."

Worry, something I rarely felt, prickled my insides as I pulled her close and scanned the room. I didn't believe what she was saying. It was the sickness. But I couldn't push away my own fear of someone truly trying to take her away. I may have treated her badly at times, but she was still mine. She had a part of me, whether I wanted to admit how big that part was or not.

"I'm going put your mind at ease. You can wear it at all times, and if for some reason I'm not with you, you will be able to defend yourself."

"You're going to give me a weapon?"

"Yes. I'm going to put my trust in you. I think it's time. Prove to me I'm not making a mistake. But a warning…if you *ever* pull it out on me, so help me, it'll be the last thing you ever do."

An arm wrapped tightly around my ribs and I lowered from my elbow, sliding her up so I could lay to face her. For minutes we stared, not saying anything. Not needing to. Tonight, the tides were turning even more. I knew my evil wasn't even close to being gone. Hell, even now, I would have loved nothing more than to fuck her ass bloody, but these new emotions were pushing the urge back.

At least for now.

"You've been so kind to me over the last few days. Now this? Thank you. I know it can't be easy for you. I couldn't even get out of bed, but you fed me, showered me. You haven't left my side once. And you're putting trust me in—something I didn't expect would ever happen."

"*You're my wife*. I told you when I married you this would come. All I needed was for you to bend, to…grow stronger, and care for me. Everleigh…" I swallowed hard, going over the colliding emotions within. I didn't want to tell her too much. I was conflicted, but I couldn't lie either. "Despite what I've done, or what I do. I did it for a reason. I know who I am, and I also know what it will take for you to survive at my side. I want that. I want ..." I stopped, making myself look back into her eyes as I searched for the right thing to say. "We can make this work. I'm sure there will be times where you hate what I do to you. Hate *me*. It would be impossible for you not to. But if you were fierce, if you could push away your hate and try to overlook the bad parts, we could share something great."

Everleigh's eyes narrowed, and I could tell she was offended by something. "*I am fierce.* Have I not proven it? You've beat me, coddled me. Cut me, bandaged me. Enslaved me, loved me. Raped me, kissed me. The old me is dead, but I am more alive now than I have ever been. How much more do you need? *I am enough*. I can survive anything you throw at me. You say we can share something great. Are we not now?"

"You want great? Drop the mask and let's speak the truth. Unless you're too much of a coward." Rage sparked in her eyes, and I knew I had her. "I won't hit you. I won't take offense to anything you say. You have my word. But be honest with me, because I'm doing the same with you. I've cared for you now for days. I've been tender. I've shown you what I am capable of this way. And sick, you had no mask. You weren't well enough to pretend. Don't start now."

Pressure settled against my shoulder, and she rolled me to my back, straddling me. "I don't know what you mean."

"That's one. Don't make me get to three."

"I haven't been pretending. I—"

"Two."

A mass of emotions swept over her face, and the last was genuine: fury. "You want honesty? I don't think you can handle it."

"Try me. I gave you my word."

"You've broken it too."

My head tilted, but I nodded. "Okay, you have me there. But I promise you right now, you have nothing to fear. Give me honesty. Brutal, ugly honesty."

Deep breaths had Everleigh's chest rising and falling through her building anger. "I hate you for what you've done. *I hate you*," she hissed, lowering more onto my chest. "There are no words for how much I want to hurt you. I look at you, and I want to claw your face off. To beat you until I can't even recognize you anymore. *You make me sick*."

My smile was automatic. "And despite all of that, you're falling for me, and you can't stand it."

A fist slammed into my shoulder, and I gripped the back of her neck hard, bringing her even closer. The resistance was there, but so was something else. Fire—lust?

"Admit it. *You want me.* No matter what I've done. Regardless of your stupid love for Bram and your pleasure for popcorn. Oh yeah," I said at her widening eyes, "I know. I saw him go to you that night after the tour. I watched you both eat popcorn… and then you cut yourself and fucked him. His true colors knocked you on your ass. But then I brought you the popcorn you so sweetly asked for. I saw your expressions as you watched me feed you. I snuffed that memory out like water to fire. You didn't see just him anymore, you saw me. You're so confused at what you feel, the mask you've gotten so good at wearing is out of reach. Do you even know who you're trying to pretend to be anymore? Or maybe you've realized you're not pretending at all."

Everleigh jerked against my hold, but I didn't let her go.

"You've tried so hard to hate me, but these last few days have confused you. They've messed with me as well. We can't escape this pull, wife. You and I may battle this need to hurt each other but look at us now. Look at where you are," I said, locking my hand on her hip. "How much longer can you go on hating me before the emotion turns to something else? Something so strong, even my worst behavior can't affect it?"

"You think I can love a man who does the things you do?"

My thumb pushed into her lower stomach, moving in circles while I watched her reaction. "I don't think you're going to have a choice. The mind can't ignore what the heart desires. You want freedom. You want power. Control. I'm the closest thing you can get to that. I may put you through hell, but the heaven you long for is already yours. What's blood, scars, and witnessing death if you're already where you want to be?"

"You forgot revenge. Power, control, and freedom don't erase the cruelty you continue to display. It doesn't make the hate I feel for you lessen."

"Ah, revenge," I said, smiling. "Are you not getting your revenge by making me fall in love with you? You're destroying the monster you hate, piece by piece. You have to get solace in that."

Nails pushed into my chest as she gripped against me. "I'd much prefer to make you bleed."

Rage didn't come. Only a perverse arousal I couldn't ignore. "Is that what you need? To hurt me for hurting you? If that's the case, I will give you a gift that will make your heart soar. Let it be proof of my…*affection* for you. One free pass to release the anger for good. To bloody me as much as you wish, without killing me. But with this gift, comes a price. You must throw away the mask and accept these feelings. Submit to them. Let's see what happens."

"I never said I had feelings for you."

"You didn't have to. I see it. I *feel* it. What are you wet for, my cock or the thought of hurting me?"

Deeper her nails sunk into my chest. "You won't beat me when I'm done? Or a week from now when you're over this generous mood you're in?"

"I gave my word," I said, letting go of her neck so she could sit up straight. "I will never use this against you. Fists only, though, wife. You change the rules and use those nails of yours, my word means nothing."

Whack! Whack! Whack!

There was no hesitation. Not so much as a warning as her fist slammed right into my mouth, repeatedly. I barely finished talking. The action happened so fast, I hadn't had time to prepare, more or less react to the blur of her coming at me.

"I hate you! I hate you!"

Whack! Whack! Whack! Whack!

Lights exploded in my vision as she connected with one eye, then the other. I gripped the mattress, tightening my jaw through the pain. Regardless of her size, she packed one hell of a punch. And she wasn't stopping. Blood filled my mouth, nearly choked me as it ran down my throat from my nose. My head turned to the side, but I let her continue, staying true to my word.

Whack! Whack! Whack...whack! Whack!

Deep breaths left her, and still, she kept trying to swing. I'd lost count of how many hits. They were so fast and hard. Everything blurred with the surprising pain she'd brought on.

"I...hate you. I..."

My head was turned to the side, and the slap cracked through my ears like an explosion. I tried blinking, noticing my left eye was already swelling shut.

"You've ruined me. You—"

"Are very surprised at my feisty little wife's temper. And power. Fuck." I spit blood across the sheet, not giving a shit. "Are you done?"

Crack!

The following slap had me nodding. "I take it you weren't. Best hurry, your time is running out."

Crack! Crack!

I flipped Everleigh over, pinning her beneath me. My vision blurred but came into focus after a few blinks. She was paler than before, and a sheen of sweat covered her hairline, but her wide, satisfied eyes that had me smiling.

"Do you love me now?"

"Never."

"Not even a little?"

"Never."

I laughed, burying my battered face into her neck. Pain shot through my lip and the stinging had me sucking against her skin harder. When my teeth tugged, she gave her shoulders a toss.

"Look at you still trying to fight it. Does it bother you so much to feel something for me?"

What sounded like a roar tore through the room while she thrashed wildly. Her hand shot up to my neck, and where I thought she was going to hit or choke me, she didn't. She held the side tight, pulling me down to crush my lips into hers. The pain was excruciating, and I felt every ounce as I thrust my tongue into her mouth. Blood and happiness. They went hand in hand with some of the best moments in my life. This one wasn't any different.

"I fucking knew it." I ripped her nightgown up, diving in to kiss her again while I tugged down my pajama pants. The moment hot wetness encircled my cock, I didn't slam into her like I needed. I let the torture carry on even more as I slowly inched inside her channel.

Blood was smeared on the side of Everleigh's face, covering her chin. It drove me even crazier. I couldn't stop my tongue from running over the curve of her jaw as I went back to give her mouth attention. She'd done this to me. She'd fucked me up so good, and it was worth it if it meant she'd drop this fake loving attitude toward me. I needed her anger. Her truth. Especially if I was going to be able to read her true motives. Just because I may have been falling in love with her didn't mean I trusted her. Not even close.

"Spread your legs wide for me, baby. Give yourself to me."

A gasp left her as I withdrew and plunged even deeper. Her legs lifted to my hips, and I buried myself, holding still while she clung to me.

"Admit it."

"No."

I let my length slide out halfway and held. The throbbing was excruciating. All I wanted to do was fuck her, but I couldn't. Not until she came clean.

"Admit it."

"There's nothing to admit."

My fingers wove through Everleigh's hair, pushing through to cradle and lift her head so I could make her face me. "Enough," I said softly. "Look at me. *At what I took for you.* Tell me."

Tears clouded her eyes, racing along her cheeks as her stare cut over to the side. "You've hurt me so much."

"And I'll hurt you again. That's a guarantee, but look at us right now. Look at how we've been since the lashing…God, doing that to you. I've never loved anything more."

Horror swept over her face, and I rolled my eyes. "It's because you gave it to me. I didn't have to threaten you. You knew what was coming, and you didn't back down. Even after the first three, you gave me more. You didn't try to escape or beg me to stop. You're mine, just as much as I'm yours. Think about how I treated you afterward. Did I not give you extra care? Did I not show you how much it meant to me by stopping the oil? I couldn't do it knowing how you truly felt. I shouldn't care, but I do. I think I lost myself to you, and maybe I'm a fool for telling you, but I know you feel something for me. Admit it."

"I feel…" she sniffled, "something."

One of my hands left her head while I moved it around to trace over the still welted lashes. "You'll always be mine now. This says so right here. These scars, you'll carry me with you forever. And I'll never forget it."

CHAPTER 42

24690

Eating was almost impossible. Sitting at the table with the Main Masters as West's wife was hard, but not like it should have been. It was the menu. It was what was not three feet from where I was sitting that made me fight the constant need to throw up. I could smell the meat. Practically taste it as the aroma seemed to stick deep within my lungs. *My sweet Julie.*

I swallowed back the bile, taking West's hand as he held his out for me. Cannibalism. West told me not to think about it, but I just wasn't sure how much longer I could last.

"Tell me more about how your face got all busted up."

I turned, seeing West smile. One of his eyes still had a dark ring around the bottom, but his lip had pretty much healed. He rubbed his thumb along mine as he spoke to Master Yahn. "Battle."

"Battling for what? Who?"

"Love."

Confusion drew in the Master's expressions, but he continued. "What are you saying? You battled your wife? Like, she beat you up?"

He smiled bigger, bringing my hand up to his lips. "Not like that. I allowed her to release her frustrations after I lashed her. You can say she didn't enjoy getting the scars as much as I did the beating. But that's okay. Hers on my face will fade. My marks never will. Everleigh is mine now, as much as she can ever be."

"Wrong," Master Kunken said, raising his fork.

"*Husband*." I moved in, keeping my voice low as I tried not to be sick all over myself. "May I please be excused? I know you all have business to discuss. I would hate to be in the way of that."

He nodded, bringing my hand closer. "What will you do?"

My eyes took in the elegance of our new dining room. The wing was like a castle. I hated being alone anywhere in this place. It was big and cast shadows I wasn't sure were there. Even now, my mind wasn't right.

"I planned to read, but…may I please have permission to visit the children? I'd like to read to them instead. Maybe put them to sleep. Their bedtime is soon." I looked over toward the door. "Eli can escort me to keep me safe if you'd prefer me not go alone."

"You never go anywhere alone. You want to go to The Cradle?"

I nodded, cautiously. "You know how much I liked being there. We talked about it last night. May I please go?"

Concern flashed within his depths, and he glanced up to Eli before coming back to me. "A bedtime story, and that's it. Don't be long."

"Thank you." I threw him a smile, then turned to look down the long table. "If you all will please excuse me, I'll be taking my leave. I'm sure there's business to discuss. Have a wonderful night, Masters."

"Husband," I said, standing and kissing West's cheek. "I will see you soon."

Fingers gripped my bicep as I went to leave. My eyes shot

back to his as he pulled me down. My pulse was racing as he continued to bring me in closer.

"I want a better kiss than that. That's how you kiss an old man or a child. I am neither."

My lips met his, and I closed my eyes, trying to keep the stiffness from my body. I had to keep telling myself West had believed me when I'd said I had feelings for him. I did, but not like he thought. For weeks, I put my plan into motion. From the manipulation to the nightmares. I couldn't afford to screw this up.

"I'll be back soon. I'll be waiting for you in the room when you finish." My teeth tugged against his lip, and West pulled me in one last time to press his lips into mine before releasing me. The moment I approached Eli and the door, the smile was long gone from my face.

"It's cold in the halls tonight. Maybe you should grab a sweater."

I didn't stop or say a word to Eli. I continued to walk until I reached the main door. It was swept open by my guard just before I could arrive. Eli was right at my side. I knew he was excited to help his sister and the children escape. I was as well. I just hoped everything worked out the way I had planned.

"Is it all ready to go?"

The door shut and Eli stayed even with me as we headed deeper into Whitlock. A chill crept up my spin and I held my arms. It was indeed cool. Winter was fast approaching, and I could feel it in my bones. The frigid chill hadn't left me since we returned. With the ice running through my veins, maybe it never would.

"Everything's ready," he confirmed. "The van is parked on the abandoned road, ready to transport the kids to random locations."

"Sheree?"

He swallowed hard, staring ahead. "Oklahoma City. I have

an aunt there. When her identity is placed, my aunt will be able to go to her. She'll be there for Sheree until my parents can arrive." He glanced over at me. "Thank you. Thank you for this. I owe you so much."

"Don't thank me until they're loaded up and leaving." I kept my voice low as we broke around a turn. "You're positive the cameras aren't working there?"

"No way. I made friends with the technician that was supposed to be installing them. He can't tie them into the main line until the password on Mr. Whitlock's computer gets broken. Whitlock is running blind until then."

"Not blind," I corrected. "Everything's still being recorded. We just can't get in to watch it."

"With Bram dead, we may never be able to."

My hands shoved into his side on instinct, knocking him into the wall. "Don't you ever say his name. *Ever.*"

Regret flashed on his face as he adjusted his shirt. "I'm sorry. Sometimes I forget about your love for Bram. You're so convincing lately with West. It's hard to tell it's a lie."

"A wise man once told me, you play the game here or the game plays you. There's no room amongst the Masters for slaves. You are either on the top, or you're not. I will not be a slave to these savages a moment longer."

"What about West? He's going to know you were involved. Even if I do hit you and you knock me out. He's going to know this was our doing. He's not stupid."

I stared ahead as we made our way down the last curved hall. The Cradle was ahead, and I was ready to break these children free. To put a new future in their path different from mine. If I could do that, they stood a chance, while my days here might very well end tonight.

"Leave West to me. I will convince him, and he will believe. If he doesn't, he may find himself not waking up come morning. That would have already been the case if I knew the Masters would have let me be free. I'm working on that. I will never be owned by another one of these devils again. At least this one I can somewhat control."

We slowed, and Eli's hand moved to the knife on his hip.

"I don't blame you. I hate this place. I don't know why you don't leave with the children. You should. You should escape and start over."

My head quickly shook. "We've talked about this. I belong here." Bram was here…or at least his memory. *His ghost.* I felt and *saw* him everywhere. "Let's get this over with."

"Yes, Mistress."

He threw me a grin, but I couldn't return it. I headed for the entrance with Eli following. A guard was outside the door and another was just inside. The children were scattered through the large main room. Some were reading, while others were watching a DVD playing in the corner.

"Mistress Harper." The guard smiled at me, and I beamed one back at him. Almost instantly, the sound of a grunt had him turning back to the door on alert. I didn't wait. Jerking up my knee-length dress, I pulled the knife from my thigh and plunged it into his chest. And I didn't stop stabbing. The guard wasn't good. He was one Eli suspected of molesting the children while he put them to bed. I couldn't let that go.

Weight hit the floor, and I slid the knife back in the holster, waving my hands at the children. "Come on. It's time to go home." For a few seconds, all they could do was stare in horror and shock. I rushed forward, hating that they had to witness this side of me. "Jessie, Renee, come on sweeties, we have to go. Your mommy and daddies are waiting."

As if reality dawned, the kids began rushing toward me. Eli raced for Sheree, a little blonde girl who was barely five. He placed her on his hip, helping me guide the children to the door. I held two of the little girls' hands, running as fast as their little feet would carry them. When the hall turned off the way we'd come, I took a right instead, weaving through the labyrinth I knew was empty of Masters.

"We have to hurry," Eli whispered loudly. "The guards have to check in every fifteen minutes. From the time, I figure we have less than ten."

I swept the smaller girl in my arms, clinging to the other as we increased our speed. Time seemed to drag on, yet I felt like we were flying. To stay out of view, I knew we were taking the longer way, but it was the only chance we stood at not being seen.

"Devon, pick Casey up. We have to go faster," Eli urged.

The hall came to a fork, and I took a quick glance to the right, jerking to a stop at the face that glared at me. A hand pushed hard into my back, and I held in the tears as I sprinted straight. *Bram.* Each time I got a glimpse of him, it got harder. Elevation began dropping. It wouldn't be long now.

"Wait. Wait. There will be a guard ahead." Eli had me pulling to a stop as we neared the last turn. He placed Sheree next to me and withdrew his knife as he crept forward. When he disappeared around the corner, my heart crashed into my throat. I looked behind me, half expecting to see those narrowed blue eyes projecting their hate—their love. Nothing.

Within moments, a voice echoed in the distance. Instinct had me pulling the kids in close as I waited. Their little breaths were ragged. They were just as afraid, if not more. Seconds passed, and my hands were shaking as I reached out and tried to touch each one to add comfort. Footsteps had me stiffen as I waited.

"Hurry." Eli appeared, waving us forward.

Blood covered his hands, but I pushed the sight away as we began moving again. He picked up Sheree, leading us through a door that cloaked us in darkness. Deep pants echoed and my fingers broke from Renee's palm, shooting up to block the blinding headlights not feet away.

"Thank God," I breathed out. "Hurry, let's get them loaded up as fast as we can."

The van door was already opening, and panic left me scooping up the first little girl in my arms as I raced over to stick her inside. One by one, Eli and I handed them over to a man. Nothing I did felt fast enough. I knew we had to hurry; I just feared any minute West would be barging through the doors after me.

"I'll see you soon, baby." Eli sniffled, hugging his sister tightly before he lifted her from in front of him. My stomach twisted into knots as I blinked passed the tears.

"Let them go," I whispered. "She'll never be safe if you don't. Hurry, we have to leave."

"Give Momma a kiss for me." He squeezed one last time, stepping back, and the door immediately slammed closed. Red lights flooded the area as the van switched gears, and I felt my pulse increase even more as it sped away. Darkness once again enveloped us, dying out as a glow emitted from Eli's phone.

"I can't believe we did it. Son of bitch, I can't fucking believe it."

"It's not over yet," I said, shaking my head. "Hit me. And do it hard."

There was no hesitation. No going easy. Lights flashed as the back of his hand connected against my cheek. Blood gushed from my nose as my body spun at the force.

"Fuck, I'm sorry. Are you okay? Can you walk? We have to try to get back fast enough for you to tie me up. We might have a five-minute window before they suspect something may have happened. They know it's bedtime."

Eli turned to lead at my nod, and all emotion drained from me. Just like it did on almost everything now. I grabbed my knife, taking three fast steps forward before plunging it into his back. *Once. Twice. Three times.* Just like with the man I loved, Eli fell to his knees, hitting hard.

"Your sister will never be safe if you're in the picture. They won't even know about the relation. I won't put her in danger because of you or anyone else. But this," I said, twisting the knife as he cried out in pain, "is from Bram and Lyle." I removed the knife, reaching around and slicing his neck. The hard thump reverberated through the room, and with it, the pitch-black sense of calm appeared. I retreated inside myself even more. I couldn't see, but I didn't care as I brought the knife up, dragging the blade slowly over my shoulder.

The halls, nothing focused as I let myself disappear into the void. Blood dripped from my fingers, and it didn't take long for lightheadedness to overtake me. I knew I'd sliced deep. Maybe deeper than I should have, but I was past the point of caring. I took my time, staying in a daze until I finally reached the main hall. I knew the van needed time to get away, but the guards would be aware soon, if they weren't already.

"Mistress Harper?"

I blinked heavily at my name, feeling my legs buckle as the guard approached and caught me.

"My husband. T-Take me to my h-husband."

"We have a situation at the main hall. All active guards head to the Harper Wing!" The guard shouted into his radio, swooping me in his arms as he took off in a sprint toward the far side of Whitlock. It didn't take but a few minutes for him to arrive. Guards were already outside the door and West pushed them out of the way, allowing room for me to be brought in. The worry on his face left me internally smiling as I was lowered to the floor.

"What the fuck happened?" he yelled, but no one knew. They stared amongst each other like lost little sheep, unaware they had all catered to the wolf. "Everleigh, baby, what happened? Where's Eli?" When I didn't answer, he got louder. "Where's Eli? He was supposed to be protecting you."

"Dead," I forced out. "I killed him."

"What?"

Pressure pushed against my arm, and I sobbed, letting my new manipulative personality take over. "He hit me and killed the guards. He took us."

"He what? *You're not making sense!*"

I took a ragged breath, breaking down even more. "I told you! I told you someone was going to take me. I woke up, and he was carrying me. The kids were so scared. Some man kept pushing them along. They took us to some dark place. A r-road. The man got the kids in and Eli tried to have them take me too, but I didn't want to go. I told him I didn't want to go, but he wouldn't listen to me. He kept saying I was safer away from here. I didn't think. I managed to get my knife and stabbed him in the back a few times. When we fell, the van took off. He tried to wrestle me for my knife, and that's when I got cut. Somehow, I broke away, but he c-caught my leg. I…I slit his throat," I sobbed.

"Son of bitch. *That motherfucker!*"

I let the sobs grow louder as he pulled me into his arms. Someone was applying even more pressure to my wound, but I barely felt it as my mind swallowed me even more. My body kept going through the motions, but I wasn't there. Not really.

"I have to get her to Medical. I want all men on this. Go down and find out what you can. Some of you hit the road and look for the van." He pulled back enough to gaze down at me. "What kind of van? Do you remember?"

I shook my head, letting confusion play out on my face. "I'm not sure. It all happened so fast, and I was over his shoulder. It was dark. I think it might have been black or blue? I don't know."

"It's okay," he said, lifting me. "You're safe now. I've got you. I won't let anyone take you away."

"You promise?"

He kissed my cheek, and I immediately lowered my head to rest in the crook of his neck. "You better believe it."

CHAPTER 43

WEST

Back and forth, I paced, getting angrier with every minute. How in the fuck had this happened? And the bigger question was, why the fuck had I put my trust in a man I was so uneasy about? I saw the way he had been overprotective of Everleigh. Especially when it came to the lashings. But hadn't I thought I put an end to that with showing him who owned her? I never expected him to try to break her free. Did he not think I'd know he was responsible? He was the high leader and her personal guard. With the children and my wife kidnapped, what made him think I wouldn't have killed him for letting them get taken in the first place? Even if he was innocent?

I glanced to Abbot, the new high leader, glaring before I took in the computer technician who had been trying to crack Bram's password since we'd been back. It was fucking impossible. He was the best, and he still couldn't get in.

"Tell me what the hell has to be done. Can we trash this system and put in a new one? Maybe tie the new one into the cameras already set up?"

The red-haired boy looked up from the screen, shaking his head. "If it were that easy, I would have suggested it weeks ago.

They're encrypted. Everything's encrypted. Without the password, everything is useless."

"God...dammit!"

"Sorry, I'm trying."

"Try. Harder. I'm not paying you a fucking fortune to type in random words. Use that brain of yours and all your fancy equipment and get to cracking. You," I said, turning to Abbot, "tell me you have something on who Eli was working with. Anything. Tell me something. It's been three fucking days."

"We're working on it, Main Master. I have people out right now trying to find out everything they can about the van. We have the files on all the children, and men are already staking out their homes."

"Jesus. I should have slaughtered the entire fucking Cradle when I had the chance. That, or had the auction earlier. Something. If one of those kids says *anything*..."

Abbott's head shook. "Won't happen. If the van is taking them home, we'll put a stop to it before they ever get within feet of the door. If it's law enforcement, we're tapped into scanners all over the place. One mention of a missing kid and we'll get in and take care of it. Even if we have to put a bullet in their head right there in the station. The identity of Whitlock won't get out."

"You better pray to God it doesn't. I'm heading back to check on my wife. She's terrified if I'm away from her for long. If she wakes up and doesn't find me there, she's going to be upset, then I'm going to be upset for making her upset. Then you're really not going to want to bring me any bad news."

"Yes, Master."

I barged out of Bram's door, walking right into Everleigh's panicked frame. Her good arm flailed, and I barely caught her before she collided with the wall.

"Jesus, what are you doing walking out here by yourself?

Did you learn nothing?" I ground out, hugging her into me tighter. "Are you hurt?"

"N-No. I couldn't find you. I got scared."

"So, you decided to come here? To Bram's?"

She paused, stepping back from my arms. "I was actually headed to the meeting room when one of the guards told me you were here."

"And the idiot didn't accompany you to make sure you made it to me safely?" I placed my hand on the middle of her back, leading her back toward our wing. "You'll show me which one it was so I can remind him why the fuck I keep him around."

"Please don't. I told him not to escort me. It's my fault. I didn't want him to get in trouble for leaving his post."

"To protect the Master's wife? Everleigh!"

At the sobs that burst from her, I couldn't help but clench my teeth. Today was not good. Not for the guards, or for her. I had to get her back to bed and try to avoid her as much as possible until this passed. If not…I knew what was going to happen. All my hard work I'd put into my wife would be for nothing. I'd tear it apart, just like I wanted to do to her. And God, did I crave it more than anything. I wanted to hear her screams. Her cries. I wanted her fear. Her fight as she tried to struggle away from me. Most of all, I wanted to be the one to physically induce a pain so great inside her, it sated the evil in me.

"I'm sorry. I…I don't want anyone around me. Only you. I don't trust anyone here."

"Not all the guards are like Eli. You have to trust them. They'll look out for you. That's one of the main things they're supposed to do. Speaking of which…"

I picked up my pace, letting the rage build and burn. The moment we rounded the turn, my eyes locked on the guard's. He took one look at me, then Everleigh. His mouth parted and he shifted as I approached.

"How did she get out?"

"I-I was only gone for a moment, Master. I promise. The restroom and right back."

"That's not the way it works! If you leave, you call in for someone to replace you until you're back."

The guard looked between us nervously. "There's no one else, Main Master. Everyone is either on patrol somewhere else or gone on the search."

Heat bubbled within me. All I wanted to do was choke the life from him. "I'll deal with you later." I threw the door open, pulling Everleigh through the large living area until we were back in the room.

"Will you be leaving me, again? *You're not going to leave me*."

"Only for a little while. I need to…" I pulled at my hair as sweat began to coat my skin. "I have to go."

"Well…if you have to…may I have my book then? The one you took when we returned. I think I'd like to read some of the poems if that's all right."

I stopped dead in my tracks, glaring over my shoulder. "Bram's book?"

"It's just poems."

I turned slowly, walking toward her. My anger knew no bounds as it surged through me like scorching lava. And she saw it. With each step I got closer, she pushed farther into her pillows. "Are you sure that's why you want it? Maybe you just miss him and want to take a trip down memory lane. Just like with your dreams. Like with the popcorn. Do you love him so much, you can't let him go!"

"I did love him, but—"

My slap to her face was automatic.

"But—"

Again, she tried to explain, and once more, I struck her. And I would have done more had I not wanted to injure her and put her healing time back even more.

"Save your excuses for someone who gives a shit. You want your stupid book, it's in my library. Let's see you go get it."

Her head shook, aware I wanted more of a fight.

"If you don't get up and go get that book right now, I'm going to go in there and burn it. How much does it mean to you? How badly do you want it?"

Everleigh threw the covers back and pushed from the bed. Not once through her light steps did she turn her back to me. She was ready to run. Ready for me to attack.

The door opened and the white nightgown she wore wisped around her ankles as she picked up the pace. The moment she made it through the living room and entered the hall, she spun, sprinting for my library door. And I was on her before she could make it through. My fingers wove in her hair, and I dragged her into the large room, not stopping until we reached the bookshelf behind my desk.

"Middle shelf, right in front of you. Take it. Pick it up."

"Don't do this, please."

"Do what? This?"

I spun her around, pushing the top of her body over the desk. Everleigh's legs went wild as she fought to turn over. I ripped up her nightgown, hearing the fabric tear in my haste to be inside her. This way. *My way.*

"Stop it! Stop!"

My hand lifted from her back, jerking the panties down. The screams that tore through the library had me moving faster, feeding my impatience.

"That stupid book was so important, you risked this? Risked us!"

I locked my arm around her throat, tearing at my belt. Within moments, I had my slacks undone and my cock out. I shoved my hand in her face, grinding my length against her ass as I put my palm over her mouth.

"Spit." A loud cry echoed while she shook her head. "Spit!"

"No! It's not too late. Stop this right now. Please. You don't have to do this."

I grabbed hair, bringing my other palm down hard on her ass. *Whack! Whack! Whack!* "Spit!"

Again, my hand went in front of her mouth.

"Fuck you! I'll kill you! I'll rip you to pieces if you do this."

A smile came to my face, and I spit in my own hand, securing her with my arm around her neck again while I stroked my cock. Still, she went crazy, kicking and trying to claw at me. I pulled her back toward me and pressed against the entrance of her ass. Slowly, I eased in, letting her fight help force my way through the tightness.

"Let's see if you make good on your threats. Let's see who rips the other apart first."

My bicep flexed, muffling her scream from the pressure while I thrust forward with everything I had. Her body jolted, going rigid through the agony she had to feel. With a single breath, her legs tried to draw up on the desk, knocking over papers as she fought for some sort of leverage. But I wouldn't give it to her in her desperate search for an escape. I kept her under my control as I eased out and basked in the warm wetness that made my thrusts easier.

"I do believe you're bleeding again, wife. Does it hurt horribly? Do you still love me? *God, I love you.* I swear I do."

Everleigh's arms were slowing as she reached for open space. With how high I had the top of her body, she had no room to grasp anything.

"K-ill you."

"Oh, here." I eased the grip on her neck. "You were saying?" The gag cut off her words before she could repeat them, but I didn't need to hear her threats. I let my thrust carry me home—carry me to the place where everything was perfect.

"God, you feel so good. I think it's been too long. We're

really going to have to do this more often. Do you want to know what I also miss?"

"You're going to be dead before I leave this room. I'm going to—"

I tightened my arm again, choking her as I began to pound my cock in hard. "I know you're upset now, but don't worry. I'll have you relaxing in no time. Soon, this will be like a dream." I pushed more of my weight on her back, leaning us forward. Pain shot into my side from her elbow, and the moment I loosened on her neck, she threw herself to the side. Before my hand could connect with her, she twisted the top of her body and pain exploded on the side of my forehead.

I blinked, barely feeling my arm rise as I reached up to the blood pouring down my face. Everleigh lay there frozen, holding a large metal paperweight fisted in her palm. I could feel myself stumbling back and falling, but I was already gone. I was already being taken over by the void of unconsciousness.

CHAPTER 44

24690

Insanity had never been far away. It had always existed within me, lurking in the depths of my mind. Waiting for the right time to strike. It wasn't about being strong enough to resist the urge to go mad but being strong enough to come back after the craziness took over.

I knew I was at the pinnacle of survive or be forever gone. I could feel myself swaying along the edge of something so significant, I would have been naive not to fear it. I did. I knew there may not have been any coming back this time.

"You fucking bitch. When I get free, I'm going to kill you."

West tugged at the ropes I had binding him to the desk, and I ignored the agonizing pain as I kicked into his face. His body curled into itself, and a growl left his bloody lips as he jerked roughly against the restraints.

"You're not getting free, husband. You're not even going to leave this room alive. I already told you that." I twisted my knife back and forth in my hand, feeling the haze of my mind continually trying to take over. I could barely remember running to the room while he lay there unconscious. How I'd even remembered the rope in our closet was beyond me. My mind knew things, even if I couldn't comprehend how.

I stepped forward, scanning over the desk. It was disheveled now. Papers were scattered all over the side and along the floor. Pens and pencils were laying along the top randomly. I stepped forward, grabbing a pair of scissors that rested close to the edge. When I walked around and lowered to face my attacker—my rapist—I couldn't stop staring into his enraged eyes. I hated him so much, I was sure hate wasn't even the emotion I harbored. He had done this to me. He turned me into what I had become. A monster. A sick, deranged thing that dreamed of blood and torture.

"What the hell are you doing with those?"

"Hmm? Which one would you prefer? The knife or the scissors?"

"Neither, you crazy bitch!"

A deep laugh left me. "I suppose I am crazy now. Did you know I see Bram? *I see him, husband.* He's everywhere. At the ends of halls, standing over me in the middle of the night. I loved him so much. He's angry at me. I guess that's because of you."

"You've lost your fucking mind. Put that shit away and untie me. We're even now. You've had your fun."

My head shook. "Oh, no. The fun hasn't even started. First, I'm going to rape you with these scissors, and then I'm going to skin off your face and make you look at it while I carve Bram's name into every inch of your body. Can you feel the blade separating your skin from your muscle? Can you feel it, *baby*? Dear. Sweet. Husband of mine?"

"You're sick. Fucking sick. God, why didn't I see it before? You need help."

"And I'm about to get it by hurting you. By skinning you, like you made me do to Julie."

"But she was dead when you cut into her!"

"You won't be."

West thrashed while I took the scissors to the bottom of my nightgown. Each snip had him getting quieter as he watched. Back and forth, my eyes went, from the lengthening white material to the cautiousness he displayed.

"Open your mouth."

"Fuck you. You want it open, do it yourself."

I lowered, unable to hold in my smile as I bunched the fabric in my palm. "If you insist, I will gladly open your mouth for you." I put down the scissors, clutching to the handle of my knife while I moved my hand in closer. West's stare stayed on my blade while he rocked his body back and forth on his stomach. When my hand lifted, I saw it. *Fear.* The sight masking his face left my hand rearing back and stabbing into the back of his shoulder.

"Fuck! You…cunt!"

I shoved the cloth into his mouth, using the other strip to tie around his head to secure it. The muffled, broken up moans and cries sent a flood of adrenaline through me. I pulled out my knife, wiping the blood along his cheek to clean it.

"Did you really think I'd let you keep hurting me? Did you think I'd let you sell off those children?" Flashes blinded me, and I could so clearly feel the pressure of my blade slicing through Eli's neck. "He told me he helped kill Bram. I can't believe Eli thought I would let him live after that. We planned it together, you know—helping the children escape. It turned out so much better than I could have hoped. He was so happy to have set them free. I can still see his smile. But…he had no clue my loyalty to my Master. My real Master." The darkness of the underground garage disappeared, and I blinked rapidly, bringing West's glare into focus. "What was your part in Bram's murder? Did you stab him yourself?"

I held tighter to my knife, lowering to my hands and knees. When I dropped to rest on my forearms so I could be closer to his face, a deep sound left West. And again, he fought against the ropes.

"No," I said, trailing the flat end of the blade along his cheek. "You're too much of a coward."

"Mmm-mmm-mmph."

"Sorry, I can't hear you. Were you saying something?"

I put my weight against his shoulder and the side of his head as I began slicing the blade down around the top of his eyebrow. The yell was gargled and loud, vibrating me as I cut around, lowering a good two inches below the side of his eye. "You let Billy do it, then murdered that guard to make yourself look like the hero. You…a hero."

Again, my mad laugh filled the room.

"My husband, always wanting to be in the spotlight. Wanting to be the leader—the one everyone looks up to. Did Bram make you feel so inadequate you had to have everything he did? That you had to kill him and take over his life so you could feel like you were worth something? I can see that." I moved my focus to the flattened blade and began sliding the tip under the skin to separate it from the muscle.

Thrashing had the knife cutting across his cheek, and I lifted enough to slap him. "Stay still or you'll lose your eye. I want you to see what I've done when I'm finished."

Yelling and a long, broken cry had me shaking my head as I stayed fixated on the skin. I moved back to the top of the eyebrow, keeping my hand steady while I made small flicking motions with my wrist. Within seconds, I was able to lift the top of his eyebrow. The scream that exploded from West was like heaven. It touched a part of my soul as I bit my bottom lip and stared down at him.

"How does that feel?" I put more of my weight on top of him, lifting the skin again. "Can you feel the cool air seeping through? Does it hurt? Burn?" I pulled down the gag, desperate to hear. "Can you feel the skin that's still attached pulling when I lift? Do you still love me with my knife peeling back your face? Tell me you love me now."

"I swear...torture…the fuck out of you." I smiled, letting his threats urge me on. "When you're dead, I'm going to fuck your corpse and tear you apart with my bare hands!"

"Oh, yes. Fucking my corpse. Is that what you like? Was that what you were going to tell me the first night you raped my unresponsive body? Your secret," I whispered.

"You just wait," he panted. "You fucking wait, you stupid psycho cunt. You have no idea what I'm capable of. I'll fuck you like I fucked those slaves I had to kill. And when I'm done, I'm going to piss all over your mutilated body before I turn that motherfucker into ashes."

"We'll see. I think you're speaking out of anger. Perhaps you need a break from your face for a little while. Let's move on to something else. We'll get back to that after you're drained from the blood loss. I do believe you'll be a lot more compliant then." My knee came down on the wound in his shoulder while I leaned forward, pushing his pants mid-thigh.

West's legs went wild. He tried drawing his knees to his chest, but the rope keeping them bound was fastened tightly to the heavy desk, as were the ropes around his hands. With the narrow distance between it and the bookshelf, he was blocked in. There was nowhere for him to move.

"I'm…going…*bitch*."

"I'm about to show you a bitch. How do you think you'll react staring back at your own face? Do you think it'll look the same when I've cut it off?"

"Ahhh! Get the fuck off me. Get! The fuck! Off!"

"Not yet. You haven't endured my rape yet."

"If you put those scissors anywhere near me…I swear I'll—"

I grabbed the scissors, pausing to look at his panicked eyes. "You'll what? What could you do that you haven't already done? Kill me? Do you think I'm afraid of death? Death and I are secret lovers. We take turns fucking each other every chance we get. Today, it's my turn to be on top." My hand flattened on one side of his ass, separating him. No matter how much he tried to tighten the muscles or move, I kept a firm grip. Drawing back my hand, I slammed the blade of scissors in West's entrance.

No scream, just a guttural explosion of a deep groan as his large frame tensed in agonizing shock. I unlocked my fingers just in time for him to catch his breath and allow the real screams to make themselves known.

"Fuck! God. God!"

"There's no God in Whitlock. Only the devil, and this one is of your creation. How may I be of assistance to you, husband? Would you like me to remove the scissors? I can put them back in a more comfortable position for you. Here, let me try."

"Get t-the fuck a-away from me." West's pale face was covered in sweat as he began to vomit.

"But I hurt you. Let me make it better. I promise, this won't hurt as much as the first time." I grabbed the handle, sliding the blades out, only to thrust slowly back in. The sobs that came as I continued my leisurely pace had a grin permanently etched on my lips. I glanced over my shoulder at West, who kept trying to catch his breath through the fast, deep inhales. It was beautiful. *He was beautiful.*

"I think you were right," I said, pausing. Harder, I looked into his bloody face. Into the eyes that feared me. Something stirred within, sparking the emotion I held for him. It was a tugging—a deeper yearning I had tried to lock away. I hadn't wanted to experience it or know what it was. But now, in this moment, I understood why it was so easy to play the role of his loving wife. Why I could endure his love-making when he wasn't drugging or raping me.

"Oh, husband." I removed the scissors, turning to lower to his lips. West tried to jerk away from me, but he couldn't move far. "Kiss me," I whispered. "Kiss me while you cry so beautifully for me."

"Stay away…no more."

"Kiss me."

"Fuck you!"

I sighed, pressing my lips into his. The moment our mouths touched, he jerked back and slammed his head forward. Blood swept over my tongue and the insides of my cheeks. The pain sent my insanity reeling. I lifted, grabbing and clutching my knife as I drew back and stabbed into his bicep.

"Ahhh! Fucking…God! I swear to—"

I stuffed the material back in his mouth and he continued to yell into the fabric. I took in the volume, realizing I was forgetting a vital part of what I was doing. There was something…*important.* I stood, coming face to face with the one thing that was truly mine. The only thing that mattered to me anymore. *Yes.* This was what I needed. I pulled the black book free, watching as blood smeared over the pages while I flipped to the one that had been marked for me.

"Mm-mmmph."

The words blurred before me, and I blinked rapidly, scanning the poem as fast as I could, afraid someone would stop me like so many times before. Lyle had been adamant I read this particular one. Looking back, he seemed to have been trying to prepare me for something. Or at least make me aware. I could still hear his words so clearly… *When you get lonely, or times are hard, I want you to go somewhere where you're alone and read this. There's a particular poem he enjoyed in the middle. I marked the page for you. Read it and have hope. Hope, above all things.*

Hope. Hope for…?

A tear fell as my heart squeezed to life, thumping and exploding into a fast rhythm. Bram was the only one who could make me feel anymore. And feel, I did. So much so, my legs almost gave out as I lowered to collapse next to West.

I took in the words again, letting my eyes rise to my husband. It was more of a muse or note…and sloppily handwritten below, another that was typed out.

Handwritten.

A loud bang filled the room and footsteps pounded toward me. I looked at the horror on the three guards' faces but turned back to West.

"Bram left us a little note, husband. I think you're *really* going to want to hear this. You're *all* going to want to hear."

I started at the beginning once again, reading each sentence aloud. My pulse increased by the second as emotions flooded back in. But not from the punishment and hell I knew I was sentenced to. The *whiteout* was coming for me—the White Room. Hell would find me there. But even that I didn't fear as much as the twisted versions of Bram haunting my mind.

"For who am I, if not a man? I've asked myself that question a million times. The answer evades me like the damned. And I must be damned to have been placed in this hell that swallows me by the day. I once thought by discovering the truth of what I queried it would set me free. But do cursed men ever find peace for their tainted souls?

"Maybe I'm asking the wrong questions," I read, glancing at West. "Maybe I've known the answer all along: love.

"I once loved a woman. Once…no, I love her still. Her presence haunts the empty cells inside me, weaving in and out of the dark crevices like a ghost seeking recognition. Death has always been my friend. Even now, *as I fight for life*, when I close my ears to the screams within, she makes her presence know. Bump-bump goes my heart. But it is not my heart I hear in the silence of my unconscious mind. It is her laugh. Her moans and sweet calls for me to come back to her. I groan at the ache she manifests in my chest. Come back to me, she says. Return my love, she pleads.

"And I cry. Does she not know I already do? Does she not feel me rushing through her bloodstream like she soars through mine? Bump-bump, she cries. And I cry back. Love me, I plead. Feel me, I beg. I am not without you, and you are not without me. We are together, even if we're apart.

"But she does not see that, *because she does not see me.*

"I'm not dead, I whisper. Close your eyes, and you will see. Close your ears, and you will hear. Bump-bump. **I am watching**. Bump-bump. **I am there**..."

To be continued...

THANK YOU FOR READING!

ABOUT THE AUTHOR

Alaska Angelini/A.A Dark is a Best Selling Author of dark, twisted happily-ever-afters. She currently resides in Mississippi but moves at the drop of a dime. Check back in a few months and she's guaranteed to live somewhere new.

Obsessive, stalking, mega-alpha hero's/anti-heroes are her thing. Throw in some rope, cuffs, and a whip or two, and watch the magic begin.

If you're looking to connect with her to learn more, feel free to email alaska_angelini@yahoo.com or find her on Facebook. You can also stop by her website madgirlpublishing.com.

Click to sign up for my Newsletter!

facebook.com/AlaskaAngelini
twitter.com/MadGirlPub
instagram.com/alaskaangelini
amazon.com/A-A-Dark
goodreads.com/alaskaangelini
pinterest.com/alaskaangelini
tiktok.com/@alaskaangelini

OTHER TITLES FROM THIS AUTHOR:

Unbearable

SLADE: Captive to the Dark

BLAKE: Captive to the Dark

GAIGE: Captive to the Dark

LILY: Captive to the Dark, Special Edition 1

CHASE: Dark and Dangerous CCTD Set 2

Watch Me: Stalked

Rush

Dom Up: Devlin Black 1

Dom Fever: Devlin Black 2

This Dom: Devlin Black 3

Dark Paranormal lover? Check out Alaska's other reads…

Wolf (Wolf River 1)

Prey: Marko Delacroix 1

Blood Bound: Marko Delacroix 2

Lure: Marko Delacroix 3

Rule: Marko Delacroix 4

Reign: Marko Delacroix 5

READ BOOK 2 IN THE 24690 SERIES NOW!

Printed in the USA
CPSIA information can be obtained
at www.ICGtesting.com
LVHW012007071224
798533LV00017B/562

* 9 7 8 1 9 3 8 0 7 6 3 9 8 *